Titanic:
The Final Voyage

A Novel By

F. Mark Granato

Titanic:
The Final Voyage

By

F. Mark Granato

Edited by
Gail A. Donahue

Published in the United States of America 2011

To Bobbie, my wife...

Perhaps you will never know
how much of this book you wrote,
and how much your love and encouragement
unlocked my imagination.

Acknowledgements

Thank you to my beloved sons, Jack and Jay, and my new daughter Andréa for bringing so much joy to my life; to my beloved Irish grandfather, William J. McGrath, the source of so many stories and characters; to Gail Donahue, my dear friend, supporter and editor who opens doors with amazing grace; to Julie Follett and Peter Potaski for their infinite compassion and wisdom; to Claudia Chamberlain and Earl Flowers who taught the irascible corporate curmudgeon the beauty of friendship as well as words; and to Groban, truly a man's best friend, for sleeping beneath my desk as I write.

Prologue

The majestic White Star passenger liner, *Titanic* rocked gently at Berth 44 in the port of Southampton, Hampshire, England, near dawn. The most temperate spring in nearly thirty years had warmed and becalmed the harbor's strong currents, and at low tide only the slightest of ripples could be detected on its glass-like surface. Still an hour before daybreak, the moonless night cast the lower decks of the forty-six thousand ton *Titanic* in nearly complete darkness. It was the perfect cloak of invisibility for visitors who would desire not to be seen.

Titanic's yellow and pitch-pine decks, only slightly weathered and bleached from exposure to the sun and elements during the many months she was being fitted out, were as polished and pristine as those found in the great castles and mansions of Europe. The lowest of the nine decks was sixty feet above the harbor waterline. They were quiet now, but in another two hours the entire ship would be teeming with activity as the crew made final preparations for the vessel's maiden voyage to New York later that day. For now, she was alone in the darkness, enjoying a temporary respite from the extraordinary attention she attracted—despite having yet to make her first ocean crossing.

Even before her keel was laid at the Harland & Wolff shipyard in Belfast, Ireland, much had been written about how the *Titanic* represented a new age of ship design. She would cruise at speeds up to twenty-four knots while her passengers basked in unrivaled opulence, comfort and safety. It was fitting, perhaps, that on her maiden voyage the greatest of all luxury liners would depart for the east coast of America from Southampton -- just as the Pilgrims had set sail for the new world on their own maiden voyage from the very same harbor nearly three hundred years before.

The air was nearly still on this morning, moved occasionally by a slight southerly breeze. The silence on the docks was broken only by the sound of brackish water lapping at *Titanic's* nearly nine hundred foot waterline, phosphorescent streaks occasionally outlining her hull where it met the sea.

From a distance all was completely quiet, save for several company guards shuffling aimlessly along the weathered planks of the berth. For the most part, these were employees of the White Star Line who were a few months or years away from retirement. When one of the big boats was in the harbor, the guards were charged with the duty of catching scalawags intent on sneaking aboard in the darkness, desperate to find somewhere within the bowels of the ship to hide during the crossing. The guards went about their duties lazily knowing they had little chance at sorting out such freeloaders.

Abruptly, the tiptoe patter of leather boots racing up the Well Deck gangplank breached the stillness. Two young boys fell to the deck on their knees, holding their breath in fear that they had been seen and would sound an alarm. They shuddered to think what their punishment would be if they were discovered. Several minutes went by, but mercifully, all remained silent.

"C'mon, move your skinny arse mate, we ain't got all night," twelve-year-old Clive Alister whispered to his henchman, Roy Markham, a boy slightly smaller but twice as adventurous. "The friggin' sun will be up in a little bit, so move it or just bugger back to your Ma's skirts."

The boys advanced to the giant black-steel anchor links on the port side of the Forecastle deck, desperate to remain hidden. They had snuck from their beds just after three in the morning, launching a caper formed days earlier to steal some artifact of the already world famous *Titanic* before she set out. They were determined to be the heroes of their school chums who had spoken of nothing but the great liner since she had arrived in Southampton. Such was the magnificence of the ship that she seduced not only the rich and famous, but the young and adventurous as well, especially school boys who could only dream of sailing her. Climbing the unguarded gangplank to the Well Deck at the bow of the ship had been too easy.

"Shut up, you twit… and don't be takin' my Ma's name in that fat gob of yours, I'm coming. I had to piss," Markham replied, in as loud a whisper as he dared.

"Piss? Where? On the deck?" Alister taunted his accomplice. "You shook your tiny little willie on the deck of the *Titanic*? Hasn't that slag of a mother ever told you about proper etiquette?"

Markham lunged at the bigger boy, his fist cocked. "Take it back you sod, take it back or I'll rip your knackers off and flush 'em down the loo."

Alister laughed aloud at the mental image his sidekick had conjured up. "Keep it in your knickers, mate. And keep your voice down. Cripes, you'll stir the gulls with your whining." He reached over and roughly tousled the redhead's scruffy hair, seeking forgiveness. He turned. "Look up there." He pointed to the main mast and the beckoning ships Crow's nest, looming some fifty feet above the Forecastle Deck.

Markham followed his finger. "So what? That's where the lookout goes. Crikey, that's high up," he said, already guessing what Clive was thinking.

"There's nothing to be found there, Roy," Alister said, shaking his head at his friend's stupidity. "Have you lost the plot so early in the day?"

The boy ignored him. "I don't care, I just want to see what it's like up there," Markham replied. Before Alister could stop him, Markham scurried forward, darting across the virgin deck to the main mast rising in front of the empty ships' Bridge. He hunkered below it for a moment, listening. "It's okay, Clive, c'mon, no one's seen us," he called back, as loudly as he could whisper. The smaller boy followed him reluctantly.

A moment later, the two boys began the laborious chore of climbing up the ladder inside the cylindrical metal mast, moving up hand over hand, eighteen inches at a time until finally hoisting themselves onto the forward Crow's nest. They huddled together, keeping their heads down.

"Jesus Christ, I thought my heart would stop when I looked down," said Alister. "I don't like being up here."

"Aw, be quiet, Clive," Markham replied in frustration with his classmate. Hearing no word of alarm from the deck below, he raised his head slowly over the Crow's nest rail and peered out at *Titanic*'s bow. "Wow, this is bloody gorgeous you fool, see for yourself."

Alister pulled himself up from the floor and sucked in his breath as he took in the whole bow of the ship. "Bloody amazing, mate. No one will believe us."

"They will if we bring back a souvenir," Markham replied. "Maybe there's something in here." He looked down below the railing to an oak cabinet, its door closed and locked. A shiny new skeleton key tagged "Property of RMS *Titanic*" dangled from a brass pull. The boy was giddy at his good fortune. He inserted the key into the lock and the door opened easily. Markham peered in and whistled in delight. "Look what we have here," he said, pulling out a heavy brown leather case. Inside was a pair of professional looking binoculars, trimmed in black leather, obviously brand new.

"What the bloody hell? Let me see those," Alister begged and wrestled them from Markham's grasp. "Lord, they're something to see." He ran his hand over the barrels, astonished by their perfection. Then he raised them to his eyes. Before he could focus the glasses, Markham wrenched them back. "I found them, you sod, I want to see." Roy raised the glasses to his eyes, fiddled with the center focus wheel and slowly scanned the harbor as his view sharpened. As he turned to the port side, he saw a tug in the distance making its way across the harbor, slowly edging towards the *Titanic*.

"Fuck, we've got to go, there's a boat coming. Let's just take the glasses and scram," Markham said.

"Are you daft?" Alister hissed. "We can't take these – what are we going to do with them? The coppers'll nail us, for sure. Just put 'em back, put 'em back and let's clear out of here."

"Bugger off, we came this far and you want to chicken out now?" Markham said a little too loudly. "We've gotta take something for the effort, you twit... wait, I have it." He hurriedly placed the binoculars back into the box and slammed the door shut, turning the key. Then he pulled the key and its fob from the lock and held it up for Roy to see.

"No one will notice these gone!" he said. Clive began to protest again, but his accomplice would not have it. "Stone me," Markham said. "This is the friggin' *Titanic*. I'm sure they've got another key lying around somewhere. C'mon, we gotta get down from here." The two boys scampered down the mast, reaching the deck just as the sun broke across the horizon and captured their shadows racing to the gangplank, caution now thrown to the wind. As Southampton began to awaken, the two boys dashed home to their cottages and crawled under the sheets of their beds. The ashes were nearly cold in their small kitchen fireplaces as dawn erupted, but neither boy felt the chill.

When their Ma's roused them from feigned sleep an hour later, the two boys behaved in most unusually good spirits as they hastily downed their porridge and milk and rushed off to school. The shiny new key in the pocket of Roy Markham's worn gabardine pants promised that he and Clive Alister would be treated like guv'nors of the playground.

One

A long Rolls Royce Grey Ghost limousine, its silver paint polished to a mirror finish, crawled slowly along the Southampton dock. The low rumble of the car's powerful six-cylinder engine was barely audible over the roar emanating from thousands of people lined up along Berth 44 where the White Star Line's newest and most luxurious ocean liner, the "*Titanic*" was moored. Some had come to board the magnificent new steam ship for her maiden voyage across the North Atlantic Ocean. Most had turned out to witness history.

A legend in its own time, the Rolls was more than the most extravagant luxury car ever conceived and built. Its sumptuous appointments and whisper-like stillness at idle deceptively hid ferocious performance that was available at a stab of the accelerator. Fittingly, its use was largely excluded to the wealthiest of the wealthy, kings, queens and noblemen.

The Rolls was built with the same grand vision of performance and opulence as the great ship it now approached. There the comparison to the *Titanic* stopped. It had taken Rolls Royce decades to earn its rightful crown in the automobile industry, and yet the brand was still an unknown to most of the world. Already, before making even a single run between Southampton and New York, *Titanic* was already the most famous ship in the world, a legend even before she sailed due to her extraordinary lavishness and size.

Everything about Titanic was bigger and better, more graceful and refined, and she represented the fashionable elite who marked the Edwardian period. Although war clouds were gathering and darkening over Europe and America had been plunged into economic depression, the very powerful and prosperous continued to take delight in their affluence and obliviousness. *Titanic* had been built for them.

The driver of the Rolls Royce, as meticulous as the car he drove, wore a black uniform and matching kidskin leather boots and gloves. Cautiously, he nursed the automobile's clutch and picked his way through the crowd. His objective was to deliver his two important passengers as close to the waiting ship's gangplank as possible. The Southampton police controlling the crowd instantly recognized the handsome man sitting in the carriage of the Rolls' open-top coach. They quickly cleared a path for his vehicle to pass. In return, he smiled and nodded as he passed with a casual friendliness that was at odds with the stiffness of his formal military dress, appropriate to the rank of Major in the United States Army. It was not every day that the policemen came within arms length of a genuine hero, who as the American President's closest advisor and loyal companion was arguably the second most important member of the American government. As such, he was a staunch and vocal ally of Great Britain and the darling of the Western European press.

Finally, the great car could move no closer, hemmed in by the excited crowd awaiting their turn to board across the gangplank reserved for Steerage passengers. Once aboard, they would be disbursed to their accommodations deep in the bowels of the ocean liner. A more dignified entrance to the ship, reserved for First and Second class passengers, was a dozen yards or so ahead. Here the ship's First Officer, standing proudly in his crisp navy blue White Star Line uniform, checked off the name of each passenger on the official manifest as they boarded *Titanic*.

Waiting at the top of the gangplank reserved for the wealthier passengers stood an imposing figure waiting to personally greet them. With his meticulously manicured full white beard and attired as always in the formal dress uniform of the ship's captain, the portly 62-year-old Edward J. Smith's appearance gave credence to his reputation as the "Millionaires' Captain". It was a tribute imposed upon him by First Class passengers who routinely requested that he be in command of the ships on which they booked passage.

Captain Smith had been quite busy all morning attending to the myriad of details required before setting sail. This included a meeting with representatives of the British Board of Trade, the government watchdog agency assigned the task of assuring that passenger-carrying vessels were seaworthy and met the strict regulations dealing with safety. The meeting was brief and almost perfunctory, as the Board had already witnessed *Titanic's* sea trials a week earlier.

Such attentiveness to detail was not new to the Captain who was celebrating a quarter century of command on the Bridge of the world's most prominent ocean liners. Having attained the rank of White Star Commander, it was customary for him to serve as Captain of the Line's newest ships on their maiden voyage. The *Titanic*, scheduled to sail the North Atlantic from Southampton to New York on April 10, 1912, was no exception.

As the esteemed captain welcomed passengers aboard the pristine new vessel, he did so with a certain melancholy. After nearly fifty years traipsing the vast oceans of the world, this would be his last voyage. Despite his love of the sea and the brilliant career, which had brought him to the pinnacle of respect in his trade, he was eager to retire to his estate at Portsmouth, Southampton. Eagerly awaiting him were his adoring wife Sarah and daughter Helen who had kept the home fires burning while he traversed the globe. On this morning, the Captain was a satisfied man reveling in his duties for the final time. The arrival of the Rolls Royce some sixty feet below his station did not escape his attention.

Finally, the driver sighed at his failure to position the car exactly at the First Officer's side. He switched off the Rolls, set the parking brake and jumped out to open a rear door for his passengers. The tall and athletically fit military officer stood in the cabin, paused for a moment to adjust his uniform, then stepped out. His colleague stood as well, but before exiting the car, turned to take in the docks.

It was pandemonium. More than nine hundred passengers had booked passage from Southampton and were making their way aboard ship. Another eight hundred ninety eight crew, four out of five that hailed from the port city, was preparing the ship for departure.

On the docks, stevedores slowly hauled mountains of steamer trunks, oversize suitcases, satchels and other luggage on board. They were especially careful in their handling of the belongings of the First Class passengers. The replacement cost of a Louis Vuitton steamer trunk was equivalent to a year's wages or more.

The ships' cranes were in constant motion as a seemingly endless supply of stores and cargo were loaded into the vast forward holds. Into her kitchens and pantries poured enough provisions to feed several thousand people for five days. She stocked two hundred fifty barrels of flour, fifteen hundred gallons of milk, twenty-two hundred pounds of coffee and ten thousand pounds of sugar. More than fifteen hundred bottles of

15

fine wines and eight hundred bottles of top shelf spirits stocked the upper class bars. Eight thousand fine Cuban cigars awaited smokers.

Having finally taken his fill of the overwhelming scene of activity, the man standing in the rear section of the Rolls turned to his host. "Have you ever seen anything like this, Archie? One wonders how in the world it all comes together and these giant ships finally make their way to the ocean."

Major Archibald Willingham Butt laughed aloud. "It always reminds me of a circus come to town, Francis. The only thing missing is an elephant and its trainer, and I suspect if we wait and watch long enough, a bull and a tender will be arriving soon."

As they watched, a crane started up near another chauffeur-driven automobile that had just arrived at the dock, but this one was to be added to the cargo manifest. The driver of the immaculate automobile, a bright red and black 1912 Renault Coupe Chauffeur, gestured wildly to the crane operator who was positioning a huge platform on the dock. Careful to avoid the forged steel chains framing the platform, the driver steered the car onto the platform carefully positioning its wooden wheels in the center of it. Satisfied that the car was accurately placed, the driver killed the engine and set the brake. He jumped out to oversee a group of stevedores who had already begun tying the vehicle down. The men moved with practiced motions, and moments later, the crane operator plucked the automobile and platform off the dock. The Renault rose in the air and was slung over the enormous opening to the cargo hold of *Titanic*'s third compartment where it was gently lowered into it.

A tall gentlemen wearing a bowler hat and a topcoat over his expensive Saville Row suit stepped out of a crowd of onlookers and placed a hand on the shoulder of the chauffeur as if to comfort him. He was First Class passenger William Ernest Carter of Pennsylvania, who was returning home with his wife Lucile, their two children, a valet, a maid and the chauffer after an extended stay in Europe. Carter had purchased the car at the Renault factory in Billancourt, France and was exporting it to the US as the first step toward establishing a North American market for the car.

"Major Butt, Mr. Millett, please forgive my inability to get you any closer to the gangplank," the driver of the Grey Ghost interrupted. "I'm afraid I'll run someone over..."

Butt brushed his concern aside. "See here, Harry, there's a better chance of this ship sinking than of you getting us any closer in this mob. Well done, and please do extend my thanks once again to Ambassador Reid. If I'd ever known that your services come with the job as US Ambassador to the Court of St. James, I might have lobbied for the appointment myself."

The driver doffed his cap and bowed dramatically. "You are too kind, Major. But I hardly think you would want to give up playing golf with President Taft for tea and crumpets with the ornery members of the aristocracy." Butt laughed roundly and slapped Harry on the back.

Tipping his hat, he returned to the drivers seat in the Rolls, carefully pulling away from the dock as Butt and Millet watched. From the corner of his eye, the Major caught a wave from Captain Smith who was leaning over the railing of the Forward Well Deck, just below the Bridge, to get his attention. Butt turned and snapped a salute to the Captain.

Major Butt -- "Archie" to his friends -- was well known to Smith and for that matter, nearly everyone who would sail his ship on this spring day. A darling of high society and Washington politics, Butt had recently been described by an admiring journalist as "one of the best-known men in American public life." It was hardly a role he could have foreseen given his humble roots.

Born in Augusta, Georgia in 1865, Archie Butt shouldered responsibility early in life, having to support his mother and two siblings when his father died when the boy was fourteen. Working day and night to provide for his family and attend the University of the South, he graduated in 1888 with a degree in journalism.

Butt pursued a newspaper career for the next decade and demonstrated a sharp eye for details. It was his refined style that attracted the attention of Matt Ransom, the US Ambassador to Mexico. Ransom, a career politician from North Carolina, was impressed with Butt's analytical mind and instinctive preference for negotiation as opposed to brute force. Butt became his secretary and accordingly got his first taste of government and politics.

When war against Mexico broke out in 1898, Butt joined the army as a lieutenant and distinguished himself during the battle for Manila. After a two year stint of duty with the Cuban pacification force, Butt was promoted to Captain and recalled to Washington to serve as chief military aide to President Theodore Roosevelt. He quickly became Roosevelt's most trusted confidant and advisor.

William Howard Taft succeeded Roosevelt in 1909 and asked Butt to remain in his role as chief military aide. Butt soon became an intimate advisor to Taft as well, playing a key role in every vital operation of the White House. Virtually all of the President's activities were overseen by the Captain, and he was the gatekeeper for those would require direct access to the Commander in Chief.

Wherever Taft went, whatever he did, Captain Archie Butt was close by. While the full military dress uniform he wore gave an aura of a formal and official relationship with the President, the attire was deceiving. For no President ever enjoyed a better friend, confidant and companion than Archie Butt.

The chief counsel to the President was indeed an enigma. He was ruggedly handsome, sporting a carefully trimmed moustache that made him appear older than his forty seven years. For a man so accomplished he was nonetheless painfully and had never married. Butt's schedule was such that he had little time for romance and its complications, and appeared to content living alone. At least three nights a week he slept at the White House after working well into the early morning hours.

He was soft spoken, too, a characteristic not unnoticed by those with whom he engaged in political chess on the President's behalf. New acquaintances were usually surprised by his demeanor which somehow made curious the dozen medals on his uniform that he had rightfully earned in service to his country. When the situation or occasion demanded a firm voice however, there was no mistaking Butt's iron will and determination to succeed. He was intimidated by no man including the President, to whom he provided frank and unbridled counsel. To those unaware of the depth of their relationship, Butt at times almost came across as insubordinate.

The strong bond between the two men came at a price, however. By late 1911 Archie Butt was nearing exhaustion from his tremendous duties and was in ill health. His close friend, Francis Davis Millet, a renowned writer and painter, convinced President Taft to send the Major on an extended tour of Europe as his ambassador in order to revitalize his spirits. Butt hesitated but ultimately followed the orders of his Commander in Chief. Now, after an eight week visit to

Europe, culminating with an audience with Pope Pius
X in Rome during which he delivered a personal message
from the President, Archie was rested and eager to return
to the US and the upcoming political primaries.

As he made his way up the gangplank, Archie Butt
took in the riotous scene on the dock and paused midway to take a deep breath. He'd have to cut down on the
cigars, he thought. But what was life without a good
Cuban leaf?

"Archie, are you feeling well?" asked Millet. He put
his hand under Archie's elbow as if to keep him from
falling. The two had been friends for more than thirty
years.

"Of course, dear Francis," he replied energetically.
"Just enjoying a bit of salt air." Even as he spoke,
Captain Smith was hurrying down the gangplank to
meet them.

"Good morning Major Butt, Mr. Millet," Smith said
eagerly. "It is my distinct pleasure to welcome you
aboard the *Titanic*. I am Captain Edward Smith. May I
be of service?"

Butt grabbed the Captain's outstretched hand and
shook it firmly. The Captain had a firm hand, Butt
thought, a sure sign of a strong personality, a leader of
men. Butt had become somewhat of an expert on
handshakes over the last four years, serving as head of
protocol for two Presidents.

"Of course, Captain Smith, but you need no
introduction and the honor is of course all mine," Butt
replied. "Actually, I just paused to take in all the activity
on the dock. It's quite bedlam down there. One wonders
how it all comes together before we sail."

"Ah, yes, Major Butt, it is quite a spectacle, but I
assure you there is strong order beneath what appears to
be chaos." He turned to Millet and vigorously shook his

hand. "I trust you both will do me the honor of joining me at the Captain's table tonight for dinner?"

Millet, always in search of recognition, jumped at the invitation. "Why of course, Captain, we would be delighted. Tell me, have you word of the weather along our path to New York?"

Smith was ready for the question, usually top of mind for First Class passengers who abhorred delays or inconveniences as some sort of personal affront. He smiled at Millet but turned his gaze back to Butt.

"This has been the mildest winter I have experienced in three decades," Smith said confidently, with an air of certainty that usually put passengers to rest immediately. "Very warm for this early in spring. The seas are calm, even polished at times in mid ocean. The only concern we have is ice. Because of the warm temperatures, it is not uncommon for large sheets of ice to break off from Greenland, calving icebergs and growlers which drift far south into the east-west shipping lanes."

Millet suddenly looked pale. Smith chuckled. "I assure you Mr. Millet, there is no reason for concern. The *Titanic* employs lookouts round the clock and we are in constant contact with other ships to keep a close watch on any ice in our path."

He turned to Butt again. "And might I add, Major, that if you pressing business in Washington, there is a strong likelihood that we will arrive in New York roughly a day earlier than scheduled. You see, *Titanic* will aim for the honor of flying the Blue Riband on her maiden voyage."

Butt was immediately intrigued. "The Blue Riband?"

Smith relished the question. "It is an honor bestowed upon the ship that captures the record for the fastest transatlantic crossing, Major Butt. Cunard's *Mauratania* currently holds the flag and it is flown from the topmast of the ship. It will be a fine companion to

Titanic's single white star on red flag which is flying now." The three men looked upward at the topmast mounted on the Forecastle deck. The *Titanic*'s White Star Line flag was indeed flying some thirty feet above the Crow's nest.

"Let us hope, my dear Captain, that the ice doesn't impede *Titanic*'s speed," Butt said, slightly uncomfortable with Smith's mixed message.

"I would never put any ship under my command at risk for any reason, Major Butt. We shall see how things proceed," the Captain said reassuringly. "Now, if you'll excuse me, I have other passengers to greet, in fact I see Mr. Guggenheim approaching as we speak. Welcome aboard the *Titanic*, gentlemen, and please do not hesitate to seek me out during our voyage. I serve for your pleasure."

The two men made their way to the First Class accommodations reserved for them, conveniently located amidships. Butt and Millet stopped for a moment to discuss plans for dinner that evening with Smith. A moment later, Benjamin Guggenheim and his entourage entered the hallway.

The fabulously wealthy Guggenheim was accompanied by his mistress, French singer Madame Léontine Aubart. At the site of Butt and Millet talking in the hallway, Guggenheim clumsily looked the other way in a vain attempt not to be recognized. There was a moment of awkward embarrassment as Butt spied Guggenheim and innocently intercepted his path.

"Benjamin, how good to see you," the affable Major greeted him. "Is Florette with you? I must say hello. Why, I haven't seen either of you since the Inaugural Ball."

Guggenheim stopped and shook Butt's hand weakly, and turned and muttered to his companion to go on ahead. He turned back to Butt. "Archie, what a wonderful surprise," he said. "No, no, Florette has not accompanied me on this trip. My wife's social calendar was full, I'm afraid."

"Ah, so that must have been your daughter, I'm so sorry I didn't have the chance to meet her..."

"Not my daughter, Archie... uh... an acquaintance... from Paris."

Butt cleared his throat, realizing the awkwardness of the situation. "Yes, well... there you have it... how rude of me," he said, then quickly turned to Francis Millet and introduced him to the millionaire.

"Yes, yes of course, how good to meet you Mr. Millet," Guggenheim responded. "I am actually quite familiar with the murals you painted in the Trinity Church in Boston. I agree with Major Butt, your work is extraordinary."

Millet beamed. There was an awkward silence. "Will you be joining us then at the Captain's table tonight for dinner?"

Guggenheim hesitated. "Perhaps some other time, Archie. I may see you in the First Class Smoking Salon later this evening for some cards."

"I suspect that *Titanic* is teeming with the rich and famous," Butt commented to his friend when they were out of earshot. "This voyage will be an eye-opener, what with the world's wealthiest industrialists, philanthropists and philanderers with nothing but time on their hands."

Over the next several days, Butt would appreciate how right his instincts were. The first-class passengers for *Titanic*'s maiden voyage included some of the most powerful and notable people of the young 20th century, combined representing more than $600,000,000 in wealth.

Titanic's passenger manifest included John Jacob Astor IV, said to be the world's richest man whose real estate portfolio was worth more than $200 million. He was traveling with his pregnant, eighteen year-old second wife, Madeleine, the subject of much lurid gossip in the American press. Also aboard was George Dunton Widener of Philadelphia, an American businessman and patron of the arts, who as Chairman of the Philadelphia Traction Company had developed the technology for cable and electric streetcar operations. Charles Hays, president of Canada's Grand Trunk Railway, had also booked passage on *Titanic*. Hays had overseen the enormous growth and expansion of the Canadian railway system that now operated coast to coast.

Macy's department store owner Isidor Straus and his devoted wife Ida were returning to New York after a brief holiday in Europe. To the delight of the card playing passengers aboard, also making the voyage was Sir Cosmo Duff-Gordon, a Scottish land baron and his wife of fifty-two years, Lady Duff-Gordon, a widely regarded fashion designer. Pennsylvania Railroad vice president John Borland Thayer was also aboard with his wife Marian and their adventurous seventeen year-old son Jack. The family had been visiting Germany as guests of the American Consul in Berlin.

Socialites who chased opportunities to rub elbows with the world's major "players" also made passage on the maiden voyage of the *Titanic* a "must do."

Among them was Margaret "Molly" Brown, an outspoken millionairess from Denver who had accompanied the Astor's on their recent journey through Europe and Egypt. She liked nothing more than beating the pants off a group of gentlemen around a poker table in a smoke filled room.

The world of journalism and the arts were also well represented aboard *Titanic*. Prolific writer William Thomas Stead, editor of London's "Pall Mall Gazette" was a peace activist who covered the Hague Peace Conferences of 1899 and 1907 with great fervor. He was traveling to New York at the invitation of President Taft to attend a Peace Congress at Carnegie Hall. Also booking passage on the *Titanic* were American journalist and prolific novelist Jacques Futrelle and his wife Lilly May Peal; Broadway producers Henry and Irene Harris; and American silent film actress Dorothy Gibson, star of sixteen silent films and the highest paid actress in the world.

J. Bruce Ismay, the White Star Line's managing director who had originally proposed the idea for the construction of the *Titanic* and two sister ships, the *Olympic* and *Brittanic,* was aboard to exploit the media attention that would accompany the anticipated wresting of the Blue Riband from Cunard's *Mauretania*. To assess any problems and the general performance of *Titanic*, the ship's architect, Thomas Andrews of Harland & Wolff, had also booked First Class passage.

There was no ship quite like her, and the preeminence of *Titanic's* passenger manifest was only one indication that she was the most exciting and advanced ocean-going vessel ever built.

Titanic's propulsion system was perhaps the most intriguing element of her design. A triple screw, *Titanic* had two three-bladed wing propellers weighing some thirty-eight tons each and a center prop which weighed in at twenty-two tons. Her twenty-nine boilers were fired by one hundred fifty-nine coal burning furnaces that gave her a cruising speed of twenty-one knots. The behemoth could make twenty-four knots if pressed.

Fed by members of the "Black Gang", the dozens of firemen and stokers who fed her furnaces twenty-four hours a day, *Titanic* consumed one pound of coal for every foot traveled. She would burn some sixty pounds of coal to move an equivalent number of feet on the ocean surface in a breathtaking one and a half seconds at top speed.

From a safety perspective, she was even more impressive.

"Shipbuilder" magazine, the leading journal of the ship building industry, ceremoniously claimed that the *Titanic* was the safest ocean liner ever conceived and "practically unsinkable". She had a double-bottom hull divided into sixteen watertight compartments, each of which had a door that was held open by electro-magnetic latches. If an emergency arose, the door to each compartment could be closed within thirty seconds by means of a switch on the bridge.

To keep her safely balanced even in the roughest sea, *Titanic* had forty-four water tanks for ballast that all but eliminated any possibility of the ship capsizing. She sailed with twenty lifeboats, only half enough for a full passenger and crew compliment that could top three thousand five hundred people, but this total exceeded the requirement of the British Board of Trade. The liner had originally been designed with thirty-six lifeboats, but White Star Line Managing Director Ismay eliminated them because of the cost and for the sake of aesthetics. The argument was moot among ship designers. There was just no conceivable circumstance under which the *Titanic* might sink. Her enormous mass simply convinced maritime experts that the ship was unsinkable.

Titanic also boasted a steam powered generator system and electrical wiring that provided hallway and cabin lights at the turn of a switch. For communications she had two of the most advanced radiotelegraphy sets yet developed by Guglielmo Marconi of Bologna, Italy. Two employees of the Marconi International Marine Communication Company, providing the ability to transmit great numbers of passenger messages, manned the fifteen hundred watt wireless radio sets around the clock. Sending a wireless message was quite the thing to do for the wealthy, and at $3 for ten transmitted words, one had to be well to do. More importantly, the Marconi wireless was a vital tool to exchange information between ocean ships about weather situations, news or the location of icebergs blocking shipping lanes.

Finally, there was *Titanic*'s sumptuous luxury that far exceeded the seduction of any of her rivals. Her First Class staterooms and suites were exquisitely appointed and lavishly large, many with private sitting rooms. They were decorated with rich, handcrafted paneling, ornate ceramic and marble tiling, and hand-turned and carved oak, mahogany and English walnut furniture.

During *Titanic*'s fitting out, features never before seen on an Atlantic steamer were added to her design. She had an Olympic sized swimming pool, Turkish Baths, squash and racquet-ball courts, and even a fully equipped gymnasium with a private trainer. There were two First Class restaurants aboard that offered world-class cuisine and ambience. There was simply nothing second rate about *Titanic*.

In fact, experienced Second Class passengers found their accommodations rivaling those of First Class on other Liners. At the lowest levels of accommodations, even Steerage passengers found lodging far more comfortable and efficient than any other steamer afloat. For many, *Titanic*'s private, flushable toilets were a new experience.

Against this exceptional backdrop *Titanic* was ready to take on the North Atlantic. Sharply at twelve noon under a blazing sun and cloudless sky, Captain Smith gave the order to cast off *Titanic'* lines. Several thousand witnesses – including school children that had been dismissed early in order to witness the historical launch – screamed their delight as the amazing vessel immediately inched away from Berth 44. With the assistance of six tugboats and South of England Royal Mail Steam Packet Limited Company, *Titanic* made her way out of the Southampton harbor bound for a stop in Cherbourg, France early that same evening where she would board another two hundred seventy-five passengers. The following morning, she called upon the port of Queenstown, Ireland at Cobh's Cork Harbour on the south side of County Cork, to pick up an additional one hundred twenty. Queenstown was the final port of call for the *Titanic* before pointed her bow towards New York City.

Then, with her remarkable cast of characters tucked safely aboard – aristocrats and immigrants, the famous and the nondescript, the powerful, the adventurers and those just simply looking for a better life in the new world – *Titanic* headed east on her maiden voyage. She would follow the southern track, a route that followed the arc of a great circle from Fastnet Rock Lighthouse to the Nantucket Shoals Lightship. The trek across the vast Atlantic Ocean would steer a course that would have her arrive in New York late in the day on Wednesday, the seventeenth of April 1912. If Ismay had his way, *Titanic* would make port a day earlier.

The mood on board was excited, with even Steerage passengers celebrating as they looked forward to a new life in America. At the other end of fate, the wealthiest of the wealthy anticipated six or more days of pampering that not even those who were most able to afford it could imagine. On the Bridge, Captain Smith, on his final voyage, ceremonially gave First Officer William M. Murdoch command of the ship carrying some 2,228 passengers and crew. He gave the Officer precise and standing orders:

"Full speed ahead, Mr. Murdoch."

Two

For the next four days, *Titanic*'s passengers reveled in the luxury and security of the great ocean-going city. The North Atlantic weather was exceptionally kind to her, with plentiful warm sunshine and unusually calm seas. The ships' iconic bandleader, Wallace Hartley and his eight-piece orchestra provided background music throughout the day and evening. The mood aboard was almost serene.

There were innumerable leisure and recreational activities to choose from, especially for First Class passengers who were easily bored. For those athletically inclined, there was the ship's heated saltwater pool, a fully equipped gymnasium, massage parlors and Turkish baths. Shuffleboard, ring toss and squash and racquet courts were also available. Many of the Second Class passengers, who could also avail themselves of First Class amenities for a surcharge, took advantage of the *Titanic*'s impressive library. Steerage passengers had their own lounge and meeting rooms in which to gather, and many an hour was passed with music and dance.

For the First Class Passengers, the exquisite dénouement following a day of leisure was the dinner hour. These were eight or nine course social events as much as they were meals, and each was a unique *Magnus Opus* with menus designed to test and delight the palettes of even those who were routinely familiar with such cuisine.

Second Class fare was hardly as extravagant, but nonetheless a memorable culinary experience. In Steerage, passengers who were accustomed to subsistence meals of potato soup were sated with menus of roast pork and fresh vegetables, fresh breads and plum pudding. Early in the development of the *Titanic*'s mission, the White Star Line consciously chose to enhance the Steerage Class passenger's experience in every category aboard the ship. The company rightfully acknowledged that the vessel's financial success would depend largely on the satisfaction of those least able to afford the journey. This segment would always represent more than half of the paying customers making the crossing and it was simply good marketing logic to cater to them.

The evening of April 14th was a thrilling time for the passengers of the *Titanic*, most of whom were excitedly anticipating her triumphant arrival in New York on the 17th, and perhaps even earlier. Throughout the day and into the evening, telegraph operators John George Phillips and Harold Bride had been extremely busy satisfying the hundreds of wishes of passengers sending messages to family, friends and business associates. As well, the two radio operators were busy fielding increasingly urgent warnings from other steamers that pack ice and icebergs lay ahead directly in *Titanic*'s path. These warnings were dutifully passed to Captain Smith, who noted quietly that the ice was farther south in the westbound shipping lanes than he could remember. On several occasions during the day, passengers had noted the Captain and Chairman Ismay locked in serious conversation. It appeared to some that the two were in disagreement over something. Perhaps it was *Titanic*'s arrival schedule.

Despite the warnings, First Officer Murdoch was instructed to hold the ships speed at twenty-two and a half knots. As a precaution, Smith had ordered round the clock manning of the Crow's Nest, and Lookouts Frederick Fleet and Reginald Lee took over the watch at 10 p.m. high above the ship. As they assumed their posts some fifty feet above the Forecastle Deck, Fleet and Lee chatted up the sudden chilling of the air as it had turned bitterly cold. Mostly they watched and scanned the horizon in silence.

The night was windless and an almost eerie calm surrounded the ship as it sped through the blackness. Despite a moonless night, the cloudless sky was brilliant with stars, a dazzling spectacle that would have filled Van Gogh with inspiration. The sea was strangely calm, almost as if *Titanic* was sailing across a great pond. The surface was flat, glasslike without as much as a ripple disturbing the calm. On the Bridge, Fleet and Lee stood in silence, somewhat awed by the most unusual seas, and leaned forward while straining to see in the blackness. They were ready to ring the alarm bell at once should ice impede the path of the regal ocean liner.

Oblivious to the efforts of the Lookouts, most passengers had already turned in for the night. Far below the Crows Nest in the First Class Smoking Salon on A Deck, a group of diehards held onto the day's last minutes, serenely enjoying a late night cognac and cigar before calling it a night. Major Archie Butt held court around one table with Harry Widener and William Carter, owner of the Renault secured safely below decks. They were sitting with Captain Smith, himself enjoying a smoke before turning in after a most entertaining dinner held in his honor by the Frederick Goodwin family. Joining them were Benjamin Guggenheim, John Jacob Astor IV and his new bride, Madeleine, and "Molly" Brown.

Without warning, the main door of the First Class Smoking Room burst open, sending a wave of icy air into the room. Through the blue gray cloud of smoke that hung heavily in the salon, Second Officer Charles Herbert Lightoller emerged wearing the heavy, woolen White Star Line issue coat that the frigid night air required. He was visually troubled as he made his way to the Captain's table. It was 9:30 p.m.

Smith stood to meet him and moved away from earshot from his guests. He was visibly agitated.

"See here, Mr. Lightoller," snapped Smith, trying to keep his voice low, "this is most unusual, interrupting the First Class passengers. Shouldn't you be on the Bridge? Who is in command?"

"Begging your pardon sir, I apologize for what I realize is a most rude interruption," Lightoller stammered. "First Officer Murdoch has just now relieved me. But I thought it important that you be informed that we have received a wireless message from the *Californian* that she is stopped for the night, surrounded by pack ice and unable to move in any direction. As well, the *Amerika* has sent us numerous messages since early this afternoon with similar warnings of bergs and large growlers. We've also just heard from the *Mesaba*. She has elected to cut her speed by half rather than risk a collision. The sea has dropped to 28 degrees, down six degrees in the last hour."

Lightoller paused, waiting for Smith to respond. The Captain remained silent.

"I wonder, sir, given these consistent and reliable reports, if we should reconsider *Titanic's* present speed?"

A look came over Smith's face that instantly told the Second Officer he had overstepped his boundaries. He moved closer to the Second Officer, just inches from his face.

"Mr. Lightoller," Smith growled, his voice steady but with a tone of unmistakable irritation. "I find it most inappropriate that you would question my orders – but yes, I have seen the wireless reports. Consequently, I have ordered round the clock lookouts above and forward on A deck. The night is exceedingly clear and I see no reason for us to slow our course. Should we intercept ice, *Titanic* will have more than enough time to alter its course accordingly."

"I understand, Captain," the Second Officer replied, bruised but insistent. "But with no moonlight and the flat sea, our lookouts will have a time of it. Without water breaking over the bergs, there is little possibility that they will catch a glimpse of ice until we are on top of it," he argued, but hesitated before going on.

Smith was infuriated but refused to show his anger in front of the passengers. "Go on, Second Officer, you have more to add?" he said.

Lightoller swallowed hard. "Begging the Captain's indulgence sir, I recommend that we slow the boat to no more than ten knots." The young officer braced for the Captain's response. "And I will be on record as having stated my position."

Smith stiffened in surprise and his face reddened perceptibly as he bristled at the impetuous behavior of the junior officer. He took a deep breath to gain composure.

"Very well, Mr. Lightoller," Smith said, aggravation gone from his voice. "But be advised that I also will be on record regarding your quite ill-thought-out recommendation. Further to my notations will be my comments concerning evidence of a lack of trust in your Captain and questions as regards your experience in dealing with the challenges of weather in a transatlantic crossing. Now I suggest that you retire to your quarters in order to get some rest and be fit for your next rotation on the Bridge, which if I am not mistaken, should occur early tomorrow afternoon."

Lightoller was dumbstruck but Smith was not finished.

"Further, Mr. Lightoller, please revisit the Bridge and repeat my instructions to Mr. Murdoch, lest there be any confusion. We will stay our present course and speed of twenty-two and a half knots." He turned back to his guests.

"Now if you will excuse me, Second Officer, I would like to finish my cigar in peace and in the company of good gentlemen. Good night, Mr. Lightoller."

With that, the officer was summarily dismissed. He stood for a moment with his mouth open, searching for a word of retort. But common sense prevailed and he turned and left without another word, proceeding to the Bridge where he repeated Captain Smith's order.

"Bloody daft, old man. I agree with you," said Murdoch after Lightoller repeated the conversation, "but I'll not challenge the Captain's orders. At least not this Captain. Try to get some rest, chum."

As Lightoller departed the Bridge for the chilled air outside, a sudden instinct made him hang back in the shadows, out of the way. He watched as Murdoch rang up the Crow's Nest. First Lookout Frederick Fleet answered the telephone.

"I say, Mr. Fleet, how are conditions from the Crow's Nest? Is the visibility agreeable?" Murdoch asked.

Fleet, never one to mince words or be intimidated by rank, shot back. "It would be a bloody sake better if some half wit hadn't lost the keys to the case where the glasses are kept," he whined. "We are up here freezing our arses with nothing more to depend upon than four tired eyeballs and our dedication, First Officer," Fleet half joked but quickly turned serious. "I see no reason for worry at the moment, visibility is alright, but we'll have a dickens of a time catching a berg awash without a moon. It's a black night, sir."

With the telegraph line still open, Murdoch shouted around the Bridge for signs of the key to the binocular cabinet, to no avail. "Do your duty, First Lookout, and let me know immediately should a mist or fog make your job more difficult," he told Fleet. "Until then, Captain's orders: we will maintain course and speed."

Fleet couldn't contain himself. "Sir, if I might make a recommendation, perhaps the Captain would consider increasing our speed," he retorted, sarcastically. "That way if we hit a berg, we can blast right through it and supply shaved ice for our First Class passengers for the remainder of the passage."

Murdoch was not amused. "That will be enough, Mr. Fleet. Save your sharpness for your work." He hung up.

The Bridge was quiet again, but the banter with the Lookout had not settled well with the ship's officers, who were rightly nervous. Unexpectedly, the door to the Bridge swung open and the Captain entered the confine, followed closely behind by an obviously ill tempered Ismay.

Smith said nothing but motioned to Murdoch for his glasses. He immediately put them to his eyes and scanned the horizon for several minutes. Nothing but clear sailing, he thought, no ice in site. Seas as flat as a cold millpond. The Captain trusted his instincts but regretted being too quick and short-tempered in dismissing the concern of one of his senior officers – a *trusted* senior officer – so quickly. The conversation with Lightoller weighed heavily on his mind. Ismay, aware of Lightoller's misgivings, was silent but did not take his eyes off the Captain.

"Mr. Murdoch, I trust you are aware and fully briefed on the ice warnings from our steamer friends out in the shipping lanes?" Smith asked the First Officer.

Murdoch hesitated for a moment, then shook his head in agreement. "That I am, Captain.'

"And may I also assume that you have discussed our present course and speed as it relates to these warnings with your junior officers?"

Reluctantly, Murdoch replied. Damn the man he thought. Why make this an inquisition. "That I have Captain."

"Well, speak up man," Smith chided Murdoch. "What is your recommendation as a result of these considerations? Let us have it, now."

Murdoch stole a glance to the back of the Bridge where Lightoller stood silently, his fists balled up in tension. Damned if you do, damned if you don't, crossed his mind. He answered instinctively, politics be damned.

"Begging the Captain's pardon, sir, I believe we should dampen the boilers somewhat for prudence sake and save the Blue Riband for another time," Murdoch replied, his voice steady. "The pennant will be ours for the taking, any time we elect to make a run for it, I'm sure of it. However, given the current conditions, it would seem irresponsible to continue to make our forward progress at this speed."

Ismay came alive and snapped to attention. "Captain Smith, I most strenuously object to this kangaroo court." He stripped off his woolen scarf for effect and knotted it into a ball in his hand. He was bristling with indignation.

Smith turned to face him as Ismay continued.

"Let me remind you Captain Smith, I am the Managing Director of the White Star Line and responsible for the success of this ship. I have no intention of being bullied about by a group of novice seamen who clearly do not have the courage to take on a slim and calculated risk. Taking the Blue Riband on its maiden voyage means a great deal to the legend and aura of this ship and the company that owns it. I might add that my personal reputation is also very much on the line." Ismay's eyes were narrowed and his voice was peaked with anger as he finished. He fully expected to be taken very seriously, and his years in the boardroom had taught him well the power of intimidation.

Later, the officers on the *Titanic*'s Bridge would remember with pride the response of their Captain who reacted without hesitation, his voice fully in control.

"Mr. Ismay, there is no doubt in my mind that I am your subordinate and that I command this ship at your appointment and pleasure. And let me also say that I know fair well the importance of the reputation of the *Titanic*, as well as your own, for that matter.

"Having said that," the Captain paused and scanned the faces of his junior officers. It was look that could melt ice. He turned back to Ismay and repeated himself.

"Having said that, Managing Director, let me also remind you that I am the Captain of this ship, and until we make berth in New York and I am relieved of command and responsibility, I ultimately answer to no one regarding the safety of each and every man, woman and child aboard this vessel. They are my responsibility and I hold the charge dearly. Consequently, I don't give a tinkers damn about the Blue Riband as it relates to the well being of this ship and everyone aboard her."

Smith paused, his eyes boring in to the face before him. "Lest there be any confusion, Mr. Ismay, let me repeat myself. I and I alone am in command of this ship."

The silence across the Bridge was deafening. Smith handed the glasses back to Murdoch. "I trust, Mr. Ismay, that in the light of day and our safe and uneventful arrival in New York that you will have had time to reconsider your considerable angst over our disagreement and will join me in my opinion of caution."

The blood drained from Ismay's face exaggerating the redness in his nose and cheeks prompted by the short walk in the blistering cold outside. Murdoch thought he looked clownish but dared not crack a smile. The White Star chairman was rendered nearly speechless by the comeuppance of his subordinate, especially in full view of his officers.

Smith ignored him and turned to His First Officer. "Mr. Murdoch, alter our course three degrees south and reduce *Titanic*'s speed to two thirds. Also, double the Lookouts on A Deck and see to it that the Crow's Nest is relieved every four hours."

Smith looked around the Bridge, seeking any doubtful eye from his officers.

"Understood?"

"Aye, Captain," Murdoch replied stone faced. He turned and scanned the horizon with his glasses, careful to hide the slight grin on his face.

Satisfied, Smith buttoned his overcoat again and turned up the collar. "Now, if there is nothing else, I will retire to my cabin for the evening. Please be sure to interrupt me with any new news of ice in our path without hesitation, and as always rouse me to the Bridge in the event of any concern." With that, he doffed his cap again, wound his scarf tightly around his neck and departed the Bridge, leaving Ismay in a fit of silent rage. Lightoller also turned his back to Ismay, who bolted from the compartment a moment later.

Murdoch wasted no time in ringing the engine room. "All ahead, two thirds," he rang on the ships engine room telegraph. Immediately, Fireman Frederick Barret, upon seeing the change in orders on the identical boiler room telegraph, ordered the dampers closed on roughly a third of the furnaces. Within minutes, there was a

perceptible slowing of her hull. Though hardly
noticed by *Titanic*'s passengers in their First and Second
Class quarters, the reduction of speed was somewhat
more obvious in Steerage where the constant vibration of
the reciprocating engines had become a kind of white
noise. The din changed from a low-key vibration to a
hum, but was hardly alarming. On the Bridge, to a man,
the officers shared a silent relief.

On A Deck, Sixth Officer Moody joined the Lookouts
in scanning the horizon for ice, even as the ship slowed.
Quartermaster George Rowe joined him on the Poop
Deck of the stern, pacing back and forth to ward off the
bitter cold. Moody returned to the Bridge and stared into
the blackness, temporarily relieving Fourth Officer
Joseph Boxhall who had stepped aft to the officer's
quarter for a change into warmer clothing. Moody stood
by the wheelhouse that was manned by Quartermaster
Hitchens who was at the ships wheel. Quartermaster
Alfred Oliver leaned down to adjust the light on the
compass. Despite the nearly complete contingent on the
ships bridge, not one Officer said a word, such was their
intensity. Each had a job to do. *Titanic* was still making
twenty knots but was gradually slowing.

The Crow's Nest rang again, and the crew's attention
fell to Murdoch, who took the receiver. "What is it now,
Mr. Fleet?" silently praying that the Lookout had not
rung the Crows Nest bell, indicating that something was
directly in the path of *Titanic*. "Beggin' the First Officer's
patience once more, have we been able to locate the key
for the glass cabinet? It's awfully dark up here without
them."

"I'm afraid not, Mr. Fleet," Murdoch responded with
a touch of irritation. You'll either have to break the lock
or go without them. Make a decision, man." Now Fleet
was aggravated.

"Mr. Murdoch, I need not remind you that by White Star policy, if I break the lock except in a moment of emergency, my pay will be docked accordingly," Fleet replied sarcastically. "Why the bloody bastards stole two schillings from my last pay packet just to replace a cap that had blown off my bald head as we were docking in Southampton. It'll be the devil with my missus should I come home again short from this voyage. I guess we'll just have to take our chances, now won't we."

Murdoch hung up the telegraph heavily, accustomed to Fleets incessant criticism of his employer. But he was troubled.

"Mr. Lightoller, at the light of day, please see to it that the key for the Crow's nest cabinet is either found or the cabinet opened without it. I will take responsibility for any damage."

"Aye, sir," Lightoller mumbled, wondering how in the world such petty problems always seem to float down the chain of command. Dutifully, he would see to it in the morning, and the man who had pocketed the key would catch the dickens.

Below decks, most passengers had now settled into their quarters for the night, turning on electric heaters to take the chill out of the air. Most of the ships upper deck lights had been doused at 10 p.m., a normal occurrence aimed at encouraging passengers to turn in. As they trundled off to bed, relief crews began working to prepare for the next day. Oranges had to be squeezed for fresh juice, bakers baked, bus boys set tables, and maintenance workers washed down the decks and tile floors in the public rooms. *Titanic* never really slept. But aside from a few late night card games in the First and Second Class Smoking Salons, the ship was mostly quiet.

Major Butt and Clarence Moore of Washington had joined Harry Widener and William Carter and were immersed in a serious poker game, despite the lounge steward's polite suggestion that they finish for the night.

"Ah, gentlemen," Archie Butt remarked politely but with an unavoidable gloating edge, "it would appear that luck is with me on our voyage. I bid your attention to my straight flush as I remove the evenings' final pot from the table."

"Archie, were you not a gentleman, a war hero and the Presidents' advocate of all matters of importance, I would think you a cad," said Carter. "Sadly, the satisfied look upon your face overwhelms my sullenness at your good fortune. Perhaps I could interest you in the purchase of a fine new Renault?"

"Ever the salesman, William," Butt chuckled. He held up his snifter of cognac. "Gentlemen, I bid you a restful night. I think I will visit the Bridge for a moment to observe the chain of command before I retire."

On the Bridge, each man of the watch busied himself with peering into the blackness ahead searching for any telltale sign of ice in *Titanic*'s path. Major Butt entered the wheelhouse with cognac in hand but immediately sensed apprehension that seemed to envelop it. The interior lights had been dimmed to help with night vision, but the resulting yellowish glow on the Bridge was inadvertently morbid.

"Mr. Murdoch," Archie greeted the normally affable First Officer, 'I trust I am not imposing. I only mean to observe your fine command crew at work. I have been most impressed throughout our passage by your ability to juggle duty with the pleasantries and endless questions with which I and my fellow guests descend upon you, quite incessantly, I might add."

Murdoch tipped the brim of his cap to the Major. "Not at all, Major Butt, it is a privilege to welcome you to the Bridge," Murdoch said, expertly hiding his irritation at the untimely social call. "Begging your pardon, sir, we are a bit busy at the moment, despite the still nature of our conversation. We have been informed of ice in these waters by several of our steamship brethren, who have been so kind as to alert us almost constantly of the danger."

"Ice, my dear man?" Butt feigned surprise. "I was of the opinion that ice was merely a bother for a ship of the *Titanic*'s seeming invulnerability."

Murdoch turned and asked Lightoller to relieve him for a moment keeping watch next to the helmsman.

"Ice is a queer problem for any ship, Major, even for one with the obvious safety design advantages of the *Titanic*. But the current weather conditions do present a challenge to this watch, sir. The clear sky and calm waters are deceiving."

Butt was impressed by the First Officer's command of presentation and his confidence. A good officer, he thought, much substance behind an understated presence. Murdoch continued, unaware that he was being measured by one of the world's great military and political minds, a master of the analytical.

"Bergs are exceedingly difficult to see on a night like this," Murdoch went on, "Because there is no moon or breaking water, it is nearly impossible to make out the base of an iceberg from any distance in dark conditions. And though some icebergs may seem small on the surface and nothing to worry about, as much as four-fifths of their mass may be hidden below the water with surprisingly sharp and strong protrusions.

"Surprisingly, even in waters this cold, icebergs do melt, and as they do so, their center of gravity shifts and often the mass will capsize and present an entirely new dimension to the open air. In this case, as it happens, the newly exposed area can be quite often dark, covered with moss growing below it. When that happens, an iceberg can be almost impossible to see at night, especially under the conditions we have before us at this moment."

Second Operator Harold McBride ducked out from the telegraph room and handed the First Officer another ice message from the *Mesaba*, just seventy-five miles to the northwest. More large bergs had been cited. *Mesaba* would be stopped for the night, hemmed in by pack ice. Her wireless was shutting down until morning. Butt quickly excused himself and quietly left the Bridge, pausing only long enough at the door to take in the blanket of brilliant stars covering the horizon. Then he was off and silence commanded the Bridge once again.

Lightoller spoke first. "Should we disturb the Captain with the latest news of the *Mesaba*?" he asked Murdoch, who shook his head "No." "No new information there, Mr. Lightoller. Let him sleep."

With the warmth of the cognac making the aspect of a good night sleep that much more appealing, Archie Butt was hurrying to his stateroom when he spied John Jacob Astor IV strolling down the hall with his young bride, Madeleine Talmadge Force. At forty-six years of age, Astor had been ridiculed and vilified by New York society for his marriage to the eighteen year old girl. When the couple learned that she was pregnant, they departed for the shores of Europe and the Middle East to avoid the hurtful gossip. Now at five months along, Madeleine was eager to return to the States to ensure her baby had proper medical care.

Butt, well aware of the scandal surrounding their marriage, nonetheless greeted the Astor's with no less enthusiasm than he had the Pope or King George. "Mr. Astor, Mrs. Astor, what a delightful way to end a delightful evening. I trust you made out well at the cardtable, John?"

"Luck never seems far from my hand, Archie," Astor retorted. "Too bad that common courtesy seems to elude my wife at nearly every turn. I appreciate your sincere greetings, old man. They are not as common as one might think."

Madeleine Astor shushed her husband. "Now John, I am fully capable of handling myself in a room full of old biddies, I dare say. Sitting alone with old maids and pretenders to society is hardly a new match for me." Nevertheless, there was a sadness to her voice.

"One wonders when those who should know better will tend to their own troubles, rather than perseverate over things that are simply not of their concern," Astor responded, having the last word.

Butt, ever the gentlemen, offered kind words of comfort. "Madeleine, should you ever be in need of companionship, please by all means seek me out. There is nothing in the world I would enjoy more than the company of a beautiful woman on my empty arm. Come to think of it, I am rather intrigued by the notion of being seen as your newborn's grandfather. Now, good night to you both, pleasant dreams, and as you rest, be concerned only with that which intrudes on your true happiness."

Astor stood for a moment and looked into the Major's eyes. Words escaped him as he stuck out his hand for a firm, if not emotional grasp. "Thank you, Major, ever a true friend," was all he could muster.

Butt sighed as the couple entered a suite down the hall from his. As a man who had experienced life at all levels, Archie Butt was nonetheless always surprised by the extreme pettiness of the wealthy and powerful. Above all others, they should have more important things to attend to, he thought to himself as he entered his stateroom. He quickly draped his evening clothes over the back of a chair and climbed into a queen-sized, down-filled bed and fell asleep, exhausted. It was 11:15 p.m.

High above the ship in the Crow's Nest, standing just forward of the First Class staterooms, Lookouts Fleet and Lee continued their lonely watch for ice in the path of the now quiet ocean liner as the ship grew quiet. The two men fought a continuous battle with the freezing cold and the nagging urge for sleep that accompanied it.

"What I wouldn't give for a steaming mug of black coffee with a tip of brandy," Lee mumbled to his superior.

Frederick Fleet scowled. "As tempting as that may be, I'd trade a mug for a good set of glasses," he said ominously.

Three

As *Titanic* finally settled into a cruising speed of just under fifteen knots, the lookouts had been vigilant in their watch, but had seen nothing as yet. The ship was at least twenty minutes into the ocean area in which large ice had been warned, but the route remained clear. At 11:30 p.m., the horizon seemed to develop a slight haze. Neither man thought if worthy of note.

Five minutes later, Fleet's eyes narrowed. He leaned forward in the awkward Crow's Nest as if doing so would bring him closer to what he was looking for. Suddenly the outline of a large black object registered in his brain. There was no mistaking it. It was ice. A massive iceberg was directly in *Titanic*'s path, a quarter of a mile distant.

"There's ice ahead," he yelled to Lee and pushed him aside for the Crow's Nest bell, ringing it three times – an indication that there was something immediately ahead of the ships path. He reached for the telephone and waited anxiously for someone to answer. Sixth Officer Moody quickly picked up the receiver.

"Yes," Moody said. "What do you see?"

"Iceberg right ahead," Fleet shouted alarmingly.

"Thank you," Moody said unemotionally and hung up.

"Iceberg right ahead," the Sixth Officer called out to Murdoch, shattering the silence of the Bridge. By this time, Murdoch had himself seen the berg coming at them and raced to reach the engine room telegraph. He yanked the telegraph lever back, channeled through the "Full Stop" gate all the way to Full Astern", thereby signaling the engine room to reverse engines. At the same time he screamed, "Hard a' starboard" to Quartermaster Hitchens, still manning the wheel, who immediately spun it forcefully left to wheel lock. Moody, witnessing Hitchens maneuver, called out, "The wheel is hard over, sir."

High above in the Crow's Nest, Fleet and Lee braced for impact. They watched helplessly as the berg grew closer second by second. As *Titanic's* engine drive shafts strained to bring the propellers to an immediate stop before they fully reversed direction, the vessel slowed but remained on a collision course. Finally the huge spiral blades churned again in the opposite direction in a bid to slow the behemoth. Slowly, begrudgingly, the bow of the great ship began to swing to port but without enough distance still appeared to be headed for a direct bow-on impact. Murdoch desperately called out "Hard a' port' in an effort to drag the ships stern around the iceberg. Then, they waited. There was simply nothing left they could think to do.

Abruptly, the door to the bridge slammed open followed by a ghastly blast of frigid night air, and Captain Smith, having heard the three warning tones from his nearby cabin, had raced to the Bridge.

His overcoat slung over his pajamas, Smith screamed at Murdoch while reaching the wheelhouse with strides betraying his advanced years. "Belay that!" he ordered emphatically. "Engine room, full speed ahead." He wrenched the wheel from Hitchens while Murdoch worked the engine telegraph, pushing the young Quartermaster aside. Smith swung the wheel back to hard a'starboard with a mighty heave, leaving the open-mouthed Hitchens in shock. "Brace yourselves," Smith bellowed, and listened, or more felt, as the ships engines, straining under her new orders, churned *Titanics* propellors back again to full forward revolutions.

Murdoch recovered quickly from the change in command and raced to ring the water-tight door alarm and throw the switch that closed them. Deep below Titanic's waterline, firemen heard the bell ring and dived under the falling steel doors into the next compartment, knowing that they had just thirty seconds to make it. The First Officer then ordered the bilge pumps fired up in the forward holds.

A great wall of ice loomed before *Titanic* even as the bow began to swing to port. There was an agonizing scraping sound along her starboard side as the liner grazed the berg and sped past the one hundred foot high mountain of ice, her speed exaggerated to onlookers by the proximity of the wall gliding by. On the Bridge, they felt rather than heard the long shriek of metal, a sound similar to dragging one's fingernails across a slate board. Throughout the ship however, little more than a groan was heard or felt. Only those passengers out for a midnight stroll on the forward deck saw or heard the roar of the impact, and they back pedaled to safety as hundreds of pounds of ice that had been calved off the berg thundered down on to *Titanic's* deck.

Far below in the engine rooms, men scrambled for safety as the first two compartments of the ship began to flood from a two foot wide, one hundred eighty foot long gash that was gouged out of *Titanic's* starboard side. Twenty eight degree sea water rushed through the opening, the freezing cold water adding to the shock of the men who had not been able to clear the first two compartments and make their way to what they presumed was safety in the third. The water's angry rush literally knocked them off their feet and sent them tumbling against steel bulkheads.

On the Bridge, Captain Smith's mind was racing. He knew his ship had been damaged but not yet how seriously. He struggled to retain control over his emotions as the full shock of the unthinkable began to sink in. Command procedure dictated that he bring the ship to a stop at once and sound it for an adequate assessment of damage before determining a course of action. But he fought back his training and imbedded instincts, later not able to explain his actions when pressed. Instead he yelled out, "Maintain full ahead, give me maximum speed on this course." He thought for an instant more and hollered out, "Belay that, make your heading due north at three degrees. And get me the chief engineer on the telephone at once."

There was confusion on the Bridge as the Officers digested Smith's orders. "Mr. Lightholler," Smith yelled, "make sure the pumps have started and relay to the engine room that they are to keep all furnances stoked to the maximum. I need speed.

"Mr. Moody," he called to the Sixth Officer, "rouse Mr. Andrews and Mr. Ismay and summon them to the Bridge immediately. Bring the ships' carpenter as well."

Without so much as a breath, Smith continued to bark out orders. "Mr. Murdoch, please give me an exact reading of our current position and a heading for Cape Sable Island southeast of St. John's."

Moments later, Murdoch handed the telephone receiver to the Captain. It was Second Engineer James Hesketh. "Mr. Hesketh, what is your situation in the No. 6 boiler room?" Smith bellowed to the twenty-three year old, who was not at all familiar with speaking to the Captain so directly. "Sir, our situation is normal, all furnaces are firing and No. 6 boiler is fully operational. Perhaps if you could provide me with the context of the question…"

Smith interupted. "Hesketh, we have struck an iceberg, there is serious damage to at least the first two compartments, perhaps more. Now listen to me... it is urgent, vital that you keep all the remaining boilers on this ship fully fired. I must maintain forward progress. Do you understand, young man?"

"Uh, yes sir, yes sir, Captain. I will do my best," the stunned engineer responded.

"I'm afraid 'your best' will not suffice, Mr. Hesketh," Smith shot back. "I demand you give me the impossible. Understood?"

"Aye, aye, sir." Hesketh heard the phone line go dead, then spent several long seconds staring at the receiver, wondering whether he had imagined the conversation.

While waiting for Andrews and Ismay, Smith further instructed Fourth Officer Joseph Boxhall to make his way as far down in the ship as he could go and assess the damage. Then he ducked into the wireless room and confronted Harold Bride and Jack Philips, still operating the powerful wireless trying to catch up on passenger messages.

"Men, we have struck a berg. Inform all nearby ships by CQD that we have sustained serious damage and are in need of assistance, details to follow immediately," he ordered. "Also inform them that we are still underway and to chase us if necessary. It is likely that we will need their boats."

Bride and Philips looked at each other incredulously, then immediately went about the task, urgently trying to reach those ships they knew to be within a hundred miles of *Titanic*, including her sister ship, *RMS Olympic*. The Cunard passenger liner *Carpathia* was fifty eight miles away and the *Virginian* and the German freighter *Frankfurt* were both more than a hundred miles away. A smaller ship could be seen off the starboard side, it's running lights blazing in the night seemingly less than ten miles away, but it could not be identified or roused by radio.

Several minutes later, *Titanic* received her first reply to the CQD from the *Frankfurt*, which although more than one hundred miles to the east, had a strong signal.

```
"We are turning course for you. What is your
situation?"
```

Bride, his finger flying over the telegraph key, immediately shot back:

```
"We are gravely damaged.
Sinking at bow.
Immediate assistance required."
```

From the *Frankfurt* came an ominous reply.

```
"We are at 18 knots; pack ice heavy.
More than seven hours to your position.
May God be with you."
```

Some four hundred miles west of *Titanic* at Cape Race, the new Marconi Company wireless station, operating twenty four hours a day, picked up the CQD, as well.

"My God, Gray," wireless operator Jack Goodwin shouted to his partner, Walter Gray, "*Titanic* has struck a berg!" He immediately began relaying the information to ships all over the dark Atlantic, and to impress a potential customer of the value of its new radiotelegraphy abilities, he also sent it to the *New York Times*. Consequently, millions of people safely on dry land would know of *Titanic*'s dire situation even before some of its own passengers.

Andrews and Ismay arrived on the Bridge simultaneously. "Gentlemen, we have struck a berg," Smith informed them, ever polite and cordial, but pulling no punches. "I'm afraid the Blue Riband will have to wait for another day, if at all," he said sarcastically, staring into the unblinking, emotionless façade of his superior. Ismay ignored Smith's look and interrupted the Captain.

"I have just now come from a chance meeting in the stair well with First Engineer Bell who assures me that although the ship is seriously damaged, he is satisfied the pumps will keep her afloat.

"Now, do you have more to tell us Captain, or may I resume my sleep?" Ismay added sarcastically.

Smith took a step toward him, his hands clenched, his face red with strain. Before he could respond, Andrews, oblivious to Ismay's incredible display of arrogance, began spreading out a large set of blueprints on the Bridge table. Fourth Officer Boxhall arrived back on the deck with the first report of damage. He was wide-eyed and obviously frightened. Smith, as much to calm his own nerves, moved quickly to steady the young officer.

"I'm sorry, Captain. We are taking on water fast," he reported, trying to catch his breath. "There is as much as fourteen feet in the first compartment, the mail hold is filling rapidly and there appears to be a gash at least several inches, if not more than a foot wide running the length of the compartment," Boxhall said. "The furnaces have yet to be damped and at the moment we are still running at full speed. Have no doubt about it, sir, we are taking on water fast," he repeated. "The second compartment already contains some eight feet of water, and it is rising quickly. The bilge pumps are running at maximum speed, but at the rate of water entering the compartments, I don't know if they are up to the task."

"Goddamitt," the normally reserved Thomas Andrews muttered under his breath as he drew red lines across the bulkheads of the first three compartments. He drew in a deep breath before he spoke. The architect was still dressed in his evening clothes,

"We have two major problems as I see it, from Mr. Boxhall's report," he said calmly, the engineer and architect in him masking his concern. "The first is that this ship is designed to float with any three compartments flooded. For now it appears that the damage is limited to the forward three, which would seem to be good news. We need inspection of four and five immediately. " He paused, not wanting to say what came next. Smith knew what was coming and caught his breath.

"If additional compartments have been breached," Andrews continued, "we have an unthinkable circumstance with which to contend. For you see, unfortunately, the concept of foundering was never confronted in the design of the *Titanic*. I'm afraid that all the talk of the 'virtually unsinkable' ship was the work of your legion of public relations men, Mr. Ismay. At this moment, I cannot tell you the depth of my regret for not being more firm in my design criteria that may have actually made *Titanic* all but unsinkable.

"You see, *Titanic*'s bulkheads rise only to E Deck," Andrews continued, now visibly shaken. "Should the water rise above that to F Deck, it will then continue to gradually lap into each of the successive thirteen compartments. Gradually – how fast I cannot say with certainty –the ship will be pulled under by the enormous weight.

"That is, of course, if *Titanic* doesn't snap her keel from the forward weight and break in two."

Ismay's smugness vanished and his face turned the color of spoilt milk. There was a collective gasp on the Bridge. The Chairman's hands began to tremble as Andrews' analysis was laid out. The ship's carpenter returned to the Bridge to report that water was rising fast in the third compartment and had been abandoned by the firemen and stokers.

"As I feared, gentlemen," Andrews said with resignation. "The second problem, but possibly our only hope, is the extensive bilge pump system installed in *Titanic*." Smith furrowed his white brows, puzzled by Andrews' statement.

"There are five ballast and three bilge pumps which are used to trim the vessel," the Harland & Wolff architect continued. "The total discharge capacity from all eight pumps is about four hundred twenty-five thousand gallons per hour That means we should be able to keep pace with what I roughly estimate to be an inflow rate of fifteen cubic feet of water per second. Theoretically, if we can keep the pumps operating, we should be able to keep Titanic afloat for days."

Smith interrupted, impatiently. "So what is the problem, Mr. Andrews. We have little time to waste, man."

"The problem," Andrews continued in as calm a voice that he could muster, "is that three of the bilge pumps are in the forward boiler rooms, and four more are in the submerged engine rooms. I suspect these will shortly become useless and unfortunately, there were no sluice valves designed into the bilge system. Consequently there are no means of mating the pumps in series which would allow water to be pumped from one compartment to another."

Smith and Ismay stared down at the drawings, lost in the complexity of Andrew's assessment. "In other words, gentlemen, unless we can keep the pumps operating in the first three compartments, the rate of influx will drag this ship to the bottom in ..." he stopped and rapidly drew penciled calculations on the chart.

"Helmsman," he hollered out, "what does the inclinometer show?" Hitchens hesitated as he checked.

"For the love of god man..." Andrews snapped impatiently.

"She is slightly down at the head and listing five degrees to starboard, sir," Hitchens replied formally."

"Five degrees... my lord... " the architect mumbled, lost in his silent calculations. Finally he spoke.

"Captain, I estimate she has less than five hours."

Smith was visibly stunned and rocked back on his heels. "Good God," he stammered, gripping the edge of the table with both hands. "I believe there is no ship less than four hours sailing time from us."

A look of fright overcame Ismay. "But surely there are the boats , Captain. They will sustain us until help arrives." He was clearly terrorized.

Smith thought to throttle the White Star executive before Andrews interrupted, a look of disgust coming over his face.

"You will recall, Mr. Ismay, that it was your decision to halve the number of life boats aboard this vessel as a means of cutting costs. There are only twenty lifeboats aboard, including the three collapsibles." He paused to allow Ismay to absorb the information. "If no help arrives and we must take to the boats and they are fully filled, at least a thousand souls will be left aboard to perish. I believe the water is at or below freezing. Hypothermia takes but minutes."

Smith, staggered to hear the nightmare spelled out before him, thought of the handgun in the safe of his quarters. The thought of so many to perish under his command was incomprehensible to the veteran commander. He could not accept it.

Smith grasped Andrew's shoulder and pleaded with him. "There must be something that can be done... we are still making headway... the passengers are not yet even aware...

Murdoch reported to the Captain with a fix on *Titanic*'s position. "We are at longitude 41 degrees, 46 minutes north and latitude 50 degrees, 14 minutes west, Captain, approximately two hundred twenty-five miles southeast of Cape Sable Island."

Smith gazed at Murdoch intensely as the words came off his lips. "Mr. Murdoch, what is our present speed?"

"We are still making seventeen knots, Captain."

"And what is the state of the passengers?" Smith probed.

"Calm, sir. Most were not roused from their quarters by the impact and they are unaware of our situation. Those who have knowledge do not seem to show any inordinate degree of distress.

"Keep it that way, as long as possible, First Officer."

"Excuse me, Captain, but shouldn't we ready the boats?" Murdoch was even more puzzled at the behavior of his Captain.

Smith snapped at the First Officer. "Under no circumstances, is that perfectly clear? We would have to stop the ship to man the boats and we cannot afford to do that. And it will cause a panic when our passengers realize they have become victims of accountants. Please check with the wireless operators as to their progress and report back to me at once."

"Aye, sir."

Smith turned to Andrews again, now having totally dismissed Ismay's presence. The White Star Line Chairman was sitting, head hung, deep in thought.

"Two hundred twenty-five miles. Mr. Andrews, what can we do to stretch the life of this vessel to ten hours rather than five?" Smith removed his glasses and placed them on the blueprints, which were rapidly filling with Andrews's calculations.

The architect looked up, incredulous. "Ten hours, Captain? A bloody miracle, that's all it would take," the architect responded sarcastically.

Smith didn't blink. "Mr. Andrews, do not waste my time or yours. We have precious little of either."

"Captain..." Andrews was shaken by the seriousness of the officer's tone. "You ask the impossible. Why..." he went to continue, then abrupty stopped. He was lost in contemplation, as if his train of thought had unexpectedly changed spurs. He sat in silence, his eyes transfixed for a long moment.

Then, as if jolted by electricity he blurted out, "Perhaps... just perhaps... we could lengthen the time afloat if we were able to lighten the load."

Smith snapped at him.

"Mr. Andrews, I am trying to save passengers, not throw them overboard," the Captain said with increasing impatience. "And even if we throw over the side every mattress, dish, the entire wine cellar, every stick of furniture and just about everything else not nailed down on this ship, we might perhaps lighten our load by a hundred thousand pounds. I can't imagine that will bring us more than another few minutes before sinking below the surface."

Andrews waved off the Captain, annoyed at how such a brilliant man could miss his thought so completely. He took a deep breath and tried again.

"Captain Smith, you are familiar with the *Titanic's* double bottom hull – which of course holds forty four water tanks for ballast." Smith's eyes narrowed.

"The tanks contain some two hundred forty thousand gallons of water weighing more than nine hundred tons. She carries another sixty tons of drinking water. That's nearly two million pounds of weight, Captain. You see, if we were able to offload our ballast and maintain our speed, there is a chance." He was dumbstruck by his own analysis.

"Yes, there is a bloody well good chance, Captain."

Smith looked startled. "Ah, yes, Mr. Andrews," Smith challenged the brilliant designer "but we can't just instantaneously dump two million pounds of ballast. The ship would capsize with the slightest roll."

"I agree... but if..." He was interrupted by a large woman dressed in a huge fur coat who unceremoniously blasted through the doorway of the Bridge, brushing past a procession of interceding officers who tried unsuccessfully to block her entrance.

"What the hell in tarnation is going on around here," said the cantankerous Margaret "Molly" Brown, the unrefined widowed millionairess from Denver who was generally as game for a confrontation as she was a conversation. "Who the hell is in charge here, boy?" she said to Lightoller, who was at the moment working with the Quartermaster to ascertain the number of lifejackets on board.

"Now see here, Mrs. Brown," Lightoller stammered, this is a busy place at the moment. Please return to your cabin."

"The hell I will," she shot back. "It just so happens that my cabin window was open a few minutes ago, and for some reason, I've got enough ice in my room to build an igloo. Some son of a bitch's got some explaining to do fast. Did this tub hit something – who the hell was driving?"

Captain Smith brushed the hapless Lightoller aside and greeted Mrs. Brown with all the élan he had learned during thirty years of command at the worst of times, and with the worst of passengers.

"Mrs. Brown, we do have a slight emergency here," Smith begged, "and I must ask you to return to your quarters. I will see to it that your steward freshens up your stateroom at once."

"Listen, E.J.," she said, glaring at the defenseless Captain. "It'll take a tougher gang of fellas than you've got to get me out of here before I get some answers. What's going on?"

Smith surrendered. "Mrs. Brown, it is imperative that we not alarm the other passengers, but I am afraid we have struck an iceberg and *Titanic* has sustained serious damage. We are just now ascertaining our situation and the proper course of action."

At that, Molly Brown's eyes rolled and she promptly fainted, crumpling to the deck. "Mr. Boxhall, please return Mrs. Brown to her cabin and see to it that she stays there for the time being. We hardly need this distraction…"

Boxhall and the two stewards called to the Bridge escorted the portly woman back to her First Class Stateroom, lucky not to be intercepted by other passengers in the process.

Smith turned back to Andrews. "I'm afraid we've only minutes until the truth begins to leak out. We must assume the Steerage passengers will soon be seeing signs of water if they have not already. Hurry, Mr. Andrews. Make sense of this, man," the Captain said with urgency. The Bridge was quickly turning to bedlam, made louder by the increasingly urgent messages being sent by the wireless operators.

"We must lighten the forward load, Captain," Andrews shot back. "Assuming that the forward bilge pumps are soon to be useless, we must raise her bow as high as possible to avert more water from spilling into the fourth and fifth compartments."

"But how, Andrews, *how* do we do it," Smith replied in frustration. "Can we offload ballast from the forward tanks without the risk of unstabilizing her?

"Yes, I believe so," Andrews said, nodding. "But they must be purged while maintaining our speed. And at all costs we must keep the midships and stern bilge pumps operating at full capacity.

"But what will this buy us, Captain – merely time?" Andrews probed. "Granted, we can be assured of help – at least from the *Carpathia* which is already steaming towards us... and blast it, that vessel to our east if we can only raise the fool... but even then, I suspect that transferring passengers in lifeboats on the open seas is a treacherous notion at best... "

Smith looked deeply into his eyes.

"Cape Sable Island is within our reach, Mr. Andrews," he said. "I need nine hours to get us there -- if we can maintain our current speed. It is known as the graveyard of the Atlantic to most seamen, one of the most hazardous navigational points on the globe. But by God... it may just turn out to be our savior. The Island is a sandy shoal about a hundred miles off the coast of Nova Scotia. Her waters are shallow, no more than fifty to seventy feet at most. I know it well, having shipped out from there as a young boy."

Smith paused and closed his eyes, composing himself. His plan was a long shot, but worth a try. He owed that much to the thousand or more people who would have no hope of survival if *Titanic* foundered. The Captain turned and faced the bow, already visibly lower in the sea.

"Mr. Andrews," he continued. "I intend to beach this young lady on her first date."

Four

Andrews took in a deep breath, dumbfounded by Smith's plan.

"My God, Captain, it may, just may, work. But time is of the essence," the architect thought aloud. "Paramount to our survival is lightening the load immediately. It's going to take some time to offload our ballast and drinking supplies safely. Perhaps too much time."

First Officer Murdoch had stood silently by his Captain while the plan was laid out. Only now did he contribute. "Captain, I know a step we can take immediately."

"Let's have it man, quickly." Murdoch hurriedly described his plan.

"Brilliant. You'll see a command of your own yet, First Officer Murdoch. Now go and rouse Major Butt and accompany him to the Bridge as soon as possible."

Five

By day, Major Archie Butt's composure and self-assurance marked him as a man of supreme discipline. At night, he fought the terrors that curse the soldier – one who has seen and felt war in all its horror. He slept the sleep of the warrior, a relentless struggle that replayed the bloodshed over and over again in his dreams.   Each night he felt the wind as bullets whistled by his head, and watched again as the bodies of comrades fell around him, torn and ruined.   Those who thought of war and glory in the same context had never slept the soldiers sleep.

The long hours of darkness came hard for Butt. Working into the early morning hours at the White House, under guise of the pressures of his esteemed office, was more an excuse for deferring the inevitability of a fitful sleep. He spoke of it to no one, ever. The scars of war would not allow him the comfort of the intimacy of another. He lived his days in bright lights, his nights, alone in the darkness.

On this night in his First Class stateroom, from somewhere deep in the inexhaustible battle Butt's subconscious railed at an incessant pounding. There was a clamor at the door that he could not place for long minutes. Finally he broke through and recognized the pounding as someone pleading with him to open the door.

He jerked his large frame out of the bed, threw on a robe and reached for the door, just as a startled steward opened it with a pass key. "Major Butt..." he stammered.

Butt had been asleep for no more than thirty minutes but the rest hung heavily in his eyes. "Yes, dear man," he replied, always the gentleman. "Whatever can be so urgent?"

First Officer Murdoch appeared behind the Steward and entered the room. Surprised, Butt greeted the Officer. "To what do I owe the pleasure, Mr. Murdoch," he spoke before seeing the worry and strain on the Officers face.

"Major Butt, dreadfully sorry to rouse you at this ungodly hour," Murdoch apologized, "but if you could please allow me to escort you to the Bridge. You are needed urgently, sir."

Butt's eyes narrowed in puzzlement, but he was accustomed to following orders as well as giving them. The soldier asked no questions and obliged the First Officer unhesitatingly. "Just give me a minute to dress."

Less then five minutes later, Butt was greeted by Captain Smith, his entire brigade of command, Thomas Andrews and J. Bruce Ismay. The White Star Chairman was uncharacteristically silent. They were all gathered around blueprints spread out on a large table. At the wheel, Quartermaster Hitchens called out *Titanic's* speed every several moments, while Second Officer Lightoller was on the telephone with the engine room.

Behind the Bridge, in the wireless room, Butt overheard Bride and Philips working feverishly to send out distress calls. Bride called out, "*Carpathia* has just responded. I told her we have struck a berg and to come at once." Philips suggested that Bride send out an "SOS" – the new international wireless distress call signals. "It's the new call, besides, it may be your last chance to use it."

"Quiet… the *Frankfurt* has heard us as well,"
Bride responded. "She's eighty miles from us."

Without being offered a single word of explanation,
Butt immediately grasped the gravity of the situation.
Titanic had struck an iceberg and the ship was sinking..
"How could that be?" he thought.

Smith abruptly noticed the Major's arrival on the
Bridge and grabbed his arm, dragging him to the group
gathered around the blueprints. "Captain Smith…what
has …?"

"Major Butt, the sad truth is that *Titanic* has struck an
iceberg and she is seriously damaged," Smith explained
gravely. "We have less than five hours before she goes
under. Without a daring action, she is doomed."

"How…?" Butt's consciousness demanded an
answer. But the soldier in him took over.

"Forgive me, Captain," Butt said, his back
straightening from instinct. "I assume you have called
me here for a reason. How may I serve?"

Smith eyed him for a moment, recognizing how
remarkable a man the President of the United States had
chosen as his most trusted advisor.   "I am grateful
for your presence, Major Butt." He sighed, deeply,
before going on. "Never in my long years…" He seemed
to be losing focus for a moment, lost in the irony that had
struck his fabled career. But his concentration, steeled by
three decades of command, was quickly recovered.

"What I need from you, Major," he went on, "is a
strong hand. I need the assistance of someone who has
experience in managing a large mass of people in a most
chaotic situation where control and discipline will be the
difference between life and death."

Butt didn't blink. "Go on, Captain."

"At this moment, we are making a dash for Cape
Sable Island, about two hundred twenty miles from here
-- nine hours sailing time if we can keep up our speed. If

we can make it," Smith paused to let his words sink in, "we will beach *Titanic* in the shallows. It is our only hope. Unfortunately, if we do nothing, there does not appear to be a ship close enough to reach us here before we founder. We have no other option."

The Major hung on every word coming off Smith's lips. "But this is not just a matter of speed, Major Butt. We have complicated maneuvers ahead of us over this long night that will, with God's grace, enable us to stay afloat while maintaining speed."

Thomas Andrews addressed the Major. "What the Captain means, is that we must lighten the *Titanic*'s load to compensate for the weight of the water she is taking on and keep her bow as high as possible. I am working with the ships engineers now to devise a plan to offload, at critical moments, most of nearly two million pounds of ballast that will give us a fighting chance."

"But that will take time, Major," Smith interjected, "and time is our enemy. There is another step we must take, without delay, and that is where we need your help."

"Get to the point, Captain. I have already unsheathed my saber." Major Archie Butt, the warrior and war hero, was now on deck.

"Most of our passengers were sleeping when the accident occurred, and with the exception of some of those in Steerage whose cabins have begun taking on water, they are unaware of the situation and danger. Unfortunately, we must reverse that quickly," Smith said firmly.

Andrews finally answered the mystery. "In order to move weight aft as quickly as possible, we need to rouse the whole ships' compliment – including non-essential crew -- and move them as far back on the stern as space will allow." He paused and looked down at his drawings.

"Without a panic," Smith finished.

Butt almost laughed out loud, only respect and the gravity of the circumstances keeping his face stolid.

"Captain Smith, I suggest the chances of that are akin to striking a match underwater… please excuse the ill-timed analogy."

"Major Butt… we have *no* time," he said, impatiently. "Now, I have much to do. Can I count on you to assume the role of an Officer of this ship and take command of the passengers?"

Butt didn't flinch. With the response of one accustomed to command crisis, he simply asked, "Who is the Chief Steward?"

Smith allowed himself the one smile he would wear on his face that night. "Mr. Pitman, hurry here please," Smith bellowed. Third Officer Herbert Pitman was also the Junior Watch Officer who was responsible for the loading and unloading of passengers and baggage. Consequently he also had command of the more than two hundred ships stewards who served aboard the Liner. At than moment, Pitman was frantically organizing the loading lists for the lifeboats, which had not been completed when *Titanic* left Southampton.

"Aye, Captain."

"Mr. Pitman, Major Butt has been appointed an officer of this ship for the duration of the crisis and you are to offer him every assistance," Smith ordered. "Understood?"

"Aye, Captain," Pitman repeated, with no visible sign of indignation at his new responsibility. He was very familiar with Major Butt, although had never met him. He turned to face the soldier. "I am at your service, Major."

Butt liked the man immediately. "Mr. Pitman, please rouse all the ships stewards and stewardesses and have them gather in the First Class Smoking Salon within the next ten minutes. I will meet you there." Pitman's immediate response was to set off to fulfill his orders, no questions asked.

Butt looked Smith in the eye. "Good luck, Captain. You deserve better than this."

Smith dropped his gaze, unable to look Butt in the eye. "Thank you Major, but I am a victim of my own arrogance and failure to command. Let us hope I am the only victim." The two men parted without another word.

As the Major left the Bridge to return to his suite for warmer clothing, he heard Smith call out to Fifth Officer Harold Lowe. "Mr. Lowe, see to it that we fire our distress rockets every three minutes, commencing immediately."

"Captain, I am sorry to report that we did not load a full compliment of rockets in Southampton," Lowe responded. "We have but a dozen, along with the usual supply of fireworks for the entertainment of the passengers."

"Blast it – has anything been seen to properly on this ship?" the Captain replied angrily, more upset with his own failure to attend to details than with the Officer. "Fire what you have until they are exhausted. Any rockets seen at this time of night should indicate we are in distress. Jump to it, man."

As Archie Butt made his way the short distance to his cabin, Steerage passengers began arriving on the deck, visibly panicked. Some had turned out in nothing but bedclothes and wore no shoes. They were desperate for some word of what was happening. Butt made mental notes to correct both situations quickly.

Several minutes later, as he entered the First Class Smoking Salon, the Ship's steam whistles began to blow, triggering the first audible indication of trouble, followed by the screeching wine of the first distress rocket exploding above *Titanic*. The rocket soared above the ship's rigging and exploded with the sound of a thunderclap, sending down a rainfall of brilliantly white stars which slowly fell to the ocean's surface.

The noise in the Salon was almost as deafening, as the tired stewards and stewardesses who had been roused unaware from their bunks were talking in raised, worried voices about the reason for them being assembled. Heads turned in his direction as he entered the room, and some of the nervous chatter died down. Butt waited a few moments more, then after getting a signal from Pitman that all were gathered, he spoke. Only later would he realize that his brief instructions were probably the most important commands he had ever given.

"Ladies and gentlemen, I am Major Archie Butt of the United States. Please forgive me for so rudely calling you here at a moment's notice." The man simply could not help himself from behaving as a gentleman first, no matter what the circumstances.

In an instant, he had their rapt attention. "As some of you may have become aware in the last few minutes, *Titanic* has struck a berg and has sustained serious damage. In fact, she is sinking." He paused for a second, allowing the words to penetrate. There was a collective gasp from the group, with some of the more emotional crew showing immediate signs of fright. Some cursed, some began to cry, others sat heavily in stunned silence.

"I have just left the Bridge where, I assure you, Captain Smith is fully in charge of this crisis," Butt continued. "As you by now have noticed, the bow is down and we are listing. Some of the Steerage passengers have been evacuated from their cabins as they have begun to flood. Given our current circumstances, even as we continue to sail, Captain Smith and the ship's designer, Mr. Andrews, have informed me that this vessel will founder in less than five hours."

There was another gasp, only louder. Several stewards made a bolt for the door as if to escape the inescapable. Pitman blocked their exit.

"Ladies and gentlemen, I am telling you the facts. I have left out only one element," Butt said, then paused, desperately aware that his next words were vital. "And that is hope." He scanned the room, staring into each of their anxious faces. "Because, despite the direness of our situation, there is hope, there is the chance of saving this ship and all the passengers and crew aboard." The room fell back into silence.

Butt stood mute for long seconds, leaving his audience thirsting for his next words.

At last, he continued. "Captain Smith has devised an ingenious, yet hardly certain plan to beach this vessel in the shallows some two hundred miles from here off Cape Sable Island."

Now the air was filled with murmurs of disbelief.

"I need not inform crew of your experience that covering more than two hundred miles of ocean, even at maximum speed and in perfect conditions, will take longer than five hours." There were several loud guffaws in the back of the room. Butt ignored them. "Consequently, in order to counter the vast weight now accumulating in the forward holds, and keep our boilers fired so that we can operate the bilge pumps at their highest output and maintain the greatest speed possible, we must shed ballast from our tanks and maintain the ships stability. The only way to do accomplish this miracle is to keep the bow from slipping lower.

"When I left the Bridge, the clinometer indicated the bow was down five degrees and listing to starboard. I assume we are deeper since then."

There came a shout. "Are you daft man?" An older chief steward, who had signed on in Belfast, called out from the back of the room, inciting a low growl of agreement with his disproval. "We'll never make it. Better to stir the passengers and set us all off on the boats now, I say. Let's get off this tub while we still can." Many in the room shouted their agreement.

"Sir!" Butt demanded attention. "Need I remind you that the difference between ships 'Steward' and ships 'Captain' is something called 'experience'?" The anxious crowd calmed immediately as Butt seized order swiftly.

"So as you are completely informed, it is also my unfortunate duty to enlighten you that *Titanic*, for reasons I do not fully comprehend, does not carry enough life boats for even half of the passengers and crew aboard this ship." There was a gasp as the Major paused again. "I need not remind you that swimming in these freezing waters is not an option.

"Ladies and gentlemen, there is only one alternative: blind confidence in Captain Smith and resolute commitment to his orders without challenge. The lives of your passengers – and your very own – depend on it." Butt was finished. Now it was up to the crew.

There was silence. Not a man spoke, until one brave enough said the only words possible. Steward Henry Samuel Etches stood and loudly cleared his throat.

"Aye, Major," he said. "The deck is already uneven beneath our feet. Let's get on with it. You've called us here for a reason.

"What is it?"

Six

Butt began rattling off orders with machine gun precision.

"I will only have time to say this once, so listen carefully, please," he began.

"First, see to it that every man, woman and child on this ship is roused from their bunks and escorted to the stern." Then, mindful of class, though he detested it, he added: "First and Second Class passengers above to the Poop deck, Steerage passengers to the general room below." If nothing else, maintenance of the cast system even in this dark hour would aid in cooperation.

"Accept no pleas or excuses to stay behind," Butt continued. "Ensure that all passengers are bundled tightly against the cold – it will be a long and frigid night with little chance for respite. Issue life jackets to each passenger without fail and provide instructions quickly but carefully to those needing assistance and as to their use.

"Once your passengers are on deck at the stern, collect blankets and warmers as you can and provide them to the neediest. Mr. Pitman?" Butt called.

"Aye, Major Butt," Pitman responded immediately. "See to it that provisions for brewing coffee are set up in the general room as far astern as possible. Instruct the galley stewards to brew barrels of the stuff. Also, all of you assigned to any of the dining facilities, gather up as much bread as possible and store it on the Docking Bridge."

He paused, running through the mental checklist he had built in the minutes after his conversation with Captain Smith. "Mr. Pitman, who is the ship's doctor and is he among us?" Butt's voice rang out with the confidence of a man who knew how to lead men.

"Dr. William Francis O'Loughlin is the ship's doctor. He is not among us."

"See to it personally that he gathers all the medical supplies available, especially revival medicines and transport them to the safest location available on the aft Well Deck. It is unlikely we will need surgical supplies, but if they are available and manageable bring them as well. Also, Mr. Pitman, lock down all alcohol provisions – regardless of class. The last thing we need is a drunken mob."

Silence greeted his last words. "Finally, I need not exaggerate the importance of efficiency. This must be carried out with absolutely no delay -- and although I realize how ridiculous this sounds – with dead calm. We cannot allow general panic or riot. The price for loss of control is doom," Butt concluded.

"Godspeed, my friends, and may your creator be with you this night."

With the Major's final words, there was a rush to the exit of the Smoking Salon. Few words were passed between the crew. Their instructions were clear. So too was the price of failure.

As the room emptied, a solitary figure stayed behind and approached Major Butt. He was still dressed in his evening clothes and clutched a violin tucked under his arm. "Begging the Major's pardon, sir, I am Wallace Hartley, conductor of the ship's orchestra. May I have a moment?"

"Those few that are left, Mr. Hartley," Butt replied stoically. "How can I help you?"

"With your permission sir, I would like to gather my small ensemble on the Docking Bridge and play through the night," Hartley requested. "Our music is generally calming, and it may help to ease the atmosphere."

Butt beamed at the suggestion. "What a splendid contribution, Mr. Hartley, and a courageous one at that. And may I ask a favor?"

"Undoubtedly, Major Butt."

"When we beach *Titanic* on the sands, might you play the chorus line from the 'Battle Hymn of the Republic'?"

Hartley thought for a moment. You mean 'Glory, Glory Hallelujah'?"

"Precisely, Mr. Hartley."

Seven

Even as Archie Butt addressed the ship's crew, Captain Smith and his chief officers were frantically identifying every means possible to lighten the load on *Titanic*'s bow, which had already slipped another two degrees under. Water had now filled the first two compartments and the surge was beginning to slip over her forward deck as she struggled ahead, her massive engines still churning with all their might against the opposing force of the filling seawater.

"Mr. Wilde," Smith called to the ship's Chief Officer, a seaman that he had not served with before *Titanic*'s departure from Belfast. Neither man had had much of a chance to surmise the other. Smith had not yet formed an opinion of him.

"Here, Captain," Henry Tingle Wilde called from the port side of the bridge, where he was working with Mr. Andrews to relay instructions to the ship's engineers to begin the delicate process of shedding ballast.

"Organize a crew with cutting torches immediately and release the main anchor and chain. It weighs close to twenty tons," Smith ordered with certainty.

"Captain, are you sure?" Wilde responded incredulously. "If we are able to beach her, the anchor will help us to stabilize the hull. And the cost…"

Smith exploded at his Chief Officer. "The cost? Damn the cost man! What is a man's life worth? Cut the bloody thing loose immediately – am I clear, Chief

Officer? And hurry, we have little time before working on the Forecastle Deck will be impossible."

As a chastened Wilde turned to hurry off to organize the crew and equipment, Smith added an order with fury. "Mr. Wilde, do not question my instructions again. Ever." There was no reason for response from the Chief Officer.

Andrews beckoned to the Captain. "We must release ballast beneath the third compartment this very moment. In another few minutes, it too will be flooded and we won't have access, Captain."

Insanity, Smith thought. The ship's already strained hull would instantly begin to destabilize. He hesitated for no more than a fraction of a second. "And then the fourth will fill, Mr. Andrews?"

Andrews shook his head in submission.

"Then so order it."

Within minutes, a purge of water was flushed out of the vessel by powerful pumps deep below the *Titanic*'s upper hull lining as engineers opened valves that emptied several of her ballast tanks of nearly seventy five tons of water. Smith watched the clinometer with Hitchens and Murdoch, urgently looking for a sign of hope. There was no indication of an improvement in *Titanic*'s list.

"If nothing else, we bought a bit of balance, Captain," Murdoch offered, in mock optimism.

"But nothing more. Mr. Andrews, should we release the tanks in the fourth compartment as well?" Smith asked.

Andrews, nearly resigned to his fate, was strangely stirred by the man's trust in him and his acceptance of doing whatever had to be done to save his passengers and crews, the risk be damned.

"Other than putting ourselves in greater danger of capsizing, I see no reason to forestall the inevitable,"

Andrews replied firmly. "Our plan will either work or it won't. It is fate, Captain."

Without hesitation, Smith gave the order. Below, engineers hurried to the fourth compartment to repeat the process. On the bridge, Smith and his men waited breathlessly for some sign of response on the clinometer.

The Captain glanced at his pocket watch. It was 12:50 a.m., Monday, April 15th. "What is our speed, Mr. Murdoch?" he asked.

"We are maintaining a speed of seventeen knots, Captain," Murdoch responded. "Since striking the berg we have traveled approximately..." He hesitated while taking a quick look at the navigational chart now spread out on the table next to Andrew's blueprints." "Approximately twenty-one miles, sir."

Smith frowned. "Are the lookouts still in place? It is imperative that we maintain speed but we cannot risk another collision."

"Fleet and Lee are still in the Crow's nest, sir and I have six hands at stations forward seeking any sign of ice. We've also managed to find some binoculars for the Crow's nest."

Smith looked up at the First Officer, staggered. "The lookouts were not equipped with glasses before sighting the berg?" he asked in disbelief.

Murdoch dropped his eyes. "No sir, they were locked in the cabinet."

For a long moment, Smith calculated the possible loss of thousands of lives and a ten million dollar ship against a three-dollar pair of glasses.

"We have been blind in every way," he said, stunned.

"God help us."

Hendricks called out from the wheel, excitedly. "Captain, the bow is up nearly one degree, although we are still listing to starboard." Smith turned to Andrews for a reaction. The ship's designer nodded, the slightest look of hope now in his eyes.

All over the liner, stewards and stewardesses were fighting their own anxieties, but went about the task of awakening and preparing their passengers with order and outward calm. The style and patience of their message was instinctively tailored, if not prejudiced to the class in which their charges were sailing.

Passengers from the Steerage quarters were first to arrive on deck, following the dozens who had been flooded from their cabins in the initial moments after the collision. Each wore a mask of fear, uncertainty and confusion. Men held on to their wives and children tightly as they struggled to comprehend cryptic orders to go astern that amounted to "Put your life belts on at once and report to the main deck."

Many simply could not understand the instructions as the lingua franca of the *Titanic*'s crew was English and they did not know that tongue. Babies cried, held close to their mother's breasts, and children whimpered from the fearful commotion and the relentless cold. The night air had dipped to nineteen degrees Fahrenheit.

In Second Class, the instructions were a little less vague, perhaps making up for the uncommonly brusque tone and lack of patience the stewards and stewardesses were displaying. Second Class Chief Steward John Hardy, in charge of twenty-four cabins, simply used a passkey to open the door of each cabin and barked. "Excuse me. We have struck an iceberg and are taking on water. Please put your life jacket on over the warmest clothes you have available and proceed to the main deck immediately." Then he would slam the door behind him, eliminating the potential for protests or questions he probably couldn't answer.

Despite the terror-filled darkness, animating the Steerage passengers was perhaps easier than those in the upper classes. Many of those on the lower decks had seen the water rising, some sloshing through it a foot deep to reach the iron staircases and a path to the open air. While there was extreme commotion, there was also order.

"Move along, please, hurry," Major Butt spoke firmly but softly as he personally met the Steerage passengers as they emerged onto the brightly lit A deck, much in the same way he had been greeted by Captain Smith when he boarded. But the world had turned upside down since that brief moment, now nearly five days past. Some of these passengers, traveling from all over Europe, stopped to ask him a question in a dialect he could not understand. Some he sensed were pleading for mercy. Most had left all or nearly all their earthly belongings behind in their cabins. He could do nothing but respond with compassion in his eyes, and to smile, confidently, as he prodded them along their two hundred yard march to the stern.

In First Class, members of the steward's group were far more gentle with their instructions, beginning with the method of announcement of their presence: a soft knock at the door. A good many of them suffered verbal abuse from people who had long ago forgotten how to fetch for themselves and felt that being served was an entitlement. After all, they thought, uniform or not, stewards were simply glorified maids.

Molly Brown, now recovered and sitting up in her bed after her invasion of the Bridge and subsequent panic attack, hurled curse after curse at the unlucky First Class steward assigned to her, and who now instead begged her to leave her quarters without resistance.

"I wish you fellas would make up your god dammed minds," she finally said with resignation. "You've got some gall ordering me around. You want to know what I paid for this undersized suite? Probably ten times your

wages." She suspended her tirade just long enough
to think up one last stab. "I'm not leaving here without
my jewelry. I know what you'll do the minute I step
outside."

In Benjamin Guggenheim's parlor, a different
reaction came from the billionaire whose mistress still lay
sleeping in the bedroom beneath fine silk sheets. When
confronted with the gravity of the situation by Chief
Steward Frank Richard Alsop, he feigned bravado.

"Mr. Alsop," Guggenheim said with outward
composure, "I am many things..." He paused as if
reflecting on his failures as a man, a husband and father,
immense contradictions to his success as a businessman.
"But above all, I am a gentleman. Please allow me a few
moments to dress accordingly. If I am to die tonight, it
will be with dignity." Five minutes later, he emerged
from his stateroom, his disheveled mistress clutching his
arm. He wore full evening clothes, a topcoat and a
bowler. Alsop persisted until he agreed, reluctantly, to
slip a life jacket over his coat.

"If I had known there were such devices on board
Titanic, I would have had one custom tailored,"
Guggenheim remarked to the bewildered steward.
"Nonetheless, I've dressed in my best, and am prepared
to go down like a gentleman."

In another First Class stateroom, John Jacob Astor
had a similar spontaneous response, as did George
Widener, Charles Hays, Sir Cosmo Duff Gordon and
other millionaires. As they emerged onto A Deck, the
group bore a resemblance to the emperor penguins of
Antarctica in their annual march to the sea, although
hardly as farcical given the deadly state of affairs. The
only notable exception was Isidor Straus, who in typical
fashion gave no inkling to his vast wealth, turning out
with his beloved Ida on his arm, in his signature black
wool topcoat, right off the rack at Macy's. He was more

concerned for the well being of his steward than of his own, reminding the young man that cold knows no class.

Seventeen-year-old Jack Thayer emerged on deck looking like he was prepared for a cricket match. He had been exercising as the *Titanic*'s bow kissed the iceberg. Francis Millet, traveling in the adjoining cabin to his long-time friend Archie Butt, knocked on the Major's door, having donned a silk smoking jacket and still wearing his evening slippers. Getting no response, he leisurely made his way to A Deck, where they promptly met.

"For heaven's sake, Archie, is all this commotion nothing more than a drill? I find this quite impertinent, if I do say so..." Butt cut him off. "Do as you're told, Francis, the situation is grave."

Millet caught the look in his friend's eye. "Oh, dear me. I didn't realize. I guess I should have known by the expression on your face. You are so easy to read, old chap. You appear to have the weight of the world on your shoulders."

"That would be a burden reduced, old friend," Butt retorted. Miller quickly entered the queue, which was becoming a wave of shocked passengers. No matter the class of society, general disbelief had replaced the celebratory ambience of the night for all passengers. But panic had yet to take grip of the situation.

Like water boiling, it happens slowly.

Eight

On the bridge of the twin-screw Cunard liner, RMS *Carpathia*, at 1 a.m. now slightly less than sixty miles away, the mood aboard had swung wildly, as well. Until now, *Carpathia*'s passage to Fiume in Italy from New York had been without incident. Her seven hundred forty passengers, predominantly third class holidaying American tourists, had mostly turned in for the night well before *Titanic*'s urgent distress call.

In lonely command of the 13,600 ton steamship was Captain Arthur Rostrom, who had not hesitated an instant after wireless operator Harold Cottam had burst into his cabin and awoken him from sleep with the desperate CQD. Even as he dressed, Rostrom ordered the helmsman to turn *Carpathia* on a course to intercept *Titanic* and over the last hour, had been fully engaged in making ready for what he hoped would be a mid-Atlantic rescue attempt. Known throughout the Cunard organization as the "Electric Spark" because of his infinite enthusiasm and relentless drive for efficiency aboard the ships he commanded, his instincts took over.

After personally dictating a message to *Titanic*'s Captain Smith that *Carpathia* was coming at once, he ordered every off duty fireman and boiler man to the engine room to stoke the ship's eight cylinder, quadruple-expansion engines to maximum speed. Then he calmly but firmly gave orders to prepare her boats, turn off heat and hot water in the passenger quarters to divert the steam to *Carpathia*'s engines, and to turn each of the ship's dining rooms into hospitals.

He was a whirlwind of leadership, containing his emotions with great internal discipline learned from twenty six years toiling at sea, yet confirming by his actions the compassion intended by his decisions. He even thought to have an extra ration of coffee made available to every crewman, recognizing the fact that they would be traveling at top speed throughout the long night in waters as dangerous as those that had imposed on *Titanic*'s future. He also instructed the ship's stewards to keep *Carpathia*'s passengers in the dark lest they panic at the turn of events. But even now, her passengers were slowly beginning to meander to the main deck, wondering why their cabins had become cold, and the ships engines were straining with a vibration that could be felt throughout the whole of the hull. In another hour, the situation would no longer be a secret.

In his ever-efficient manner, Rostrom had already calculated that at a maximum speed of fourteen and a half knots, his ship would not arrive until hours after Thomas Andrews had predicted the sea would at last swallow *Titanic*. Even that performance would depend on the struggle of *Carpathia*'s engines to sustain their exhaustive effort -- and the night itself. In just the last hour, Rostrom had seen six icebergs loom precariously out of the darkness with little advance warning from the ship's lookouts which he had tripled in deployment.

Cottam suddenly entered the bridge forgetting to close the door and the excruciating cold blew into the darkened room. He was clutching the newest message from *Titanic*. "She's steering a course for Cape Sable Island, Captain, and has asked us to chase her," he reported excitedly.

"Cape Sable Island? Why that's..." he paused for a moment to calculate in his head. "That's more than 200 miles from the position she indicated. What the devil is he doing?" he pondered, holding his fist to his chin. There was silence from his officers.

Then First Officer William Prothero spit out, "The bloody hell... they're aiming to beach her, Captain... why else would they make their way so south... I used to sail there as a child. Cape Sable Island is surrounded by shallows!"

Rostrom looked at his First Officer with a look of disbelief. "My God, man, you're right. But can he keep her afloat that long?" His thought trailed off for a brief moment.

"Helmsman, make your heading due east for Cape Sable Island," Rostrom announced, his decision made.

"I'll be dammed if we're going to be late to the bloody party."

Nine

The stream of passengers, rousted from the peace of their beds in the middle of the freezing night with little information as to what was happening, gradually became a mob. As the throng continued to gather on the stern, Butt watched carefully for signs of panic.

Stewards handed out blankets and poured coffee, while there were those passengers who cast their own fears aside, perhaps in silent capitulation to the crisis, and showed care instead for others.

Molly Brown, recovered from her fit of anger over the "barbaric" treatment at the hands of the White Star Line, succumbed to the whimpering of a little girl of eight years of age, who by the cut of her clothes was obviously traveling in Steerage.

She was sitting on the deck, shivering, holding her knees and rocking, back and forth. Tears rolled down her small face. She was desperately afraid. There were no sign of her parents, and Molly couldn't help but give in to her motherly instincts, despite the fact that at dinner that very evening before, she had referred to children traveling in Steerage as "unripe vermin." Her unkind words were ringing in her head as she approached the girl with atypical caution, not desiring to further the young child's angst, and knelt down on one knee beside her.

"There, there, little one. Be brave. We'll all have a good laugh about this in a short time. Now don't you be afraid," she said in her best corn pone accent.

The girl looked up at her, her disheveled brown hair hiding some of her pale skin. Her brown eyes were full of fear and uncertainty and the ends of her thin lips were drooping with sadness. What she really needed was a hug, Molly decided, and without invitation wrapped her two beefy arms around the child and comforted her.

John Jacob Astor, who really couldn't recall the names of his own personal servants if tested, found himself surrounded by young men, Steerage passengers who somehow found confidence in the company of the world's wealthiest man. A fatherly persona came over Astor from somewhere deep inside. He did not know where it came from, for it was certainly not a trait handed down to him.

"We will survive this, all of us, have faith boys," Astor said calmly and with what sounded like conviction, despite his own fears to the contrary. In his evening clothes and dark coat, he could almost have been mistaken for a priest or man of God.

"So tell me how the 'Reds' season is progressing boys?" he asked, attempting to get the group of late teens to focus their minds elsewhere. "I'm afraid we don't get much news of the Liverpool Football Club in the New York papers, although I continually harp on it with the *Times* publisher, Mr. Ochs. A good chap, but I've told him several times: Adolph, you are far too prone to that boring baseball game."

He hit a nerve. No young man from Liverpool could scarcely contain himself when if it came to the mighty Reds. The half dozen boys began talking excitedly, all at once.

Despite the efforts of some, disquiet was brewing amongst the horde, fed mainly by the lack of information and no signs of activity in launching the lifeboats. Major Butt was not surprised as he witnessed small groups beginning to form spontaneously on the fan tail, and their whispered conversations and furtive looks at the officers assisting him slowly grew to a buzz, getting louder by the moment.

Butt took notice of Benjamin Guggenheim, sitting in a deck chair near a small gathering of Irish men as the millionaire playboy abruptly stood and interrupted the conversation he was having with young Jack Thayer. Guggenheim and the seventeen year old Thayer, both wearing their evening suits, began talking with the men and tried to calm one of them who was particularly excited. An argument broke out.

The Major casually wandered over to Second Officer Lightoller, noticing as he did the increasing downward pitch of the deck. "Mr. Lightoller," he said. "Are you carrying a weapon?"

Lightoller's was alarmed, being completely taken aback by the question. He did not respond straight away, unsure of the authority of the newest member of the *Titanic*'s officer corp.

"I said, do you have a gun?" Butt repeated.

"Yes Major, I have a sidearm. I have authority to carry it per White Star policy," Lightoller finally responded, agitated and off balance from the question.

"Policy…" Butt muttered. "I've often reflected on the integrity of that word. For example, is it also the policy of your employer to equip its ships with half enough lifeboats for its passengers?" The statement dripped with sarcasm.

"Major Butt…"

The military officer frowned and caught himself. "Forgive me Second Officer Lightoller. That was unwarranted and hardly the time.

"Let me have your pistol," he ordered.

Lightoller took a half step back. "Sir, what is your intention?" he asked, further alarmed.

"Only to get the attention I need. I promise not to embarrass the White Star Line anymore that it has already done itself.

Lightoller was unconvinced. "If the gun has to be used, Second Officer, far better for you if it is me holding it," Butt responded.

Lightoller let the words sink in. He shook his head. "May God help you, Major." He opened his pea coat to reveal the holstered weapon.

"Careful, old man. Don't let this be seen," he warned. "What is the situation on the bridge?" It was now 1:30 a.m.

"I've just come from there. She is down six degrees with the water just under the bow rails. But she is stable. The list has been corrected with the offloading of ballast. Water is pouring into the fifth compartment. We will go deeper, I'm afraid. But there is no plan to launch the boats. It is impossible at this speed. Captain Smith still believes we can beach her in the shallows – another one hundred forty miles."

Butt allowed himself a half smile for the Officer's benefit. "Mr. Lightoller, remind me never to ask you for a report if I am inclined to hear good news. You pull no punches, young man, I like that."

Out of the corner of his eye, Butt saw a tall, strongly built Irish man with forearms a foot around, perhaps in his late twenties, break away from Guggenheim and Thayer and accost Fifth Officer Lowe standing beneath the Docking Bridge. Lowe was adjusting the life jacket straps for a five year old. The man approached him menacingly, gesticulating wildly with his hands as he spoke.

"When will they launch the bleeding boats? You're wearing the stripes, tell us for God's sake!" He waited for a response. When none was forthcoming from Lowe, who stood his ground before the angry man nearly twice his size, the Irishman screamed in Lowes face. "Now, dammit, or we'll do it ourselves!"

"Now calm down sir," Lowe attempted to assuage the man speaking as forcefully as he was able, "I assure you that everything is being done that can..." *Titanic's* hull dropped a foot beneath his feet, as water pouring into the hull forced an air pocket to fill, jarring the officer and his confrontator. The Irishman jiggled backward trying to regain his balance.

"Are you daft, man?" he bellowed at Lowe. "What are you waiting for?" Lightoller was already running to assist his fellow officer, as were Wilde, Pitman and Boxhall from other parts of the stern.

"The hell with you all, you bastards," he shouted furiously. "'C'mon mates, if the boats are to be launched, we'll bleedin' well have to do it ourselves!" He took the three steps to reach the officer in one giant stride and gave Lowe a shove that sent him to the deck.

Immediately, several dozen of the man's comrades rushed the Poop deck staircase to the aft Well deck, then raced to the Second Class entrance that would bring them to the Boat deck. There, the aft, most port side lifeboat hung in its davits, unguarded.

Thomas Guggenheim, resplendent in his splendid evening dress, inexplicably joined the group, elbowing his way to the front of the pack just as it reached the Second Class entrance. Jack Thayer was only a step behind. As the Irish leader reached for the first rung on the steel stairwell leading to the boats, Guggenheim leapt onto the panicked man's back and forced him to the ground. Several behind them fell onto the pile and blocked the forward progress of the mutinous mob. Thayer leapt over the prone men and took a position on the stairwell, his fists raised and cocked. One of the Irish took a wild swing at the boy, but young Jack was all business. Sidestepping the punch, he crouched low and sent his right fist into the solar plexus of his assailant. The man dropped to the deck like a rock.

A shot rang out from the Docking Bridge, where Major Archie Butt clung precariously to the wheel with one hand, the gun in his other. To several witnesses, he resembled the caricature of Teddy Roosevelt storming San Juan Hill, flag in one hand, pistol in the other. There was one deciding difference: Butt's pose was real and intimidating.

"Halt, all of you! Or I will be forced to adjust my aim!" Butt shouted even as he fired a second and third round into the air. Almost simultaneously, a mighty explosion occurred over their heads. It was the last of the distress rockets, and its brilliant white exploding charge illuminated the stern in a ghastly pallor, outlining each passenger's shadow on the deck where they stood, struggling to remain upright.

The thunderclap retorted over the ships rigging and masts, and a rainfall of fiery white ash rained down among them. The mob's dangerous energy was immediately discharged.

At the Docking Bridge wheel, Butt recognized his moment and shouted to regain control. "Stop, I order you," he roared, a vapor trail following each word out of his mouth in the freezing cold night air. "We must remain calm -- there is no other way for us to survive, do you hear me?" His words echoed across the now still deck.

A hush descended over the multitude as Butt spoke. "I have just had information from the Bridge, from Captain Smith, whom I assure you is fully in control of this crisis." Every eye on the stern was on the war hero.

"We are making our way to the shallows, about 100 miles from here," Butt exaggerated to lesson the shock. "All engines are still running at their maximum and we are making good speed to Cape Sable Island. We should the spy the lights of the coastline near dawn."

Women caught their breath, men cheered.

"Everything that can be done and more is being executed by the crew of *Titanic* to ensure our safety," the Major continued. "But it is imperative that we maintain calm, lest our panic dash any hopes of survival. While we are making speed, the boats cannot be launched – to attempt to do so would be the makings of another disaster.

"Furthermore, any rush of people to either side of the ship will likely capsize her – we will turnover into the freezing water – and there will be no hope of survival.

"Do you understand me?" Butt challenged the rapt and terrified mass. Not a word was heard in response. Only the sound of weeping could be heard across the deck.

He paused for a moment, letting his words sink in, and allowing time for translation. "Ladies and gentlemen, you must put your trust in Captain Smith – and in me, as his faithful emissary. You are in no immediate danger. *Titanic* will not sink beneath you. We will be saved, every last one of us. I swear to it.

"I believe this as I stand here before God as my witness -- the *Titanic* will not desert you in this extraordinary hour."

He paused again, aware that he had calmed them.

"Rescue ships are racing to us as I speak," Butt continued. They have been instructed to intercept us at Cape Sable Island where, after *Titanic* has been beached, an orderly transfer to the safety or our rescuers will be accomplished.

"For now," he went on, "I urge you to pray to your God and have faith. Find something to hang on to, for the ship will continue its downward pitch for a while, as the pumps work to clear out her holds.

"But know that with every minute that passes, we are closer to safety."

The leader of the mob slowly stood to his feet and sheepishly extended a hand to help Thomas Guggenheim to his feet. His followers quietly walked back to their families. Guggenheim was bleeding heavily from a gash over his left eye, and the collar and bib of his starched white evening shirt were stained red.

"Thank you, my good man," Guggeneheim said to the Irishman, just moments ago a terrified and flustered antagonist. He became aware of the blood streaming down his face and dripping on to his shirt.

Without a moment's hesitation he brushed across his shirt with his fingers as if whisking away a piece of lint, and said loudly enough for the crowd assembled around him to hear: "Oh, dear me, another shirt ruined. I will have to change for breakfast."

Molly Brown, still clutching the terrified little girl whom she had rescued, was the first to laugh, a great, heaving laugh that continued and slowly spread to those within earshot, depressurizing the crisis, at least momentarily.

"You tell 'em, Bennie. Ain't no gentleman worth his salt show's up at the table in a dirty shirt," she hollered. With that the laughter intensified in the brief fleeting moment of a man at his best. Thayer's assailant eyed the boy for a moment, then grinned and stuck his hand out to him in respect.

Butt slid down the staircase, barely touching the steps to reach Guggenheim. "That was a terribly brave thing to do, Benjamin. We are in your debt," the Major congratulated him. "Most impressive, chap, especially how fast you moved. Not bad for a middle-aged codger."

Guggenheim, woozy on his feet, feigned ignorance of the attention, and winked at Butt.

"Well, my dear friend," he said while dabbing at his eye, "when you've royally fouled up your life as well as I have, it's any wonder there's any man left in me at all. However, I do not intend to go down without a fight." He paused, looking down at his shirt. "Although I must say the sight of one's own blood is most distressful."

Butt turned to Thayer. "And as for you, young man – I assume you have learned such behavior from your father?"

The teen looked cautiously at the Major. "Of course, sir. My father taught me how to box when I was young."

Butt laughed. "When you were young? I daresay Jack, it was not your boxing skills to which I referred, although they are quite impressive. I was speaking of your courage."

Thayer beamed. "Then of course, Major Butt. My father is the bravest man I know."

The soldier smiled. "We shall talk more about courage someday, young man, when all this is behind us. Until then, let me just say that your father has every reason to be proud of his son."

Without another word, Butt spun on his heals in search of Wallace Hartley and his orchestra, which had already begun playing again. A gloomy arrangement of "Till There Was You" wafted over the fantail, and the music, while intended to be calming, made the situation even more chilling.

"We shall need something a little more lively," Butt muttered to himself as he eyed the bandleader in the starboard corner of the Poop deck.

"I do not intend to sing at my own funeral."

Ten

On the Bridge of the steamship, it's profile now of a boat clearly sinking by the bow, Andrews was scratching the small bald spot on the back of his head, frantically searching his mind for other measures to keep the liner afloat. As *Titanic* pushed relentlessly against the sea, waves of her own making were already washing across the bow deck.

Smith nervously glanced again at his pocket watch. It was nearly 5 a.m. His inability to act more decisively was rubbing at his nerves.

"What is her speed?" he barked to no one in particular. Still at the wheel, Quartermaster Hitchens replied. "We are making fifteen and a half knots, Captain. We've slowed considerably in the last hour."

"How much of the ballast remains, Mr. Andrews?"

"Approximately forty percent," he responded, not looking up from his scribbled calculations. "I believe we should dump another fifteen percent within the next few minutes to keep the bow from slipping under – but I am unsure as to the effect it will have on her list. She is already precariously top heavy."

"This is no time for indecision, Mr. Andrews," Smith said sternly. "Do we drop the ballast or not?"

Andrews finally looked up, his eyes red with strain of the last hours, his face pale and drawn. "I am an engineer and architect, Captain," he snapped. "I am not clairvoyant."

"Dammit man -- do we lighten the load or not? We are already at eight degrees down!" Smith roared. "At this rate the Bridge will be underwater in less than two hours." He stared at the clinometer, as if willing it to rise.

Andrews, frustrated at the wreckage of his design and its failures, shouted his reply. "Do it, god dammit. And quickly."

Within a few minutes, deep below the Bridge, seacock valves were opened by ships engineers who remained at their posts despite the rising waters and the potential for their own entombment. Then *Titanic* began to shudder as another three hundred thousand pounds of water was furiously purged from her holding tanks.

Not able to wait for the clinometer to respond, Smith barked anew.

"What is our distance to Cape Sable Island?"

First Officer Murdoch had been plotting *Titanic*'s progress towards safety throughout the night. The only other officer on the Bridge was Hitchens, at the wheel. All other officers had been dispatched to the stern to help manage the passengers.

"We are just less than 100 miles away, Captain. We only need another five hours if we can maintain speed."

"Five hours..." Smith repeated, reflecting on the enormity of their challenge. "If we go much deeper, moving her forward with any speed will be like the four of us trying to push a locomotive up a hill. We cannot allow the bow to submerge."

Without so much as a breath, he turned to his First Officer. "What is the situation below?"

"I just spoke to the chief engineer," Murdoch responded. "Water is entering the sixth compartment as we speak. But the pumps are holding their own against the influx rate. It's our very weight that is pulling us down. The pumps need time to catch up."

"Look!" Hitchens shouted. "The clinometer – we're up by almost two degrees!"

"How is her balance, Mr. Hitchens?" Smith called out without taking a second to celebrate.

"We're rolling, Captain, I can feel it in the wheel. If the seas pick up..."

"See to it that they don't," Smith fallaciously ordered his crewman.

"Begging the Captains pardon, sir, I hardly..." In the tension, Hitchens had failed to see the humor.

"Stow it, quartermaster," Murdoch ordered impatiently.

Hitchens ignored him. "She's up another quarter degree, Captain," he reported with relief.

Wireless operator Jack Phillips burst onto the Bridge and breathlessly handed Smith a new telegram from *Carpathia*.

"She's chasing us, Captain, at full speed," Phillips reported. "*Carpathia* is about 45 miles to the west of us but has turned for Cape Sable Island where she will intercept *Titanic*."

Smith dug into his pocket and retrieved his pocket watch again, glanced at it, then absent-mindedly began winding it from habit.

"Good news," the Captain said. "But unfortunately, nothing has really changed. We've only bought more time. The inevitable will happen if we don't make the shallows.

"And what of *Frankfurt* and *Mesaba*?" he probed.

"Both have turned towards us, but each is more than one hundred miles away. *Frankfurt* is making twenty-two knots, through ice on a heading for Cape Sable Island, but she will be five to six hours behind us if we're able to beach *Titanic*," Philips responded. "*Mesaba* is much slower, perhaps fourteen knots, and will be several hours behind the *Frankfurt*."

Murdoch interrupted. "So even if we are able to reach the shallows, it will be hours before we can expect assistance."

"I'm afraid those are the facts, First Officer," Smith answered. "Even if we're able to stay afloat until then, *Titanic* will need all the steam she can muster to ride high up on the sands to stabilize her. We will be in jeopardy of keeling over unless we can grab a strong foothold."

He turned to the wireless operator again. "Mr. Phillips, see if you can raise someone on Cape Sable Island. I'm not sure that Marconi has set up shop there yet. If you can't reach anyone, transmit to Cape Race and see what they can do to organize assistance from the Islanders."

Phillips turned on his heels, lost his footing on the sloping deck, and fell heavily to the floor. He waved off a helping hand from Murdoch and crept to the door, where he raised himself to his feet. "Sorry, Captain."

"Mr. Phillips, we cannot afford any slipups," he chided the young wireless man, tongue in cheek. Phillips allowed himself a chuckle then scurried to the radio room.

Smith calmly stepped up behind Quartermaster Hitchens, who had not had relief at the wheel for more than seven hours, and placed his hand on the helmsman's shoulder. "Keep her steady, son," he said to the startled young man. Such displays of affection, however slight, were unheard of on the Bridge. "There are twenty-two hundred helpless gathered on the stern who are counting on your skill – and courage."

Hitchens swallowed hard at his words. "Aye, Captain," he responded through gritted teeth." For a brief moment, he thought of his father, an elderly widower, alone in Liverpool, waiting for his return.

"Aye, Captain."

Eleven

Some three hundred fifty miles west at Cape Race, Marconi wireless operator Walter Gray, desperate for news of *Titanic*'s situation, squirmed in his seat as the message came in. Phillips was on the other end.

```
"On heading for Cape Sable Island.
Will run aground if possible.
Can you provide assistance?"
```

Gray shouted to his partner, Jack Goodwin.

"There's no wireless there, man, I don't know what we can do," said Gray.

"Yes, but the local constable has a wireless set for emergencies. He'll know what to do."

On the small Canadian island at the southernmost point of the Nova Scotia peninsula, in the fishing port of Clark's Harbour, Chief Constable Harold Renaud had already been in his tiny, shack-like office for an hour. He sipped his black coffee as he sat at his desk made of old lobster crates and plywood and read the *Boston Globe*. It was dated five days earlier and had arrived by ferry only the evening before. He dropped the newspaper at the sound of the telegraph.

```
"Cape Race to Renaud, Cape Sable Island.
Titanic has hit a berg and is sinking.
On course for your front yard - hope to beach
ship.
Nearest vessel five hours behind.  Can you
offer
assistance?"
```

Renaud nearly choked on his last sip of coffee.
"My God," he said out loud. He sat hard and
immediately responded, trying not to waste time on
questions with no answers.

```
"Please instruct Titanic's estimated time
arrival and how many aboard.
What is her course here?"
```

He waited impatiently for a reply, his coffee growing
cold, his brain racing with dread and excitement. About
the biggest crisis the twenty-nine year old father of two
had ever handled involved the ferry running aground
fifteen feet from the dock at Clark's Harbour, her Captain
dead drunk at the wheel. He fought down the fear that
churns up a man's stomach at the thought of being in
way over his head.

Renaud rang up the telephone and called his best
friend who happened to own the largest fishing boats of
the tiny community. There were only two hundred
twenty-seven inhabitants on the island, nearly all
fishermen.

Gilles Quimmet, like Harold Renaud, had been born
and raised on the tiny island, and could count on the
fingers of one hand the number of times they had
escaped it for the excitement of Halifax, Portland or Cape
Cod since their first birthdays. Life was difficult on Cape
Sable Island, hardly as romantic as its name. It was a
cold, rainy outcrop of Nova Scotia that was directly in
the path of frequent Nor'easters and hurricanes
contributing to hundreds of shipwrecks. It was only after
the wreck of the *Hungarian*, a Liverpool ship destined for
Portland, Maine which ran aground and sank on the west
side of the island in 1860 with the loss of over two
hundred, that the Canadian government established the
Cape Light lighthouse to warn seafarers of the potential
for disaster ahead in the island's shallows.

The seven mile long, three mile wide Cape Sable Island, the Atlantic lapping on all sides, was the only world Renaud and Quimet knew. But there was virtually nothing the two men didn't know about it. Every rock, every shoal, every change of tide, they knew indelibly and by instinct.

"They're going to try and run her aground? That's insane!" Quimet barked at Renaud when he informed him of Smith's plan. "My God, man, they must be a desperate lot, hey?"

"I don't know Gilles, I only know the ship is coming and it's sinking. How they're continuing to make headway toward us is a mystery. Cape Race says they expect her to appear over our horizon within four hours from now – say 9:30 a.m. – and there's not a large craft able to reach her for five hours after that.

"What the hell do we do, Gilles?" Renaud asked urgently, the bile of panic already churning in his knotted stomach. "We don't have time to raise tugs from the mainland..."

"Hell no," Quimet agreed instantaneously. "I'm afraid it falls to us, old friend. Get over to the Light as quickly as you can and make sure she's blazing. I'll alert my boats and let them know we have new plans for the morning. From where should we expect her to approach?" he probed.

"Just received a new message," Renaud said. "Confirms that Titanic should be expected on the horizon off the west end of the Island about 9:30 a.m. She's eighty miles away." He paused to read the rest of the message.

"My God, Gilles, what in the name of Christ..." Renaud gasped. "She's carrying twenty-two hundred people – with lifeboats for about half."

There was a long silence on the other end of the telephone.

"Two thousand people and no boats – they must have thought her invincible."

"Aye, Gilles. But now it seems only God himself can keep her afloat."

Quimet was silent for a moment.

"Yes, God," Quimet responded.

"But perhaps Cape Sable Island can give the Good Lord a hand."

Twelve

Smith's pocket watch read 7:30 a.m.

"How far?" he asked, looking down from the Bridge. The bow of *Titanic* was now completely submerged, her deck awash with the sea. Waves churned by her forward surge were splashing up as high as the Bridge.

"About thirty-five miles, Captain," Murdoch answered. Anticipating the next question, he added, "Somehow, she's still making twelve knots."

Smith raised his eye at the seemingly impossible.

"We must keep pushing her ahead," he responded, hoping that saying the words out loud would make it happen. "What is the situation aft, Mr. Murdoch?"

"I've just come from the stern, Captain," the First Officer responded, his teeth chattering from the cold and his wet clothes. He had ventured onto the bow an hour ago to dog a small hatch that had been carelessly left open and had caught the full brunt of an icy wave, soaking him through.

"Major Butt has done hero's work in quelling the panic," Murdoch reported. "Our passengers are cold but quiet, though if we dip much farther, it won't take much to spark another run for the boats. They'll go to pieces, I'm sure."

"How much of the ballast remains, Mr. Andrews?" Smith inquired, even now electing to retain the formality he was accustomed to on a Bridge under his command.

He watched Andrews as he scribbled new calculations on a scrap of paper. The ship's designer shook his head.

"Perhaps twenty percent, Captain," Andrews responded. I fear we will roll if we let any more go."

Smith stared at him for several minutes, silent. Andrews became uncomfortable, expecting the beleaguered Officer to lash out.

"There is another problem we must address Mr. Andrews," the Captain finally replied. "And I have no idea how to analyze it."

Andrews looked up at Smith, his eyes squinting, waiting for the answer.

"If the bow sinks much lower," he said, shaking his head, "she will raise her propellers out of the sea. Rather quickly, we will be dead in the water. And if that happens, we are lost."

Andrews slumped lower. Hitchens, still at the wheel, kept his eyes ahead, trying desperately to make out the first signs of land. All he could see was ocean. The helmsman had never felt so alone.

"Then we are between a rock and a hard place," Andrews said. "She is already so top heavy, we could capsize with any kind of following sea or heavy current from her port or starboard side..." Andrews concluded, his voice trailing off as he tried to analyze the problem from a new perspective.

"If we have had any good fortune this night, it is that the seas remain polished, Mr. Andrews," Smith responded. "I see nothing in the skies that tells me anything will change until we get much closer to the Island." Indeed, *Titanic* has been blessed with a dawn that found the sky clear and the sun warm. After a night of wretched cold, the temperature had risen nearly twenty degrees, tickling the high 40's, and there was no wind.

Andrews looked up, despondent. "Captain, I have no more rabbits in my hat. ..." He hesitated, and then went on, the stress of the night's work showing clearly in his drawn face. He spoke haltingly.

"We have nothing to lose. I recommend that we release the balance of the ballast, at once."

Smith swallowed hard. The moment of no return had come.

"Mr. Murdoch, pass word to Major Butt of what we are about to do. If the ship begins to roll to one side, he will have a mass panic on his hands.

"It will be every man for him self."

Murdoch went to say something, then thought better of it and left the Bridge.

"It will take him the better part of fifteen minutes to go back and forth. Is there anything else we can do in the meantime?" Smith asked of Andrews.

This time he didn't hesitate, somewhat refreshed again at the sign of Smith's calm and strong hand under unimaginable circumstances. His own burden of failure was nearly unbearable, and he had resigned himself to the hand of God. What was going on in Smith's mind, Andrews thought, he could not imagine.

"Yes. We should drain the drinking water. There are almost seven tons to be had. "

Smith picked up the Bridge telephone and rang for the Chief Engineer, who was now in compartment eight with a crew of men, doing everything he could imagine to keeps the engines and pumps running.

"Aye, Captain," Chief Engineer Joseph Bell answered after several rings. He sounded out of breath but not rattled. "If we survive, it will be the result of men like this," Smith thought to himself.

"Mr. Bell, please release the drinking water immediately and prepare to drain the remaining ballast tanks. Do not open the seacocks until Mr. Murdoch or I tell you to do so, but be prepared.

Bell was alarmed at the order. "All of the drinking water, sir? What will the passengers do without...?"

"Mr. Bell, thank you for your concern, but we will have no need of drinking water for the foreseeable future. In fact, the less our passengers see of water, the happier I will be."

"Aye, Captain. Thank you sir," the chief engineer responded.

"No, Mr. Bell – thank you. God be with you, you're a good man, Joe," Smith told him, his emotions finally getting the better of his ingrained rules of officer etiquette. Before the startled Bell could respond, Smith hung the receiver back in its cradle.

Far below the bridge, in a lonely, artificially illuminated hold amidships, Joseph Bell said a silent prayer and thought of his wife and children, who were waiting for him in Queenstown. Then he growled to his crewmates.

"Boys, open the drinking water tanks, quickly, drain it all," he said, sloshing around in a foot of water. He tried to ease the tension. "And get ready to open the valves for the last ballast tanks. It looks like we're going to lighten the Lady's bottom."

A fireman called back with a grin in his face.

"Let's hope she hasn't put on any weight up top," he yelled.

No one laughed.

Thirteen

"Mr. Murdoch, thank you for informing me. I trust there is nothing else that can be done? We are so close…" Butt responded as the First Officer informed the Major of Smith's intention of depleting *Titanic's* remaining ballast.

"Sir, I've never served with another Captain I have had more faith in," Murdoch said. " I'm afraid this desperate measure is in order, considering the irrevocable consequences of inaction. If her propellers leave the water, we are simply doomed."

"And the nearest rescue ship?" Butt queried.

"At least four hours away, maybe more. Perhaps the only more frightening place to be right now would be on the Bridge of *Carpathia*. She is making full steam through a minefield of ice to get to us," Murdoch offered. "I know Captain Rostrom personally. You would like him, Major. The word 'failure' is not in his vocabulary. Like you, sir."

"Mr. Murdoch, you overestimate me ," Butt replied, surprised.

"I don't believe so, Major." He hung his head in shame before going on, his hands twisting the brim of his hat in frustration. "I'm afraid failure is what I will be remembered for."

"Why would you possibly say such a thing, First Officer?" Butt retorted. "From what I have seen of your conduct, I would hardly say you are a failure."

Murdoch dropped his head, staring at his shoes.

"I steered *Titanic* into the berg. The blood of these people are on my hands." He turned and hurried off to the Bridge before Butt could respond. The Major watched as the First Officer made his way down the sloping deck of the First Class Promenade Deck, sliding precariously. Then he slowly made his way up the staircase to the Docking Bridge and rested against the wheel housing.

From somewhere on the poop deck, a man who sounded deeply intoxicated hollered up at him, causing conversations to stop in mid sentence.

"When are you going to launch the fucking boats, general?" he slurred, angrily. "I'm in no mood for a swim. Or at least open the fucking bar, will you mate?"

Butt motioned to Lightoller to get to the man and quiet him. The Second Officer nodded and hastened to the drunk who was leaning against the port side rail.

The Major then took advantage of the sudden silence that ensconced the crowd at seeing him.

He cleared his throat. "Ladies and gentleman. Captain Smith has just informed me that we are less than forty miles from our destination and safety. *Titanic* is still making good speed and the seas should remain calm for the remainder of our journey." A small cheer went up from a group of men on the starboard side. The Major could almost hear the utter relief that his words had released.

"What's the bad news, Major, let's have it," George Widener yelled from the starboard rail.

Butt stared at the industrialist while he frantically searched for the right words.

"It is not bad news, Mr. Widener... simply another challenge." Just as quickly as it had been removed, the look of fear descended again on the thousands of people who hung helplessly on Butt's next words.

"It is gravely important that we continue every effort to lighten *Titanic's* load to keep her from going any farther under. Her propellers must remain in the water or we will be powerless to move and fall short of the shallows. We cannot allow that to happen.

"Thus, in a few moments, Captain Smith will order that the remainder of the ship's ballast be released." A general look of bewilderment descended upon the throng.

"There is a chance that once the ballast is released, *Titanic* will..." A loud terrified voice interrupted him.

"She'll keel right the bloody hell over!" he shrieked, putting words in Butt's mouth.

Those of the group who hadn't already risen to their feet at the sight of the Major on the Docking Bridge, now stood, many looking around frantically for something to hold on to. Others sought a place to hide, as if being hidden would protect them from the unforgiving Atlantic. Some wailed, some screamed, some swore. A hideous fear descended over the mass and Butt knew he was in trouble.

He wasted no time, firing the pistol twice more at the sky to get attention. The shots echoed across the deck. Little children screamed at this new, deafening threat.

"Stay calm, please, remain calm!" he hollered, struggling to be heard above the din. Bone tired, Archie Butt willed himself to stand erect, head up, shoulders back, in the classic stance of a warrior.

"Let me explain... there is no need for panic..." Before he could finish, he became aware of a commotion at his back. He turned, pistol at the ready, to find Fourth Officer Boxhall restraining a tall, wild-eyed man, his long hair and beard matted and tangled, who struggled for release. Boxhall had a firm grip on him, pinning his right arm behind his back and holding the neck of his soiled topcoat with the other.

"Let me speak, please... allow me to be heard," the seemingly psychotic man yelled. "I have the answer they need to hear."

Butt took two strides to the man. He appeared deranged – perhaps suffering from a mental breakdown of some sort as a consequence of the night filled with terror.

"Sir," Butt addressed the man sternly, "this is hardly the time."

The strange man clasped his hands together as if to pray and beseeched the Major.

"I mean no harm. I have a message that must be heard," he begged.

Every instinct in Butt's body, honed by years of leadership under the most trying of circumstances, told him to keep the man restrained. But what he saw in his wide eyes told him differently. Despite his wild appearance, he saw calm, almost serenity in them.

He took a risk. "Let him go, Mr. Boxhall – and we shall let him be heard."

Boxhall looked puzzled, but released his grip and the man quickly stepped to the wheel next to Butt.

"My fellow passengers," the man said slowly, in a booming voice that was at the same time remarkably soft. "My name is William Thomas Stead. I am an English journalist from Darlington and the son of a minister. Some of you may know of me, I am the editor of the *Pall Mall Gazette* in London."

His audience fell silent, in rapt regard of the man. Almost at once, he had a strangely reassuring influence on the tormented men, women and children below him.

Something about him was familiar, Butt thought and he kept trying to place the face. It came to him, suddenly. He realized that he was in the audience of one of Britain's most famous men. A journalist, editor, author, spiritualist and pacifist, he was a powerful voice of the poor and a tireless seeker of world peace. He was traveling to New York to attend the 1912 Peace Conference at Carnegie Hall at the invitation of President Taft.

Butt had judged Stead correctly.

"But I am also a spiritualist who has bridged the abyss between the world we live in and the 'Other Side' – through my dear Friend, 'Julia', dead some fifteen years," he continued. "Julia and I speak most regularly, and she has never once shared with me an outcome that did not, in fact, come to be."

The horde hung on his every word, with nary a cry of derision. The man spoke like a lunatic – but they were desperate for hope.

"I spoke to Julia last evening, hours before *Titanic* struck the berg. She warned me of grave danger ahead that men would disregard."

The hair on the back of Butt's neck stood up and a chill traveled the length of his spine. There was a gasp at Stead's words, and he was afraid for a moment that panic would finally ensue.

"We know that these facts have proven true, beyond a doubt," Stead continued. "But know this – I have a further message from Julia that she wishes me to share with you."

A young mother, holding an infant in her arms and with two young boys fearfully holding her skirt, cried out in fear. "We are lost!" she wailed.

Stead did not hesitate. "We are not lost… this is the message Julia wishes me to share with you. She has promised that *Titanic* will not founder.

"We will all be saved." He said the last words in a staccato voice and raised his arms to the sky. "No man, woman or child will die today at the hands of this behemoth vessel – and the blind capitalists who own her."

Later, Butt would recall a rush of wind emanating behind Stead's uplifted arms, as if the heavens were opening up to absorb the massive fears of the twenty-two hundred innocents. He himself inexplicably felt a wave of relief.

"Believe in Julia, believe in the God whom she kneels before. For he will save us. Now join me – all of you, in prayer." Stead reached out to Butt with his left hand and to Boxhall with his right. "Join hands – quickly!"

In all his years of command, Butt had never seen orders executed with such haste. In a matter of moments, every passenger and crewman of the *Titanic* had clasped their hands together.

On the Bridge, Smith ordered Murdoch to relay the message to purge the ballast. Bell personally manned one seacock while his crewmates tackled three others. "Turn, you bastards!" he shouted, raging at the valve as he used all his might to force it open. In two minutes, every seacock was open, and the last of *Titanic*'s ballast was bled from her hull, following the drinking water that had been loosed minutes before.

"Our Father, which art in heaven, hallowed be thy name," Stead's voice rang steadily across the stern with the most famous prayer in all of Christianity, and with a great roar, the mass of humanity beneath him followed. As they began to pray, there was a sudden motion from the ship's deck, as if it were rising.

"Thy kingdom come; thy will be done…" the ship rolled slightly to port, causing some passengers to lurch… "On earth as it is in heaven." Their voices, in enormous spiritual unison, rang to the skies even as *Titanic* recovered, but rolled slightly to starboard just as fast. Cries of terror rang out.

Stead redoubled the sound of his booming voice. "Give us this day our daily bread…" On the Bridge, Smith, Andrews, Murdoch and Hitchens joined in the recital that echoed along the promenade to the water that was slowly filling their command post. *Titanic* rolled again to port, with alarming momentum, causing Smith to instinctively shout "Hold on, boys!" and he waited for the swaying impetus to carry her back to starboard, and finally, to keel over.

"And forgive us our trespasses, as we forgive them that trespass against us. And lead us not into temptation; but deliver us from evil..." *Titanic* lurched dangerously back to center as the throng finished the stanza.

And stopped.

"For thine is the kingdom," Stead bellowed at the heavens, his arms uplifted in praise of his God, urging the innocents to join him, "the power, and the glory..." *Titanic* once again became stable, sitting heavily in the water but with the clinometer up two degrees, her three propellers continued to churn up the sea leaving great swaths of froth in her wake.

The prayer reached a crescendo. "Forever and ever... Amen."

Hundreds dropped to their knees, physically sapped of strength. At the same moment, a gust of warm wind raced from the south. As if on cue, an Atlantic Brant goose and her mate appeared over the deck and settled on the Docking Bridge rail, oblivious to *Titanic's* peril.

"It is a sign, my friends," announced Stead. "We are nearing land."

Butt quickly spoke up. "Please remain where you are. The ship is balanced – any sudden shift in her weight could rock her. I will announce it if we see land.

"Have faith, good people."

Stead had already left the Docking Bridge, preferring to retire to the port side and pick up the book of Holy Scriptures that he had been reading all night. People instinctively cleared a small circle around the strange man and stared at him. Stead was oblivious to it.

On the Bridge, Murdoch reported to his Captain.

"Sir, the ballast is away, *Titanic* is bone dry," he announced after a quick conversation with Bell.

Smith's mouth curled up in one corner. He looked over the horizon, anxiously scanning it for the first signs of land, now only twenty-five miles distant.

"If only that were true, First Officer."

Fourteen

Twenty miles off the northwestern tip of Cape Sable Island, Gilles Quimet fired flares from his fifteen ton trawler, the *Nightingale*. The rocket alerted Constable Harold Renaud, stationed five miles offshore in a smaller boat that he was in position, along with the other fishing boats of his fleet, the *Sparrow*, *Robin*, and *Eagle*. Slightly smaller, the three fishing vessels, along with *Nightingale*, seemed hardly a match for the *Titanic* at more than forty-six thousand tons. But if Quimet had his way, they wouldn't need to be.

Their plan was a hurried one, but with no time to arrange for larger, more powerful diesel-powered tugs to meet her, and only Quimet's ships to lend assistance, it was the only one they could contrive.

"Brian," he shouted over his bow to the captain of the *Sparrow*, Brian Ross, a Cape Cod mainlander who had given up the easy life for a chance to command his own boat with Quimet. "*Sparrow* will approach *Titanic* from the starboard side. Pass on word to Simon to ease into her on the port side. I'll see to it that *Nightingale* and *Eagle* get lines on her bow."

The four ships were huddled together, twelve feet apart in holding positions, waiting for the White Star Line's pride to appear on the horizon. They had not heard from Cape Race in more than an hour, and had no way of knowing if she was still even afloat. Simon Tallier, at the helm of the *Robin*, and Glenn Anders of the

Eagle took their orders and waited in the warm morning sun. On all four ships, adrenalin was racing.

Each of the ships carried crews of five. They were twenty men who were eager to help orchestrate the most outrageous seagoing run for safety in maritime history. Between them, the fishermen had nearly two hundred years of experience in some of the most difficult ocean waters known to man. But today, the sea was showing mercy. The boats rocked slightly on the surface of what almost appeared to be polished plate glass. The current was still and they were filled with hope.

Tallier, at the wheel of *Sparrow*, saw her first.

The great ocean liner appeared over the horizon as just a speck, but her funnels, spewing heavy black smoke, gave *Titanic*'s approach away. Within her engine rooms, every available fireman had worked for the past nine hours to keep the ship's furnaces stoked with coal, squeezing every last possible ounce of steam energy from her boilers, and then some more. The temperature had risen to nearly one hundred forty degrees Fahrenheit in the engine rooms. The crew of fifty men was nearly done for yet still they shoveled furiously. There was no choice.

Tallier shouted across the bow to Ross who relayed the message to Quimet.

"Let's fire off some flares, boys – and hope that she sees us," Quimet hollered. "I'm sure it will be good for her spirits."

Fifteen miles inland, off Clark's Harbour, Renaud saw the red flares and fired off two green rockets of his own – signaling the small assembly of doctors and nurses standing by at the Island Hospital that *Titanic* was in view. They were as ready for her as they could be, although knowing inside that even more than a few dozen casualties would overwhelm their ability to provide medical care. Their plan was simple as well.

Tend to the children first, women next and hope the men were strong.

Hitchens saw the first rocket and let out a whoop. "Begging the Captain's pardon, that's a fucking rocket!" he yelled across the Bridge. He quickly caught himself. "Sorry, sir. There is a rocket about three degrees to starboard – they're waiting for us."

Smith raced to the side of his helmsman, ignoring the curse, and raised the pair of binoculars to his face. "By God, they are, young man. Mr. Murdoch, do we have anything left to signal her?"

I'm afraid not, Captain. But I'm sure she's spied our steam."

"Lay on the horns for a moment. Maybe the wind will carry the sound," he ordered the First Officer. Thomas Andrews still sat at his makeshift desk, peering over his drawings and calculations.

"What's our distance?" he inquired, worriedly.

"Less than twenty-two miles, sir," Murdoch responded.

Andrews scribbled another calculation.

"And to the shallows?" he asked.

"Make that eleven miles, sir."

Andrews sighed and broke his pencil in two in frustration. "Captain, I don't think we can make it. There is water entering the eighth compartment and with her list I am afraid the propellers will leave the water in the next ten minutes."

"God dammit, Andrews, can't you ever offer good news?" Smith bellowed, immediately sorry that he had. He had a sudden idea.

"Mr. Murdoch, stay on the horns – use Morse code for the SOS signal. Perhaps we can draw the boats to us. If they are large enough, they can drag us to shore."

"Aye, Captain." At his order, Murdoch began tapping out the signal for SOS – three quick blips of the horn, followed by three longer blasts and then three quick blips again – over and over again.

Several minutes followed with no sign of activity from the three boats that were coming into view. "I can't tell how big they are, Captain," Murdoch said.

"So long as they're larger than a rowboat, Mr. Murdoch."

"Wait – they're making smoke, Captain, they're moving towards us," Hitchens cried out in excitement. "Should I try to turn to them, Captain?"

"My God, no Hitchens!" Andrews shouted. "Any turn could cause her to capsize. Stay the course, please man!"

Hitchens looked to the Captain, who nodded agreement.

On board the *Nightingale*, Quimet had heard *Titanic's* horns and just made out the SOS Morse signal. "She in real trouble, we can't wait for her. Full speed ahead, boys."

The four boats separated and took an immediate bead on the luxury liner and to their assigned stations. Drawing closer, Quimet recognized how low *Titanic* was in the water.

"How in bloody hell has she gotten this far?" he shouted out loud. "Christ -- only half her hull is showing! How is she still moving?"

On *Titanic's* stern, prayer groups had sprung up all over the deck, as those closest to the rail could look down the First Class Enclosed Promenade and spy the water that was gradually moving up the sloped deck toward them. Those who could see prayed the loudest.

Lightoller approached Butt still standing on the Docking Bridge. "Begging your pardon sir," he whispered to the Major, "I thought you might be interested in the chap below, sitting against the port side crane turret. The one crouched down wearing a women's shawl over his head."

Butt scanned the deck to the crane and immediately saw the man. It was Ismay, managing director of the White Star Line who had been attempting to hide his identity through the long night.

"Pity," Butt said after watching him, staring motionless at the decking between his legs. "It appears Mr. Ismay has traded his silk Blue Riband for a woolen stole." Lightoller laughed out loud.

"Careful, Mr. Lightoller," Butt interrupted him. "I know of no man who is without terror and weakness born of reckless decisions. Do you?" Lightoller nodded, somewhat chastened by his cruelty, itself born of anger at Ismay's insistence on blindly challenging the north Atlantic.

"Aye, Major, I would not trade places with that man, even with all his wealth and power. He will have much to attest to when we make port."

"And I believe we will make port, Mr. Lightoller," Butt said, and turned to see the rockets from Quimet's boats announcing their coming. Murmurs grew to loud cheers as the word was passed among the passengers and crewmen.

Fifteen minutes later, Quimet's boats were in position around the *Titanic*, and although dwarfed by her, were the most welcome sight the twenty-two hundred people on board had ever witnessed. From the port and starboard sides, the *Sparrow* and *Robin* managed to throw lines over her rails, which were hurriedly tied off to cleats on her deck, then throttled back to pace the great steamship.

On the *Nightingale*, Quimet pondered the question of how to get a hawser cable on her bow. With the giant vessel continuing to make way, but at just five knots, he maneuvered his boat to run adjacent to the Bridge. Smith went to the Bridge door and yelled to him.

"By God, Captain, you are a sight for sore eyes," Smith hollered over the *Nightingale*'s diesel engines.

"I am Gilles Quimet, sir, at your service,' he responded.

Smith saluted the seaman. "May God bless you and your crews, Captain Quimet."

"What is your situation, Captain Smith?" Quimet hollered.

"We are moments from foundering. Her propellers are nearly clearing the water and we have dumped all her ballast. We have no bottom weight, she is completely top heavy. You must exercise great caution or you will roll us over."

Quimet whistled at the report. "We have tied off to your stern starboard and port sides, sir," he responded immediately. "Now we must get lines on her bow cleats. The question is how?"

Murdoch appeared next to Smith and saluted their rescuers. "Bring your boats abreast of the bow crane, the capstans are about eight feet below. When I get into position, throw me the lines and I will secure them," he said with dead calm, as if he really believed that it would be so easy.

Smith turned to his First Officer. "Are you crazy man? You'll never make it! We're still moving..."

Murdoch interrupted him. "Captain, I have learned never to question your authority, but this is one time I must. There is no other way. I know this ship by heart. I will find the capstans." Smith at once saw the pain in the eyes of his First Officer and understood. He nodded.

"Move your boats into position, Captain Quimet," Murdoch hollered. "I will signal when I have reached the area where the cleats should be."

The First Officer turned and began wading deeper into the water, ignoring Smith's protests. "Mr. Murdoch, I forbid this! I will not have your blood on my hands!"

"You won't, Captain Smith. And you will permit me the pleasure of washing the blood off my hands," Murdoch called back. He waded forward another two steps and the water was now at his neck.

"Captain?"

"What is it, Murdoch?" Smith hollered over the roar of the diesels that had picked up speed to reach the bow.

"It has been my pleasure to serve with you, sir. You are the finest man I've ever sailed with."

Smith choked up at the unexpected tribute, but said nothing. Then he stood to attention, and snapped off a crisp salute to his First Officer. "May God be with you, son."

"And you, Captain," he called. And then he was gone. Murdoch kicked off from his precarious foothold on the sloping deck and dove headfirst into the water across her Well Deck and towards the Forecastle Deck. He surfaced a moment later and began stroking his way to the forward crane, about sixty feet away. Halfway there, he stopped, looked around to get a bearing, then dove below the surface to check his position. Then he swam the rest of the distance to the crane and rested, his arms wrapped around the top of the machine, now just barely breaking the surface. He knew the capstans were eight to ten feet below it.

Just feet away from *Titanic's* bow, Quimet held *Nightingale* in position and waved instructions for *Eagle* to do so on the port side. When Murdoch called for the line, a crewman stationed on the bow sent it whistling through the air at him with a mighty throw. The heavy steel hook at the end of the line just missed his head and quickly sank as it splashed into the water. Murdoch dove and retrieved it before it could sink all the way to the submerged deck. "Give me plenty of slack," he called on surfacing in a voice barely audible over the rush of water still sweeping over *Titanic*'s and *Nightingale*'s diesels.

Gripping the steel hawser line in his hand, Murdoch took a deep breath and dove beneath the surface. The heavy line actually helped him sink to the deck quickly, some nine feet below the surface. He frantically tried to see the capstan, but could not in the dark Atlantic water. After another minute, he kicked back to the surface, a much more difficult task given the weight of the line. He was nearly exhausted when he reached the surface and gasped for air, struggling to remain on the surface with the weight of the line upon him.

On the Bridge, Smith and Andrews helplessly followed Murdoch's efforts. Without warning, Hitchens released the wheel, ran to the door and dove into the water to join the First Officer. He ignored Smith's frustrated calls for him to return immediately.

Several minutes later, Hitchens had joined Murdoch at the crane.

"God dammit, Hitchens, you disobeyed a direct order of the Captain. I'll have you on report for this," Murdoch shouted at the young man. Hitchens stared at him for a moment, bewildered. Then he laughed out loud.

"Begging your pardon, sir," Hitchens replied, " but I suggest you may have more important things for your report than my indiscretion. So fuck you, mate!"

Murdoch was incredulous at his response, then burst into laughter himself at the lunacy of their situation. "Let's get this done, Quartermaster, I need a beer and a blanket."

"Aye, sir, and I'll be happy to join you for a few pints."

"It's too dark, I can't see the capstans. I'm going to have to feel for it, okay?" Murdoch warned the helmsman. "Ready?"

Each holding a long section of the cable, they dove beneath the surface back to *Titanic*'s forward deck. Murdoch left the cable in Hitchen's hands and pushed himself prone, his belly scraping the yellow pine surface.

He blindly felt ahead for the capstan, Hitchens holding on to his leg. He scanned right then left, then bumped his head on the base of the huge starboard bow capstan. Reaching back, he pulled the cable from Hitchens and furiously pulled fifteen feet of slack forward, wrapping it as tightly as he could muster by hand and hooked it around the barrel. Then with his last ounce of air expired, he kicked off for the surface, Hitchens behind him.

Both men held on to the crane for dear life, bone weary and struggling for breath, but knowing the feat would have to be repeated on the port side. *Eagle* moved into position and tossed her line. Murdoch caught it, the heavy hook striking him in the shoulder. He winced with pain.

"I'll do it, take a blow, mate," Hitchens yelled to Murdoch, then taking the line, wasted time and dove to the bottom. Two minutes later, he broke the surface. "It's on," he gasped. Murdoch turned and waved to Quimet, anxiously waiting on the Bridge of the *Nightingale*.

The Captain gave a signal to Glenn Anders on the *Eagle*, and a crewman stationed aft on each boat relayed the signal to the *Sparrow* and *Robin*, tied off at *Titanic*'s stern. Slowly, the four boats applied power and eight, ten thousand horsepower diesels began pulling in unison on the hawser lines, quickly taking up the slack. "Easy, Captain, she is unbalanced," Murdoch screamed to Quimet who waved acknowledgement.

Without warning, there was a fierce ripping sound, and the port side cable attached to *Eagle* flew out of the water. Its hook had not set. Hitchens looked down into the water to see the trouble, uttering "What the blazes...", but before he could move, the hook caught him in the abdomen as if he was a large game fish.

Murdoch watched in horror as Hitchens was pulled toward *Eagle*, which immediately cut its engines. *Titanic* reeled to the port side, rolling over two degrees with the sudden unequal torque, then miraculously righted herself as the remaining boats cut their power. The hawser lines went slack again. Hitchens bobbed to the surface, blood pouring from his nose and ears.

Murdoch kicked off from his hold on the crane turret and swam quickly to the helmsman, who was motionless in the flat sea, great plumes of red blood churning upwards.

"Hitchens, are you alright?" he screamed anxiously. There was no response. Murdoch wrapped his arms around the young Quartermaster's lifeless body and realized how light he was. He reached down to grab his belt in order to drag him back to the crane, but he could not find it. To his shock and horror, he found the boy had been cut in half, his lower torso shorn completely off. He was dead.

Murdoch let him go, quelling the scream he felt roiling up inside him and signaled the *Eagle* to throw the line again. He swam back to the turret and let the line splash into the water next to him, grabbed it, then dove to the port side capstan and attached it, setting the hook once again around the barrel. He surfaced, nearly spent, but managed to wave to Quimet to try again. The signals were passed and the lines tightened on command.

From his perch on the *Titanic*'s bridge, Smith and Andrews watched in mute dismay at the sight of Hitchens' body slowly floating away from the ship. The burden of their helplessness was immense, their guilt even heavier, and Smith had to wrench himself away from the scene to take command of the wheel.

"You will not have died in vain, my boy, you will not have died in vain, I swear to you!" he cried, at once repulsed by the young man's horrific end and his own abject failure of command.

"I will beach this bitch if I have to fill her bottom with sand myself!"

Fifteen

"We've got her, boys!" Quimet shouted excitedly over the roar of *Nightingale*'s straining diesels. Behind him, *Titanic* was once again picking up speed even though her propellers were half exposed. Slowly, agonizingly, they towed her towards the shallows and safety.

On the Bridge, the ashen-faced Smith held onto the wheel even though it was nearly useless, the ship's gigantic rudder almost completely uncovered. He swore to remain in command until he had fulfilled his vow, but the feel of the helm was numb in his hands. The image of young Hitchens body would not leave his eyes.

His mind wandered back to his early days at sea, to the first time he had ever taken a ship's wheel and remembered the great surge of adrenalin that had course through his body as he alone controlled her direction. Now he was racked with guilt. The water on the Bridge had receded slightly, the pull of the fishing boats having raised the bow slightly. Nonetheless, the Captain struck an unnatural pose, standing at the wheel, grasping it with both hands with Atlantic seawater almost up to his waist.

At the stern, all was calm, and save for the recitation of a thousand rosaries and incantations, the poop deck was eerily quiet. *Titanic*'s stern had become a cathedral of sorts, beckoning the mass to the safety of her sanctuary.

William Carter, dozing against a port side rail, woke up, startled, but not knowing why. He sensed something new was amiss and glanced over the side, just in time to see Hitchen's dismembered body float by.

"Dear God in heaven, have mercy on that boy's soul..." he said softly. Others saw him too, but were too shocked by the night's peril, and most simply looked away and renewed their prayers.

At precisely 10:14 a.m. in the morning sun of April 15th, 1912, *Nightingale*, *Sparrow*, *Robin* and *Eagle* killed their engines having dragged the gargantuan *Titanic*, the largest ship ever built by man, firmly onto a sandy shoal some ten miles off the coast of Cape Sable Island. Their work was done. Forever more, Quimet would be known as "Captain Gilles, the giant killer."

The end was almost anticlimactic, as Butt announced to the throng, following a report from Murdoch, now safely back on board, that the Liner would soon beach herself: "Hold on, we shall soon be digging into the bottom." His words were met with a roar that Islanders, for years afterward, would swear they heard, even though the boat was still over the horizon, out of sight.

Captain Smith finally left his Bridge and made his way aft where he wandered through the crowd, embracing startled passengers, hugging small children and crying mothers. He was seeking forgiveness, even if not asking for it, and tears rolled freely down his cheeks.

Four hours later, the brave *Carpathia* arrived, Captain Rostrom still on the Bridge, joyously waving to the mass of humanity that was celebrating as if there were to be no tomorrow. But there was to be another day – for nearly everyone.

By day's end, all two thousand two hundred and eight passengers and crew, save for one who gave his life so others might live, had been safely transported to the *Carpathia* using *Titanic*'s finally useful lifeboats. Major

Butt personally saw to the exacting enterprise, and was amazed by the spontaneous assistance of the group of millionaires who had sailed her. For many, it was the first real work they had ever performed. Some of them were irrevocably changed by the experience of helping others.

For some of the First Class passengers, their actions bordered on the heroic.

In the Engine Rooms, the firemen who had so valiantly fueled the *Titanic*'s boilers non stop for more than ten hours, were too exhausted to climb out of their sweltering dungeons to the clean, fresh, cool air. Astor, Widener, Carter, young Jack Thayer and Thomas Guggenheim, still wearing his bloodied shirt, virtually carried each of the men on their backs up fifty feet to the surface.

Several who could barely walk but had no patience for waiting to be hoisted out of the sweatboxes took the guiding hand of Molly Brown, who had taken it upon herself to march down into the bowels of the ship to help. When she arrived, she announced her presence in true Molly Brown fashion: "One hell of a job, fella's. I bet you boys would like nothing better than a cold beer and a thick steak. Well, you're all invited to the ranch once we get the hell off this god forsaken tub!" To the bitter end, Molly spoke her piece – to anyone who would listen.

That night, *Titanic* was dark again for the first time since she left Southampton, five days earlier, against another brilliantly clear night, the stars dazzling in the heavens. But now she was completely empty, save for a small compliment of guards, perched high on the sand at low tide.

Just before midnight, on the bow of *Carpathia*, Second Officer Lightoller, exhausted beyond sleep, leaned over the rail smoking a cigarette. He was luxuriating in the peace and quiet. He turned to an unexpected visitor who joined him at the rail, a large lit Cuban cigar in one hand, a pistol in the other.

"Mr. Lightoller, I believe this is yours," Archie Butt said to him, spreading his coat and placing the revolver back into the Second Officer's empty leather holster.

"Major Butt..." Lightoller managed to utter, finally breaking down from the enormous emotions that had been raging in him for nearly the last twenty-four hours.

The military officer faced the ship's officer, proudly proffering his hand. "Mr. Lightoller, there are no words required or necessary. I am proud to have served with you."

Lightoller wiped his eyes, shaking the Major's hand. Then the two men did an entirely un-officer like thing.

They embraced. The battle was over, the war was won.

Sixteen

It was April 14th, 1932.

Nearly twenty years had passed since the morning twenty-two hundred and seven passengers and crew of the British steamship *Titanic* had been given a second chance at their futures. At least half, if not all had cheated death because of the brave efforts of people they did not know. Most remembered the date of the terror filled night, especially those for whom the experience had served as a reawakening. Many had gone off and fulfilled their great promise. Otherwise, the day came and went without notice, and not a mention of the *Titanic* "miracle" could be found in the world's press.

For Washingtonians, what was more important about this day was that it was also the twentieth anniversary of the gift to the city of three thousand cherry trees by the Mayor of Tokyo to celebrate and grow the warming friendship between the United States and Japan. The first two trees had been ceremoniously planted on the north bank of the Tidal Basin in West Potomac Park even as the news of *Titanic*'s brush with disaster began trickling into the nation's Capital.

The day dawned almost identical to that morning in the North Atlantic Ocean two decades before. The sun was brilliant, the skies were clear, and a gentle, soft wind was blowing almost imperceptibly off the Potomac. The cherry blossoms were in their full glory, filling the air with an intense rose-like fragrance and painting the city a pale pink.

Those who lived in the Capital city often said that if there was ever a truly happy time in the most political of all places, it was the three days the cherry blossoms were at their full peak. The city just slowed down. Even taxi drivers pulled over occasionally just to take in the perfumed air and to bathe in the warm light that the blossoms seem to bring out in a metropolis built of aged marble and washed granite.

In the White House, Archibald Willingham Butt, the thirty-first President of the United States, sat in his favorite wooden rocker, a gift from his beloved friend, former President William Howard Taft. He stared out at the Rose Garden, deep in reflection. This was his favorite time in the Capital, even if he wasn't allowed to walk the city or even the White House grounds to enjoy the cherry blossoms directly. The assassination of President McKinley, some three decades prior, had the effect of making his successors virtual captives of their office, their lives guarded twenty four hours a day, seven days a week.

Despite his imposed captivity, Butt actually enjoyed working from his desk in the Oval Office, a room that Taft himself had created when the West Wing of the White House had been expanded in 1909, with the intention of signaling a more hands-on approach to the presidency. But in December 1929, in the first year of Butt's presidency, fire destroyed much of the West Wing and heavily damaged the Oval Office, so it was left to Archie, who had never married, to restore the symbolic grandeur of the Commander in Chief's place of work.

Having little time to devote to such extravagant priorities given the pressure of his duties and the nation's troubled economy, he turned to the wife of Vice President Dan Moody to oversee the work.

With silent recognition of the potential for her own husband to sit in the Oval Office at some time in the future, Mildred Moody used the opportunity to create an environment that was architecturally more grand and impressive. She placed emphasis on Georgian details such as ornate, hand-carved pediment hoods over its four doors, set bookcases into wall niches, installed heavy crown moldings, and had the symbol of presidential power, the Presidential Seal, set into a ceiling medallion in plaster relief. A hand sculpted, white marble mantel, imported from the village of Pietrasanta, Italy during Taft's presidency was retained as were the two flags behind the president's desk, Old Glory and the President's Flag.

Over the mantle hung a masterpiece, Dutch post-impressionist artist Vincent Van Gogh's "Starry Night on the Rhone". Since that fateful night in the mid-Atlantic twenty years before, Butt had somehow been drawn to the painting with its extraordinary juxtaposition of chaos and tranquility. He studied it often and was always drawn back to the deck of *Titanic*, gradually sinking below a most beautiful moonless sky, dazzling with the brilliance of countless diamond-like stars. The space over the mantle was empty on this day. White House staff had been informed that "Starry Night" had been in need of "cleaning". No questions were asked.

Set in front of the fireplace were two high-back chairs upholstered in a silken mauve fabric imported from Paris, on a deep magenta carpet that had been woven in a broadloom factory in Lowell, Massachusetts. The only time Butt intervened in the redecorating process was when he had insisted on an American made rug.

"You see, Mildred, that way I'll remember the plight of the working man every time I walk across it," he said.

Working in the solitude of this inviting environment was not the problem. It was getting out of it – unseen -- that was. The thought occupied his mind for several valuable minutes.

For time was Archie Butt's enemy. And the plight he had referenced to Mildred Moody was as real to the former "Major" Butt as the night he had stood on the Docking Bridge of *Titanic*, pistol in hand trying to quell what would have been a cataclysmic uprising. He had been successful that night.

Now, as he gazed out the window at the Rose Garden, his mind silently wandered to the question he carried every waking minute, and which had begun invading his already difficult attempts to sleep at night. He wondered if he had the intelligence, strength and courage to lead America out of the worst economic depression in its history – and to prevent her from becoming embroiled in another, unthinkably more horrific, world war. And for perhaps the millionth time since being elected President, he asked himself how it was that he now found himself in the battle of his life.

Butt's image and reputation soared around the world when the story of the near sinking of the *Titanic* was reported. The man who had sailed from Southampton a world recognized military and political personality arrived in New York on April 17, 1912 on the *RMS Carpathia*, and to his consternation, found that he had become a full fledged hero.

Despite his visible role in the White House and his growing importance in world affairs as the president's advisor, he was an unassuming man who was still uncomfortable in the glare of the spotlight. He struggled with what he thought was undeserved recognition.

"There were many heroes that night," he would say, anytime someone would congratulate him on being one. This self-deprecating sense of importance only grew his iconic status around the world. Instead of basking in the glory, Butt instead threw himself even more deeply into his work.

When Democrat Woodrow Wilson was elected the twenty-eighth President of the United States in 1912, Archie Butt's status on the world stage prompted the new chief executive to ask him to stay on in the White House despite his Republican affiliation. Butt was to have a new role, however, as Wilson's Secretary of State. For the next eight years, he served Wilson with determination and was a significant force in supporting the President's passionate desire to keep America out of the World War pitting the "Entente Powers" – France, the United Kingdom, Italy and Russia – against the "Central Powers" of Germany and Austria-Hungary and their empires, and later, the Ottoman Empire.

With Butt's powerful influence in the capitals of the Central Powers, Wilson was able to avoid direct US involvement in the fight, allowing him to focus on domestic affairs. That concentration ended abruptly on May 7, 1915 when a German submarine torpedoed the British steamer *Lusitania* within sight of the coast of Old Head of Kinsale, Ireland. The *Lusitania* sank in just eighteen minutes, faster than she was able to load her boats. Nearly twelve hundred were lost, including one hundred twenty-eight Americans.

The barbarous attack sparked a global condemnation of Germany, particularly in the United States, where opinion had leaned heavily towards isolationism. Reluctantly, Wilson presented a declaration of war to Congress in April 1917.

An armistice brought a halt to the fighting a year and a half later. The *Treaty of Versailles*, in which Germany was forced to accept unconditional surrender and the "14 Points" that were largely drafted by the Secretary of State, was signed seven months later in June 1919. The consequence of the four-year conflict was some forty million casualties, including more than three hundred thousand "Doughboys" killed or wounded.

Butt, who had philosophically opposed the war even more stringently than Wilson, did his best to bury his emotions when drafting the *14 Points*, but the enormous number of American casualties overwhelmed his normally sharp sense of justice. The ensuing *Treaty* he wrote was tinged with vengeance and the intent to leave the Germans unable to ever rearm again. The *14 Points* ultimately included Germany's admission of sole responsibility for the war and its consequences, the evacuation and return of all land the country had acquired through aggression since its colonial times, and a huge punitive reparations bill of more than US$33 billion to be paid to France, England and the Soviet Union. Germany's treatment at Versailles was brutal and left a deep and bitter resentment among the German people – particularly the veterans who had lost everything, including their pride, fighting for their beloved homeland. Among them was a young army corporal named Adolph Hitler.

Had he fully appreciated the blow to German pride that was the invisible byproduct of the Treaty, the Archie Butt would have fought with more passion to build peace with a wooden scythe rather than a forged saber.

Shortly after the end of the war, Wilson was struck by a devastating stroke that left him paralyzed and reclusive for the remainder of his second term. The extent of his incapacitation was hidden from view of the American people and the business of the Oval Office was largely tended by his loving wife Edith, with a strong supporting role by Archie Butt. The Secretary of State carefully selected the issues that Wilson personally addressed in his weakened state. For all intents, Butt was the de facto President of the United States from October of 1919 until the inauguration of March 1921, but he successfully remained in Wilson's shadow, at least in the public eye.

Consequently, both the Democratic and Republican party leaders saw in the "Major" the kind of man to lead the country, however reluctant he was to officially take the oath of office. Butt, however, was entirely satisfied to leave Washington and its cherry blossoms to others. He retired to his home in Augusta, Georgia, but remained cerebrally active by writing a syndicated column entitled *"View from the Butt"* for the *The Macon Telegraph*.

The task of leadership fell to Senator Warren G. Harding but little was accomplished during the two years he served as President. The US economy sunk into deep recession and the country was also plagued by urban violence sparked by race riots and returning troops who found themselves homeless and jobless. When Harding died of a heart attack in August of 1923, he left the task of rebuilding prosperity and confidence to Vice President Calvin Coolidge of Vermont, who was completely devoid of foreign policy experience. Coolidge delved headlong into domestic issues favoring the poor and middle class and steadfastly supported America's growing isolationist stance. Fittingly, when he left office in March of 1929, the country was enjoying prosperity, optimism – and peace.

In Europe, however, the outlook was bleak. Despite the rapid reconstruction of infrastructure and tremendous economic recovery, the discontent of the Germans, still burdened with enormous financial reparations and limited in their ability to openly rebuild their military, was growing deeper with each year's distance from the *Versailles Treaty*.

At the Republican National Convention in August 1928, Herbert Hoover, former Secretary of Commerce under Harding and Coolidge, emerged as the Party's candidate on the first ballot. In contrast, the 1928

Democratic Convention held earlier in late June was chaotic.

In the steaming heat and humidity of the Sam Houston Hall in Houston, Texas, the Democrats held the South's first political convention since the Civil War. Al Smith was the Democratic favorite and appeared to hold a lock on the nomination. However, his Irish, Roman Catholic roots, prohibitionist stance and loudly vocal opposition to the Ku Klux Klan drew strong resistance from a minority of the delegates. Among them were the delegation from Texas, a bastion of the secretive, white-hooded KKK. The opposition caught fire, and Smith was unable to swing the first ballot nomination and Senator Joseph T. Robinson of Arkansas became a strong challenger.

The Texans, led by Governor Dan Moody, still weren't appeased and successfully blocked either man from getting enough delegate votes to win the nomination through eight ballots. By mid-week, the delegates were drained from the blistering temperature in the hall and the round the clock negotiations that had not produced a solution. Many delegates were threatening to leave the convention all together without having nominated a candidate and the election was less than five months away.

Governor Moody invited Democratic Party leaders to join him on the veranda of his private Victorian mansion at 18th Street and Harvard in Houston. It was here that most of the most important political deals of his long and successful career in Texas politics had been hammered out.

"Boys," he lectured the Democratic leadership, "what we have here is a god dammed embarrassment. We might just as well give the Presidency to Hoover if you insist on giving this pansy-waist city slicker Smith the nomination. I tell you, it's a mistake. Hoover will cut his

balls off just like a god dammed steer and look him
right in the eye while he's doing it. If you want a
Republican in the god dammed White House for another
four years who'll force us to pay even more taxes – hell,
what's it up to now – sixty-three fucking percent? Then
you go ahead and nominate Al Smith. But you'll do it
without the support of the great state of Texas, pardners,
cuz we're leaving, I tell you."

Congressman Cordell Hull of Tennessee was the first
of Moody's guest to challenge him.

"Well, that's all and god dammed good, Dan," he
said uncharacteristically crude, hoping that falling into
the Governors vulgar style would help calm him down.
"I'm a bit worried myself. But who in hell is it that you
have in mind – you must have a candidate in that big
back pocket of yours or you wouldn't be so god dammed
persistent. Who the hell is it?"

A wicked grin came slowly to Moody's face. "You
know Cordell, you'll make a fine Senator come
November. You get right to the god dammed point,
don't you?" He took a long drag from the six-inch stogy
he held to his mouth, inhaled, then blew the acrid blue
smoke across the hot orange ember. "You know Cordell,
if I'm not mistaken, one of your constituents wrapped
this fine cigar."

After a long drink of his ever-present Kentucky mash
bourbon and branch water over ice, Moody sat up in his
high-backed wicker rocker and leaned over to face Hull.
"Well, that's the thing, Cordell, the name I have in mind
isn't in my back pocket. In fact, he's the only man I know
who's not in anyone's back pocket."

There was silence as he paused for another pull at his
drink and a drag on the cigar.

"For Christ's sake, Dan, who is it?" Hull asked,
completely out of patience. The man was making a fool
of them all.

Moody zeroed in for the kill. Like shooting ducks in a barrel, he thought.

"The hero of the '*Titanic*'," he finally said.

Every head looked up. "The what?" Hull queried, confused.

"Why Cordell, we must get you the hell out of Washington more often," Moody taunted. "You've never heard of the '*Titanic*'?"

"Why hell yes I've heard of the '*Titanic*', you condescending son of a bitch, but who are you talking about?" Hull demanded. "They were all fucking British!"

"Save for one, pardner, one of them was a god dammed, born in the USA, Yankee."

Hull's assistant said it first. "Archie Butt," he murmured from a chair against the railing. "God dammit... he's talking about Archie Butt."

Mouths dropped. "You mean 'Secretary of State' Archie Butt'? That Archie Butt?" Hull blurted.

"The one and only, Congressman," Moody gloated. "I tell you, god himself couldn't beat that boy at the polls – he is one tough son of a bitch who can charm the balls off a ballroom full of rattlesnakes.

"And he's as pure as a frigging virgin. Not a dark spot on his record," Moody finished and sat back slowly in his chair, exhilarating in his performance.

"Extraordinary!" Hull exclaimed before quickly composing himself. "What a brilliant..."

"And I," Moody cut him off, "would be pleased to corral the Senate for him," he said, referring to the vice president's primary role as president and presiding officer of the government's most esteemed elected body.

A reluctant Archie Butt finally agreed. Not surprisingly, he was nominated on the next ballot of the convention by unanimous acclaim and became the 1928 Democratic Presidential candidate in a most extraordinary moment in political history. The November election was no contest and Butt won in a landslide campaigning on a platform of continued prosperity, jobs for every man and woman who needed one, proportionate taxation for all citizens, and a conservative foreign policy that would limit US support to those countries struggling to build or defend democracy.

He had no idea how difficult his Presidency was to be. A scant seven months after he was inaugurated, the bottom was ripped out of the US economy as unexpectedly as the *Titanic*'s hull was opened to the sea seventeen years earlier. "Blindness" was a similar cause.

On October 29, 1929, "Black Tuesday," as Butt was addressing a Boy Scout troop from Boise, Idaho in the Rose Garden, he was handed an urgent message from his Chief of Staff, Jack Thayer. Thayer was no longer the courageous teen Butt had encountered on the *Titanic*. He was now one of the savviest and most capable political operatives the Major had ever known.

"I was good," Butt admitted in private to Coolidge, whom he counseled with regularly, "but not as good as Jack Thayer. He is that rare man who is not only supremely intelligent and articulate, but he is a warm and approachable personality and an addict for his work. And by God, he is loyal and honest to a fault.

Thayer, like Butt, was calm and soft-spoken and carried himself with self-deprecating humor and exquisite poise. So it was that the President picked up his body language even as Thayer handed him the note. "Trouble?" President Butt asked before reading it.

"Yes, Mr. President, we'll just have to add it to the list, sir." The bell had just been rung ending the days' business on the New York Stock Exchange, and the news was grim. The stock market had traded down another twelve percent and nearly thirteen million shares in a single day. Following two previous sessions that had ended in double-digit losses, in less than one week, $30 billion dollars of investor wealth had simply evaporated.

"Oh, my God," was all Butt could manage to mumble and he gazed forward, momentarily oblivious to the young Scouts. Not one of the boys could have appreciated the news the President was trying to assimilate. but for each of them, that moment in the Rose Garden was their introduction to the hardest times America had seen since the Revolutionary War.

No American was spared from the Great Depression and the new President, who prided himself for actually listening to his constituents, knew it. He wasted no time or effort to get the country back on its feet.

Literally ramming tens of thousands of pages of legislation through Congress, President Butt took direct aim at providing relief for those most in need, while also instituting wholesale reforms on Wall Street and bringing to task banks and corporations that had fueled the economic disaster. If there were any doubters as he assumed the presidency, they were silenced as Butt more than lived up to the proclivity to action that was his reputation. Long days and nights in cabinet meetings and private sessions with leaders of the Congress produced bill after bill. Butt worked tirelessly in behalf of the people who had put him in office as well as those few who hadn't. His stamina was remarkable.

Now, gazing out the window of the Oval office, he wondered once again if he had done all that was possible. The answer was always the same. Of course not, there was more to be done. But with the economy having carved out a precarious toehold on the path of recovery, it was time for the already exhausted President to address another crucial and potentially devastating issue that was growing with a ferocity and speed that made him dreadfully fearful of the future. The drums of war were once again thundering in Europe, and the sleeping dragon of Asia was showing signs of awakening.

For the first time in three years he resolved to set aside his domestic agenda, at least for the moment entrusting it to Vice President Moody, while he turned his considerable energies towards averting a crisis of potentially more staggering proportions. Butt had come to believe that the proposition of continued peace could only be brokered by America.

The President was brought back to reality by the sudden presence of his Chief of Staff, who cleared his throat to get Butt's attention.

"Is it time, Jack?" he asked wearily from his rocker. Stuffing papers from the President's desk into a valise, Thayer answered. "Yes, Mr. President, it will be dark soon."

"Is Van Gogh assembling?"

Thayer stopped what he was doing and addressed the President.

"Mr. President, I have confirming telegrams from all members," Thayer said. Even after three years at his constant side, he was still not entirely comfortable with the notion that he was addressing the President of the United States face to face.

"To a man – and woman – they are in route as we speak. It's time to go, Mr. President," Thayer assured him. "Everything is in order."

Butt looked around the Oval Office as if taking leave of its security.

"Jack?"

"Yes, Mr. President."

"Before we go, pray with me a moment, won't you?" Thayer nodded in silence, slightly humbled by the request.

The two walked to the center of the room, directly beneath the Presidential Seal embossed in plaster on the ceiling. They knelt together.

Butt began, head bowed, his hands clasped in reverence.

"Our Father, who art in heaven..."

Seventeen

The White Star Line was justifiably leery of a US government investigation into the near-disaster, which might impound the ship in a New York Harbor for months. The company wasted no time in arranging to patch *Titanic*'s hull and make her seaworthy for the voyage back to a drydock in Liverpool. Less than forty-eight hours after *Carpathia* departed the shallows of Cape Sable Island with her crew compartments and decks awash with survivors of the wreck, powerful tug boats arrived on the scene from several ports on Cape Cod. Salvage crews immediately invaded the hull with huge pumps.

As luck would have it, the tidal cycle was in their favor. *Titanic* had beached in high water at mid morning. The ebb tide began and the ocean receded until low water was reached in the late afternoon. Dead low tide completely exposed the 185-foot-long gash along *Titanic*'s starboard side which had torn a two-foot wide hole through her first two compartments.

Thomas Andrews stood with Captain Smith of the *Titanic* and Guilles Quimet, captain of the *Nightingale* and surveyed the damage. "Another fifty feet of berg and you would not have made it, Captain Smith. It's a miracle that you're alive to see this," Quimet observed.

Smith was silent for a long moment. "I am afraid, Captain, that I would rather not be alive to see this." He turned his back on the great liner and went below to a hammock the *Nightingale* Captain had hung for him near the ship's galley. He pulled out his pocket watch, not so much to check the time, but to look again at the engraving on the back. "May warm tides and our everlasting love always keep you safe." It was signed by his wife Sarah and his daughter Helen, whom he supposed were just now being informed of the *Titanic's* incident and hopefully of his safety. He sighed, rubbing his thumb over the words carved out of the watch casing. "I'm coming home, my ladies, for the sea is done with me," he whispered to himself before closing his eyes for the first time in more than two days.

By evening of the following day, *Titanic's* bow had been successfully patched and the drainage of her hull was going well. She would be seaworthy by noon the next day, and with the assistance of high water, the four tugs standing by would be able to help drag her off the sandy shoal that held her. But before that could happen, *Titanic's* ballast tanks amidships would have to be filled to ensure she would not capsize when the tugs began to pull at her hull. Even as bilge water was being pumped out of the massive steamers' forward compartments, fresh seawater was being sucked into her ballast tanks.

Fittingly, the bulk of the work to free *Titanic* would fall to the great liner itself by "kedging" off the sandy bottom. Shortly after eleven o'clock in the morning on the nineteenth of April, a crew of firemen fed coal into several of *Titanic's* still burning furnaces and built enough steam to power the stern winches. Slowly, using one of her massive, mushroom-shaped, deck-mounted stern capstans, *Titanic* began winching in her own Poop Deck anchor, which had been laboriously ferried by a tug and laid more than two hundred yards off her stern. The anchor held, and *Titanic* effectively began to pull itself towards the anchor and freedom. At the same time, the hawser lines that the remaining three tugs had cleated to the ship snapped tight as their thirty thousand horsepower diesels began pulling. An hour later, *Titanic* found water beneath her bow again, but this time her nose was as high and proud as it had been in Southampton Port just nine days earlier.

The ship's interior hadn't fared as well. More than half her guts were soaking wet, contaminated with saltwater and mold up to the First Class Lounge which had been nearly 90 feet above *Titanic*'s waterline. Back in Liverpool, Harland & Wolff would coordinate the refitting at a cost of several million dollars. Even with her survival and the loss of only one life, *Titanic*'s brush with infamy might still bankrupt the White Star Line.

Thomas Andrews knocked on the door of Quimet's cabin following a quick inspection of the vessel. Inside, in complete solitude as he had been since being evacuated from the *Titanic* three days earlier, J. Bruce Ismay was in despair. Desperate to avoid the inevitable questions his presence In New York would prompt and fearful of an investigation, he elected to hide out on the *Nightingale* and return to England aboard *Titanic*'s sister ship, *Olympic*, which had been diverted to pick him up.

"Mr. Ismay, may I have a word, sir," Andrews asked after poking his head into Ismay's cabin. The general manager of the White Star Line sat in a chair next to a porthole that was the only source of light in the small compartment. He looked ashen, almost waxen, his eyes closed but not asleep. He did not acknowledge Andrews' presence.

"I have inspected her, just now, Mr. Ismay. She is a wreck up to her midships, but can be refit if the White Star Line chooses to do so," he reported. "The hull has been pumped out and patched and she will be able to make it back to Liverpool under tow." Ismay did not respond.

"Unfortunately, her engines will need complete overhauling and we have several cracked boilers. We were very fortunate that they did not explode." Only then did Ismay recognize the presence of the ship's designer.

"How old was that boy who died?" Ismay asked, barely audible above the Nightingale's engines. His sunken eyes bored into Andrews.

"I don't know, Mr. Ismay. Perhaps his early twenties," Andrews responded, caught off guard by the question. The sight of Hitchens' lifeless body was very much on the architect's mind as well.

"Did he have family?"

"I'm sorry, sir, I hardly knew the young man."

Ismay looked up in anguish, his eyes red-stained. He obviously had not slept. Andrews noticed a bottle of scotch whiskey, three quarters drawn on the deck beside him. He felt a surge of pity for the man. His arrogance had completely disappeared.

Andrews dropped the formality. "Bruce, we all have our regrets of the *Titanic*. Let us focus on tomorrow to ensure that it never happens again." The managing director, now a shell of the man he was, said nothing.

Andrews turned to leave. "I will let you know when the launch is here to ferry you to *Olympic*," he said, and closed the door softly behind him.

Ismay sat in silence for a while, his eyes closed. Abruptly, he leaned forward and reached for the bottle on the floor. He put it to his lips and drank deeply, draining it, then threw the bottle on the bunk. He waited while the strong liquor coursed through his system, numbing him. His eyes felt heavy.

Then, before he might fall asleep or lose his courage, he unhesitatingly reached below the mattress, pulled out a handgun, cocked it, placed the barrel into his opened mouth and pulled the trigger. The bullet blew out the back of his skull and brain matter splashed across the white interior hull. As the gore slowly dripped down the cold steel wall, Ismay's body fell forward, teetered slightly, then settled into place in the chair in an upright position, his head down, eerily imitating *Titanic*'s last hours.

It took two tries, but Titanic had finally revenged the orders that nearly sank her.

Eighteen

After changing into casual clothing, President Butt was escorted by a handpicked Secret Service detail into a secret passageway, hidden behind a heavily wainscoted wall in the north side of the Oval Office. As always, Jack Thayer was at his side. Butt had been in the tunnel only once before during a briefing on how the Secret Service would evacuate him from the Oval Office in the event of a terrorist attack. Only the President, Thayer, the three agents accompanying him and one other knew of the secret escape path.

The electrically illuminated tunnel ran down two levels beneath the White House and then six hundred yards north under the grounds to Pennsylvania Avenue at Lafayette Park. There, the brick lined tunnel, secretly constructed when the White House was rebuilt following its burning by the British during the War of 1812, ended at three flights of stairs that rose into a nondescript locked utility shed in the center of the Park. A fourth agent was waiting outside, sitting on a park bench fifty yards away, reading a newspaper under a streetlamp. Darkness had fallen. They were on schedule. Outside Renwick Gallery on Pennsylvania Avenue, a large black sedan devoid of official government markings, awaited the President and his party.

As the door of the shed opened a crack, the fourth agent casually folded his newspaper and tucked it under his left arm. He unbuttoned his suit jacket for easier access to the .38 caliber handgun he carried in a leather holster, just in case. The park was quiet, and other than a few tourists walking the grounds and admiring the view of the White House, nothing was amiss.

President Butt emerged from the shed with Thayer following, both men minding the instructions of the lead agent who strode briskly towards the waiting car. Crowds of tourists lined Pennsylvania Avenue, oblivious to the President in their midst. Wearing a navy blue cardigan sweater over a white oxford shirt and khaki trousers, Archie Butt looked like any other middle-class American come to see the most recognizable homestead in the country. Another agent opened the back door of the car without stepping out and Butt and Thayer smoothly took their seats beside him. The three-man detail that would accompany Butt on the trip jumped into another car parked behind the President's and slammed the doors. Without hesitation, the two cars pulled away from the curb simultaneously and blended into the normally heavy traffic. The cars turned left onto Independence Avenue and continued on to the Arlington Memorial Bridge where they exited the highway. The escape had gone flawlessly.

Ten minutes later, the two black cars pulled up to a remote pier on the Potomac. Their headlights provided the only illumination of a ramshackle marina. Butt's driver pulled to a stop, turned off his lights, and then blinked them on and off, twice. Twenty-five yards away, another Secret Service Agent flicked his flashlight similarly in response. The lead agent got out of the car and walked to his colleague.

"Already?" Butt heard him say.

"Give me a minute. We'll pull the boat up," the agent, dressed head to toe in black, replied. Butt heard the distinct sound of twin marine diesel engines roar into life, and a few minutes later watched as a sixty foot long mahogany and navy blue wooden cruiser appeared at the dock. She cast no shadow in the moonless night. Across her stern was stenciled the name, *EXCALIBUR.*

"She'll be there?" Butt asked Thayer in the darkness.

"Yes, sir. I have her word," he responded crisply.

An agent knocked on the back window of Butt's car and opened the door, motioning for him and Thayer to step out.

"Mr. President, your battleship awaits," he exaggerated in jest. "Everything has been seen to and to the best of our knowledge you were not detected leaving the White House."

Butt smiled and energetically shook the young man's hand. The Secret Service Agent beamed with pride. "A job well done, Stan, as always."

"Thank you, Mr. President. And God be with you sir," he replied.

The President looked him in the eye and winked.

"Yes, Stan," he said. "God and a little bit of persuasion."

Butt strode briskly down the dock sandwiched between two agents. What he wasn't aware of were the half dozen Secret Service men who were hidden in the shadows around the marina, each armed with a high powered sniper rifle. They left nothing to chance.

He stepped into the boat and was immediately met by Secretary of State Henry Lewis Simpson. Simpson, a staunch Republican, had been drafted by Butt for his considerable experience and ability, party affiliation be damned. The career statesman from New York had just returned from the *Geneva Disarmament Conference,* and was prepared to brief the President on the state of international affairs and overseas military buildups. A young man, perhaps in his late twenties whom Butt did not recognize, stood behind Simpson with Jack Thayer. The President's old friend, Francis Millet was also on board, but was resting in his cabin.

"Good evening, gentlemen. I'm sorry to take you from the comfort of your beds," the President greeted the men. "I needn't remind you of the importance of our mission."

Simpson spoke for both of them. "Mr. President, it is our privilege to support you on this most critical undertaking. It's a daring concept. I dare say we will all sleep better should you be successful."

"*We* will be successful, Henry," Butt assured him, emphasizing the plural. He turned to the stranger. "I have not had the pleasure, Mr....?"

The younger man, caught off guard by Butt's question and informality, cleared his throat quickly. "Yes, Mr. President, I am Robert Maldonia, director of domestic intelligence for MI-8."

"Ah," Butt responded. "MI-8, the eavesdroppers," he said, referring to the little known US intelligence group that intercepted and analyzed daily some thousands of telephone and wire communications transmitted by or in behalf of the world's most important, powerful and influential individuals and their holdings. Known only to a small group of Washington insiders, MI-8 was commonly referred to as the "Black Society" as their operations and activities came under the cloak of "Top Secret". Only the President and two members of his cabinet, Stimpson and the Secretary of Defense, were authorized to receive briefings from the intelligence unit, which operated secretly out of the basement of a large grocery store in Alexandria, Virginia.

"It's important that you get some rest before our meeting, Mr. President, so perhaps we should begin the briefing," Simpson interjected.

"I agree Henry," Butt replied. "It seems the older we get, the shorter the nights become, hey? I trust that all of you will be agreeable to a brandy and perhaps a cigar while we chat? It's a luxury I can rarely afford working in the Oval Office."

All four cheerfully agreed and as they settled into chairs around a large table in the stateroom set up for the President's journey, a porter appeared carrying a large crystal decanter of fine French brandy and a handful of Cuban cigars. "Above all, gentlemen," he joked, "we must be sure that Cuba remains an ally. How could we possibly deal with affairs of state without Cuban cigars?"

Maldonia, in his first exposure to the legendary President, was struck by his calm demeanor despite the burden of his responsibility and all that was dependent on the outcome of the next thirty six hours.

Simpson, the most formal of the men, began his presentation to the President.

"Perhaps I should begin with a summary of the *Geneva Disarmament Conference*, Mr. President," Stimpson said. "I have just returned from Switzerland a fortnight ago, and I am sorry to report to you that the conference was not only an abject failure, but also most alarming."

Butt fidgeted nervously in his seat, despite the relaxing respite the brandy promised.

"As you know," Simpson began, "the key players at the talks were the US, whose delegation I personally led, the Soviet Union, the Germans, French and the Brits. Our goal was to finally put into action the disarmament accords that were reached in Versailles in 1918. Your message was well received, at least in principal."

Butt had sent a carefully worded letter to the Conference, which was read by Simpson. "If all nations will agree wholly to eliminate from possession and use the weapons which make possible a successful offensive attack, defenses automatically will become impregnable and the frontiers and independence of every nation will become secure."

"I believe this was the final attempt," Simpson continued, "at least through formal negotiations, to concur to act on the agreements which were signed at the end of the war, limiting military buildups of the Allied Powers and to enforce the continued disarmament of Germany and her allies.

"Ostensibly, the Soviet Union agreed to uphold its signature on the treaty, but Stalin's word and actions to do not always compliment each other."

Butt interrupted the Secretary of State. "I suppose that it is a polite way of saying you don't trust the bastard, hey Henry?"

Simpson smiled. "I would not be so bold, sir... but that is precisely my point. All of our intelligence, largely gleaned via MI-8 and our Soviet Embassy, leads me to believe that the Russians have already ramped up their substantial military production, and indeed will lead an arms race among European nations.

"Frankly, I found the Soviets' a little too agreeable. I had the distinct impression they were going through the motions and giving us the answers we all wanted to hear. Because on the contrary, Russia has placed twenty full divisions on their most western border with Germany and are poised for an offensive, although they will, and did, argue that their western fortifications were strictly defensively minded."

"Good Lord," Butt said, shaking his head. "No peace time economy can afford to support – what is that, three hundred thousand troops?"

"Approximately, yes sir."

"No peace time economy," Butt repeated," especially one that is as agriculturally founded as the Soviet Union, can afford to support an army that big and that far from home for any considerable period of time. I believe you are correct in saying that they are 'poised' for some imminent action.

"But what is their motivation?" the President probed. "Do we have any idea why the Russians are attracted to Germany or the other western European countries?" he asked, but already knew the answer.

"The Soviet Union still has the taste of blood in its mouth, Mr. President," Simpson responded. "In the case of Germany, it wants vengeance. As to the balance of Western Europe, I believe Stalin's ultimate objective is complete domination of the continent by 1940. And in that regard, the man is so treacherous that I could actually envision him throwing in with the Germans, at least until he had the opportunity to stab them in the back."

"He is a madman," Thayer interjected.

"Perhaps," Simpson replied, "but he has good company in the Bavarian corporal who will most assuredly be named Chancellor of Germany within the next few weeks. Bismark is exhausted by the continual pressure and growing Nazi party power, and he will have no choice but to hand the Chancellorship to Adolph Hitler."

"Hitler..." Butt interrupted. "What do we know of him besides what I read in the papers?"

Simpson looked down at his papers arranged carefully on the table and removed his glasses. He rubbed his eyes. "Mr. President, I have had two meetings with young Mr. Hitler in the last year. Suffice it to say that I think him a lunatic."

"A lunatic?" Butt asked. "How is it that the vast majority of sixty- five million Germans can be taken with him if he is a lunatic? Surely you must underestimate the man."

"On the contrary, Mr. President," Simpson snapped back. Butt thought he saw a glint of fear in his eyes. "To underestimate Hitler would be a mistake we would live to regret, I'm afraid. He is a fiery brand of orator, angry and animated, and he appeals to the enormous sense of pride the German people still have for their motherland. There is grave bitterness amongst the people over what they feel was racist treatment in Versailles.

"Hitler continually rubs their noses in the pain the Allies inflicted on Germany following the Armistice, and he speaks the message of revenge to a people who are hungry for it. I am afraid that we must hold ourselves somewhat accountable for the sentiment of the German people. I suggest that if we were constructing the Treaty today, our approach would be significantly less punitive."

Butt wiped his brow with a handkerchief from his coat pocket. "Unfortunately, the blood of the war caused many people, including me, to be blinded to the seeds of hate that we sowed with the enforcement of the *14 Points*, he said. Not a day goes by that I don't revisit that god dammed document," the President admitted, shamefully.

"Nonetheless, it happened and we must concentrate on diffusing the intent of the Versailles treaty with a far more appropriate and realistic approach." He took a long drink from his brandy, the conversation dredging up memories he wished he could bury.

"Getting back to the Soviets – what do they need?" Butt asked, getting right to the point.

"Need, Mr. President? The most basic of commodities," Simpson responded. "Despite their agricultural bent and the implementation of state run farms, they are in desperate need of food. Natural resources – iron, copper, coal, oil – are all plentiful and are not bartering chips. But the Russians are starving."

"And Germany?"

"On the contrary, the German people can sustain themselves, but natural resources are a significant challenge for the nation. A similar situation is occurring in Japan, which is highly dependent on oil imports to fuel their economy. They are desperate for oil – which makes the Chinese, Koreans and Malays inviting targets of aggression."

Butt sat in silence for a moment, turning to stare out a large porthole at the banks of the Potomac as the cruiser rushed upriver in the darkness. The boat had no running lights, and except for the yellow glow ensuing from the President's stateroom, was completely blacked out and running at full speed. It reminded him of another such night long ago.

"What was the final outcome, Henry? As dismal as I expect?" the President asked.

"Worse," Simpson replied, shaking his head. "The outcome was in serious jeopardy almost from the outset. The talks quickly got bogged down with semantics over what constituted 'offensive' and 'defensive' weapons. The French were adamant that the continued stranglehold on German military armaments was the only assurance they had that Germany would not attack them again. For their part, the Germans were equally insistent that they had the right to maintain armaments equal to that of the French and British. The hatred between the three countries is deep and bitter. I dare say it will be many generations before normal relations between those two countries can be possible.

"Consequently," Simpson reported, "in typical fashion, the French demanded additional security from the US and Great Britain in exchange for limitations on their military armaments, which neither of us was willing to commit to."

Butt responded in frustration. "When it comes to France, sometimes I think the best course of action would be for the US to declare it a state within the American Union. Their expectations of US military and economic support know no bounds, yet we seem never to be able to count on French support when we need it most urgently." The President reflected a large body of American opinion that would support his position.

Simpson said nothing, but smiled his taciturn agreement. "Finally, Hitler's delegation threw up its hands in disgust, and with his approval, withdrew from the conference. In short, gentlemen," Simpson concluded, sadly shaking his head and removing his eye glasses, "it was an unmitigated disaster and a personal disappointment of the highest order. I had great expectations of success this time." He concluded his briefing to the President and rubbed his eyes, red from fatigue.

"Don't be so hard on yourself, Henry," Butt said, reaching over to gave his trusted friend, confidant and counselor a deserved pat on the back. "We cannot expect to solve the tribulations of Europe when the seeds were sown for them many generations before we arrived. Nevertheless, we must do everything in our power to influence the course of history as it regards war. I only regret your disappointment, Henry. The Lord knows of your commitment to our country."

He turned to Maldonia who had been listening in silence. "Robert, I am most eager to hear from you. Should I assume you were able to garner the information I requested without being detected?"

"Mr. President, the act of discovery is not a difficult challenge for MI-8," Maldonia began without hesitation. He had been preparing his remarks for the better part of a day, despite being interrupted constantly by newly arriving data. "You have been very generous in your support of our classified operations as it regards resources both here and abroad, and thus we have been able to retrieve a substantial amount of data, and yes, without concern of detection. People at this level of society are surprisingly casual as it concerns the transmission of business information by telephone and wire, much more so than they would be in face to face conversation." Butt shook his head in agreement.

"As is almost always the case for MI-8," Maldonia continued, "the challenge for us is not so much interception or retrieval, but interpretation. Consequently, without knowing precisely your motivation or exactly what you are looking for, it is difficult for us to offer you a professional summary of our analysis."

Butt grinned, satisfied that the true nature of his mission was still unknown.

"Robert, perhaps it would be best if you told me what you know," the President replied. "I will, with your understanding, interrupt you when I need clarification or additional analysis. Please, do not hesitate to give me your personal opinion as it relates to understanding or interpreting what you have learned." The young cryptologist nodded his head, grateful for the President's invitation to be a meaningful contributor to their conversation.

"Thank you, Mr. President, I will do my best, sir," responded.

"So begin, please. I am impatient to hear what has transpired over these last twenty years. A greater understanding of the achievements and disappointments of my former shipmates, as well as a peek into their personal lives will be most helpful as it regards my message tomorrow."

An hour later, the President sat alone in silence reflecting on Maldonia's report. How was it, he marveled, that so few could wield such power and influence? Their accomplishments were extraordinary, their successes indisputable.

It came to him that the success or failure of his plan was ultimately contingent on the way each of them responded to a question. Since that terror filled April night twenty years ago, had success quenched their thirst for significance? Or, like himself, were they hungry to make a greater contribution?

The question was profound, he thought. But he would have the answer within hours.

Nineteen

The White Star Line front office moved quickly to secure *Titanic* a berth in the dry docks of Harland & Wolff in Liverpool to make permanent repairs to her torn hull and refit the vessel. The humiliating journey home took seven long days under tow of four ocean-going tugs. In contrast to the jubilation of her departure from Southhampton just days before, the great steamship was met with the eerie silence of thousands of spectators – many of whom had helped to build her. The crowd grew even larger after *Titanic* was settled in dry dock, incongruously out of the water, and the gash in her starboard hull became completely visible.

The scene was funereal. The curious shook their heads in wonder, while the morbid mourned the vessel that had left Liverpool with the community's pride entrenched in her hull. Some cried, many sighed. The general reaction was one of shock and amazement, the damage being so severe they understood that it was a miracle they were able to see her at all.

The cost of the damage was in the millions. But as all who viewed her resting peacefully in the dry dock understood, there was no price on the lives of the more than two thousand passengers and crew who had been saved, somehow.

Through the end of the year and well into the fall of 1913, *Titanic* underwent an extensive overhaul, including the removal and replacement of her three massive engines. The seventeen-month overhaul concluded with

Titanic refreshed and resplendent, as if her first voyage was no more than a bad memory. The White Star Line had no trouble filling her cabins for her second, and hopefully successful voyage.

A British Board of Inquiry was convened shortly after *Titanic* had returned to Liverpool, and testimony was heard from Captain Smith and most of his officers regarding the facts and events of the fourteenth and fifteenth of April 1912. The Board was particularly incensed by Smith's reckless disregard of ice warnings, but their true fury was held back as they listened to witnesses who testified about J. Bruce Ismay's continual haranguing of the Captain regarding the Blue Riband.

Ultimately, the circumstances surrounding Ismay's death were read into the record, and largely because of the support of his fellow officers, Smith was censored but exonerated of any criminal or civil wrongdoing.

Also taken to task was the British Board of Trade, the government body responsible for regulations drafted in 1902 that required a minimum of only sixteen lifeboats on passenger liners, no matter their ultimate passenger and crew count.

The White Star Line paid several hundred thousand dollars to settle claims against passenger losses, most notably the new Peugeot that William Carter was shipping to the United States. He received a settlement equal to the purchase price of the car, but was also provided the wreck. Carter promptly had it completely restored and sold the Peugot for more than his original investment, trading on the notoriety of the *Titanic* incident.

In the United States, a congressional investigation led by Senator William Alden Smith was high theater but actually productive. Despite the lack of participation by the White Star officers including the Captain, Senator Smith was able to push new regulations through

Congress requiring any passenger ship making port
in the United States to have enough lifeboats for all
passengers and crews, radio operators on duty twenty
four hours a day, more powerful pumps, watertight
doors and a host of other safety improvements.

Later that year, with the *Titanic*'s near disaster still
top of mind in the media and taking advantage of
election year politics, Senator Al Smith pushed another
bill through congress authorizing the creation of the fifth
arm of the US military service, the United States Coast
Guard. Ocean rescue and the oversight of US maritime
safety regulations were the two highest priorities for this
new branch of the military.

Now ship-shape and fully compliant with the new
US required safety features, *Titanic* made more than a
dozen trans-Atlantic crossings without incident. Aside
from even more opulent First Class accommodations, the
only modification to the ship was the installation of a
small bronze plaque, cemented to the portside forward
capstan dedicated to the memory of Quartermaster
Robert Hitchens. The young man had given his life to
save the passengers and crew of the *Titanic*. William
Murdock, now Captain of the steamship, visited the spot
each night of a voyage before turning in. Hitchens had
saved his life, too.

Titanic's royal stature on the North Atlantic route
was short lived. With the outbreak of war in June 1914
she was conscripted by the British government to serve
as a troop carrier. The vessel was once again hauled into
dry dock in Liverpool, where her staterooms and
kitchens were stripped and equipped for the
transportation of as many as five thousand troops. Steel
plating, armaments and camouflage paint turned the
most beautiful steamer afloat into an ugly juggernaut.

For the next four years, *Titanic* served the British
Admiralty with distinction, transporting more than one

half million British and American troops to the front lines in France. She survived five different U-boat attacks, only once sustaining damage when a torpedo grazed her rudder. The great lady made port safely and without casualty, an event that once again raised the specter of her invincibility.

Upon his safe return home on *Titanic* after a harrowing confrontation with a German submarine deep in the North Atlantic, a young field artillery captain by the name of Prescott Sheldon Bush, who had survived two years of savage fighting at the front with the *American Expeditionary Forces*, remarked to a New York Times reporter that, "It's true what they say about *Titanic*.

"God himself could not sink this ship."

Twenty

The darkened wooden cruiser broke out of the
Potomac River and into the headwaters of the
Chesapeake Bay at daybreak, still not having been
recognized as any more than a chartered pleasure cruise.
The boat turned southwest at Point Lookout, a peninsula
formed by the confluence of the Potomac and the Bay
which marks the end of the river's 400-mile run from the
West Virginia mountains. A lighthouse was built by the
federal government in 1830 at the tip of the point as a
navigational aid and to warn ships away from its rocky
outcrops.

The Chesapeake Bay was windy and choppy,
bouncing the sixty-foot craft around. The motion was
enough to wake the President from his much-needed
rest. As usual, he had slept poorly, his mind still racing
even at rest. For the few hours he slept each night, he
dreamt of war and the hideous deaths of young boys
naively rushing into battle spurred by their patriotism
and dreams of glory.

Only Francis Millet and Jack Thayer knew of Butt's
nighttime terrors. Each night was a reminder to the
Major that he must do everything in his power to avoid
embroiling his beloved country in another war. When he
took the Oath of Office as the thirty-first President of the
United States, he swore to himself that at least during his
tenure, there would never be cause for him to have to
write to the inconsolable mother of a boy soldier who lay

dead on foreign soil. He had already written too many such letters.

"There is no glory in war, Francis, only pain, blood, death and despair," he once remarked to Millet over a brandy and cigar. "Dying on the battlefield is perhaps the worst way for a man to meet his end. A lucky man may have a brief sense of satisfaction believing he will die for his country. But the majority dies with one question on their lips: 'Why?'"

"How many young men have I seen die, Francis..." he asked himself aloud, his mind unwillingly carrying him back to blood-drenched battlefields.

Butt rose from the sweat soaked sheets of his bed and asked for coffee. Then he sat at the table and began writing notes that he hoped would gain the support of the small group of people he would meet later in the day. Support that just might enable him to head off the war he knew was coming.

At 10 a.m., the cruiser arrived at its destination, three miles off White Stone Beach in Lancaster County. The Bay was wide here, almost eleven miles shore to shore. They would be far enough off shore to avoid detection and far enough removed from the normal shipping channels that the chances of being seen and identified were very limited.

A small launch appeared next to *EXCALIBUR*, and Archie Butt, now wearing a dark suit, spryly stepped aboard, followed by Thayer, Secretary Simpson, Maldonia, Millet and three Secret Service Agents. The driver of the boat nodded recognition to the President and then pushed the throttle to its limit. The launch jumped into the rippling current of the Bay and cruised at top speed towards a large vessel anchored some three quarters of a mile to the north.

As the launch approached, Butt took in the clean lines of the two hundred sixty foot yacht, the *Nourmahal,* in which their meeting was to take place. A stretched bow steamship built in 1928, Butt thought to himself that the elegant vessel *Nourmahal* (Arabic for "Light Of My Soul") was as impressive as her owner, John Jacob Astor IV, the world's wealthiest man.

A few minutes later, the launch idled up to *Nourmaha's* starboard side stairway and the driver killed the engine. Astor, who had been nervously awaiting the President's arrival from the ship's Bridge, made his way quickly down the stairs to the loading platform to welcome him aboard.

A tall, thin man in his early sixties, Astor also wore a dark suit to greet the President, but sported a straw boater hat replete with its flat crown and brim. It was the kind of hat only a very wealthy gentleman could wear without looking comical. Butt watched as the man waved and then turned to instruct his crew to be at the ready.

"Mr. President, this is an honor sir. It is so good to see you again," John Jacob Astor, the world's wealthiest man greeted Butt.

"Hello, John," the President reacted. "You have my undying gratitude for arranging for the Van Gogh meeting. I trust you will understand the importance I am attaching to our discussion after you hear my remarks."

"Mr. President...," the man began.

"John, my friend, at least in private could you please do me the pleasure of addressing me as 'Archie'? We've known each other too long for..."

"Say no more, Mr. President," Astor smiled. " 'Archie' it is. As I was about to say, I have no doubt that whatever the reason you have called us together, it will be a wise investment of my time. I've never known you to be frivolous, Mr. President... uh, Archie."

The President returned the smile. "I will have plenty of time for frivolity in my final retirement, John, at which time I hope you and I will find plenty of time for golf together."

"Splendid, Mr. President. Now let me show you to your quarters. We have another hour before we gather."

"Are they all here, John?"

"To a man, Mr. President," Astor said, having already given up on Butt's request for informality. "And of course, our group could not be complete without the western charms of the lovely lady from Denver."

"Excellent. I knew you wouldn't let me down, just like that long night some twenty years ago."

"I dare say…two decades," Astor reflected. "It's hard to believe that so much time has passed. I learned many things about myself that night – among them, the concept of humility."

"As I did, John." Butt felt the heat of the late morning sun and slowly climbed the stairs to the aft deck. He was beginning to feel the enormous burdens of his first term in office, going on four years without a day of relaxation, and he was bone tired.

Butt was giving serious consideration to declining the Democratic Party's invitation to nominate him for a second term. In his heart, he knew he could not make that decision until he had seen his plan to the end, whether it be bitter or sweet.

As he rested in his cabin, the large plate glass sliding windows on either side were opened to afford the strong breeze that continually moved across the Bay, and the President was refreshed by the cool clean air. He allowed himself a few minutes to reflect on his friend and fellow *Titanic* survivor, John Jacob Astor .

What was truly impressive about the man was what he had become since that long night aboard *Titanic*, Butt thought. At sixty-eight, the richest man in the world was renowned for his philanthropic work. Despite the repeated callings of society for him to support the arts and cultural projects that were the playground of the rich and famous, Astor declined, focusing the power of his vast resources on the poor and the destitute.

"I tell you, Archie," Astor commented to him at the Inaugural Ball, "something happened to me that night. It took me many years to realize it, but those poor boys I spent time with on the aft deck knocked whatever ingrained pretensions I had about the role of the wealthy right out of my mostly useless head."

After the stock market crash laid waste to the economic security of millions of Americans, Butt summoned his friend to the White House. Astor, unlike many of his millionaire colleagues, had been largely unscathed by the crash. His focus on real estate and investing in "things that I can touch and feel" had protected his vast holdings.

"John, I'm doing just about everything I can on Capital Hill to help the millions of Americans who've lost everything, but it's just a plain fact that government cannot solve all problems," Butt shared with Astor. "Sometimes it just falls to the man to pick himself up with resolve and his own god dammed self respect. But it's also true that sometimes a good man just needs a break."

Butt talked for an hour about the plight of the America farmers, many of whom had been wiped out when cash strapped banks had called their mortgages. On top of that, Middle America had become a dust bowl because of a prolonged drought and soil that had been over-farmed.

"Those banker sons a' bitches just laid their own failure right on the noggin's of a million farmers, John," Butt argued. "Wiped them out overnight to fill up their cash drawers again. These people are tough minded though, my friend. They've spent their entire lives scraping and clawing, never asking for a handout or a break. Give them a fighting chance and they'll not only survive, they'll help the god dammed United States of America build an agricultural industry that will humble the socialists in the Soviet Union."

Butt finally leaned forward in his chair and flicked a long ash from his cigar into the fireplace. He sighed and looked Astor straight in the eye. "With a little help from a friendly banker, John...'

Astor had heard enough.

"Mr. President, can you arrange for me to meet with the Secretary of the Treasury?" the millionaire responded, stone faced.

"When?"

"Right now," Astor said, already impatient. "I believe I've just received a calling to go into the banking business."

By the spring of 1932, "The Astor Bank" was the second largest lending institution in America, specializing in "recovery" mortgages with extraordinary low interest rates and grace periods of up to ten years. In the three years since it's founding, Astor Bank had never once foreclosed on a farm or residential property, extending the loan term as the situation dictated on a handshake and with no penalties. The once reviled "playboy" became a hero to nearly a million American citizens who found themselves down on their luck.

Now, with a warm late morning breeze filling his suite, the President felt refreshed just thinking about the difference one man could make. By God, he thought, there were a bakers dozen people just like Astor in the next room. Was there anything they couldn't accomplish together?

Twenty-One

Promptly at noon, John Jacob Astor IV proudly opened the double oversized mahogany doors at the entrance to the *Nourmahal*'s grand ballroom and announced the President of the United States. The thirteen invited guests turned and applauded in unison. Butt glanced to the front of the room and saw Van Gogh's "Starry Night" hanging on the wall, beautifully illuminated. Astor had left no detail unfinished.

As he strode into the room, he scanned the faces – some of whom he had not seen since that night so many years ago. Some of them had accepted his personal, handwritten invitation to his inaugural ball with delight. Others were not so delighted. These were the few who had refused to support him politically, despite their high regard for him as a man, simply because a continuation and expansion of Coolidge's' agenda was more than they could bear financially. But not one of them had turned down this invitation. Whatever Archie Butt had up his sleeve, he would not have summoned them on a whim. You could cut the anticipation in the room with a knife.

Arriving since early the evening before in carefully orchestrated shuttles from White Stone Beach to Astor's yacht, none of them was aware of who the other guests would be. In fact, it was not until they had gathered in the grand ballroom of the *Nourmahal* that they realized they were among the elite of the elite, the wealthiest, most powerful and influential private citizens – a dozen men and a single woman – in the world. It only took them a few minutes to realize that they had each been passengers aboard the *Titanic* on its maiden voyage -- an event that had left them all humbled in their realization that fate knew no social class. When all was said and done, when they faced death together, their fantastic wealth and power simply didn't matter.

They were assembled in a room eerily similar to the *Titanic*'s grand ballroom, albeit on a smaller scale. The opulence was breathtaking. The golden silk-lined walls, framed by solid mahogany wainscoting literally glistened beneath a neoclassical chandelier of French design, twinkling in its gilt bronze plating. The refractive glass absorbed the radiance of the steel blue Cararra marble floor as well as the soft sunlight poring into the room from large glass-paned windows on both the port and starboard sides. Several white-jacketed stewards circulated through the room, serving a particularly fine 1907 Heidsieck Diamant bleu vintage champagne from France.

Eagerly wading into the roomful of his guests, the President took his time greeting each one by name and made a point of looking directly into their eyes.

"Benjamin, my dear old friend," Butt said to the mining magnate Benjamin Guggenheim, a man whose personal fortune had swelled by three times since April 15, 1912.

"Mr. President, it was my good fortune to be under your command on that terrible night," Guggenheim responded. "You taught me courage, Archie... forgive me, 'Mr. President'.

"I believe I recall you teaching me a thing or two that night, Benjamin," Butt responded, referring to Guggenheims own heroics.

George Dunton Widener of Philadelphia grabbed the President's hand with the grasp of a ship's stoker. He was still Chairman of the Philadelphia Traction

Company, but over the last twenty years the firm he built had gained complete control of the streetcar market, supplying not only equipment but infrastructure as well. Now, in the last years of his business career, he was working longer hours than ever developing and installing underground subway systems in major cities all over America. Widener had gladly accepted the President's invitation, hoping to get his ear and support for expanding the company's operations into Europe. The burly man shook Butt's hand vigorously, making no attempt to hide his enchantment at being in the President's audience.

"George, you still have the strength of two men, I see," Butt replied. "Do you remember hauling those exhausted men up to the deck that morning?"

"Best work I've ever done, Mr. President," Widener said, a broad grin on his face. "I actually got my hands dirty."

Charles Hays moved Widener aside. "George, do be polite and make room for us smaller folk."

The diminutive Hays had more than made up for his lack of physical stature with incredible business acumen. The result was the Canadian railway system that was now the envy of the world. As Chairman of the Grand Trunk Railway, his light and heavy rail systems were in place from Calgary to Nova Scotia, and in recent years, Hays had expanded lines into the US. Detroit auto manufacturers, who had built substantial sales infrastructure throughout Canada, depended heavily on his railways to move cars across the border.

"Nonsense, Charles," the President laughed. "You're one of the biggest men I've ever known, my friend," Butt said. He had a particular affinity to the railroad man. Hays had personally contributed more than $10 million dollars to help Canadians who had also suffered from the consequences of the Great Depression.

Sir Cosmo Duff-Gordon, the Scottish land baron and two time Olympic fencing medalist, cleared his throat loudly and reached over Hay's head to reach for the President's hand.

"Baronet Duff-Gordon, we meet again, dear chap," Butt greeted him. "Why you don't look a day older since the incident!" he jested, admiring Sir Cosmo's full head of hair that had turned completely white by age fifty.

"One of the luxuries of royalty, Mr. President," Duff-Gordon responded jubilantly at the compliment. "You may be the only other person in this room who knows what a 'Baronet' is," he added referring to his title as the fifth baronet of Halkin, a distinction that had been passed down to him from a great uncle who had served the monarchy in some long forgotten capacity. Duff Gordon had no appreciable fortune of his own, his wealth coming from the stipend he received as royalty and the income of his wife, Lucy, a widely regarded fashion designer. What he lacked in personal wealth he made up for with his enormous grasp of Western Europe politics and diplomatic skills. With a simple telephone call, he could arrange for an invitation to visit with most of the heads of state of the continent, including Stalin.

"I'm looking forward to chatting with you, Cosmo. I greatly value your insights as it regards affairs across the pond," Butt said.

"And I you, Mr. President. I am more excited about this visit than the day I was knighted by the Queen Mum."

"If I know you Cosmo, what you're excited about is my brandy and Cuban cigars, of which we will enjoy together," Butt teased. Duff-Gordon beamed.

Out of the corner of his eye, Butt caught a solitary figure hanging back from the group who appeared deeply uncomfortable and unsure of himself. The President excused himself from his guests and strode to

the tall, almost gaunt man, who still wore the full
beard and unkempt long hair as he had on *Titanic*'s
Docking Bridge those many years before.

"William Thomas Stead," the President called ahead,
his hand extended. "I dare say it is the man who saved
us all." Now nearly eighty years old, the great British
journalist appeared startled by Butt's attention. The
eccentric writer, now perhaps the most recognized
newspaper columnist in the world, still wrote with a
clarity and ferocity that astonished the President. Stead
was employed by no single journal, although the biggest
of them had tried in vain to employ his talents, but he
was held in such high regard that whatever he wrote
would be published immediately without question by
whichever newspaper he chose. He continued to lobby
for peace and was as active in the anti-war movement
today as he was when Butt met him on *Titanic*.

Stead shakily took the President's hand. "Mr.
President... I must say this gathering has conjured up
some memories I've oft times tried to bury. I was
unaware..." he stammered.

"As all my guests were, William," Butt said, feeling
compassion for the man, obviously uncomfortable in his
own skin and somewhat overwhelmed to be part of this
extraordinary group. "Take comfort knowing that if not
for your courage and remarkable ability to calm the
multitude on that dreadful night, this room would be
empty."

The wild look in Stead's eyes seemed to soften.
"How kind of you to say that, Mr. President. Indeed, I
had forgotten what a remarkable man you are. How is it
that the President of the United States can have a
moments' thought of compassion?"

"You flatter me, William," Butt said, genuinely
touched by the remark. "I hope you will look as kindly

on the mission I propose today – in which your role will be vital."

The aged journalist appeared startled again. "But how can I...?

Butt placed his hand on Stead's shoulder. "Trust me, William."

"You may be the only person I ever have, Mr. President," he said with a slight grin. Butt was aware of someone pulling at his coat sleeve. He turned and was abruptly pulled into the arms of Margaret "Molly" Brown.

"Well I'll be a son of a bitch, it's true, you are the god dammed President, Archie Butt. I had to see it for myself," the heavy set woman said to him. Butt laughed out loud. As an actress, singer, cowhand, philanthropist and suffragist, Molly Brown had experienced life to its fullest over the years, the President thought, but nothing had smoothed out her rough edges.

"Molly, dear Molly," Butt said, looking into her eyes. "I knew I could depend on you to come – even if you didn't vote for me," he chided her.

"What in hell ever gave you that idea, Archie?" she roared, releasing her grip on the President's waist. The sound of heavy jewelry jingling on her wrists only added to her charms. "Any son of a bitch who's got the stones to stand up in front of two thousand, scared-shitless non swimmers is good enough to be President in my book. Hell, I voted for you twice before they caught me!"

Butt leaned back and took her in. Behind the bravado, Molly Brown was perhaps the most benevolent human being he had ever known. Despite the sudden death of her beloved husband after being married only a year, she had "picked up her britches and got back on the saddle."

A life-long cowgirl from Denver, she had inherited millions from her husband's silver-mining estate.

Although her demeanor suggested otherwise, Brown had had the intellectual foresight to invest heavily in oil and grew her fortune to more than $300 million. But making money wasn't what drove Molly Brown. Money was only the tool that allowed her to follow her heart. She had invested heavily in orphanages all over the West Coast, never being able to shake off her memories of the little French girl she had befriended on a bitterly cold night on which she thought they both were going to die.

"Still a bit salty I see, Mrs. Brown. But I dare say you give a sense of elegance to the art of foul language," Butt laughed. "My God Molly, you look as beautiful as the day I met you all those years ago." Despite her advancing years, molly Brown was still a fetching woman. A bit on the heavy side, she wore it well, and her face was still radiant and her eyes full of mischief.

"What the hell is the party for, Archie? I only packed this one dammed dress, so it better be quick. Besides, I've got young ones to feed, 'Mr. President'," Molly taunted, unable to resist.

"If it's all the same to you Molly, 'Archie' is just fine," he said. "And I promise not to keep you beyond dinner tonight, at which I sincerely hope you will sit to my right so I can flirt with you a bit."

She roared with laughter. "Well 'Archie', that's the best offer I've had in years. You never know, even a god dammed President gets lucky now and then!"

Archie felt the red coming into his face. "Molly Brown, my dear, you may be the only person on earth who can make the President of the United States blush. Now I must greet our other guests, lovely lady, so until tonight…"

She smiled and wrinkled her nose teasingly. "I'll even wear some of that perfume you sent me when I got named president of the Red Cross, you naughty boy."

From his right, William Ernest Carter saw the opening and seized it. "Mr. President," he said politely, "might I interest you in the newest Carter limousine? No President should be relegated to being chauffeured in a Cadillac. So bourgeois, if you don't mind me saying so."

"Mr. Carter, my dear friend. You have the keys to the new car in your pocket, no doubt."

"That they are Mr. President, jingling with my pocket change," Carter laughed. "Gold plated, I must add."

"William, I believe you could sell ice to the Eskimos," Butt said jokingly, but always somewhat amazed by the tenacity of his guest. "How one man could parlay the sodden wreck of a French motorcar into a billion dollar enterprise is beyond my wildest imaginations. But here you stand in front of me, proof positive."

"Mr. President!" Carter laughed, feigning indignation. "Why that Peugeot was a fine motor car and might have had a future in the United States if not for its poorly designed engine, transmission, suspension and steering, and the occasional fuel related fire. But it certainly was a beautiful car."

"The Eskimos won't stand a chance, William." Carter just thirty-six years old as a passenger on the *Titanic*, had indeed forged a challenge to General Motors, Ford and Chrysler with his upstart Carter Motor Corporation, and made his fortune doing so. He credited the notoriety and press attention he received from the *Titanic* incident for providing him the the leverage to get financing for his Carter luxury automobiles. The tale of the forlorn Peugeot, the only automobile aboard the vessel had become front page news all across the US, and the newspapers followed the cars restoration and resale with detailed attention.

Carter, never one to pass up an opportunity, quickly changed the subject to the manufacturing practices of the big three automakers in Detroit. "I tell you, Mr.

President, unless General Motors, Ford and Chrysler begin to invest in their processes, the Europeans will make a serious challenge to their leadership. Mercedes, BMW and Renault are forces to be recognized. And I needn't remind you that what is ultimately at stake is American manufacturing jobs," he argued. Butt shook his head sadly.

"I've had several direct conversations with your competitors," the President responded, referring to Alfred P. Sloan, Henry Ford and Walter Chrysler. "They argue that the assembly line concept Mr. Ford conceived will continue to meet the challenge of a growing market place and the ability to mass produce."

Carter winced. "I know their arguments well, Mr. President," he said rolling his eyes. "They don't know it yet, but their inability to quickly change over tooling to produce new models will in time lead to their ruin."

Carter was right, of course and Butt knew it, and it was not only the European manufacturers that posed a threat to Detroit. The businessman had traveled to Japan frequently over the last decade, gleaning new manufacturing techniques from the Japanese who employed the "kaizen" philosophy of production in virtually all of its factories. The Japanese were rapidly becoming a manufacturing and engineering juggernaut, a fact that left Butt very troubled. Carter had brought "kaizen" to his own factories which as a result, now focused on standardization of operations, cycle time, in-process inventory, and creating a work environment that encouraged and rewarded product and process innovations. America needed more minds like Carters', he thought.

"Bring that new model by the White House for a look see, William. I am intrigued by your accomplishments."

"Thank you, Mr. President," Carter winked. "You will be the first to know when Detroit newspapers deem it appropriate to refer to the "Big Four.""

As he shook Carter's hand, a tall thin man, slightly stooped at the shoulders, approached. "Mr. President, I am John Borland Thayer. Unfortunately, we did not have the chance to meet aboard the *Titanic*. Jack is my son..."

"John," Butt roared. "Finally we meet! I too regret not having made your acquaintance – but destiny has decreed it would happen because of that young man you reared. I tell you, John, he is one of the most remarkable men I have ever known. What you see around you has been orchestrated almost totally by him."

"You make me proud, Mr. President," Thayer said, his face radiating with gratification. "I look forward to the time you release your grasp of him so I can have the daily pleasure of his company again. Hopefully, it will be in time for him to be prepared to succeed me."

John Borland Thayer's business, indeed his life, was the railroads. He had sailed on the *Titanic* as a vice president of the Pennsylvania Railroad, but had since been elected its Chairman Emeritus. Known as the "PRR", it had grown to become the largest railroad in the United States, controlling nearly 10,000 miles of rail line and employing more than a quarter of a million Americans.

Now in his late 70's, Thayer still cut a dashing profile, and Archie understood where Jack got his matinee idol handsomeness. In his earlier days, Thayer was a renowned US cricket player and a heartthrob for female admirers of the sport. He and his wife Marian, joined by their adventurous son, then seventeen years old, had been visiting Germany as guests of the American Consul in Berlin at the time of the *Titanic*'s near disaster. And that is precisely why Butt had invited him.

An admirer of the German culture since his youth, Thayer had visited the country regularly and had developed a strong friendship with the American Consul General in Berlin. Through this relationship, he became fascinated with the political workings of the country and in fact, by 1932, he had become a key, unofficial advisor to US Ambassador Joseph C. Grew. Thayer met Adolph Hitler in the late 1920's and had an extraordinary grasp of the history of the Nazi Party and insight into its motives and intentions. Over the last two decades, he had developed an unparalleled right of entry to Hitler and his most powerful Nazi Party advisors. Butt knew that Thayer's connections could be vital.

"John, the time for Jack to rejoin the family may be closer than you think," Butt responded with a chuckle.

Knowingly, John Thayer sighed. "I understand, Mr. President. It's taken me the last several years to come to terms with the fact that it's the body that grows fatigued, not the mind. Whatever your decision, sir, you have served our country beyond America's expectations, even if they already recognized you as a hero."

"You are too kind, John. I am grateful that we've finally had the chance to meet. There is much we need to talk about, as will become clear in a few moments."

Butt pulled out his pocket watch and stole a glance. The proceedings were set to begin at 12:30 p.m. He had just a few moments. Francis Millet was holding court with three other survivors: Edward G. Crosby, chairman of the Great Lakes Shipping Company; George D. Wick, chairman and chief executive of the Youngstown Sheet and Tube Company, the only real competitor to US Steel's market dominance; and Thomas Andrews, the naval architect who designed the the *Titanic* and its two sister ships, *Olympic* and *Britannic*. He was now a partner in Harland & Wolff, the British ship builder that had constructed the three vessels.

"Archie," Francis greeted him in his usual carefree manner, despite the level of anxiety in the room. "I saw you glancing at your watch so I know the time is upon us, but please take a moment to say hello to my colleagues."

The President turned to Crosby and Wick, both of whom he saw occasionally as they served, at his invitation, on a Commerce Department task force on creating new opportunities for employment within the industrial sector. He had visited with them both in the Oval Office on two occasions for briefings, the last just five weeks before.

"Edward, George, so good of you to accept my invitation," Butt greeted them. "If nothing else, it is an opportunity for me to thank you for your tireless efforts with the Commerce Department. Secretary Lamont recently told me your work is showing great promise."

"Both Edward and I are very pleased to serve, Mr. President," Wick responded, "and we are happy to report to you that we have developed a plan that will infuse the economy with up to a quarter of a million new jobs in the industrial sector, which of course includes The Great Lakes Shipping Company and Youngstown Sheet and Tube Company. We alone will hire between five to seven thousand men before the first of the year."

"Splendid!" Butt said, greatly impressed by the report. "I knew I could count on you both." He turned to Andrews.

"Thomas, I don't know how we were able to drag you across the pond considering your travel schedule, but I am grateful that you accepted. It is hard to believe that I have not seen you in twenty years. In fact, the last time I spoke to you was on the Bridge of *Titanic* after you and Captain Smith had come up with your remarkable plan."

"Hardly remarkable, Mr. President, considering all that went before the mishap," Andrews said sheepishly. "I remember our conversation well. In fact I am reminded of it nearly every night when I sleep."

"Then we have something in common, Thomas." The President grasped his hand in friendship, fully aware of the breakdown that Andrews had suffered several weeks after the *Titanic* incident. He held the death of the young seaman as his personal responsibility and was still, after all these years, trying to cope with the burden.

"Trust me, we all have our demons," he said with compassion. "But there is nothing better for the soul than plain old fashion work, and I dare say I have a mission for you that should take your mind off the ghosts of *Titanic*."

Right on schedule, Butt heard the voice of Jack Thayer behind him. The young man stood at the podium, poised and ready to begin the meeting that had occupied his every thought for the last two months.

"Lady and gentlemen," Thayer said, in deference to a grinning Mrs. Brown, "if I may have the courtesy of your attention. Please take a seat anywhere you will be comfortable." Thayer, fastidious in his attention to details, had wisely left the seating casual, with three round tables and thirteen chairs. In the game of power, he knew one must pay attention to even the most fallacious of ideas, and at this level of success and influence, any one seen to be situated nearest the President might get as much attention as the President himself.

The guests moved quickly and took seats, silently pleased that there was no game involved. Thayer went on, quickly.

"I appreciate that time is perhaps your only limited asset," Thayer joked, rising a titter of laughter from the group, so without further adieu, please let me first introduce our host, Mr. John Jacob Astor." The group applauded politely and Molly Brown made a show of rattling the considerable jewelry adorning her wrists, which quite amused them, and for a moment, took some steam out of the room.

Astor stood at the podium.

"I dare say it is good to see you all again. I find it impossible that so many years have passed since I've last seen some of you," Astor said. Butt thought he heard a catch in the man's voice.

"While you are aboard *Nourmahal*, the ship is yours and please do not hesitate to speak up if there is anything my fine crew can do to make your brief stay more pleasurable. Some of you may remember a similar invitation from Captain Smith, which of course had its caveats…" George Widener roared with laughter and it was contagious.

"But I do promise, at the end of your cruise you will be high and dry, just as we left that magnificent steamer now some two decades ago.

"And with that, 'Lady'," he nodded to Molly in respect, "and gentlemen, I am humbled to introduce to you a real American hero, the President of the United States."

The gathered guests all stood and applauded, genuinely appreciating the honor of being selected to be in the company of this great leader – no matter what the message. Although there was a smattering of different opinions among them regarding his aggressive political agenda, each truly did respect Archibald W. Butt, the thirty-first President of the United States.

Perhaps, much more importantly, they respected Archie Butt, the man.

Twenty-Two

Butt slowly made his way to the podium, aware that every eye in the room was upon him. Stepping to the podium, he reached into his jacket pocket for his notes, carefully placed them on the dais and put on his glasses. His movements were unhurried, rehearsed in a thousand other speeches. Only then did he look out over his audience.

He was hit with a sudden deja vue. Awkwardly, he stared at them for more than a minute, trying to regain his focus.

"Gentlemen... and Mrs. Brown of course..." he began, and then paused again in silence.

"My friends, please forgive me for the inelegance of my presence before you," he began, somewhat halting. "You see, looking up at you just a moment ago, I was overcome by a sense that I had been here before."

The audience was rapt in their attention of the President, but his strange behavior caused several of them to rustle slightly in their seats.

"Perhaps seeing you all together again has resurrected long buried emotions. I suddenly recalled standing in *Titanic*'s First Class Lounge, preparing to speak at Captain Smith's request to several hundred stewards aboard the ship. I remembered thinking that this was the most important speech I would ever give – that my words might mean the difference between order and rescue, or chaos and doom. I felt uncomfortable. Nothing in my life had ever prepared me to deliver a message of such great importance – and with so little time to do it.

"None of you were there. Suffice it to say that Captain Smith asked me to assemble the stewards so that we could charge them with the onerous task of rousing all the passengers and to get them to move to the stern of the boat – with order, discipline and calm under the most trying of circumstances. Without their help and professionalism, all would have been lost. The stewards were frightened, with good reason. What they didn't know, was that I was the most fearful of all. I have faced death many times as a soldier. But I assure you, the blackness of the North Atlantic Ocean on that night chilled me to the core.

"You know the rest of the story. With God's help, I was successful in my motivational attempt and the stewards performed valiantly in rousing frightened and angry passengers, asleep in their berths, with little to offer as explanation."

The former First Class passengers hung on Butt's every word, silent and motionless. The sound of an ice cube melting would have echoed through the ballroom.

"Now lest you think this is some vainglorious attempt by the President to resurrect memories of my vastly overrated role in the *Titanic* incident," Butt continued, "please allow me to put what I have just said into context."

He paused again, gathering himself.

"I was wrong about that night. That was not the most important speech of my life. Those were not the words of my epitaph. No my friends, my speech on that frigid night was not the most important I have ever given."

He looked up and scanned the room, meeting the gaze of his guests. "This is."

Standing silently in the back of the room, the *Nourmahal's* First Officer quietly entered from the aft entrance to the ballroom and handed Jack Thayer a note. The Chief of Staff quickly left the room, unnoticed but for the President. He paused for a long moment to gather himself.

"You see," he continued, "today I am once again standing before a group of people whom I must convince are the difference between salvation and destruction. This time, however, my message has to do with world peace -- or world war."

Butt watched as his guests shifted uneasily.

"Perhaps some of you who have traveled abroad in the last year have felt the building tensions on the European continent. Perhaps you have also sensed that the world is simply not the same frivolous stage we all enjoyed as much younger, relatively carefree people in 1912. There is danger today. And it is lurking right before our eyes."

He had forgotten Thayer's exit, building steam behind his message.

"Our own blessed country has experienced a most unkind journey over these past several years. Just as it seemed that the policies of my predecessor were taking root and leading America out of the depression, a great hammer fell on our economy. I needn't lecture you on the consequences of the stock market crash and the rampant unemployment that followed. Indeed, I have done little else these past three years than tend to our crippled workforce. But in doing so, I'm afraid that I have contributed to the isolationist spirit that grips America. Perhaps I am guilty of the same arrogant blindness that almost cost us our lives some twenty years ago.

"However, today there is good news on the home front. Our energized administration and congress have performed admirably in taking the steps necessary to get the United States back on a strong financial and economic footing. Many of you have helped in that regard, and I am deeply grateful for your support. Now, to a large degree, like turning a huge passenger liners bow, it takes time to know if we have clearing sailing ahead. Only time will tell if we are truly on the right path.

"But even as I observe progress in America, I also see the makings of a new, potentially devastating disaster ahead of us. The drums of war are beating, my friends, just as sure as we are together in this room today.

"The allied success in the great war -- a calamity of monstrous proportions that claimed the lives of so many million innocents -- was at the same time a brilliant moment for those who fought for peace. Unfortunately, our success was tinged with the inescapable arrogance of the victor, and our decisions following the Armistice were tinged with vengeance. The *14 Points*, of which I admit to you included my dedicated hand, were, in hindsight, the seeds of further and future discontent on the European continent. We felt satisfaction in disarming Germany and in squeezing vast repatriations out of our fallen enemy. Unfortunately, we also humbled, embarrassed, and demonstrated great prejudice against him. In so doing, we have inadvertently sown the seeds of renewed hatred and anger in the next generation of Germans, Austrians and the people of the former countries of the Ottoman Empire. At the same time, for some, like the Soviet's, the *14 Points* was not nearly punitive enough, and the Russian hatred of the Central powers runs deep, as does their mistrust of Western Europe, and I dare say, the United States."

Guggenheim coughed, startled at the unexpected admission by the President. Several others looked uncomfortable.

"It is a fact," Butt continued, "that our punitive disregard for the respect and pride of those millions who fought for their countries -- misguided or not -- has laid the kindling for another great conflagration. And there exists any number of potential sparks to set off the blaze.

"Secretary of State Simpson has just returned from the *Geneva Disarmament Conference,* where he represented the United States in an effort to finally coerce all participants in the Great War to live up to the accords struck in the *Versailles Treaty.* To his great frustration and my disappointment, the efforts failed. Adolph Hitler -- a man whose name will cause you to grimace when you hear it in the days ahead -- essentially ordered the German delegation to withdraw from the Conference. Why? Because it clear that his demand for the German right to rebuild it's military to an equitable position as it regards France and Great Britain was unacceptable to the Allied position, crafted at Versailles in 1918.

"The German position was clearly espoused by its delegation. Germany stated her claim to equality of status as the basis of future talks, arguing that 'continued discriminatory treatment would not be compatible with the sentiments of national honor and international justice among the German people'. Hitler's delegation demanded recognition, without further delay, of the equality of all states in the matter of national security and the application of all the provisions of the Geneva Convention."

Butt paused again and sipped from a glass of water on the stand.

"My friends, I regret to tell you that I believe that demand, dictated by Hitler -- who as the iron-gripped leader of the vicious Nazi Party will soon be named Chancellor of Germany -- was the first step toward war. It seems that Hitler has the match in his hand. He needs only to strike it to start the inferno. If he does, the consequences will be unimaginable. France, Poland and the Soviet Union will have no choice but to engage German forces, which will march immediately into their countries and territories.

"How can that happen, you might ask, if Germany has not yet rebuilt its military might?

"It can happen, my friends, because the position of the German delegation was more evilly premeditated and deceptive than any official government position that I have ever encountered in all my years as a statesmen."

A look of alarm spread through the room.

"Despite the rhetoric displayed at the *Geneva Disarmament Conference,* and in earlier discussions in the Hague and other countless peace talks since 1918, Germany has never lived up to the Versailles Treaty, and has in fact been rebuilding their military since the early 1920's. Today Germany's land forces are larger and better equipped than ever before in its history, and their naval fleet is larger than the United States and Great Britain combined. The German government, under the guise of building commercial ships with which to resurrect their foreign trade, has secretly built the greatest naval force the world has ever known. A similar revival has occurred in the German Luftwaffe. The German air arm now dwarfs that of the US, England, France and the Soviet's -- combined."

There was a soft, collective gasp from the Presidents' audience. Butt watched as John Jacob Astor dropped his head in disbelief.

"All this has occurred in secrecy. It is only because of our recently revitalized intelligence efforts that we have been able to ascertain the degree to which Germany has rearmed. There is no other way to say it than that Adolph Hitler, at this moment in our history, is poised to unleash a military fury the likes of which we have never see -- and which the nations of free people are painfully ill prepared to defend against."

He paused again, letting the urgency of his message sink in.

"If the situation on the continent is not worrisome enough, the tigers of Asia, particularly Japan, are also waving their swords. Japan has had no limits on its ability to expand its military -- which it claims is a homeland defense against their sworn enemies, the Chinese and Koreans. It is simply unfeasible for Japan's economy to support this massive military buildup, unless it has plans to use it.

"I am embarrassed to admit, while all this has been happening around the world, your government has had it head buried in the sand. Now, the time for isolationism is passed. The situation demands that we respond -- immediately."

Butt could feel every eye in the room boring into his skull, expecting him to say the word 'war'. What they heard instead was a shock.

"I suppose that I've led you to believe that our only course of action is to prepare for war," the President continued. "On the contrary, the reason I have requested your presence today is to enlist your support in avoiding war and maintaining the peace, forever.

"My friends, I have had enough of war. I am sickened at the mere thought of another world confrontation. If there is to be an epitaph for Archie Butt, it will include the words 'He sought peace'. I cannot imagine a higher calling."

He paused again, taking a long drink from his glass. He felt himself tiring.

"Now before you jump to the conclusion that what I am after is a chunk of your wealth..." There was a nervous snigger of laughter at the comment, but the

President thought he saw them also breathe a sigh of relief.

"Before we can take any action, it is vitally important, perhaps for the first time in our history, that America truly understands the motivation for war. What is it that drives the German, or Austrians or Soviets to hatred? Why is the gun the weapon of choice rather than understanding and action?

"I suggest to you that we need not look any farther than our own backyards to understand. Why is it that at the onslaught of the depression, after the market crashed and Wall Street collapsed, that foreclosure became a weapon? I find it sad to recognize that millions of our countrymen lost their homes and farms before the government intervened. But why did this happen?

"Because, unfortunately, power, in the hands of a few, abetted by greed and avarice, is corrupting. And only a firm hand - and an alternative -- can stop the pillage. However, the consequence of this inhumanity is to rob good people -- hard working men and women -- of their pride, and to instill in them a deep sense of frustration, despair and finally, anger. But give these same people the chance to survive, to put food on the table and a roof over their heads, and they will rise to the opportunity. We have seen it work in our own backyard. I firmly believe that the situation in Europe can and will change if we provide such opportunities in Germany."

The President paused, waiting a moment for his message to sink home.

"The vast fortune Germany is spending on rearmament is coming at a severe price to its people. Like our own American farmers, they have been pillaged and have had no recourse to contest or reject the policies of their government. And they too, like the millions of American citizens who were financially raped, are filled with frustration, despair and anger. In turn, they seek vengeance, because there is no other salve to heal their wounds, and they naturally look to the government to exact it.

"I also believe that the leadership of Germany, the Soviet Union, and to some lesser degree the British and French, are war bent. Hitler and Stalin do not fundamentally represent the desires of their people, but think only of their place in history that is to be engraved as a result of their conquests. They think in terms of blood rather than wheat. In Western Europe, the years of threat have jaded the judgment of British Prime Minister Ramsay MacDonald and French President Paul Doumer to the degree that they seemingly only think in terms of their own national interests and in preparation for war.

"My colleagues," Butt continued, drawing his fellow *Titanic* survivors closer to his fold, "I suggest to you that if all the energy that has and is being expended to wage war were concentrated on the rights of the people, to provide for them a means to earn a living, to building schools, universities and hospitals, bridges and roadways, in mining their national natural resources, in developing their agricultural means -- then the warmongers could not hope to maintain the support of the people in building their war machines. The key to avoiding war and more bloodshed can be found in the hearts and minds of those who would otherwise be conscripted to do battle at the whim of their dictators.

"In short, it is not the leadership we must continue to lobby for peace, but the common man. Only then can we begin to dream about ending this cursed folly of war and bring true peace to the world."

The President reached for his water glass once more. The hook had been set.

"Where is all this leading us, my friends...?" The President glanced at his notes for the first time.

"As I look out among you, I see people whose eyes were opened wide on the night of April 15, 1912, twenty years ago to this day, to the plight of men, women and children of innumerous nationalities and social levels that were living in fear, not only of their immediate crisis, but of the future. I dare say that at least for me, I can look back at that night as a sort of epiphany. My desires, motivation and understanding of self respect and importance have never been the same. I have no doubt, based on your own behavior over these last two decades that you did not each experience your own illuminating enlightenments.

"Collectively, you represent the highest achievers of our generation and your expertise and wisdom is matched only by your compassion. If only I could convince you to run for political office..." They laughed, relieved of Butt's intensity if only for a fleeting moment.

The time had come for the President to lay out his plan.

"In this room, we have the power of industrial giants. Steel makers, automobile, ship and bridge builders. Men who know how to drill deep beneath the earth's crust to mine its natural resources. Others who have literally built the great railroads that now connect the United States and Canada coast to coast and across the border. And those who have developed the technology of light rail to the point that it is being deployed now in every metropolis of our country in the form of streetcars and underground subways.

"We have among us men who know the intricacies of moving freight across the Great Lakes and into Canada on great cargo steamers. A man who knows the value of land, how to develop it, how to rebuild cities and towns -- and who has the financial banking prowess to capitalize and finance it. And a woman who has learned all there is to know about the oil industry -- where to find it, how to drill for it, bring it to the surface and distribute it, while also managing the worldwide operations of the Red Cross. Simply astonishing," Butt said in praise, tipping his head slightly to Molly Brown out of respect. She glowed.

"And finally, we have in this room two of the most esteemed artists of the twentieth century. Mr. Stead, recognized around the globe as the greatest journalist of our age, with the ability to reach hundreds of millions of people by newspapers and radio with his opinions, learned facts and judgments. And my dear old friend, Francis Millet, a brilliant painter in his own right who has, over these last years focused his considerable energies on protecting the world's masterpieces and ensuring that they are accessible to those they were painted for: people. The dozens of wars and conflicts waged throughout Europe over the last several hundred years has resulted in the wholesale theft of national artistic treasures. What belongs to Germany may in fact be hanging on the walls of Le Louvre in Paris. Or Belgian masterpieces that have been stolen now decorate German museums. My friend Millet knows how to find these priceless artifacts, steeped in national pride, and return them to their rightful owners -- an effort that in itself will ease tensions between European nations and heal wounds.

"My dear friends, it is not your fortunes that motivated me to ask you to come together. No, it is simply your great wisdom, knowledge, experience and compassion that have done so. For without your help, I do not believe the United States can propose any plan that will avoid the war that I am certain is coming.

"Specifically, what I propose is this. At my invitation, I plan to bring the heads of state of France, Great Britain, Germany, Spain, Italy and Russia to a secret meeting to be held here in the United States in early September. I do not mean their national disarmament delegations. I speak of MacDonald, Doumer, Hitler, President Niceto Alcalá-Zamora of Spain, Mussolini of Italy, Stalin, and of course, myself. The seven heads of state who, if willing, can head off war."

Every eye in the room widened. The thought of bringing the most powerful European leaders, many of whom had not been abroad since the signing of the Versailles Treaty, together under one roof -- in the United States of all places -- was nearly laughable. Except that it was Archie Butt who was suggesting it, and he wasn't joking.

"My objective is simply stated: bring a halt to military rearmament by making the progenitors an offer they can't refuse. And that's where I urgently need your assistance."

Butt scanned the room looking for signs of rebellion among them. He glanced quickly at "Starry Night" for fortitude before going on. The painting hung alone, illuminated by the sun off the port side.

"The offer I intend to make to them has several components. First I will demand an immediate halt to German rearmament, but as a quid pro quo, I will also agree to put an end to the German reparations payments. In lieu of these funds, the United States will provide instead an immediate transfer of technology in the areas most needed by all parties. This will come largely in the form of mining and drilling technology to aid these countries in the pursuit of their goal towards self sufficiency in minerals, ores, and petroleum oil.

"Second, I will propose to Germany specifically a massive infusion of financial aid from the United States, which will allow the country to undertake the construction of the schools and hospitals they desperately need, as well as major infrastructure improvements such as bridges, roads, power generation and urban development. Both of these proposals will nearly instantly create a huge number of jobs, not only in Germany, but throughout Western Europe, a means to convince the common man that the sickle is stronger than the sword.

"Finally, with your support, America will offer the Europeans your commitment and hands on efforts to make the US proposals a reality. In this role, each of you becomes the most vital and corroborative component of my scheme. Without your involvement and dedication, I fear that any investment we make will either be lost or corrupted.

"As to the Soviet Union, admittedly a nation whose leader I do not trust, I intend to make it clear to Mr. Stalin that our proposal, if acceptable to Germany, its allies and ours, will result in the signature of non-aggression and mutual aid pacts that will effectively bond all of Europe as allies of the United States. Consequently, if Stalin becomes an aggressor he will face our combined strength -- and that my friends will make him think long and hard about starting a war on any front."

Again the President scanned the room. He was relieved to see no signs of outward rejection. Butt noticed that Jack Thayer had come back into the room. Jack caught his eye with a quick shake of his head to indicate there was nothing to worry about.

The President continued. "If the leadership of the seven invited nations cannot reach agreement to accept my proposal, I will make it clear that it will be my intention to appear before the *League of Nations* to share with its members the intelligence that we have gleaned regarding the Germans. Further, I will describe in detail the rejected United States proposal to buoy the European continent with jobs and cash. That alone should prompt riots in the streets and cause considerable undermining of their power and governments. If nothing else, Hitler will have little time for planning a war.

"Mr. Stead, I would presume to have your support for this presentation and to help foster understanding through the media." The journalist nodded his head in acquiescence.

"In the coming weeks, if you are agreeable, I will ask each of you to join me in Washington for individual discussions so that we may vet this plan further, and detail your specific roles. I would further propose that you join with me at the summit meeting in order to have clear access to Europe's leaders and to share with them first hand your proposals."

The President was nearly spent, but adrenalin coursed through his body urging him on.

"My friends, I have thought of little else over these last several months than of this opportunity to garner your support. I hope that I have been clear and trustworthy in my remarks, and most importantly that I leave you knowing my passion for the avoidance of another war. Without your help, I believe we are lost.

"Now I will leave you to discuss the viability of my plan, and of course, your considerable role in its success. I would appreciate your reply tonight at the dinner Mr. Astor has planned for us in this very same room.

"Until then, I thank you for your courtesy… as well as your friendship," Butt finished.

There was dead silence in the room as the President left the room. Not a comment or question, just silence. Thayer met him on the other side of the door.

"Brilliant Mr. President. I do not believe I have ever heard you deliver a more powerful or important message," Jack told him.

"I can only hope that they understand my urgency, and that they are prepared to support me," Butt responded.

"Frankly, Jack, I do not have any inkling as to what to do without them."

He remembered his Chief of Staff leaving the room. "Any trouble, Jack?"

Thayer knew it was important for Butt to stay focused.

"Nothing I can't handle, Mr. President."

He hoped.

Twenty-Three

A mile off White Stone Beach, a small skiff floated far off from *Nourmahal's* starboard side, a lone figure standing in its flat bottomed hull apparently fishing. The boat had gone unnoticed by Astor's security until about ten minutes into the President's speech.

Jack Thayer had been particularly worried about the possibility of the extraordinary gathering being discovered, knowing the press would have a field day with the story and that the coverage would cause great concern. Thayer winced at the thought of the headlines

Upon discovery of the fishing boat, *Nourmahal's* launch had been immediately dispatched to investigate. The crew made a fast pass by the fisherman then turned around for a slow drive by.

"What's your business here, mate?" a crew member called to the short heavyset man in the boat.

"Jest fishin, for Christs sakes. Did I break a god dammed law or something'?" he responded, clearly agitated by the unwelcome interruption of a quiet afternoon's fishing.

The crewman was satisfied. "Have a good day, sir." The launch peeled off to inform Thayer of a false alarm, leaving the skiff rocking in its wake.

The fisherman sat down heavily in his boat, cursing the intruder, started a small outboard motor and headed back to shore. It would appear that he had been scared off. A half hour later he dropped anchor about a mile off land and leaned down to open a large canvas satchel he had carried on to the skiff before sunrise when White Stone Beach resembled a ghost town. He was confident he hadn't been seen.

The man pulled out a wireless radio set from the satchel and quickly powered it up. When he had acquired the signal he needed, he proceeded to inform a radio operator on the other end exactly all that he had seen through a pair of high powered binoculars now hidden beneath a blanket. The maestro would have a great time with this information he knew, and expected to be handsomely rewarded for his efforts. He ended his message with two words:

"Heil Hitler."

Twenty-Four

They talked for no more than thirty minutes. Thayer watched the door to the grand ballroom but didn't dare to impose upon the discussion. At 3:00 p.m., John Jacob Astor was the first to emerge, Molly Brown on his arm smiling and having the time of her life. The others followed. Thayer could see no signs of distress on their faces. It was if they just finished a high-spirited luncheon.

Francis Millet was the last to come out and he immediately took Thayer aside.

"Well done, Jack. I will leave it to Astor to announce our decision tonight in the company of the President."

"Thank you Mr. Millet. I trust the President's message was an eye opener for his guests?" Thayer asked.

"Jack, our eyes have never been more open. Now if you will excuse me, I must take some rest in my cabin. I feel that excellent champagne about to impinge on my sense of good judgment." He turned to walk away.

"Jack? Just one thing before I go."

"Yes, Mr. Millet. Anything."

"Archie failed to mention how critical it is that our meeting today be held in the strictest confidence. Perhaps you might mention to the President my concern and he can bring it up this evening in his own way."

"I will do so, Mr. Millet. It is an important point, although I trust our guests understand the vital nature of secrecy already," Thayer responded. The comment had caught him off guard.

"Perhaps, my good chap. But one never knows. Mr. Maldonia's comment last night about the loose lips of the wealthy and powerful have taken root in my subconscious, I'm afraid. I might be overly concerned."

Thayer said nothing, and Millet sensed he had misspoken.

"Something wrong, Jack?"

"Uh, no sir... it's just that..."

"What is it?" Millet probed.

"It's just that I was not aware that the President had discussed with you the details of his briefing by Secretary Simpson and Mr. Maldonia," Jack responded.

Millet looked startled, then gathered himself and replied calmly. "Archie simply mentioned Maldonia's comment to me this morning before the start," he answered.

"Ah, I see. Well good afternoon, Mr. Millet. I hope you get some rest."

Millet turned and walked casually back to his cabin situated near the Poop deck. He didn't turn to look back at Thayer, fearful of showing the least bit of concern over the question.

Entering his room, Millet saw that his bed had been made with new linens and there were fresh cut roses on the nightstand. He saw to his pleasure that none of his personal belongings had been touched, with the exception of his smoking jacket that had been laid out with the artistry of a valet at the Georges V hotel, at the base of his bed.

He went directly to his closet and retrieved a single large Louis Vuitton leather trunk from the bedroom closet, unlocked it and removed a hardbound, olive green book, about the size of a postcard. Then he sat at the table in the center of his sitting room and began to write furiously, recollecting all that he had heard in the last twenty four hours, often opening the small book for reference.

In the President's suite, Archie Butt opened a glass wall on the port side and sat heavily in a chair, drained. Fatigue was becoming a problem, he thought silently, although resolute that he would not succumb to it so near success. Thayer knocked at the door.

"They remained together for perhaps thirty minutes, Mr. President," the Chief of Staff reported, "and did not display any particular distress on emerging from the grand ballroom. In fact, I would categorize the ambience as rather energized, yet relaxed. They seemed to be enjoying each others company. Perhaps a sort of bonding. My instincts tell me that you will be satisfied at their response tonight."

Butt thought for a moment, staring across the windswept Bay, the waters picking up a stronger chop in the late afternoon.

"I dare not be optimistic, Jack. This is an amazingly powerful group of people, each with their own battle scars. Some of them could look right into your eyes while picking your pocket. They haven't become who they are by being 'nice'," the President responded. "My fellow *Titanic* survivors are experts in the art of deception."

He waited for a response. "Ah, yes, forgive me... present company excluded, my friend," Butt added, recalling that Jack Thayer had been a seventeen year old teenager when he had met him onboard the vessel. 'Deceptive' was not a word one would use to describe the young Thayer. He was the epitome of candor and forthrightness.

Thayer laughed, although he was feeling himself beginning to succumb to the lack of sleep over the last thirty-six hours. "No forgiveness necessary sir, but I am flattered by what you think I am not."

Butt turned to the horizon again, watching as the sun began to set across the Bay. The sun's radiance splashed across his face, warming him, exaggerating the urge for a quick nap before dinner.

"I think I will lie down for a few minutes Jack, just to restore a bit of vitality in these old bones."

"Of course, Mr. President, I will see to it that you are not disturbed and I will personally call on you at seven. Dinner is at eight o'clock and I may need to brief you on some last minute details."

He turned to leave. "By the way, sir, before I take my leave, I was wondering if you had shared Mr. Maldonia's comment last night about the wealthy having 'loose lips' with Mr. Millet this morning? Perhaps at breakfast?" Thayer knew he had to be careful when it came to anything to do with Francis Millet. The artist and the Major had been friends since they were born, and were inseparably close.

Butt thought for a second. "Why I don't believe so, Jack. I don't recall that. But my mind was elsewhere this morning. Perhaps I could have.

"Why, is there something wrong?" he asked, staring into the young man's face, which never lied.

"It's nothing sir. Just for a moment, based on some things that Mr. Millet said, I thought perhaps you might have. Nothing to worry about. I'm sure it was just a coincidence. Good afternoon, sir, I will rouse you at seven," he said, and left the room, making sure to hear the lock on the door engage as he closed it.

Butt didn't give Thayer's question a second thought. He removed his jacket, loosened his tie and lay down on the bed. In minutes he was asleep. He had learned to take advantage of those few occasions when fatigue forced him to sleep, but inevitably, his 'night time friends' would join him, robbing him of the rest that he was becoming desperately in need of.

As he reached to turn out the bed lamp, he accidentally jostled a large bouquet of roses on the bed stand. The motion sent a loud explosion into the ears of the German fisherman, who now sat in the small skiff wearing a pair of oversized earphones.

Within the flower arrangement was buried a small object about the size and shape of a pencil. It was a "Buran" listening device -- a Russian developed eavesdropping "bug" that had the ability to monitor the sounds of conversations by means of the detection of the vibration of window glass. It had no power supply of it own, nor wires that might expose it. An ultra-high frequency signal beamed to it from the canvas satchel in the fisherman's boat allowed him to hear the entire exchange between Butt and Thayer. Similar devices had been planted all over the *Nourmahal,* unbeknownst to John Jacob Astor, while it been sitting in dry-dock less than a month ago for refitting before the President's visit. Ironically, the only room on the vessel not monitored by the listening devices was the grand ballroom. The black uniformed agents who had clamored all over the ship one night to plant the bugs had been interrupted in their work by a slow witted night watchman, who never saw them, but whose presence nevertheless caused them to flee without completing their mission. There had not been a second opportunity. As luck would have it, listening devices in the ballroom were unnecessary. The artist had a front seat to the actual proceedings.

He began to write. There was much to be done before dinner.

Twenty-Five

The President appeared in the grand ballroom promptly at eight o'clock, followed closely by his Chief of Staff appearing refreshed with a bit more color in his cheeks than earlier in the day.

Butt looked striking dressed in his well tailored evening suit. It was an odd agreement between such a large man and an elegant cut of cloth. Wearing a white silk bow tie and black tails, a white boutonniere and gold cufflinks, more than one of his guests had their own deja vue of Major Archibald Butt on the Docking Bridge of *Titanic*.

Butt had his own sudden reminiscence as he greeted his individual guests, each man wearing their own custom tailored tuxedos. For a moment he saw them once again, gentlemen to the bitter end, making their way up the *Titanic's* Promenade Deck to the stern as in the "March of the Penguins".

As chance would have it more than etiquette, Molly Brown was the first to greet him, looking nothing less than dazzling in a black Chanel crepe evening dress. The "V" neckline gown was trimmed with black sequins in an arrow design that ran down the front of the bodice to the waist, which then became a straight line of sequins to the hem. Famed designer Coco Chanel had surprised Molly with the dress, re-cut to fit her less than petite frame after the Denver socialite sent the designer a personal note of congratulations on her spring 1932 collection as displayed in *Harper's Bazaar*. Chanel's skill was evident and Molly's presentation was literally stunning. She wore her hair up and had chosen a double strand of exceedingly rare matched, natural Indonesian pearls for her still shapely neck. Butt was immediately taken by her unexpected loveliness, and wasted no time telling her so.

"Why Mrs. Brown, you look absolutely radiant. I have never been more struck by your natural beauty," he complimented her, bringing her hand to his lips. "You make me wish I had asked Mr. Astor to bring an orchestra. I would have filled your dance card."

"Get outta here, you romantic. Do they teach President's how to flirt or something?" she responded, secretly loving the attention, but helpless to hide her less than lady-like elocution. Butt ignored it. Her language was simply part of her endearing charms.

"Molly, I must tell you that I am looking forward with great anticipation to the day that I can be nothing more than a common Washington tourist. Because when that day comes, there will be nothing more in life that I will aspire to -- except to have you on my arm."

Her eyes went wide, and for the first in her life, Margaret Brown simply could not immediately find words to respond to the President's surprising flirtatiousness.

"I would like that very much, Mr. President," she finally stammered, her voice uncharacteristically soft and lilting. More importantly, she meant it.

"I have been alone for many years, Margaret. Perhaps it is time for me…"

"So when do you get off work?" she interrupted him softly, but with the playfulness that helped her hide her own loneliness . With that, the two roared with laughter, all but oblivious to the others.

"Give a man some room, will you darling?" William Guggenheim interrupted the couple. "I may not match your beauty, but I'll give you a run for your money in the oil game," he boasted.

"The hell you will," Molly retorted, reverting to form. "Why you city slickers couldn't smell oil unless you were taking a bath in it!"

"That's not a vision I care to entertain, Mrs. Brown, unless of course you would care to join me in my bath?" Guggenhiem teased her.

Molly roared again. "What in tarnation has gotten into you boys tonight? I'm getting more attention than Mae West. I'll have to wear a fancy dress more often for sure."

"Careful, William," the President said, sticking a finger in Guggenheim's starched white shirt. "Her dance card is full."

"Ah, I see Mr. President. Well, the more I think about it and remember that you have the FBI and Secret Service at your disposal, not to mention the IRS, perhaps I will rejoin my colleagues as wall flowers," the Philadelphian joked.

"A wise decision, old friend," Butt responded in jest. Guggenheim laughed, but for a moment wondered if the President might be serious.

One by one, the President's guests came forward to greet him. John Jacob Astor, like a nervous house mother, peered over his shoulder to ensure everything was in order. The grand ballroom had been reset and was no less sparkling than Cinderella's Castle. White coated servants were everywhere in the room, once again serving a breathtaking champagne from the French winery Moët Chandon. Astor delighted in telling his guests that the 1872 vintage Brut Imperial was a champagne that Moët Chandon had dedicated to the memory of Napolean I, who along with his substantial entourage, had been among the winery's most prestigious early 19th century customers. The sixty year old champagne, worth more than $1,000 a bottle, was poured generously for the entire evening much to the delight of Astor's guests.

Promptly at eight o'clock, Astor invited his guests to be seated at a long African hard wood table, covered with a delicate eighteenth century hand-woven Japanese silk tablecloth that was an antiquity even before his mother purchased it. Small placards at each setting announced the seat assignments. The solution to the problem of selecting those guests who would sit nearest the President was offered by Jack Thayer. "We simply sit them alphabetically. If anyone has a problem with that, they need only to lay the blame on their forefathers."

Consequently, the President, seated at the head of the table was flanked on his right by Thomas Andrews and on his left by Astor himself. Molly Brown was next in line. Astor, with his exquisite manners, graciously offered her his seat nearest the President. She blushed at the offer, but didn't refuse. At the end of the table sat the ubiquitous George Widener, grinning like the proverbial Cheshire Cat.

Waiters scurried around the table, filling their fluted crystal champagne glasses once more. Butt wasted no time. He stood.

"My dear lady," he began, bowing to Molly, "and gentlemen, good evening.

"I trust that you were able to enjoy the rest of your afternoon. I'm sure that it will come as no surprise that Mr. Astor has arranged perfect weather for us." There was a smattering of laughter and applause.

"Indeed, as I sat in my cabin looking across the harbor earlier this evening, watching as the sun set across the Bay, I wondered for a moment if I should consider a new line of work. Perhaps something involving a small boat and a fishing pole." They laughed aloud, now very comfortable together. "Life in Washington is so tedious..." he added, glancing down at Molly, who caught the look and smiled.

"But that is another story."

"Tonight," the President continued, his voice taking a more serious tone, "I want to celebrate a single event in our lives that changed each of us irrevocably. Of course I speak of the twentieth anniversary of the *Titanic* incident. It seems fate drove us together that night with quite ironic results. I am sure you will agree that we are all the better for an experience that taught each of us something about humility, compassion and the true meaning of courage. " The President paused, letting his words ring for a moment.

"My dear friends, as I stand before you tonight, it is with the clear cognizance that fate has brought us together again. Only now the fate of millions hangs in the balance.

"So it is with deep humility, and the recognition that I stand before the most accomplished group of people to ever gather in one room, and with honor that I may call them 'friends', that I offer this toast."

The President reached for his champagne glass.

"To *Titanic*: Our undying gratitude that you did not fail us. May your strength and beauty remain etched in our minds eye forever. As well, we offer our perpetual thanks for the enchanting spell you have cast over each of us, which has given our many and diverse life's journeys not only purpose and passion, but has forever richened our sense of compassion."

He raised his glass. "Salut!" he finished with a French flourish.

"Salut!" his guests echoed, each sipping from their crystal flutes. Immediately, at the other end of the table, George Dunton Widener seized the center of attention.

"Lady and gentlemen, please be seated," Widener began as confident as if he was addressing his own

Board. "I too would like to propose a toast, but first I would like to address the President."

The room became very quiet and Widener took on a solemn pose. Butt had a fleeting thought that he would not want to engage this man over a negotiating table. For all his good-natured clowning and lighthearted manner, Widener was a bull when it came to getting his way. Thank God, Butt thought, that he was dedicated to always doing the right thing.

When they were seated, Widener began.

"Mr. President, first I must inform you that my colleagues had the enormous good sense to elect me as spokesman for the Van Gogh Society," he said, raising his glass and silently toasting them. And may I add that after seeing Vincent's masterpiece, a "Starry Night", first hand, I must compliment you on your choice of distinctiveness for our covert efforts. How poignant, yet how elegant.

"Second, I must also inform you that neither Mr. Astor's guests nor I have any intention of letting the world's troubles ruin a simply smashing dinner party. So we must take care of our business, quickly and surgically."

Butt tensed, hardly able to maintain the amused look on his face. "I have no "Plan B", he thought to himself, panicking.

"Finally, I must inform you that you have insulted us, Mr. President. Allow me to explain, as you are obviously immune to this most grievous affront." Widener's face was as stoic as chiseled marble.

"We do recognize that you, as President, have both the moral compass and the military on your side, essentially allowing you to insult anyone you please at your slightest whim. However, as 'Major Butt', a fellow *Titanic* survivor, you must understand that we consider you our equal.

"Unfortunately Mr. President you have vastly underestimated your fellow survivors."

Butt could feel the punch line coming, and was afraid it was going to hurt. The other twelve chosen had the same poker face as Widener. He was sure he had failed.

"Mr. President, you have insulted us by entertaining personal doubt that we might decline your request, put to us in the most articulate and concise manner that I could ever have imagined.

"Simply stated, Mr. President, the thirteen of us will support you --as my dear friend, Mrs. Brown would say..." He paused and leaned towards the President for emphasis. "Come hell or high-water."

Butt was momentarily speechless as the room erupted in applause. Widener finished him off. "You know, I hate to keep quoting Molly, but she does have an amazingly succinct way of putting things into perspective. As we were talking this afternoon, she finally said: 'For Christ's sake, he saved our asses once and you can be damn sure he'll do it again. I'm hitching up to his wagon, pronto."

The room was filled with laughter, and Butt dropped his head into his hands in amazement. Molly Brown reached over and shook the President's sleeve.

"So allow me to propose a toast, Mr. President," Widener continued.

"To the President of the United States, a man who has invited us to be counted among his friends, but as well to Archie Butt, the man who cast his own regard aside twenty years ago to this day to lead us to safety. May God guide you and give you the strength to lead our country and the world through this new great crisis. But as the gale winds of war threaten your odyssey in search of lasting peace, always know that we stand behind you, immoveable and unswerving Apostles dedicated to your ultimate success.

"Salut, Mr. President," the street car man from Philadelphia concluded. His colleagues drank to the toast, followed by John Jacob Astor launching a hearty round of applause.

Twenty-Six

Rear Admiral Konrad Patzig bounded up the stairs
to the clay-tiled terrace entrance of "The Berghof",
Adolph Hitler's headquarters high in the Bavarian Alps
near Berchtesgaden, Germany. It was early May and an
exceptionally warm spring had prompted the elaborate
gardens of the chalet to erupt into the full bloom of an
artist's palette. Hitler cherished these impeccably
manicured grounds and often walked in the garden with
guests for private conversations. Patzig ignored the
beauty surrounding him. Today he had much more
urgent matters on his mind.

The naval officer was met in the chalet's entrance hall
by a fully uniformed SS Colonel. Patzig had been to The
Berghof on several other occasions and always found the
hallway a rather strange room. It was filled with foreign
cactus plants in large Italian tin-glazed pots known as
Maiolica, and there were dozens of yellow canaries in
separate cages. The birds sustained a cacophony of sorts,
being as incongruous to the ambience as the plants.
Someday, he thought, he would ask the new Chancellor
the meaning of the odd flora and fauna, but then quickly
wiped the idea from his mind.

The man obviously destined to be named Führer of
Germany was proving to be an oddity himself, mercurial
by nature, capable of the most charming etiquette but
also to animal-like outbursts of vicious behavior over the
most trivial of things. Patzig feared the news he brought
to the Chancellor today might provoke such behavior.

The aging German President, von Hindenburg, must have been under extreme pressure to have named Hitler Chancellor, he mused, because the man who was the leader of the newly empowered Nazi Party literally reeked of evil.

The SS officer quickly showed him to Hitler's study. This too was a curious room, he thought as he entered the library and walked past an elaborate telephone switchboard off to one side in what he guessed had previously been a servant's pantry.

On the other side of the room, completely flanked by floor to ceiling, heavy, dark walnut bookcases containing hundreds of volumes on history, architecture, painting and music, was a large motion picture projection screen. In the center, behind Hitler's oversized, ornately carved Teutonic desk was a tall Italian red marble fireplace mantel, beneath a large portrait of the Chancellor himself wearing his signature khaki dress military uniform with a bold, black and blood-red armband adorned with a spreading eagle atop a swastika, the formal symbol of the Nazi Party.

"The Chancellor will be with you in a moment, Admiral," the officer informed him. As he turned to leave, he flipped an electrical switch near the projection screen causing a small electric motor to turn and slowly raise it into a cavity in the ceiling. As it rose it revealed a large picture window that looked out over the highest peaks of the snow covered Alps. The view was spectacular.

A servant, one of twenty employed to see to the Chancellor's every need and whim, entered the room with a magnificent antique silver coffee set and placed it carefully on a large round, solid oak table that could seat as many as ten people. The older gentleman walked with a slight stoop, and as he exited, he stopped and bent over to pick up a piece of lint that had somehow been tracked into the room, interrupting the purity of the handmade, deep pile maroon Tabriz rug that virtually filled the vast study.

"Power," he whispered out loud. That is what drives this madman, Patzig thought to himself. He had never been in a more intimidating environment, and the room's overstated opulence was a shock to the eyes of a man who had commanded large military ships nearly his entire career in the German Navy and was accustomed to substantially smaller and more austere work environments.

As the head of the *Abwhehr*, the German intelligence organization of the Deutsches Reich, Patzig was one of only a handful of the advisors who had complete access to Hitler. The information he carried in his locked, leather satchel had not been shared with anyone else, nor would it be unless the Chancellor dictated it. The Admiral looked upon his ability to see Hitler at a moments notice as a mixed blessing.

On one hand, it offered him the ever present opportunity to impress the German leader with his intellect, cunning and patriotism, and thus heightened his chance for advancement in Hitler's inner circle. On the other, it made him a target. It was well know that Hitler despised bad news of any kind, and consequently was surrounded by corrupt, corpulent sycophants who would enthusiastically tell the Chancellor whatever it was he wanted to hear despite the truth, and whose orders they acted upon without reflection or debate.

Patzig was not such a man, but worried that his frank nature would ultimately be the cause of his downfall in the rat's nest that was the Third Reich. Secretly, he longed for a new command and a return to the sea where he might be in charge of his own fate once again.

The name "Abwehr", meaning "defense" in the German language, was a sordid misnomer. Upon his

promotion to intelligence chief, Patzig had expected
to spend his time on matters of national security and
administering to the legion of agents the intelligence
agency had planted in dozens of nations, often at the
highest level of government. But it quickly became clear
that Hitler was more interested in a different kind of
intelligence, and more often than not Patzig found
himself responsible for clandestine operations aimed at
uncovering weaknesses in those Hitler did not implicitly
trust. The intelligence chief's files were thick with
information obtained on Hitler's closest allies in their
most base states, often accompanied with photographs of
them satisfying their most primal urges, whether it be the
abuse of drugs, sexual depravity, or worse. He found
himself sickened each time he reviewed or added new
information to the files, which were carefully labeled
"Top Secret" and locked in an iron safe in his office to
which only he had the combinations to its double locks.
He had never looked at the photographs in his files more
than once.

Today, Patzig was visiting the Chancellor to share
with him information that he truly believed posed a
danger to the national security interests of his fatherland.
It was an attempt at blackmail, he would tell Hitler.
Further, he did not intend to just hand this bomb to the
Chancellor. Indeed, he would lay out a recommended
course of response -- and retaliation.

Ten minutes later Hitler entered the room
surprisingly without his usual entourage. The
Chancellor had taken Patzig's word that this was a
matter for his ears only.

"Admiral Patzig, welcome to The Berghof," Hitler
called out as he strode across the thick carpet to meet
him. "I apologize for keeping you. I hope you have been
comfortable while waiting?"

"Of course, Herr Chancellor, I have been amusing myself by taking in the beauty of this remarkable library and the breathtaking view of the Alps," Patzig said cordially, but conscious that the German leader did not take kindly to casual conversation.

"Please be seated. Would you like coffee? I have an extraordinary Brazilian blend on hand for my special guests."

"Thank you, Herr Chancellor."

Hitler poured two steaming cups from the polished silver pot and presented one to Patzig. Each took a sip of the thick, aromatic liquid that had been carried back to Germany for Hitler by a U-Boat commander who had visited the Port of Santos, in Sao Paulo Brazil on a goodwill mission. The coffee was not a gift from the German commander. The officer had been ordered to procure and deliver it by his superior. "It is delectable, Herr Chancellor. I am pleased to know that you consider me a 'special' guest," Patzig said.

Hitler laughed softly. "Admiral Patzig, if I cannot trust you, who can I trust? You know that you are always welcome to visit with me. Now what is it you have to tell me?"

Patzig took another sip of the hot coffee, swallowed hard, and began his presentation.

"Yes, Herr Chancellor. Two of my operatives in the United States recently discovered an extraordinary stream of communications between the White House and some of the wealthiest and most influential individuals in America, as well as two Europeans. The information was obtained via the use of listening devices we have in the Oval Office and in other rooms of the President's mansion."

"You have been able to penetrate the White House, Admiral?" Hitler asked, astonished.

"Yes, Herr Chancellor, even the White House. We took advantage of some remodeling that occurred recently. Our American network is beginning to pay off handsomely, as I hope to convince you today."

"I am already impressed," Hitler said dryly, without the hint of amusement.

Patzig allowed himself to feel more at ease. "The intelligence we gathered indicates that President Butt was eager to invite this select group to a secret meeting in Chesapeake Bay, but no details were forthcoming in his request. What especially caught our eye was a name -- most certainly a code name -- that was assigned to the twelve men and one woman who were asked to attend. The code name was "Van Gogh."

"Van Gogh?" Hitler probed. "The artist, of course. I have underestimated President Butt once again. I hardly would have expected that buffoon to have any appreciation for the works of the Dutch master."

"Unfortunately, we have not yet reached a conclusion as to the meaning of this designation, Herr Chancellor, but we are working on it," Patzig added.

"Go on," Hitler said. Patzig picked up on the Chancellor's impatience, usually a first sign of trouble when presenting a briefing summary to the former wallpaper hanger and army corporal. He wondered what Hitler's own appreciation of art was based on. Certainly not his upbringing.

"We were able to further decipher the communications which ultimately enabled us to pinpoint the exact time and place of the meeting. It was held on John Jacob Astor's yacht at noon on 15 April."

"Astor? The playboy prince who once bought his way into the military?" Hitler asked. "I hardly think he would be of any interest to Germany, other than that he represents all that the Nazi Party opposes. Who else attended this meeting?" Hitler asked, now intrigued by what Patzig was informing him.

The intelligence chief quickly summarized the list of invited guests and their extraordinary credentials. Hitler raised his brow and turned to stare out at the Alps.

"A fascinatingly eclectic troupe, known as 'Van Gogh'," Hitler said, searching for a link. "I haven't the faintest idea why the President would want to bring them together unless he was appealing to their ability to underwrite his re-election campaign. But that would not explain the secrecy, Herr Patzig."

"I agree Herr Chancellor. As well there is considerable speculation in Washington that the President will not seek re-election. It seems he is weary of the fight against the economic depression that still plagues his nation."

Hitler's eyes went wide and his mouth quivered slightly. He was fighting to maintain his composure, but Patzig could see the sudden rage on his face. "Depression? What would Archie Butt know about depression? He almost single-handily has kept Germany in the throes of bankruptcy since the Versailles Treaty. I hope the economic collapse of the United States has left him sleepless for the last three years," he fumed.

Patzig did not dare to respond for fear of saying the wrong thing. "Yes, Herr Chancellor."

His face beet red, Hitler leaned forward across the table. "I am tiring, Patzig. I assume you have uncovered the reason for this 'Van Gogh' gathering – or you would not be here."

Patzig heard a slight tremor in his own voice as he continued. "We have, Herr Chancellor.

"The American is launching a plan to blackmail the German government, your Excellency."

"Blödes arschloc!" Hitler exploded, drawing a connection between Butt's brain and his anus.

Patzig cringed. He had to finish quickly and get to his plan.

"Herr Chancellor, allow me to summarize what we were able to learn of the meeting of 'Van Gogh" – and then, with your permission, I would like to propose a plan of response."

"Go on," Hitler growled, barely in control.

The intelligence chief summarized the report of the "fisherman" and the inside mole. Although he could not say exactly what had been discussed in the actual meeting of Van Gogh, it was not difficult to extrapolate the President's message based on the overheard briefing of Secretary Simpson and Maldonia, as well as the eye witness account that had been drawn from memory.

Hitler had regained his composure. "The German people are tired of war," Hitler responded, "but at the same time they are angry and they will fight for their homeland if it means recapturing the territories we lost in Versailles. They will do anything, I am sure, anything to break out of the economic malaise which is suffocating us.

"But I compliment the President. He is correct in his assumption that by placating the German people and providing them with economic relief, they will lose their resiliency to fight.

"And he has also correctly concluded that the United States is the only real Allied Power. He feels he can buy the cooperation of England, France and Italy and he is willing to stare down Stalin. He is not even concerned with the weakling Spaniards. You will see, Patzig. It is only a matter of time before I crush MacDonald, Doume, and Mussolini… and even that dirty old pervert, Stalin," he said emphatically.

"Europe *will* be ours, Patzig," he raged, having lost the focus of their meeting. "Remember this conversation well."

Hitler turned his back on Patzig and turned to the Alps. He was silent for more than five minutes. Patzig had to restrain himself from interrupting. Finally the Chancellor spoke.

"We must not let this happen, Herr Patzig," he said softly and slowly without looking at his intelligence advisor. "It is important that the German people remain angry." He turned to Patzig and pounded a fist on the oak table. The response shocked the Admiral.

"You see," Hitler continued, his voice building as he spoke, "fury is a key assumption of my strategy for the future of the Reich. I will not allow the German people to be treated like dogs begging for a bone! Do you understand me, Herr Patzig." It was a statement, not a question.

His response was quick. "Absolutely, Herr Chancellor."

"So then... what is it you propose to do about this problem?"

The moment of truth had arrived for Patzig, and he seized the opportunity.

An hour later, an elated Hitler personally showed Rear Admiral Patzig to the door. "I have great faith in you, Herr Patzig," he said to the somewhat stunned intelligence chief. "I want to know more soon."

"Yes, Herr Chancellor."

"Good day then. Perhaps the next time you visit, we should conduct our business in the garden," Hitler said.

"I would like that Herr Chancellor. And perhaps it would be a more secure environment in which to chat," Patzig responded, bringing a slight grin to his mouth.

Hitler laughed. "Ah, yes... we must be very careful."

Patzig turned to walk across the great terrace and down the steps to his waiting staff car and military escort that would return him to Abwehr's Headquarters in

Berlin, adjacent to the offices of the German High
Command of the Armed Forces

"Herr Chancellor?" he called back.

"Yes, Herr Patzig," Hitler responded, with a tinge of
impatience in his voice, "What is it?"

Bouyed by his successful briefing, Patzig said: "Ich
bin stolz, ein Deutscher zu sein."

Hitler, unimpressed, turned his back without
comment and returned to his library, muttering as he
walked.

"Yes, Herr Patzig, I am proud to be a German as
well," he said out of earshot.

"But if you fail me, I will wrap you in your flag and
bury you alive."

Twenty-Seven

Unbeknownst to the President, John Jacob Astor had launched a plan of his own.

After the last guest departed his beloved *Nourmahal* on the morning of April 16, Astor had returned to the ship's grand ballroom just as two of his crew was preparing to take down "Starry Night" for shipment back to Washington.

"Leave it for the moment," he instructed the men.

Alone with the masterpiece, Astor stood before the painting and studied it for nearly an hour, completely lost in his thoughts. He recalled how deeply terrified he had been on the fateful night *Titanic* had struck an iceberg in the frigid North Atlantic. One of his most vivid recollections was standing on the Poop deck, watching as the icy water slowly crept up the Promenade, threatening to engulf him and the mass of humanity gathered on the stern. Another was chatting up the group of young men who had surrounded him, seeking the security of an older man in what they thought was to be their final moments.

Finally, he recalled watching *Titanic* from the bow of the *Carpathia* as the vessel departed for New York. Aside from the tugs surrounding the great ocean liner, she looked as grand and fit as the day they had first sailed her from Southampton. With her four orange funnels profiled against the bright blue sky off Cape Sable Island, he remembered just how beautiful she was. "I will never see *Titanic* again," he had thought to himself romantically in a fleeting moment of sadness at the liner's fate.

But on this morning, aboard his own vessel anchored in Chesapeake Bay, Astor had another thought.

"Perhaps I was wrong," he said to himself, invigorated.

He walked briskly to the radio shack on the Bridge and placed a call to New York. "Please get Mr. Colvin on the line," he asked the radio operator.

Several minutes later, Phillip Colvin, his closest business advisor, answered the call. "Phillip, find *RMS Titanic*," he instructed his bewildered aid.

"I will explain later."

Twenty-Eight

Through the balance of spring and into early summer, Jack Thayer was a busy man.

Working eighteen hour days, the Chief of Staff carried the enormous responsibility of making the pledge of support won from the extraordinary people gathered on the *Nourmahal* a reality. The noble task consumed him, day and night.

He was more than up to the job. At the young age of thirty-seven, Thayer, who had sailed from Southampton aboard *Titanic* with his father, John Boreland Thayer II and his mother Marion some twenty years ago, held perhaps the most important position in the Butt administration. In his rare moments of reflection, or when he occasionally suffered from a crisis of confidence, he would sometimes wonder how he had ever become a captain and captive of Capital Hill.

After surviving the *Titanic* wreck, Thayer had experienced a quite remarkable epiphany of his own from the experience. From a lighthearted, carefree young man, almost overnight he became driven to succeed.

"Something tells me my stay in this world will be brief, Father, so I intend to make the most of it," he told the senior Thayer upon his enrollment at the University of Pennsylvania that same fall. *Titanic* had influenced him in many ways. He often told friends at school that the high-pitched hum of Cicada's on a summer night in his hometown of Bryn Mawr reminded him of the crying

and moaning of the terrified mass of people on
Titanic's stern.

Thayer graduated summa cum laude from the
University in May 1916, and without so much assistance
from his father as a phone call, he landed a job on Wall
Street as an investment banker, a rather heady
opportunity for such a young man. Jack excelled in the
high powered financial world, and before the age of
twenty-five found himself a vice president of The Bank of
New York, occupying an enormous corner office on the
fourth floor of its prestigious address at the corner of
Wall and Williams Streets in the heart of the financial
district. When the Bank merged with the New York Life
Insurance and Trust Company in 1922, making it the
largest investment bank in the country, he was elected
executive vice president and a director of the company.
It seemed that whatever Jack Thayer touched turned to
gold, and his reputation as a modern day Midas grew
rapidly.

By 1927 however, just fifteen years removed from
Titanic and already a very wealthy man, he lost interest
in Wall Street and privately worried about its' future.

"The foundation of the stock market is now debt," he
wrote to his father. "I fear that this whole system of
investment is nothing more than a house of cards, which
eventually will experience a minor shake that will
ultimately become a calamity." His words of concern
were fortuitously correct.

He left the bank in 1927 and was named Financial
Vice President and Treasurer of his alma mater, the
University of Pennsylvania. "It is too late to correct the
blindness at the top of the investment world," he told his
father over a brandy and cigar one winters' evening in
front of a roaring fire at the University's storied faculty
club. "But perhaps we can beat some sense into these

young minds before they repeat the cycle of blind avarice."

Whatever academic pummeling Thayer had in mind had to wait, as following Archie Butt's election in November 1928 he was summoned to Washington by the President elect. Butt had been taken with the young man when he met him on the *Titanic*, and from a distance followed his career with great satisfaction. The job he had in mind for him now was White House Chief of Staff, a critical role served as the President's primary liaison with congress and his cabinet members.

At times the Chief of Staff was not only the President's right hand, but his left one as well, far more involved in the day to day program and key priorities of the Commander in Chief than even the Vice President. Tall and handsome like his father and exceedingly articulate, Thayer had proven particularly adept at managing Butt's legislative agenda. His banking experience was also a major plus to the President. Archie Butt often referred to "remarkable presence" when describing Jack's key professional attributes.

Butt was also taken with Thayer's intellect and deeply analytical style of problem solving, and most importantly that he was not afraid to speak his mind when invited, which the President ensured was often. There were few going's on in the Oval Office in which his Chief of Staff was not an equal participant or a witness. Archie simply trusted him that much.

Like the President, his few personal hours were spent alone and somewhat empty. He had just never had the time to fill the void in his life, or so he told himself. The truth was that Washington's most eligible bachelor was extremely shy. He could argue and debate with senior advisors and diplomats with aplomb and considerable success, but leave him alone with a debutante and he was completely tongue-tied. Instead, he threw himself at his work with the energy of three men.

The President had been impressed with how expertly he handled the Van Gogh invitation with the elder Thayer. Although he and his father were very close, John Thayer knew no more about the agenda of their meeting than the others, but trusted his son enough to sign up with enthusiasm.

Finally, Archie Butt cherished Jack Thayer's loyalty. He was not dedicated to the point of blind allegiance, an illness that plagued many aides in the high-powered world of Washington politics. As long as it was his watch, Jack Thayer simply would not allow the President to misstep because he was not adequately informed, about to be bushwhacked or used politically. Jack Thayer worked tirelessly to keep his President completely and fully aware of the facts, the issues and their possible solutions and the path he must follow through the most difficult political minefield. Above all, he was resolute in his commitment to tell the President what he needed to hear, even if he didn't want to hear it.

So it was by June of 1932 that Jack Thayer was effectively running the Van Gogh operation. He saw to it that each member, as promised, was scheduled for discussions with the President and other key advisors, as appropriate to the subject, and he personally prepared the President's briefing and script for each session.

Thayer spent hundreds of hours that spring and early summer analyzing intelligence and prodding state and commerce department statesmen to think in boldly creative terms about what the Europeans needed, wanted or fantasized about. By the time the face-to-face meeting between Archie Butt and the Van Gogh members took place, the deal was essentially done. The President more often than not was left with only the task of wringing out the cherished words, "I do" from his new strategic partner.

By the end of July, the plan that President Butt would propose to the leaders of the United Kingdom, France, Italy, Spain, Germany and the Soviets was solidly in place and each member of Van Gogh had signed on to their pledges of support and action with satisfaction and enthusiasm. Each left the meeting with the Commander in Chief truly believing that they had a noble mission and could make a difference.

William Stead was ready to bombard the world's media with editorials aimed at the common man. Butt was convinced that Stead, armed with a pen instead of a sword, was the man to convince the Brits, French, Spaniards, Italians, Germans and Russians that industry and commerce, construction and development were far more advantageous than battle and bloodshed.

Margaret Brown was prepared to launch an offensive on two fronts. First was the operation of the Red Cross, an organization predominantly visible in war times. She was convinced that the vast army of Red Cross employees and volunteers at her command could offer as great a support network during peacetime, catering to the homeless and destitute, the hungry, sick and infirm and those who were desperate for jobs. As well, Molly had the wherewithal to bring to the table the chief executives of each of the world's major oil suppliers, and together with their vast resources she was convinced they could find a way to refuel Europe -- in peace.

Benjamin Guggenheim, with his decades of experience in the field of mining, was ready to dedicate his huge resources in drilling into the earth's core to uncover desperately needed new natural resources -- and wealth -- for Europe.

Sir Cosmo Duff-Gordon and John Thayer were primed to do what they did best - to reach the highest members of the target governments, including Hitler and Stalin -- and get them to the same table.

Thomas Andrews and Edward Crosby proffered the ability to rebuild the Europeans' transatlantic commercial shipping industry, and to transform the vast naval investments in ships of war to ships of industry, thus supplying the means to reopen ports all across the continental edge to free trade.

George Wick stood ready to supply steel for ships, the construction of new buildings, bridges and other infrastructure, efforts that were now starved for resources.

George Widener and Charles Hays, acting upon their own impetus, had devised a plan that would open the land borders of the interlocked European nations to new rail lines and auto traffic. Additionally, he was ready to help construct new mass transit systems that could expand the land footprint of the major metropolises of Europe and open the way for new urban development. And with John Jacob Astor's vast knowledge of real estate, development and financing, he would unlock the key to major expansion and economic growth.

William Carter was literally drooling over the opportunity to design new, kaizen-style automobile production plants that would build similar designs under national brands in each of the European countries. He was so excited that he had already charged his design team with the mission of designing a car for all Europe.

Together, the twelve men and one woman represented enormous experience and abilities, but more importantly, new found passion for their commitment to make a contribution to the goal of world peace. Like the morning of April 15, 1912 when each of them had experienced a profound change in their outlook on life, they had been reborn, again.

Archie Butt thought Margaret Brown summed it up perfectly.

"Ain't nothin' better than gettin' outta bed in the morning knowing you got a new bronco to bust," she said.

"Cuz when it's all over, you and the horse can look each other in the eye knowin' you did a god dammed good days work and you've got a new friend."

By the Fourth of July, they were ready to change the world.

Twenty-Nine

As John Jacob Astor stepped off the *Nourmahal* in New York Harbor, Phillip Colvin was waiting for him with the information requested.

They drove through Central Park in Astor's long, black chauffer-driven Cadillac. The Park was in full bloom and overflowing with tourists, and romantic horse drawn rental carriages were doing a brisk business. Traffic moved slowly, but for once in his life, John Jacob Astor was in no rush.

He was still basking in the success of the meeting on the *Nourmahal*, which he personally had spent many hours worrying. It was rare for him to be so involved with the details of any project, but this indeed had been a rare opportunity. He must send the President a box of the finest Cuban cigars and a note of congratulations, he thought to himself.

"Tell me what you've learned," Astor asked Colvin, anxious to hear of the whereabouts of the famous *Titanic*.

"Well, John it's a rather long story, so allow me to summarize it," Colvin said. Astor's tall, lanky assistant was a Princeton graduate and had been with the Astor organization for more than twelve years. The last three had been exhilarating for the thirty-four year old, who, as an accountant by training, had hardly anticipated such a career. As the most senior advisor to the Chairman, Colvin had Astor's ear and unreserved trust -- two characteristics that made him not only unique, but powerful as well. Colvin read his boss like a book and made every attempt to stay one step ahead of him. He had not failed him yet. And when Astor entrusted him with an assignment, Colvin produced with the anticipated results in half the time given. He was handsome, glib and one of New York's most eligible bachelors, but life as John Jacob Astor's right hand man left little time for distractions, including the ladies.

He began. "I'm sure you know that *Titanic* was refit at the outset of the war and served with distinction as a troop carrier in the North Atlantic."

"Yes, I know," Astor said, "but frankly that's when I lost touch with her."

"We know that *Titanic* survived at least five specific attempts by the Germans to sink her," Colvin continued. "Actually the Germans were more interested in sinking the ship that God couldn't for the sheer publicity and propaganda. In somewhat of a miracle she did survive, and at the end of the war was returned to the White Star Line. The British government, in gratitude, underwrote her complete refitting again as a luxury passenger steamer. That was in 1918. She sailed again for the first time in late 1919 to a bit of fanfare, but only the British press was much interested and that was largely in the Liverpool and Southampton markets."

"Interesting. Come to think about it, I never saw any news stories about her in the New York press," Astor replied, eager for the tale to continue.

"That's because she no longer sailed the Southampton to New York route," Colvin reported. "White Star saw a great opportunity to exploit the South American market and set her on a Southampton -- Cherbourg -- Rio de Janeiro route. *Titanic* spent the last ten years of her adult life plying the warm waters off Brazil. The company actually made a profit off the old girl."

"I see," Astor said, a flash of disappointment in his eyes. "The last ten years you say? She's no longer active?"

"White Star retired the vessel in 1930, right after the depression hit. She simply couldn't fill her steerage cabins anymore, which is where the profits actually came from, and most of her First and Second Class cabins were either sold at steep discounts or were empty when the ship sailed. The bottom fell out of the whole luxury liner industry about six months after the Wall Street crash. Interestingly enough, by that time *Titanic* was a tired out old tramp anyway, in need of a complete overhaul. White Star could never have afforded to refit her anyway."

Astor looked crestfallen. "So she's been scrapped?" he asked.

Colvin smiled, already a couple of steps ahead of his boss, which was exactly what Astor paid him handsomely to do. He also knew that Astor had very little patience. He answered directly.

"No, she has not been scrapped. The last run *Titanic* made was back to Liverpool, where she was originally built, and right now she's sitting out in the harbor."

"Waiting to be scrapped then?" Astor responded. Colvin could tell his boss was very disappointed. "I would imagine she's no longer seaworthy."

"No sir, not to be scrapped, and *Titanic* is very definitely still seaworthy according to the White Star engineers I spoke with." Astor stared at him in puzzlement.

"Then what...?" the Chairman began.

"She is to be sold."

The senior aide to the richest man in the world always reveled in pleasing his supervisor. His year-end bonus depended on it. "White Star thought they'd put the vessel on the market in case any eccentric millionaires

might be interested in buying her. *Titanic* is famous
you know, John."

Astor laughed and felt a wave of relief. "Tell me
about. She has a permanent place in my dreams in the
wee hours. Have there been any bids?" he asked,
anxiously.

"Just one," Colvin replied.

"Who?"

"It's already been sold, John."

"God dammit," Astor sulked. "Let's get a hold of the
son of a bitch who bought it and buy it from him, then.
Double his price if you must, damn it."

"You don't have to."

Astor looked at him, puzzled. "What?"

"You already own it. Yours was the only bid."
Colvin had set the hook and reeled the millionaire in. He
stifled a laugh.

Astor's mouth gaped. "You son of a bitch," he
roared, delighted.

"You're fired," he added.

"Fine then, I'll return it. Shouldn't be too hard to
unload." The aid was familiar with the game and enjoyed
it.

"Never mind. I'll need you to manage this."

"Manage what? Are you going to turn it into a hotel
or museum or something?" Colvin asked.

"A hotel? Are you daft, man? We, my good friend,
are going to return *Titanic* to all her splendid glory. By
the time we're done she'll look, feel, smell, taste… hell,
even sail better than the day she left Southampton on her
maiden voyage. April 10, 1912."

Now it was time for Colvin's jaw to drop. "John, as
your financial advisor, I have to tell you I think you've
lost the plot," Colvin replied in surprise. "In my research
I discovered that it cost White Star ten million bucks in
1912 dollars to build her. It just cost you slightly more

than three million just to keep her off the scrap heap and I'll bet it will take at least another thirty to thirty-five million more to, as you say, 'return her to her glory'."

Astor did not reply. For that matter, Colvin wasn't sure his boss had even heard what he said. It was obvious that Titanic fit into some grander scheme than he understood.

"John, did you hear me?" Colvin asked in frustration.

"I don't care what it costs," Astor abruptly responded.

"Sir," his assistant responded without hesitation. "With all due respect, have *you* gone daft?"

"Hardly, Phillip," Astor replied with a delighted grin. "And she'll only sail once more. From Southampton to New York on a one way voyage," Astor added. "*Titanic* will have a chance at a maiden voyage to New York after all".

Colvin was aghast. "John, seriously, are you crazy? What in hell were you smoking on that cruise in Chesapeake Bay? The return on investment would be..." Colvin said, astonished.

Astor stopped him cold.

"Priceless, old friend. Literally priceless. I can only tell you that millions - no, make that tens of millions -- will be saved if we are successful."

"Millions of dollars? Pounds? But how..." Colvin was totally confused.

"Not dollars, Phillip," Astor said.

"People."

Colvin stared at Astor for long moments, waiting for the rest of the story. It was not forthcoming.

"I can't tell you more, yet, Phillip," Astor finally said, mysteriously but firmly. "When I can, I will. For now, you have your orders. I want you to leave for Liverpool on the next crossing. Get there as soon as possible and devote your complete attention to the project until it is completed."

Colvin knew when his boss was serious. He had never seen him more so.

The two sat in silence until the limousine pulled up in front of the Waldorf-Astoria hotel where Astor occupied a suite that took up the entire top floor. A uniformed boy wearing a red cap opened the door and greeted him by name.

Astor stepped out of the car without another word to Colvin, who was already deep in thought about the project, wondering how long it would take him. As if reading his loyal assistant's mind, Aston turned back and answered the question for him.

"Phillip. One other thing. I forgot to mention by what date I need the vessel completed."

Still trying to gather himself after the strange conversation, Colvin said that he would immediately gather the resources needed and develop a timetable.

"I'm assuming that it will take at least a year to eighteen months to complete, depending of course on the availability of materials," Colvin said.

Astor stared at him, incredulous.

"A year? Eighteen months?" he barked through the half opened window.

"Why, you were expecting it soon…"

Astor cut him right off.

"You have until Labor Day. I will expect an update every afternoon until then," Astor ordered.

"What?" Colvin began to protest, not sure he had heard correctly.

"We sail on Labor Day, 1932," Astor said, completely serious. "You have a little more than four months. Good day Phillip."

The millionaire tipped his hat and strode briskly into the hotel lobby, feeling more alive than ever before in his life. Colvin stared as he watched him walk away, noticing the energy in his step.

"What the bloody hell…" Colvin murmured to himself, without having the foggiest notion of how he would pull this rabbit out of a hat. Almost immediately, he laughed to himself, recognizing the complete waste of time it was to fret over the answer. When John Astor made up his mind to something, the decision was resolute.

"Ok, boss, you got it," he said out loud to no one in particular, then hollered to his chauffer. "Freddy, get me back to the office as quickly as you can please. I've literally no time to waste."

Astor didn't give Colvin's dilemma another thought. His thoughts had already turned to his next step.

He couldn't wait to share the news of *Titanic* with President Archibald Butt.

Thirty

Francis Millet sat with his friend in front of the Oval Office fireplace. The two were admiring "Starry Night", which had been returned from its temporary loan to the *Nourmahal*.

"It is an extraordinary work," Millet observed. "But did you know that Vincent Van Gogh was quite mad when he painted it? He was actually being held in a hospital for the insane when he was inspired."

"The turmoil in his life is quite evident," Archie Butt responded. "But that is one of the reasons I have been attracted to the work since the *Titanic* incident. It is hard to forget the chaos we experienced that night, my old friend."

"Yes… I think of it often, Archie, as I'm sure you do."

Butt finally took his eyes off the painting and turned to his comrade.

"So how do your efforts go, Francis?" Butt asked, sipping a brandy. Millet had been exceedingly busy trying to track down works of art stolen by the German military in their occupation of Belgium in 1914.

Millet let out a sigh, always enjoying the drama of discussing issues of importance with the President.

"It is sad work, Archie," he responded. "I find it difficult to separate the horror of the occupation and all that led to the theft of countless masterpieces from the inanimate objects themselves, no matter how precious or beautiful."

"Ah, yes, Francis, the Germans were heavy handed," Butt said with empathy.

Millet nearly choked on his drink. "I hardly think 'heavy handed' describes the behavior of the Huns. They were brutal. Cold blooded. They bayoneted women and children in the streets of Louvain, Malines, Dinant, and Termonde. Hunted men like animals and then complimented each other on their marksmanship. Rape, pillage and plunder were their objective, Archie. They were savages – not heavy handed."

Butt did not respond, staring deeply into the cold fireplace. They sat in silence for several minutes.

"If I knew the answer to man's inhumanity and cruelty to each other..." the President paused. "But I don't and never will. Unfortunately, I believe that the only antidote to some men's bloodlust and cruelty is to satisfy their greed. We must rob the bastards of the one thing that empowers them, Francis, and that is malaise. To do that we must incite the anger of their people. Men like Hitler don't stand a chance if the common man has the security of knowing that he can put food on the table for his family, a roof over their heads and a book in the hands of his children. If he has the requirements of a peaceful life, he will live peacefully -- and he won't follow blindly, as you put it so succinctly, after 'savages' like Hitler. The dictator will lose his power, control and lust for war to the disinterest of a satisfied people."

Millet studied his friend as he spoke. He and Butt had been friends almost their entire adult lives. The man who was now President had stood by him through a failed marriage, several scandals involving other men, and had even bailed him out on several occasions when his outlandish bohemian lifestyle had put him in serious financial jeopardy. He admired nearly everything about him -- with the exception of his politics.

"You may be right. Archie," Millet said after awhile. "The only way I can rationalize such behavior is that the anger of the German soldier in the Great War allowed him to do unconscionable, unspeakable things."

The fact was, Francis Davis Millet spoke from experience.

The accomplished painter and frequent world traveler had a darker side of which Archie Butt was oblivious. By day, he was a respected member of the world art community, serving as a trustee of the Metropolitan Museum of Art and as a member of the advisory committee of the National Gallery of Art. He was heavily involved in the American Academy in Rome and was a founder of the Boston Museum of Fine Arts. He counted among his eclectic circle of friends the writer Mark Twain, who was best man at his wedding, and the American painter John Singer Sargent.

He thrived in this world, which not only allowed him to live a decidedly unconventional lifestyle, but encouraged it. He mimicked the French, spoke fluent Italian, could adapt a British persona at the mere mention of London, and even felt comfortable in the more austere German culture. He tended to dress unconventionally as well, preferring pastel suits and elegant Italian leather shoes to the more mundane business dress of his associates. By day, he was a character of distinction.

By night, in his closely guarded secret life, Francis Millet tended towards the lifestyle congregated by sexual deviates and other tortured minds, and he had a particularly bizarre taste for young boys and the art of sexual dominance and sadism. Had the Washington set that had grown to admire and even love him had any inkling of his dark side, they would have quickly labeled him a pervert and shunned him. That fear of rejection caused Francis Millet to battle severe insomnia and an ever growing opium habit.

"I despise the Germans, dear friend," Millet exaggerated. "However, I have not lost sight of the fact that you are counting on me as it relates to the repatriation of works of art stolen before and during the war. In that regard, I have made some progress and should be able to address the subject in detail when you call the summit meeting."

"I see you are concentrating on the Belgian issue at this moment?" Butt asked, thankful that the philosophical portion of their conversation had been laid to rest.

"That is correct, Archie," he responded. "As you well know, throughout the period 1914 to 1918 Belgium was occupied by the Germans and many of its major cities were used as passing grounds in the military move toward the Western Front. It is safe to say the Germans looted any artwork of value in the cultural capitals of Antwerp, Louvain, Marlines, Dinant, and Kermode, and destroyed many other works, including some masterpieces by Rubin and Roden. Priceless pieces, gone.

"The library at the University of Louvain was burned to the ground and with it hundreds of thousands of irreplaceable books, manuscripts, maps and other antiquities were lost. The library itself was a masterpiece of architecture."

"Art knows many forms... how sad," Butt said. "I assume the works that were stolen were not returned after the signing of the Treaty?"

"Article 247 of the Treaty of Versailles calls for the immediate return of any work of art removed illegally from Belgium and all other involved nations," Millet said with studied certainty. "Suffice it to say that fourteen years later it has never been attempted, let alone accomplished. In this regard, at least, the Versailles accord has been a dismal failure."

Butt sighed. "I'm afraid the Treaty has failed on nearly all accounts, Francis, except the unintended consequence of making the world an even more dangerous place."

"Nonetheless," Millet continued, "with a little bit of cooperation from the Germans, many important works could be returned to the Belgian government. I am personally aware of several stolen masterpieces that hang on German museum walls in Berlin. But so long as the Third Reich turns a blind eye to the fraud, we will be unable to return them to their rightful owners -- short of stealing them back." Millet watched the President's face for a sign that he would consider such a thought.

Butt read his mind. "Christ no, Francis," he snorted. "That's out of the question. I'll be god dammed if we're going to go to war over this."

"Just a quick in and out under cover of darkness, Archie... it's done all the time in my world," Millet protested.

"And to what end, Francis? Would two wrongs make a right? I hardly think so."

Chastised, Millet sulked in his chair and sipped on his brandy.

Butt would not accept Millet's suggestion as the only option. "Have you considered appealing directly to Hitler?" He was dead serious.

Millet laughed. "You expect me to get an audience with the Chancellor? Perhaps if I wore my Mayfair Street suit..." he jested, referring to his prized Savile Row pinstripe. "I'm told I look fetching in it."

Butt was not amused. He disliked Millett's habit of becoming affected when he was disappointed. Such an effeminate style was not appropriate in Butt's world and he had warned his friend that such behavior would hurt his standing in the public eye.

"Dammit, Francis, I've asked you not to…" Millet finished his sentence.

"Act like a dammed fairy, Mr. President?"

"Francis, please."

Millet laughed, always amused by Butt's reaction to his "delicate" side. The President stewed for a few minutes.

"Perhaps I could discuss this with John Thayer," Millet said, breaking the silence. "He appears to have some access to Hitler. Do you think he would be willing to bring up such a subject with the Chancellor?"

Archie thought for a moment. "I think so, if I was to ask him personally. But I do not want this to interfere with his efforts to ensure that Hitler attends the summit."

"I understand," Millet said. "I'll speak to John and feel him out on the subject. Perhaps he could just deliver a letter for me."

"Excellent idea, Francis, do it. Now since we've tossed away most of the afternoon and, if you can believe it, I have the evening off, perhaps you would care to join me in a round of golf. We have time for nine holes if we hurry before it gets dark."

Millet was staring into the fireplace and did not respond. He was already thinking about his letter to Hitler – and what other information it might include. Opportunity was knocking.

"Francis?" Butt woke him from his trance.

"Why yes, Mr. President, golf is a splendid idea," Millet responded. In fact, unless I'm mistaken, if you get nine holes in this afternoon it will bring your total attention to golf since you took the oath of office to a staggering – let me count -- nine holes."

The President sighed. "I guess it has been a while."

"Pity, I love the way your hips swing when you strike the ball."

Butt flinched at the joke.

"God dammit, Francis!" he snapped at his friend, then couldn't keep a straight face and laughed out loud.

Thirty-One

"John, I'll die trying, but I don't know how in the hell I'm going to get this done by Labor Day," Phillip Colvin reported to John Jacob Astor from Liverpool.

"She's a god dammed tub, for Christ's sake. Look, I've got good news and bad, boss." Astor was silent.

"Much to my surprise, most of the pieces are still here, but there aren't many that don't need to be reworked or repaired," Colvin continued despite knowing how bad news irritated Astor.

"The hull is in good shape, thank God, but it's riddled with rust and needs to be scraped, primed and painted. The engines need a complete overhaul. At least two boilers must be replaced. We've got at least one bent propeller. Every piece of millwork, the floors, teak decks and ceilings need to stripped, sanded, stained and varnished. There's not a dish, a fork or knife to be found, the gallery equipment has disappeared, there is no bedding or linens, and most of the toilets are busted. "I mean Christ, John, what did I do to deserve this?" Colvin pleaded for mercy.

"Stop your whining," the voice on the other end of the transatlantic phone call said. "I'm not paying you to tell me all the problems, I need answers. So what's the good news?"

Colvin sighed. He'd arrived in Liverpool on Monday morning and hadn't had much more than a few hours of sleep in the last three days. He was on *Titanic*'s Bridge, surveying the repair work with a half dozen engineers when Astor's call came in. It wasn't lost on Colvin that the ship's wheel he was holding onto belonged to one of the most famous steamers to ever set sail.

"Well, the only chance I have to pull this off depends on the availability of labor, and at least on that front, there's plenty of it. Harland & Wolf hasn't laid a new keel in almost three years and they've got only a skeleton crew working the dry docks. Unemployment here is nearly forty percent, so I'll have no problem hiring the thousands of men I'm going to need to get this wreck shipshape. I'm told that a lot of the guys who worked on her twenty years ago are still around."

Astor didn't blink. "Phillip, I don't care what it costs. I'm counting on you to get it done. You have a blank check and twenty-four hours per day seven days a week. Spend my money and your time wisely."

Colvin could hear the excitement in Astor's voice. He didn't have a bloody clue why this tired old ship was so important to him, but he knew and respected John Jacob Astor well enough to know he must have one hell of a good reason.

"Ok, John, I'm you're man," Colvin pledged. "Bring your bags on Labor day. *Titanic* will be set to sail, I promise you. She'll look as beautiful as the day she left Southampton twenty years ago."

That's what Astor wanted to hear. "Thank you, Phillip. And I promise to fill you in on what this is all about as soon as I can. For now, trust me, it's important. By the way, I'm sending someone to help you. He should be there in three or four days. You'll like him," Astor added.

"Who?"

"Thomas Andrews. The man who designed and built the ship that God himself could not sink."

Thirty-Two

Sir Cosmo Duff Gordon sat quietly in the back seat of a chauffeur driven Bentley as it made its way through heavy traffic across Charing Cross at the southern-most end of Trafalgar Square. The car had been sent for him by British Minister Ramsay MacDonald who had been delighted to learn that Duff-Gordon was in London. Sir Cosmo placed the call to Number 10 Downing Street only the afternoon before, but a luncheon meeting between he and the PM was set immediately for the next day.

A gentle rain was falling across London as Duff Gordon enjoyed observing the bustle in the heart of the great city. A frequent visitor to the offices of many of the leadership of Great Britain, he particularly liked Trafalgar Square and the Westminster area where all the political posturing took place. They passed Nelson's Column, surrounded by tourists, and headed north to Westminster.

As the driver maneuvered through the slow moving noon time traffic, Duff Gordon was feeling elated at what he had accomplished over the last several weeks. In the short span of time since the Van Gogh gathering in Chesapeake Bay he had crisscrossed Europe for meetings at the highest levels of government. Just three days prior he had been the guest of French President Paul Doumer at the Élysée Palace in Paris, and the week before that he had visited President Niceto Alcalá-Zamora in Madrid and Benito Mussolini in Rome. In each case the message he delivered from President Butt was received with even more enthusiasm than he hoped. Duff Gordon extracted commitments from each to attend the summit and expected no less from Ramsay MacDonald, an old friend.

To the casual observer, the dapper Sir Cosmo Duff Gordon was a loveable gadfly, always lighthearted with a ready joke and a penchant for trivial conversations. He carried himself in such a way that most acquaintances held him in kind regard, although they did not take him as a man of much substance. Sir Cosmo would have it no other way.

Duff Gordon enjoyed his carefully self-cultivated reputation as a flirtatious aristocrat and philanderer, a ruse that was completely at odds with the boundless love he had for Lucy, his wife. He often wondered how it was that people accepted the deception so easily, and that they couldn't see the truth in his eyes when he was with her. His devotion to Britain was second to none, yet it was a distant passion to the love and devotion he felt for his Lucy.

The reason he played the "playboy" was to help ease his way into the social and government circles that were vitally important to his value as a spy for the British Secret Service, a joint agency of the Admiralty and the War Office formed in 1909.

Beneath the sham, Sir Cosmo was also a political broker, at seventy years of age able to open virtually any door of influence across Europe. He was a brilliant student of history who recognized that to have any hope of brightening the future, one must first have an enlightened appreciation for the past. Consequently, when in the company of a head of state, Sir Cosmo generally understood the man's motivation, was familiar with the influences that had shaped his life and had a firm grasp of his political agenda.

He was perhaps one of the few men who really knew the answer to why the Germans hated the French, and vice versa, and how men like Mussolini and Hitler were actually able to come to power. He was a political broker without peer, often called upon by one head of state to deliver a message to another, thus sidestepping the normal, bureaucratically constipated channels of communications that cursed any hope of real discussion or negotiations. It was a little known fact that in the fall of 1918, at the insistence of Secretary of State Archie Butt, President Woodrow Wilson had asked Sir Cosmo Duff Gordon to meet quietly with the German leadership to test their appetite for an armistice. The Scotsman met secretly with Kaiser Wilhelm II and made it clear no truce was possible unless the German Government agreed to an immediate retreat of the military from all occupied territories, the cessation of submarine warfare and the Emperor's own renunciation of the throne.

Wilhelm was shocked by Duff Gordon's frankness. Despite weeks of preceding discussions by negotiating parties from both sides seeking an end to hostilities, Sir Cosmo's message to Wilhelm was the first time the Kaiser really understood the reality of his country's situation – as well as his own.

The Bentley pulled up in front of Number 10 Downing Street, the most famous address in London, and stopped. The Prime Minister met him personally.

"Cosmo, you are a sight for sore eyes," MacDonald greeted him. Duff Gordon extended his hand but was silently shocked by the PM's appearance. He was haggard and looked bone tired. Here was a man with the weight of the world on his shoulders, the Scot thought to himself.

"Prime Minister, how good of you to see me. I always look forward to my visits to London, but having the chance to speak with you sets this journey apart as particularly memorable," Duff Gordon said.

"My, my Cosmo, you bloody well know how to stoke a man, don't you?" he said, but secretly enjoyed the compliment.

"Come, my friend, I have an extraordinary bottle of champagne awaiting us. We have much to talk about," the PM said.

"Indeed we do, Prime Minister," Duff Gordon said, still gripping his hand, allowing the PM to satisfy the always present press corps gathered outside the centre of British government.

"I take it then that you are here for more than my champagne?" MacDonald whispered to him while facing the sea of reporters.

"Actually, Prime Minister, I have a message from the President of the United States," Duff Gordon, carefull to keep his voice low.

MacDonald forgot about the cameras, cocked one eye and looked into those of his friend. "Well, then… if he has chosen you to deliver the message, it must be of great importance," he said, caught off guard.

"Yes, it is a matter of great importance," Duff Gordon replied. "More precisely, Prime Minister, it is a matter of grave importance."

On that note, the two disappeared into the PM's private residence. At three o'clock, the door opened again and MacDonald walked Duff Gordon to his waiting car.

"Tell the President that I am forever in his gratitude," MacDonald said to his friend. "Even if nothing of consequence comes of his efforts, he will be remembered by the British people as a man of peace," the PM said, shaking Sir Cosmo's hand energetically.

"If you know Archie Butt," the diplomat responded, "then it would behoove you to bet heavily on his success,

Prime Minister. He is a man who accomplishes his goals, quickly and neatly. And he has no greater passion than peace.

MacDonald shook his head in agreement ."Until September, my good friend."

"Until September, Prime Minister."

As the car pulled away, Duff Gordon watched as MacDonald walked back to his office.

"A bit more life in the old boys' step, hey?" he said to himself. "Three down, two to go."

Thirty-Three

John Thayer's visit to Berlin was hardly so cordial.

Upon arriving from Berlin, Thayer had lingered patiently in his hotel room for the next four long days waiting for the telephone to ring. President Butt had sent a carefully worded telegram to the Chancellor's office seeking an appointment for Thayer, who was hardly an unknown to Hitler. The two had spoken before on several occasions. Still, no word had come from the Reich Chancellery regarding his visit, and Thayer was about to admit defeat.

On the morning of his fifth day in Berlin, the telephone finally rang. A voice on the line, speaking in curt, clipped sentences, identified the caller as SS Oberguppenführer Philipp Bouhler, head of the Reich Chancellery operations.

"Mr. Thayer, I have not had the pleasure of your acquaintance," Bouhler said, icily. "You wish to see the Chancellor?"

"Thank you for the call, Oberguppenführer Bouhler," in a calm but friendly voice . "Yes, I have a message to deliver to Chancellor Hitler from the President of the United States," Thayer responded, trying to sound unthreatening.

"May I ask the nature of your business with the Chancellor , Mr. Thayer?"

Thayer knew this game was coming. In the German government, information was power.

"I'm afraid that I cannot share the purpose of my visit except to the Chancellor. Suffice it to say that it is a matter of some urgency."

There was silence. "I see, Mr. Thayer. In that case I assume you will not mind waiting for your audience with the Führer?" He expected this too.

"No, Oberguppenführer Bouhler, I will be patient."

"Then perhaps we can make arrangements within the next forty-eight hours. Please be available and ready to meet the Chancellor at a moment's notice. His schedule is quite full of 'urgent' matters," he added, his voice dripping with sarcasm.

"I await your call, Oberguppenführer Bouhler. Good day." Thayer hung up the phone slowly, careful not to give any indication of the rage he was feeling. He felt insulted by the senior SS Officer, but had no recourse but to wait.

Just after midnight the phone in his hotel room rang again, waking Thayer from a deep sleep. It was not Bouhler.

A woman's voice said, "The Chancellor can meet with you now, Mr. Thayer. A Reich car will be outside your hotel within the next fifteen minutes. Please be ready and carry your passport." The phone went dead.

Thayer leapt from the bed, threw cold water on his face and dressed, managing to exit the door of his hotel just as the Reich car, driven by an SS Officer, pulled up. He opened the door and got in. The car was empty except for the driver.

As they drove up to the Reich Chancellery ten minutes later, Thayer was already unnerved. In previous visits to Berlin, he had always been impressed with how alive the city was, even in the early morning hours. It reminded him of New York City in that it never seemed to sleep. Café's that were normally full and streets that were typically clogged with tourists all were empty tonight. It was as if the City of Berlin had gone into deep hibernation, dark and deserted.

He asked the driver, in the little German he knew, if there was a curfew in effect. The driver did not acknowledge his question other than to glance in the rear view mirror. Thayer caught his eyes. They were a deep, piercing blue, and they made the American uneasy. The German officer continued to drive in utter silence.

The car pulled through the towering entrance gates of the new Reich Chancellery, which was flanked by two huge bronze sculptures entitled "Wehrmacht" (Armed Forces) and "Partei" (Party). The driver parked the car and opened the door for Thayer, who stepped out at the base of a grand staircase made of marble. There was no one to meet him.

The driver motioned for him to follow. Thayer hesitated for a moment and took in his first glimpse of the new headquarters of Hitler's Nazi government. It had been completed just several months ago by more than four thousand Germans who had worked three shifts, seven days a week for more than a year to complete the immense, steel frame building on schedule. It was said that architect Albert Speers, a close confidante of the Chancellor, had a blank check to build the structure. It was completed less than two days before Hitler's deadline.

Thayer's immediate reaction was that Speer's design was very similar to the Germans post war outlook on life. Stern, austere, even cold. The massive government complex had been designed to impress, and in that regard it succeeded brilliantly, if only by its gargantuan footprint. Yet, it was heavily imposing on the city of Berlin, an oddity in both its size and architectural style. The sight of it, combined with streets empty of people made Thayer uncomfortable again and he felt a sudden chill on the back of his neck.

The driver led Thayer up the stairs to a small reception area in front of seventeen foot high, solid German walnut double doors. These led to another set of stairs that emptied into a circular room featuring a breathtaking glass domed ceiling. For a moment, Thayer thought he had entered a cathedral. In effect, he had.

At the entrance, Thayer gazed upon a grand gallery that stretched nearly five hundred feet in length, its walls adorned with framed paintings. He recognized some of them as masterpieces of the European art world. The collection was breathtaking. The Officer beckoned him to follow him through the gallery to the main reception area. Thayer found it difficult to concentrate on the long walk, overwhelmed by the artwork that surrounded him. He wondered how many of them had been "borrowed" during German occupations and conquests.

Upon reaching the reception hall, a tall and strikingly beautiful young woman dressed in a military uniform with skirt, welcomed Thayer and dismissed the SS Officer. The driver walked away in silence, still not having spoken a word to his guest. "Come with me, please," the blond haired, blue eyed woman said to him and led him down a long corridor to the reception area of the Chancellors suite of offices.

There he was told to sit in a sparse, dimly lit foyer and to wait for instructions. It was nearly 2 a.m., and Thayer was exhausted. The waiting area was odd, he thought, a most antiseptic place in which to welcome a visitor. He sat in a vinyl chair, the kind one would find in a hospital waiting room. An hour passed, then two, in which time he never saw or spoke to anyone. Thayer began to fume. In all his years of dealing with members of the German government, including Hitler, he had never been treated so shabbily.

Finally, the young woman appeared again and informed him that the Führer would see him in a few moments. Thayer followed the girl through a short hallway that appeared to be the back entrance for Hitler's personal office. It struck him that the military aide had escorted him through the servant's entrance.

She brought him over to a large rectangular black marble table, perhaps twenty feet in length and motioned for him to sit at it. Thayer did as he was told, now completely unhinged by his treatment.

Before he had an opportunity to take in the room, which might have been as much as four hundred square meters in size, the main door to Hitler's office and library opened and in walked the Chancellor, seemingly as fresh as one would be at mid day. He was alone.

"Mr. Thayer," Hitler called to his guest as he made the long walk to the table. "How nice of you to come. I hope you have enjoyed your tour of the new Reich Chancellery. It is spectacular, wouldn't you agree?"

Thayer did not respond immediately, taken aback by Hitler's cordial greeting. He had half expected the man to scream at him.

"Is something wrong, Mr. Thayer?" the Chancellor asked, appearing to be seriously concerned about his guests' well being.

"I am sorry, Herr Chancellor. I did not expect..." Hitler cut him off with a motion of his hand.

"You did not expect such a rude welcome, my old friend?" His tone of voice changed. "Are you surprised that I did not personally greet you at the entrance to the Reich Chancellory?

"Now it is I who am confused, Mr. Thayer -- or may I call you 'John' as does your President?" Hitler's face was turning a deep red, and John Boreland Thayer felt very afraid of the man.

"John is fine, Herr Chancellor," he stammered.

"Good, because now I have at least one thing in common with President Archie Butt. I have yet to find any other qualities that I can relate to. On second thought, perhaps I can associate with his intelligence. I am told he is a very smart man. Well, Mr. Thayer, so am I."

Thayer was flustered by the awkwardness of Hitler's remarks. "Herr Chancellor, I have asked for this meeting with you to..." He was cut off again.

"I know exactly why you are here, Mr. Thayer!" Hitler screamed.

There was a long, uncomfortable silence. Hitler had yet to sit at the table. He seemed to enjoy talking down to his guest. The tone of his voice abruptly calmed as he continued.

"Before you deliver your message to me from President Butt, Mr. Thayer, I ask you to consider what you have seen of this building, of my office, of our surroundings here. Did you not enjoy your walk through the Reich Gallery? Did you know that it is more than twice as long as the 'Hall of Mirrors' at Versailles? Did you not enjoy the works by Caravaggio, Rembrandt, Rubens, Velázquez, Poussin, Vermeer, Michelangelo and Raphael?"

He began to rage again. "Have you not yet seen and tasted the power and glory of the Third Reich? Are all American's blind?"

Thayer was convinced he was dealing with a madman and he was terrified.

"Mr... I mean, Herr Chancellor, if I have offended you in any way..." Thayer stuttered.

Hitler reared back and laughed, once again changing his persona. "Mr. Thayer you must forgive me. I have been under great pressure. However, I must admit that I feel insulted by your President. He should have delivered this message himself. It is unfortunate that he does not take Germany seriously. Others have made that same mistake."

The color drained from Hitler's face as he calmed down. Now it was Thayer who became red faced with anger.

"What?" he hollered back at Hitler. "He should have delivered it himself? Would you have shown him through the servant's door too, Herr Chancellor?" The President's delegate was enraged. He'd been pushed too far.

"Forgive me if Americans are not always the first to salute Germany's newly found power, Herr Chancellor. But you may recall that the United States left some boys to be buried in Europe as a result of the mindless actions of some of your predecessors." Hitler sat quietly, now listening. His eyes were getting wider by the second.

"And I'll be god dammed if you think I'm going to listen to you insult my President -- who has proven he is a man of peace. Can you claim that Herr Chancellor? So far the world has heard that what you seek for your country is freedom and prosperity. Well, your rhetoric is certainly interesting, but don't blame America if we all don't stand up and salute. Too much American blood has already been spilt on account of Germany's dreams. "

Hitler could not believe his ears nor could he remember the last time anyone had spoken to him with such disdain -- and lived to talk about it. He was about to interrupt, but Thayer wouldn't let him. Once John Boreland Thayer's back was up, it stayed up.

"Yes, Herr Chancellor, I bring a message from my President to you. I am sorry if I am not worthy enough in your eyes to deliver it. The message has to do with real peace and actions to sustain it. Archie Butt is tired of wasted efforts on the diplomatic front. He feels strongly that if there is to be a sustainable peace, it must be brokered by those leaders who will be held accountable to its success or failure.

"And that, Herr Chancellor, includes you," he concluded, raising a finger and stabbing at the air in Hitler's direction .

Before Hitler could say another word, Thayer stood up and removed an envelope entrusted to him by Archie Butt. In it was a summary of the American President's ardent desire for peace and his intention to gather European leaders together to build a plan not only of intent, but also of action.

"Herr Chancellor, I will take no more of your time. This is the letter from President Butt." He tossed it on the table. "I will leave it here for you should you desire to review it." Then he turned and began walking out of the room the way he had come in. He abruptly stopped and instead pointedly walked out the doors Hitler had used to enter the room.

Behind him, an enraged Adolf Hitler stood alone. In the cavernous office. His hands shook with anger. Finally, he reached for the envelope and tore it open. He read the contents, then threw it back on the table.

"Mrs. Janz," come here at once," he screamed to his secretary.

A middle-aged woman entered the room immediately holding a steno pad. Her face showed no emotion.

"Find Herr Patzig and have him brought here. Now."

As Thayer retraced his steps through the long gallery alone, his mind was a jumble of emotions. He could barely remember all that had been said, his adrenalin was pumping so hard.

He was also upset with himself. Archie Butt had made him promise to come back with a complete blow by blow description of the dictator's office to compare to his own. "I'll bet his is a lot bigger but mine's a lot warmer," Butt had bet him. For the life of him, John

Thayer couldn't remember one thing about Hitler's office.

Except that it was very large, very cold and very scary.

Thirty-Four

As August came and members of Congress headed home for the summer adjournment, Washington D.C. took on a friendlier tone and the newspapers were hard pressed to fill their pages with political news. Normally at this time of year reporters assigned to the White House would follow the President to wherever his summer retreat was located, but since Archie Butt had taken office, there was no summer break. The man simply didn't take vacations and wouldn't hesitate to call Congress back to work in an emergency.

The President actually owned a magnificent antebellum mansion and estate on St. Simons Island off the Georgia coast, where he would occasionally entertain foreign dignitaries. The home was a former Sea Island Cotton plantation that produced the finest quality chambray and lace prior to the Civil War. It was set on thirteen hundred acres adjacent to the St. Simons Lighthouse and spanned nearly a mile of ocean front. Inland, the property was dotted with clusters of great oak trees garlanded with thick, emerald colored Spanish moss, and was awash with waves of olive green ferns along salt marshes.

The island was famous for its cooling ocean breezes that were laden with the smell of salt air, and its brilliant white beaches that grew and shrank with the tides. Hundreds of species of birds populated the island and Archie thoroughly enjoyed hiking his property with a guest in tow while excitedly pointing them out. His favorite moments on St. Simons Island were spent alone on his veranda, however, when he watched the sun settle over the horizon with a good Cuban cigar and a tall snifter of brandy. He hadn't had one of those moments in quite some time.

Since occupying the Oval Office, Butt had been to St. Simon's Island just three times and on each occasion for diplomatic work. He was badly in need of a vacation but would not allow himself to be distracted from his urgent schedule. There would be plenty of time to get reacquainted, he often reminded himself when Georgia beckoned in his heart. But for now, the Capital was where he needed to be.

It was Jack Thayer who suggested that he take a few days at the Island to hear briefings from John Jacob Astor, Sir Cosmo Duff Gordon and John Thayer. The Chief of Staff was secretly worried about the President's health. Butt had been working day and night since April and needed rest. His pallor was quite wan and the dark circles under his eyes had become pronounced. Even the Commander in Chief of the world's most powerful nation could wear out, and Thayer saw signs that it was happening right before his eyes.

It had taken Jack Thayer's arm twisting to convince the President that escaping Washington's intensely humid mid-summer weather for the cool breezes of the Island would do him good, physically and spiritually. The closer was Jack's suggestion that he might even find a few hours of the solitude he so enjoyed while walking the beaches and dunes. The Chief of Staff informed the President that Astor, Duff-Gordon and the senior Thayer would be his guests as well as "one or two others." Butt didn't press for details and Thayer didn't offer any.

In briefing the ubiquitous White House reporters about the visit to the Island, Thayer had made it clear that this was simply a break in the President's arduous schedule, and that although he might entertain a few guests, there was no official business to be conducted. He refused to answer questions regarding the identity of any guests who might be invited to visit or accompany him, suggesting only that those few were close friends of the President. He was purposely vague so as to ensure that he did not arouse their inherent suspicions.

Privately, Jack Thayer had been scheming for an excuse to get the President out of the White House, and especially the Oval Office, so that counter surveillance experts could conduct a complete "sweep" of the building. He was becoming increasingly concerned that either the White House was "bugged" with eavesdropping equipment, or worse, that there was a spy among them, a mole buried somewhere within. His father's conversation with Hitler had deeply alarmed him. It seemed that the Chancellor knew more about the reason for the senior Thayer's visit than he should have.

A week later, the President, his Chief of Staff and an entourage of Secret Service Agents arrived at St. Simons Island on the USS Sequoia, the official Presidential Yacht. USS Sequoia had been transferred to the White House from the Department of Commerce, which had purchased the boat to use as a decoy while hunting Mississippi River rum runners during prohibition. A 104-foot-long wooden hulled vessel designed by master ship builder John A. Trumpy in 1925, it had been refit to include a Presidential suite, a sophisticated communications system, a large meeting room and quarters for several guests and Secret Service Agents. Butt had used the craft sparingly during his Presidency, in fact only for entertaining heads of state. His Chief of Staff directed its use for the cruise to St. Simons Island instead of making the exhausting and tedious fifteen hour drive from Washington.

As the yacht approached the Island the sun was full. A warm breeze blew across the vessel's teak decks. Thayer saw an almost immediate change in the President who already looked rejuvenated as the *Sequoia* docked some five hundred yards from the veranda of his estate.

"I have to hand it to you Jack. I needed this," Butt complimented his Chief of Staff, and for perhaps the first time in his long career was grateful for having someone to look after him.

"I'm sure your stay will be therapeutic, Mr. President," Thayer responded. "To tell you the truth, I needed to get out of Washington for a few days myself. The place is stifling, in all respects."

While they were gone, Thayer was counting on Robert Maldonia to ensure the White House was not broadcasting its business to foreign ears. "This is a good move, Jack," Maldonia had commented to the Chief of Staff. "The technology of eavesdropping is developing at a pace that alarms me. The White House probably should be swept on a continuous basis, and we should consider installing some new anti-eavesdropping equipment."

"All in do time, Robert," Thayer replied. "We'll have to revisit this, perhaps in October," Thayer said. He did not want to risk the observance of concern about eavesdropping so close to the summit, for fear it would only serve to fuel the already suspicious minds of its intended participants.

Astor, Duff Gordon and the senior Thayer arrived the next morning, and found the President already relaxed and enjoying breakfast on the veranda. The salt air and aroma of Sweetbay magnolias growing around the mansion were thick in the air, and the creamy white blossoms softened the stately, multi-columned white veranda. The three men were ready to begin their briefings to the President, but Archie Butt had something else in mind. "Gentlemen, we are going fishing," he announced to the group, who were genuinely surprised yet equally pleased with the opportunity for a few hours of relaxation themselves. The President also invited Jack, knowing that he and his father had very little opportunity to spend any real time together. Jack beamed at the invitation but was not surprised. Whatever history wrote about Archie Butt, the younger Thayer was determined the world would know that besides being a strong President, Archie Butt was simply a good man.

After lunch that afternoon, Sir Cosmo Duff Gordon and John Thayer gave summaries of their visits to the heads of state of England, France, Spain and Germany. Butt was delighted by the warm welcome that Duff Gordon had received from Prime Minister MacDonald, French President Paul Doumer, President Niceto Alcalá-Zamora of Spain, and surprisingly by Italy's "Il Duce". On the other hand, he was quite concerned by Thayer's report of his confrontational meeting with Hitler.

"Based on your preliminary report, John, I must admit that I was quite astounded by Hitler's letter to me indicating he would attend the summit. I had feared the opposite," Butt said. "However, his acceptance has had the intended effect on Mr. Stalin. Once the bastard recognized that Hitler would attend the meeting, his curiosity, if nothing else, couldn't keep Uncle Joe away. I doubt that the presence of MacDonald, Doumer, Alcalá-Zamora and Mussolini had anything to do with Stalin's decision. Like all of us, Hitler is the guy he's worried about," the President added. Thayer shook his head, still bewildered by the reception he received from the new German dictator.

"Hitler is quite mad, Mr. President, I am sure of it, and dangerously so, I would add. Consequently, I am not surprised by his acceptance, nor would I have been surprised by his decline," Thayer said. "I have never felt more intimidated by any man, and he accomplished my extreme unease in a matter of moments. I am embarrassed to admit that I was terrified by him..." Jack Thayer swallowed hard for his father, knowing how embarrassed such an admission was for a man who had stared down fear more than once in his life without so much as a blink.

The other four men in the room stared at John Boreland Thayer, not quite sure of how to respond. They had the utmost respect for him, not only as a self-made king of US industry, but also as an extraordinary benefactor of the rights and fair treatment for the American worker.

Awkward silence filled the room until the senior Thayer finished his sentence. "...Until he pissed me off, that it is," he added. They all roared with laughter, and silent relief.

He continued. "Hitler is not a particularly imposing individual, rather short, somewhat 'Napoleonic', I would say. Nor is he physically unappealing or remarkable in any way -- with the exception of the 'Charlie Chaplin' moustache, of course, which certainly is very theatrical, if not even a bit clownish," Thayer mused.

"However, his eyes are indeed striking," he continued. "They are uncomfortably piercing and blood red, presumably of fatigue because of the absurd schedule the man keeps. His facial expressions too are puzzling. At one moment he is the picture of charm. In the next split second, he is grinding his teeth in rage, barely able to control himself. The son of a bitch has charisma, but I will suggest to you that he gets his way by scaring the bejeezus out of anyone who dares challenge him. I half expected the crazy bastard to either strangle me when I challenged him or shoot me in the back as I abruptly adjourned our meeting and walked out on him," Thayer confessed.

"I sincerely do believe the man is psychologically imbalanced to the point of insanity and therefore quite capable of any level of evil behavior. We must never underestimate him or pretend to think we can anticipate his reaction -- to anything."

The room was silent once again as the group pondered Thayer's description of the German dictator.

Jack Thayer finally piped in. "Dad, you mentioned to the President that you had the sense Hitler knew more about the summit than you planned to share with him. Can you add anything to that?"

The senior Thayer reflected on the question for a moment before speaking. Just then, Butt's valet entered the room, carrying large crystal snifters of brandy and a box of Cuban cigars. Thayer waited for him to leave before responding.

"It was very strange," he said after lighting his cigar. "I recall – and please remember that I was somewhat in shock at this point by his behavior -- that he said, and I quote: 'I know exactly why you are here, Mr. Thayer!'

"I'm not sure he intended to say that, gentlemen," Thayer continued. "It just came off his lips in his rage. But it was if we had threatened him in some way. Which of course, is exactly what we intend to do should he not agree to cooperate. So to answer your question, yes, I believe he knew more than he was letting on."

"Dammit," the President cursed. "That's not possible. The circle of knowledge of our plan is exceedingly small. Only the Secretary of State, Maldonia of MI-8, each of us here and the other ten members of Van Gogh have any knowledge of what we intend. I dare say I would be shocked speechless to learn that any one of the Apostles had dared to break our silence. They simply have too much integrity and personal reputation on the line.

John Thayer spoke first. "Nevertheless, Mr. President, Hitler's statement speaks volumes. We must be extremely cautious of our communications between now and September. Giving a man like Hitler the opportunity to prepare a response -- verbal or otherwise," he let his last word hand in the air for a moment, "could be catastrophic and may even lead to him doing the preposterous."

"What do you mean by 'otherwise', John?" the President asked, obviously alarmed.

Sir Cosmo Duff Gordon interjected. "Mr. President, I doubt that it would surprise any of us if Hitler launched a pre-meditated attack on an unsuspecting European nation, if given the opportunity to plan it. We have to consider him in the same light as a cornered animal. He is capable of lashing out blindly, even against the odds, if he believes he is in danger."

"Good Lord," the President responded, leaning forward in his armchair in angst. There was silence.

His Chief of Staff finally broke it. "Mr. President, you should know that I have initiated an eavesdropping sweep of the White House in your absence. We'll know by tomorrow afternoon if we have anything to worry about."

Good call, Jack," the President responded. "Let's be sure. Is there anything else we can do?"

"MI-8 vetted each member of Van Gogh before our meeting in April, Mr. President. Nothing untoward or worrisome was uncovered at that time."

At the Chief of Staff's comment, Astor, Duff Gordon and John Thayer each looked at the President. Thayer had inadvertently let them know that their business dealings and personal affairs had been analyzed by the government's intelligence agency. Butt picked up on the slip before Jack did.

"I am sorry, gentlemen. I had to be sure," he apologized. The statement hung in the air.

John Thayer was first to speak. "Aw hell, we would have done the same god dammed thing, Archie. Come to think about it, we all do the same thing from time to time as it relates to business -- or our wives." They laughed and the moment passed.

Butt turned to John Jacob Astor. "John, you had something you wanted to speak to me about -- or do we need to talk in private?"

"Privacy is not an issue, Mr. President," the world's richest man responded. "But I would like to put off my report until after dinner this evening, if you don't object. I'm waiting for some last minute information which I should have by the end of the day."

"So be it, John. Gentlemen," he turned to Duff Gordon and Thayer, "I thank you from the bottom of my heart for your valiant efforts in Europe. You must be tired. Would you like to rest for the remainder of the afternoon?"

Duff Gordon looked apoplectic. "Rest? Hell, that's for old folks. "Don't you have a bloody golf course on this morsel of paradise?"

A phone call later, Jack Thayer had secured them a late afternoon tee time at The Hampton Club, a picturesque golf course on the northernmost tip of St. Simon's Island, with long, brilliant green fairways, thick forests and enormous salt marshes. After some frantic arrangements by the Secret Service and with the help of the local police, Butt and his party played eighteen holes on the meticulously maintained course , thoroughly enjoying its natural beauty, the cool ocean breezes and good company. Through a round of golf filled with 'whiffs', 'mulligans' and 'gimmes', the foursome devoted their total energies to relaxation, the aspect of another world war off the agenda, at least for the moment.

At the start of play, Astor mentioned to the President that the course seemed familiar. "But I do not recall playing it before," he said. He scribbled a quick note on the back of a scorecard and gave it to a Secret Service Agent.

"Please call my office," he asked, "and tell them I need an immediate response. Some thirty minutes later, on the fourth tee, the agent returned with a response which he whispered to Astor.

"Ha, I thought so," he laughed. "I knew the course was familiar. I own it."

At dinner that evening, Astor, Duff Gordon, John Thayer and the President's Chief of Staff joined the President in the mansion's inviting formal dining room. The room faced the ocean and the servants had thrown the windows open wide for the evening. A mild breeze swept through the room throughout the night, making for a most comfortable dinner and conversation.

The dining room was filled with hearty laughter throughout the long evening. The conversation was as delicious as the excellent five course meal and a half a dozen bottles of Archie's own private stock of native Georgian wines.

Delighted at not being the center of attention, the President reveled in the stories told by his three millionaire friends. Each was a seasoned international traveler capable of closing business deals in any port of the world, despite the barriers of language, culture and the varying degrees and depths of government oversight and intervention. To dine at the table of a head of state was nothing new to these gentlemen. The only difference on this night was the fact that the deal had already been done.

Finally, as the clock approached midnight, John Jacob Astor finished his last tall tale of the evening and turned to the President.

Now straight-faced and surprisingly sober, Astor began.

"Mr. President, I thank you for a most remarkable afternoon and evening and for giving me the opportunity to know you better. As to my good friends Sir Cosmo and John, I can only say that it has been my exquisite pleasure to make your acquaintance out of the spotlight of industry, and I am proud to call you my friends."

Before any of them could utter similar respects, Astor began again.

"And that is why I am particularly pleased to share with all of you some news tonight regarding a lady who once tried to kill us all but ultimately failed." Butt looked at him, puzzled.

"For some unknown reason, despite her dogged attempts to pass us on to our maker well ahead of schedule, I fell in love with her and have been captivated by her mysterious charms for more than twenty years.

"And no, Sir Cosmo," Astor continued in jest, "I am not speaking of any of the femme fatales with whom you are rumored to have dallied…" There was laughter as Sir Cosmo smirked, thoroughly enjoying the backhanded compliment to his reputation.

"No, I am speaking of another larger, yet even more exquisite seducer of men."

Butt could not help himself.

"*Titanic*," he said, softly, the word rolling off the tip of his tongue as if perpetually in waiting, his eyes riveted on Astor.

"Precisely, Mr. President," Astor responded jubilantly. "I am not the least bit surprised that it was you that solved the riddle. In fact I believe it is possible that over the last twenty years, you among all of us have been most influenced by the allure of the charming young lady we last saw on April 15, 1912."

Butt was thoroughly enjoying the touch of entertainment Astor had brought to the evening, but had no idea where the real estate mogul was taking them.

"She must be scrapped by now," the senior Thayer said, shaking his head sadly. "By God, she was a thing of beauty. Who could ever forget such a lady? "

Astor paused for a moment, letting Thayer's thought sink in. It was the perfect segue to the rest of his story.

"By way of background, I'm sure you all know that *Titanic* was refit almost immediately after the incident but was commandeered by the British government in 1914 for service as a troop transport. What you may not know is that during the war, the Germans launched no less than five pre-meditated attempts to sink her for the benefit of their own propaganda efforts. After all, what better way to dishearten the British than to send its legendary 'unsinkable' *Titanic* to the bottom? It seems the lady who occupies each of our dreams has always found a way to skirt disaster, however, and the Germans were entirely unsuccessful."

"Jolly good," interrupted Sir Cosmo. He turned to Butt. "I shall have to share with you more details of the events John speaks of, Mr. President. It just so happens that I was somewhat involved in that business."

The President smiled. "Should I have expected any less from the man who purportedly seduced the Mata Hari?" Laughter filled the room again.

"Of course it helped immensely that the British Admiralty protected the most celebrated Queen of the Royal Mail Ships with all the fury it could muster to keep *Titanic's* legend and the spirit of the United Kingdom alive" Astor added.

"Precisely," Sir Cosmo interrupted again, winking at the President.

"After the war," Astor continued, *Titanic* was refit as a luxury ocean liner again at the government's expense, and for the next ten years admirably and profitably serviced a route from Southampton to Rio de Janeiro with a stop in Cherbourg. When the market crashed in '29 however, the whole bottom fell out of the luxury steamer market and *Titanic* was finally retired. By that time she was a tired old lady badly in need of tender loving care. The White Star Line was itself in shaky financial condition and had no choice but to drop her anchors."

"So they did scrap the old girl," the President said, somewhat sadly. Astor noticed that Sir Cosmo was grinning mischievously, but kept silent. There was little that happened on the British Isles that escaped Duff Gordon's notice.

"No, Mr. President, she was not scrapped," Astor said, a noticeable gleam coming to his eyes. "After her last return from Rio to Southampton, a skeleton crew sailed *Titanic* back to Liverpool, where she was sold off after two years of rusting in the harbor."

"Dammit, Astor, get to the point man!" Thayer chided him. "So you mean that she was sold for scrap, then?"

"No, John, that is not what I mean. She was still seaworthy, I assure you. Breaking her was an option, most assuredly, but the White Star Line had a hunch that some eccentric millionaire might be interested in purchasing the old girl for the sake of her reputation," Astor responded. "Or perhaps just for giggles."

"Why that's preposterous," the President said. "Not even someone with all your money would be crazy enough to sink it into a rusting old tub, John. Why, it would cost tens of millions to restore her to her glory."

Astor smiled. "'Restore her to her glory'." How enchanting, that is exactly the phrase I used. Well, Mr. President, perhaps I am crazy and eccentric, and most assuredly I am a millionaire many times over.

"You see, I purchased the remains of *Titanic*. And by the time I have finished with her -- on Labor day by the way -- I will have invested more than $40 million in restoring her to the grace and beauty that we first saw on April 10, 1912. She will have been completely refit to her original condition with the exception of two important modifications: *Titanic* will now carry a Presidential suite and accommodations befitting heads of state, and her First Class Lounge is being converted into a conference room the likes of which will embarrass the *League of Nations* for its technology, comfort and the ideal seating arrangement. Everyone at the table will be equals."

Butt was silent, a look of disbelief coming over his face. He was stunned as Astor produced photographs and drawings of the great liner. The eight by ten inch black and white pictures captured hundreds of dock workers gutting the vessel and refitting her.

"More than four thousand men have labored over *Titanic* nonstop in three shifts spanning twenty four hours a day, seven days a week for these last months. She will be completed by Labor Day, so help me," he said triumphantly.

Archie Butt was in utter awe of what he saw in the pictures.

In the latest series of photographs that Astor had couriered to St. Simons Island just that afternoon, the President saw that *Titanic* had already been removed from dry-dock and was being completed in Liverpool Harbor. Her hull was once again a gleaming coat of black, while her superstructure was brilliant white. The lower sections of the four steam funnels that had made her so unique in shipping design in 1912 had been repainted in their original "White Star Buff" and the upper sections had been given a fresh coat of black paint. There was not a speck of rust to be found on her. A final picture in the bunch caught his eye.

"For heaven's sake. Is that Thomas Andrews?" Butt inquired of Astor.

"The one and only," Astor answered. "And if I dare say, the rebirth of *Titanic* has done wonders for him. I saw him in New York last week to go over the plans for the final time and I almost didn't recognize him. He was radiant. He thanked me, in his words, for giving him 'the opportunity to get it right this time'. It was an exquisitely poignant moment."

The Thayer's were as flabbergasted as the President. Sir Cosmo continued to sit quietly, grinning. Astor laughed when Jack Thayer suggested the millionaire could buy a small country for less money than it was costing him to restore the *Titanic*.

"Yes, Jack, perhaps," he replied with a smile. "And I could even name myself Emperor. But I find owning the *Titanic* so much more romantic."

"Mr. President," Sir Cosmo finally said. "Would you do us all the kindness of putting this poor rich bastard out of his misery? If someone doesn't ask him "Why?" soon, I think the old chap will suffer a stroke."

The President turned to Astor, who was still smiling.

"Well, John... why? What could possibly have possessed you," the President asked.

Astor looked relieved to finally have his moment.

"Mr. President, I am a millionaire so many times over I've lost count. I give to charities, the homeless, hospitals and just about anyone who needs a hand. No bank of mine has ever foreclosed on a man's house just because he's down and out. One would think I am a generous man, but the truth is that my business dealings are virtually always a success and my money makes money." It almost sounded like an apology.

He took a long drink from a snifter of brandy, offering a casual toast to the President as he set the glass down. "However, and I beg you to forgive the cliché, it is true that money does not buy happiness." He reached for the brandy again then put it down again without drinking.

"Madeline left me some years ago, as you know, and my children have grown and gone with little time for their father. I live in a hotel, and the people I call friends are not really my friends in the true sense of the word, but mostly subordinates who like to tell people that they are my friend." He dropped his gaze from the President and his voice went soft.

"In short Mr. President, my life is empty. I have everything, yet I have nothing."

The table grew silent, in respect for the man's humility and unnerving candor. Astor drew long on his cigar, savoring the moment of complete integrity. It occurs so seldom in one's life, he thought.

"John," the President said, reaching over to put his hand on Astor's shoulder, "you give yourself no credit for the countless acts of kindness and generosity that you are responsible for."

"Thank you, Mr. President. But I have to admit that when a man has everything, sometimes he is left to wonder only about his epitaph. I am not satisfied with mine," Astor responded.

He paused for another moment, reflecting on what he had just said.

"On April 15th of this year, you lit a fire in me, Mr. President. You invited me to have a hand in the makings of world peace. As I studied 'Starry Night' after everyone had gone from *Nourmahal*, it struck me that I had finally found meaning in my life again. Could there be a nobler destiny for any man than to have helped to build peace? And I dare say, not just by throwing money at the problem, but by committing mind and heart to the proposition. Frankly, it is something I have never done before in my life."

He took another long draw on the cigar followed by a long taste of his brandy. He looked vibrant for the hour and the drink as if suddenly relieved.

"And what of *Titanic*, John? I appreciate all you have said, but I still do not understand the connection with the lady," Butt said to him softly.

"I'm getting to it, Mr. President. You see while working with Jack Thayer on our meeting on the *Nourmahal*, I was amazed to learn how difficult security can be for a meeting of more than two people that is intended to take place in secrecy. Even as our meeting took place, I worried that we were being watched.

"Then I multiplied the degree of difficulty by a hundred thousand and came to the conclusion that there was absolutely no entirely safe place to hold our summit meeting. No island, no hotel, castle or fort anywhere on the earth could possibly contain the heads of state of seven major nations in absolute concealment and safety."

Butt leaned forward in his chair, in rapt attention. Jack Thayer could smell it coming and he felt a rush of relief.

"Why? Because no matter where we hold the meeting, one man would always have the advantage. Hold it in the United States, advantage Butt. In Paris, advantage Doumer, and so on. Each of the others would be at risk because they will be forced to trust their host. From what I have heard about this fellow Hitler, I would suggest this is a very real dilemma.

"But there was one place, just one place I could think of where every man would be an equal. It is a place where no one individual can have an advantage. If you think back to that long night twenty years ago, one of the things that struck us all was that at the end of the day, all men were equal. For each of us, *Titanic* was the great equalizer requiring us to fend off disaster together and as equals."

Butt was stunned. "You mean to have the summit aboard the *Titanic*," he said, a statement rather than a question, "In the middle of the god dammed North Atlantic." He paused for a long moment, then leaned forward, looking into the millionaire's eyes.

"How brilliant, John. How profoundly brilliant." Astor beamed.

"Jack, have you had any luck yet in identifying a location?" Butt queried his Chief of Staff. He was full of energy again.

Jack Thayer shook his head, still in disbelief. "No Mr. President, for exactly the reason Mr. Astor cited. I was losing hope but didn't want to approach you without a plan. The requirement for secrecy makes it so difficult. And the ego's involved..." he didn't need to finish the sentence. "*Titanic* truly is a safe haven. Each man aboard will have to trust the integrity of the others."

"Worry no more, Jack," Astor said." I will see to every detail. All you need to do, Mr. President, is inform our guests of the location and the date."

"Not so fast, gentlemen," Duff Gordon interrupted. "I suggest we set the date, but leave the location secret until the last possible moment, for obvious reasons."

"I agree," said the President. "When will you be ready, John?"

"*Titanic* will be set to sail the day after Labor Day, Tuesday, the sixth of September," Astor responded. "I suggest we meet in Southampton the day before, greet Prime Minister MacDonald the following morning, then sail to Cherbourg to pick up the remaining participants. I believe Hitler will have fewer problems touching French soil than British."

"Screw the bastard," Sir Cosmo mumbled, draining the last drops from his well used brandy snifter.

"Done," the President said. "I can hardly wait to see her." Astor stood and picked up his glass, raising it.

"To *Titanic*," he toasted. All nodded in agreement.

"May she deliver us from evil once more."

Thirty-Five

Archie Butt awoke from a night filled with memories of *Titanic*. His dreams were unusually lighthearted and fanciful, recollections of the few days he had spent relaxing aboard the great ship. He felt refreshed and oddly at ease for the first time in many months.

The President spent the morning in his library, catching up on legislative readings, then shared lunch with Jack Thayer on the veranda. The cool winds, salt air and aroma of magnolias were most intoxicating, but not enough to turn his thoughts away from the coming election.

"I'm not sure I can build up a head of steam for another run, Jack," the President informed Thayer.

The Chief of Staff was not totally unprepared for the conversation. "I can appreciate your longing for retirement, Mr. President. However, I do hope you will delay making a decision until after the summit. Success of the Van Gogh plan may hinge on your continued leadership."

"I suppose you're right, Jack, it is too soon to make up my mind," Butt answered, knowing Thayer was right.

"On another note, Mr. President, Astor, Sir Cosmo and my father will be departing shortly. I have taken the liberty of inviting two new guests for dinner this evening."

The President looked surprised. "Who are they?"

Thayer hesitated. "Begging your pardon, Mr. President, if you wouldn't mind a little suspense, I'd prefer to answer that question this evening when they arrive."

Butt cocked his eye at the response. It was not like Jack Thayer to play games.

The President returned to his library for several hours before dinner, absolutely enjoying the solitude. Thayer knocked on the door just as the sun was beginning to set and the room had taken on a warm, yellow pallor.

"Excuse me, Mr. President, but your guests have arrived. Perhaps you might care to greet them in the foyer," Thayer said, still not providing an inkling of who they might be. Butt dutifully followed his Chief of Staff to the front entrance of the mansion.

The President caught his breath as Jack stepped aside, revealing Molly Brown framed in the doorway. She looked radiant and more beautiful than he had ever seen her. The President was speechless and felt a heat rising to his face. He hardly noticed that Francis Millet was escorting her.

"Mrs. Brown, Molly, how… He rushed across the marble floor and took her hand. Then, succumbing to his emotions, he embraced her. Millet stood in silence. He thought for a moment that Archie had not noticed his presence.

"Molly, I am overjoyed by your visit. How did you possibly get here? How long are you staying? You must be tired, let me get you something to drink," he rambled, and then caught himself. He stepped back. "My God, you look stunning."

Molly Brown stifled a laugh, slightly heady from the President's excitement upon seeing her. It wasn't easy primping yourself in a train car, even one as sumptuous as that which John Thayer had arranged for her travel. But she had help. Given a few days notice by Jack Thayer, she had been able to speak to her friend, Coco

Chanel who arranged for an entire "Island" wardrobe to be delivered to her door in Denver.

Wearing a long, pale blue, free-flowing rayon dress with a pleated skirt and a moderately low "V" neckline that pronounced her decidedly new figure, there was a softness about Molly that Butt had not noticed before. She wore light makeup which emphasized the natural beauty of her face with a fresh, summer look. Archie Butt was simply dazzled.

"Why thank you, Mr. President," she said softly. Even the tone of her voice seemed to have tempered, Butt thought as he took her in. She seemed to have left the "cowgirl" back in Denver.

Only then did the President notice his other guest. Reluctantly taking his eyes off Molly, he turned to his old friend. "Francis, how good of you to come. What a wonderful surprise," he said, turning to grin at Jack Thayer. "It seems my Chief of Staff feels I need a little uplift in my schedule. Thank you, Jack, this means a lot to me." Thayer beamed with satisfaction.

"How did you ever manage to get here Molly?" he asked her.

"Well it just so happens that this young man's father owns a railroad," Molly said turning to Thayer. "I'll be, I think he turned the world upside down to get me a private car from Denver to Washington, where I met Francis. Then we rode the rest of the way together to West Palm Beach where we sailed to St. Simons Island on that marvelous boat of yours. It could not have been a more relaxing journey and the company was wonderful." She leaned over and took Millet's arm. "He was the perfect gentlemen."

Butt smiled. John Thayer was proving to be a particularly good friend. "How kind of your father, Jack. I must call tomorrow to thank him."

"So noted, Mr. President," Thayer replied dutifully, but secretly pleased that the President thought so highly of his father.

"Well, I'm sure you want to rest for a little while before dinner," the President said. "Knowing Jack, your rooms are all ready, so I will take your leave and spend the time remaining anticipating our dinner together."

Thayer looked at Millet. "Uh, Mr. President, there's been a slight change of plans. Mr. Millet and I have some urgent matters to attend to regarding some art works discovered in Berlin. I'm afraid it will be just you and Mrs. Brown for dinner."

Butt took a long look at Thayer's knowing face, and caught him winking at Millet. "I see, how unfortunate..." he played along. "Or perhaps I should say unfortunate for the two of you and so deliciously fortunate for me." They laughed together as Butt took Molly's hand again and squeezed it.

"Until dinner then, my beautiful lady," the President said. Then he turned and left them, a glorious twinkle in his eyes and with the energetic step of a man twenty years younger. Thayer thought he had never seen the man so happy.

Promptly at eight o'clock, Molly Brown made her entrance unto the veranda as the President waited anxiously to greet her. A white-jacketed servant stood at the ready holding a silver tray with two crystal champagne flutes. Archie had personally inspected the table, set on the north side of the veranda, just in front of a magnificent magnolia tree. A butler had actually caught him polishing a silver fork from the two settings.

When all was to his satisfaction, Butt asked the butler to play some background music from the record player in the library. "Just something to take a bit of the edge off," he said. The Butler smiled, amused that the most

powerful man in the world might be intimidated at
the prospect of dinner with a lady.

For all his preparation, Archie Butt could only stare
as Molly approached him. Chanel had envisioned this
wardrobe as well. Having shed nearly thirty pounds
since the last time she had seen the President in April,
Molly had decided to take advantage of her curvaceous
figure. Her gown was sheer black silk, sleeveless with a
high loose neck and long sash thrown over her shoulder
that reached nearly to the floor. The bodice and hips
were pleated and drew snugly around her newly defined
waist. The effect was elegant, if not a touch bewitching.

With the awkwardness of an adolescent boy on his
first date, the President hurried to meet her, a single
crimson rose in his left hand. He bowed slightly and
took her proffered hand to his lips, holding the pose for a
few extra seconds just to inhale the scent of her light
perfume.

"Why Mrs. Brown... you look astonishingly
beautiful. Simply ravishing. Where have you been all
my life?" he said, handing her the rose.

She blushed, the color coming to her cheeks in a
wave, and sighed.

"Right here waiting, Mr. President," she said softly,
none of the daredevil cowgirl behavior in sight. "You
look pretty handsome yourself." The President looked
down at his white evening dinner jacket, which he had
sent back to his valet for pressing twice, and swung his
hands out to each side, palms up.

"I'd like to say that I dress like this for all my lady
friends, but that would be a gross exaggeration, Mrs.
Brown. The fact is, you are the first woman I've
entertained in a very long time."

Ever the rapier wit, Molly teased him. "My dear boy,
a lady likes a little mystery. I'll just pretend I am the first
woman in your life."

285

The President laughed. "You wouldn't be far off, Molly."

They stood against the railing of the veranda sipping champagne and looking out over the horizon. The sun was setting, casting long rays of orange across the sea, and the rush of the mild surf in the near distance filled the night. The lemony smell of magnolias hung in the cool air, a soft breeze blowing off the ocean.

"Hemingway himself could not have described a more beautiful scene, Molly," the President said to his radiant guest. "He could not have, for he could not have imagined you in it."

Already nearly swept off her feet, Molly complimented her host as they sat for dinner. "Do all men from Georgia have such wonderful manners?" she asked him. He just smiled, grateful that she had noticed his attempts to be the perfect gentlemen. The music of Ira and George Gershwin, a romantic blend of piano and strings, floated to their table.

"Why Mr. President, I'll bet you ordered that up just for us," she said.

"Caught in the act, Mrs. Brown. Somehow tonight I wanted to appeal to your every sense."

"'Every sense', Mr. President?" Now she was toying with him with a sensuality that reawakened in her.

They talked for hours as the night passed and the darkness revealed a full moon and a sky lit with thousands of brilliant stars. The cool ocean breeze was the only thing that kept Archie from perspiring. Molly Brown had that kind of effect on him.

He talked of growing up in Georgia, of his parents and his love of journalism. She spoke of life as a young girl on a ranch, surrounded by brothers and cow hands hardened by what had been an untamed west. She regaled him with stories of busting wild Mustangs and running from even wilder bulls. He was amazed to learn that she had even taken up the art of boxing as a young girl, just so she could keep up with the boys.

Despite their openness, the President never spoke of the war, and the scars he bore from it. In turn, Molly Brown never once brought up her late husband. It was as if they both knew that some things were better left unsaid, no matter how deeply they were felt.

Later, Archie Butt summoned up the nerve to ask her to dance. "Why, I've never had a more charming invitation, Mr. President. Who leads?" Molly answered, just for a moment reverting to form. They danced under the moonlight, holding each other tightly, until early morning.

"Well, Molly, it seems we have danced the night away," he said, looking into her eyes, sad that their evening together was coming to a close. Abruptly she leaned forward and kissed him, softly but with a taste of longing that ran through him to his soul. It lasted only a moment, but the kiss was electric. It served to finally erase the President's last ounce of reserve.

He took Molly's hand, and without a word between them, they left the veranda and climbed the stairs to the President's master suite. He opened the door for her, but she stopped and gently kissed him again, this time a long passionate embrace that put the house of Archie Butt in its proper order.

Inside, he flicked on the lights to find that his bed had been drawn and a single large candle was flickering on a bed stand. The windows were open and the curtains tied back, allowing the moonlight to illuminate the bedroom with a soft silvery glow. Molly stepped back quickly and turned off the lights. "It's just perfect without them, Mr. President," she said and embraced him again. He pushed her lightly away from him.

"My God, Molly, I hardly think this the time to refer to me as 'Mr. President' for Christ's sakes," he said, a bit bewildered. "I would be indebted if you would simply call me 'Archie'. In fact it will bring me fond memories just to hear it come from your lips."

She leaned forward again and kissed him without responding. He embraced her with arms that threatened to suffocate her. She pulled back. "Archie", she whispered. "Careful, I break." They laughed together, holding each other as if afraid to let go. She felt his hands at the back of her dress, fumbling with the hidden zipper. After a few minutes and sensing his embarrassment, she said softly, "Let me do it." In a moment, the dress was at her feet along with her undergarments.

Archie sucked in his breath at the site of her, shamelessly naked in front of him. "My God, Molly," he whispered, "you are the most beautiful woman these tired eyes have ever seen." He couldn't say more. The most powerful man in the world felt like an adolescent boy. He reached out and drew her close to him again, reveling in the softness of her body.

"There's nothing tired about you, Archie," she said, opening his belt buckle and fondling him as he grew hard in her hand. "Why am I not surprised?" she said, nuzzling against his neck.

All inhibitions gone, he stepped out of his pants, scooped her off her feet and carried her to the bed. He cupped her breasts and kissed her with a passion he thought had long since died, and could feel her moving beneath him. He stopped.

"Molly, it's been a very, very long time," he said, almost embarrassed.

She smiled and brushed his thinning hair off his forehead.

"Tell me about it," she replied. For several long moments they couldn't stop laughing, half from the humor of it all, half from their relief at allowing the feelings that had been smoldering so long to finally flame.

She held his face in her hands. "You know, I don't care if you are the most powerful man in the world, 'Mr. President'. All you are to me, at this moment, is the man I have loved silently for twenty years. So you god dammed well better convince me that the wait was worth it."

She paused.
"Right now!"

Thirty-Six

Several days later, candles were also burning into the night in a room in Berlin, but for decidedly less romantic reasons.

"Finally!" Adolph Hitler, Chancellor of the Third Reich screamed as the door to his office suddenly burst open and Rear Admiral Conrad Patzig, head of the Abwehr military intelligence agency entered. The naval officer was carrying a briefcase that was handcuffed to his left wrist. It was four o'clock in the morning.

"Heil Hitler," Patzig saluted in the awkward, right arm extended with palm forward address that the new Chancellor had instituted. "Forgive me, I have been collecting some last minute information for our discussion." Patzig had been forewarned that Hitler had been frantically pacing his office for hours awaiting the intelligence chief's arrival and he feared the worst.

"I will not have this, do you understand", Hitler screamed in Patzig's face, waving a fist in front of him. "When I call for you it is not an invitation, it is a command!"

There was no point in arguing, yet Patzig tried to explain. "Yes, Herr Chancellor, it will not happen again. Unfortunately, I did not expect our meeting to occur until later this afternoon as I requested."

Hitler's patience had been exhausted and he would not accept an excuse of any kind.

"I cannot wait until this afternoon, Patzig, can't you understand this? There is too much at stake. Now what have you learned? Hurry, speak to me."

Hitler sat at his giant conference table leaving the intelligence chief to stand. "Herr Chancellor, late yesterday our network in the United States was able to share with us the location of the American President's 'summit', as it is referred to." Hitler was silent. "This has not been announced by the Americans yet. They are planning on waiting until the last possible moment to advise you of the location and schedule."

Surprised by Hitler's patience, Patzig continued. "I believe you know that the heads of state of England, France, Spain, Italy and Russia have already agreed to attend." Hitler eyes were wild as he took in the information but said nothing. "The meeting will take place beginning on the sixth of September. All participants are to gather at Cherbourg, France in the early evening."

Hitler finally exploded and lunged at Patzig. He grabbed the lapels of the Admiral's uniform and shook him. "France?" he screamed. "The madmen expect me to attend a meeting of this magnitude on French soil? Are they insane?" Patzig grimly hid emotion from his face at Hitler's use of the word 'insane". The man was behaving like a rabid dog, he thought.

"No, Herr Chancellor. Please allow me to explain," Patzig responded. "The meeting will be held in the North Atlantic Ocean off the coast of New Foundland. On a ship."

Hitler's eyes narrowed. "A ship? Go on, quickly."

"The American Astor..."

"The playboy?"

"Yes, Herr Chancellor, John Jacob Astor," he replied trying to pacify the enraged Chancellor. "It seems the millionaire has purchased the remains of the *RMS*

Titanic, a luxury steamship he sailed with President
Butt in 1912 that struck an iceberg on its maiden voyage
and nearly foundered in the North Atlantic. He has had
the vessel completely rehabilitated and restored, and the
Americans plan to use it as the venue for your talks."

Hitler sat in silence, pondering this latest news. "A
boat," he finally said, appearing to calm down. "The
American president is an interesting character, very
imaginative. I wonder how this *Titanic* figures into his
plans."

"Interestingly enough, Herr Chancellor, we have also
discovered that all members of the Van Gogh are
survivors of the *Titanic's* brush with disaster."

Hitler laughed in ridicule. "So they are romantics
enjoying a reunion," he said sarcastically. "How utterly
adolescent."

Patzig was silent. The Chancellor did not like to be
corrected. But it was necessary.

"Perhaps, Herr Chancellor," Patzig replied, "but our
contact has informed us that the American President
made the decision to use *Titanic* after reasoning it would
be the most private and secure environment possible. He
desires this to be a meeting of equals."

The Chancellor erupted again.

"Equals? The man dares to compare the master race
with the scum of Europe? The pigs have trampled
Germany enough. It is time to turn the tables, Patzig, do
you understand?" His hands shook as he spoke and the
Chancellor was almost blind with rage again. Patzig sat
silently, at once embarrassed by the performance and
terrified of the man.

Hitler sat down at the table again, placing his hands
in front of him, folded as if in prayer. He stared ahead in
absolute silence, motionless, as if in a trance. Patzig
dared not interrupt.

Finally, after long minutes of agonizing stillness, Hitler turned to his intelligence chief again.

"I assume you have developed a plan, let us say, to imbalance the equality?"

"Yes, Herr Chancellor. I have pledged never to hand you a problem without a solution," Patzig replied.

"This is true, Herr Patzig, you have not failed me yet. But I need not tell you the consequence of failure in this matter. If the American is successful, it could cause the downfall of the Reich. And we cannot let that happen."

Patzig swallowed hard. He didn't fear for his own life, having already recognized that he was in a trap set by his own blind desire for recognition and power. He was resigned to his fate, knowing that he would ultimately be a victim of the Reich. He did not fear for himself but agonized over the safety of his Helga and their three children. If they only knew what a monster he was dealing with. Patzig shook off the thought.

"Yes, Herr Chancellor, I have a plan, and I will not fail you."

"Very well, take me through it and exclude no details. I want to hear it all."

For the next hour, the two men, one sane and trapped, the other quite insane but free to wreak havoc with the most powerful military on the continent, talked through a scheme. If successful, it would result in the Chancellor's seizing absolute power over Europe. In the process, Germany would become an instant and deadly threat to the United States of America. While they talked, Hitler's mind raced with visions of conquest, with him as a Napoleonic emperor leading Germany to her rightful place as the most powerful nation on Earth.

All that stood between him and world dominance was the murder of the leaders of Europe – and the President of the United States.

And as Patzig explained, it was all quite possible.

"Then you will leave for Moscow immediately?" Hitler asked as Patzig concluded.

"Yes, Herr Chancellor. I am certain Stalin will receive me following your message," the intelligence chief responded.

"And I will dispatch Goebbels to Rome, immediately. Mussolini will offer no resistance," Hitler added.

As Patzig collected his documents from the table, his hands were shaking. He had successfully hidden his real sentiments from the madman. Hitler was insane, he was sure of it. He was equally confident that the American President genuinely wanted peace. A sudden chill went down the length of his spine at the supreme irony.

To protect his wife and children, he had become the architect of the murder of the only man who might save Germany from Hitler's madness.

Thirty-Eight

Under cover of darkness, President Archibald Butt boarded the heavy cruiser *USS Augusta* at the mouth of the Chesapeake Bay on the moonless night of September 1, 1932 with Jack Thayer and eleven of the thirteen Apostles. John Jacob Astor and Thomas Andrews were awaiting them in Southampton.

The President's voyage was classified top secret and his public schedule had been virtually erased. Jack Thayer told the press that for the next ten days, the President would be secluded in the Oval Office working intensely in preparation for the upcoming fall congressional session. In truth, four days from now he would be in Southampton for the long awaited European summit.

The President and his party were greeted by the *Augusta*'s five star fleet Admiral, Chester W. Nimitz, who was the commander of the new ninety-five ton Northampton Class heavy cruiser. Bristling with heavy guns and anti-aircraft weapons, she was the newest pride of the United States Navy and had been built with special provisions to serve as a Presidential Flagship. She had a crew compliment of seven hundred thirty-five officers and enlisted men.

Recalled seven days prior from the West Coast, *Augusta* had remained anchored out of view of the Delaware coast while awaiting the President and his guests who arrived via the *USS Sequoia*. Nimitz had hosted some high-powered visitors on his ship before, but no one quite like this. Along with the President were the world's most wealthy and influential private citizens. He shook his head at the list of names, and could only guess as to the kind of mission that would bring them together aboard his ship.

During the long journey across the North Atlantic, with the *Augusta* averaging nearly thirty knots across calm seas, Van Gogh met several times to polish their proposals and to ensure no details had been left unattended. The mood was somber and intense among the group as they worked, and the President was pleased to see that all were taking on the challenge with seriousness and purpose. There was no need to remind them of the gravity of their mission.

For their part, Molly and the President appeared before them not as lovers, but as two people who had grown remarkably close. Having been raised in the art of social intrigue and gossip, their friends could not help but breathe a taste of scandal into every whispered conversation, but they did so with pleasure at the knowledge that a man and woman whom they deeply respected had found each other at long last. Molly and Archie did not flaunt their relationship, but didn't attempt to hide it either. They were simply too long in years and too happy to care what others thought.

Jack Thayer had seen to it that the ship had been swept clean in search of eavesdropping equipment, a concept that defied logic for her commander.

"Need I remind you that this is a US Navy flagship, Mr. Thayer? I hardly think it necessary to conduct such an effort on any ship under my command," Admiral Nimitz remarked, somewhat put off.

"I apologize, Admiral, but we must be absolutely certain," Thayer had responded. A similar effort in the White House had uncovered listening devices in the Oval Office -- in the Presidential Seal embossed on the ceiling -

- in Thayer's own office and in the Cabinet room. The discovery had shocked the President, who had even considered postponing the summit until they could analyze the potential damage done. The President had finally been insistent that the summit proceed as planned.

"As Molly would say," the President remarked, "come hell or high water, Jack, we're going ahead. It's just too god dammed important to be delayed by some insecure idiot. Let's do it."

The *Augusta* pulled within five miles of Southampton Harbor on the evening of the fourth of September and dropped anchor for the night. At three in the morning, a launch bearing no visible military insignia pulled up to the cruiser and picked up the President's party and two Secret Service Agents. By the rules of the game, each of the heads of state was allowed to travel with a single advisor and two security men. The Apostles were alone. The playing field would be level on every account.

The sun was still hidden behind the horizon as the launch came within view of the born-again *RMS Titanic*. The ship was resting at Berth number 44 just as she had the morning Archie Butt and the members of Van Gogh boarded her for the great vessel's maiden voyage across the Atlantic. As the launch pulled closer, the President sucked in his breath at sight of the remarkable steamer, and he heard a collective gasp from his party.

As stately and elegant as she had appeared more than twenty years before with her distinctive four funnel silhouette, *Titanic* waited for them again. She was even more beautiful than they could remember. It was if they were taking a step back in time -- a time when life for each of them had been carefree and fanciful and they had looked upon the *Titanic's* opulence as more of an entitlement than a novelty. She held their gaze for nearly an hour as they approached. Not a word transpired among them, each lost in memories that held little fondness.

The irony struck them all. Here was the vessel that had nearly killed them yet which now represented the cathedral from which they hoped to hammer out an agreement that would keep the world safe from war. Once they had all been blinded by power, success and achievement, and the world had been their playground. Now, their eyes were open, more mature, compassionate and enlightened, and they were wise enough to know that the world might be their undoing.

Astor and Andrews met Butt and the party as the launch docked.

The President shook Astor's hand and searched for words. "My God, gentlemen, you have done it. Words cannot express how I feel at this moment. I am torn with memories..."

"I know well the emotions you are feeling, Mr. President," Thomas Andrews replied. "It took me some weeks to get over seeing her again. It was like I was trying to drag a ghost back into the real world. But I assure you, there are no more ghosts aboard her than when we all first met. You will find only the sweet fragrance of an elegant lady who has served admirably despite the failures of men.

"Having had a hand in bringing her back to life, I hope *Titanic* will now forgive me for my own arrogance so many years ago."

The President would not have it. "Thomas, if not for you on that long night, none of us would be standing here, it is that simple. Now let that demon rest once and for all," the President said, gripping the naval architects hand.

Astor turned to a tall man standing directly behind him. "Mr. President, please allow me to introduce Mr. Phillip Colvin of my firm. He is the man directly responsible for this amazing recovery. I gave him less than five months to accomplish this miracle, and by God he has not failed us. Let us just say that I think of Phillip Colvin in the same regard as you do Jack Thayer."

Butt stuck out his hand and shook Colvin's firmly. "Mr. Colvin, I don't know if you realize it but your boss just gave you the highest compliment possible. I want to personally thank you from the bottom of my heart for what you have done to breathe life back into the *Titanic*. "

"Thank you, Mr. President," Colvin responded, exhausted but relieved that once again he had not failed his mentor. The rest was just icing on the cupcake. "Let us just say it was a difficult process made simpler by my boss' outspoken – and let us just say, 'constant' – encouragement," he added in sarcastic jest, bringing a laugh from the President.

As they walked the boarding plank up to *Titanic*'s Well Deck, a face familiar yet far more matured greeted them. It was William Murdoch, now retired Commandant of the White Star Line whom Astor had dragged from his estate in Moorhead to once again take the helm of *Titanic*.

"Mr. Murdoch," Butt said, "or should that be Commandant Murdoch? You are forever ingrained in my memory as the First Officer of this great vessel who risked his life that all might live to sail another day."

Murdoch dropped his gaze, embarrassed. His own failures on that fateful night were still never far from his thoughts. "Begging the President's pardon, but if you ask me to take a similar dip on this cruise, I believe I shall have to decline. The old flippers don't work as well these days, Mr. President."

"We shall not count on you to swim for us Commandant, just steer us to safety. Your cargo on this voyage is quite important."

"As it is every voyage, Mr. President," smiling as he corrected Butt. "As to steering her course, you can count on it," Murdoch replied, impishly. "I've made it a habit never to make the same mistake twice." The two men laughed somewhat nervously. Archie had not intended to open old wounds. He put his hand on Murdoch's shoulder, grasping it.

"I have complete faith in you Commandant, just as I did in the First Officer who sailed this magnificent vessel twenty years ago."

"You are still an exceedingly generous man," Murdoch complimented the President. "I will do my best to ensure that your faith in me is not ill placed."

Astor moved them to the new Presidential Suite that Andrews had designed specifically for Butt. It was extraordinary, not by its lavishness, but rather in the environment the rooms created.

Unlike the dark walnut and mahogany fittings and Persian carpets adorning other First Class accommodations aboard ship, the large Presidential suite of rooms was decorated in fine grained, bleached ash paneling with a deep, navy blue woolen carpeting. The Presidential seal was embroidered in the rug at the center of the sitting room. It had large expanses of glass on both the starboard and port sides, allowing copious amounts of natural light to fill the room right up until sunset. The ambience reeked of confidence and strength.

At midmorning, Prime Minister Ramsay MacDonald arrived in a Southampton police car. He walked up the gangplank quickly and was met by Murdoch who escorted him to the President's suite.

"Ramsay, my old friend," the President greeted him with open arms, "why I almost didn't recognize you."

"Yes, dear chap, I did miss the Rolls, but for the sake of success, the police car did just fine. I assume we were not noticed." Jack Thayer arrived shortly after to confirm it.

"Actually, that was rather fun," MacDonald mused. "Having to be spot on all the time in public does get terribly boring, wouldn't you agree , Archie?

"Whole heartedly," Butt agreed. "All the constant attention does make the heart grow fonder at the thought of retirement."

MacDonald and Butt passed pleasantries on the balcony adjoining the President's suite, enjoying a cigar and comparing the plight of the Liverpool Soccer Club with the Washington Senators. Only as MacDonald took his leave did business come up.

"Archie, I'm not quite certain what you have in store," MacDonald said, "but I know you well enough to believe that whatever it is will be good for us all. Godspeed, my friend, and God bless your intervention. It has long been desired. I believe this will be your finest hour, my friend."

"With your support, Prime Minister, I assure you our discussions will be kindly remembered by the writers of history," Butt replied, flattered by the PM's kind words.

At noon, the *Titanic* set sail for Cherbourg, with only a small crowd on hand to see her go. Her arrival in Southampton four days prior had sparked the jubilant interest of thousands of spectators, some of whom had sailed on her abbreviated maiden voyage, others whose fathers and grandfathers had worked the docks supporting her. The crowds had dwindled since, and Colvin had arranged for a press release indicating that the ship would be leaving Southampton for several days of sea trials and would return later in the week. Thankfully, the announcement stirred very little interest and only a few hundred people were on hand to see *Titanic* leave her berth.

By six o'clock, as the afternoon sun was beginning to fall, *Titanic* arrived off the coast of Cherbourg, France to greet the remainder of her urgently important passengers. The vessel was anchored well off shore. Five separate launches, all stripped of insignia and operated by the United States Navy, visited the *Titanic* in quick succession, delivering the heads of state of France, Spain, Italy, Russia, and finally Germany. Each launch, with the exception of Stalin's, carried exactly four passengers, as agreed. Watching the proceedings, Archie Butt silently prayed that nothing trivial would occur that might incense the ego of one of Europe's leaders.

Far from the prying eyes of news reporters, Butt personally greeted each of the envoys, doing his best to meet them with lighthearted cordiality and humility. He had previously been in the company of French President Paul Doumer and President Niceto Alcalá-Zamora of Spain, and had worked with each in his prior capacity as Secretary of State under Wilson. But he had not had the pleasure of meeting the Italian dictator, Benito Mussolini, Joseph Stalin of Russia or Hitler. The latter weighed heavily on his mind.

Thayer had timed each of the launches to arrive in such a manner as to board one party, clear the decks and greet the next. They agreed that the first gathering of the leaders should be more formally arranged, a sort of rehearsed "ice breaker".

The President was at the top of his form as host, having enjoyed extensive briefings by operatives in the State Department who were exceedingly knowledgeable of each man as well as their native cultures. He first welcomed Paul Doumer with open arms, embracing the French President as the old friend and trusted colleague that he was. For a few moments the two traded innocent banter of times in Washington and Paris, ending with a promise to swap stories of their adventures as younger men in France and America.

The President exchanged similar pleasantries with Niceto Alcalá-Zamora of Spain, as always a perfect gentleman whom Archie wished he had had the opportunity to know better. Stalin stepped onto *Titanic's* deck with an unexpectedly warm, almost mischievous grin on his face, greeting the President with a bear hug. The Russian leader was a big man, with hands the size of small canned hams, and he sported an enormous mustache that helped to hide his badly scarred face, the result of smallpox as a boy. In his strong Georgian accent, Stalin spoke through an interpreter who accompanied him.

"Mister President, I have long anticipated the grasp of your hand in friendship. You should know that I am an admirer," Joseph Stalin began. "I have been most impressed by your compassion for the American worker." Butt winced at the irony of Stalin's words, recalling the State Department report that held him responsible for the deaths of millions of innocent Russians as he reshaped the Soviet Union into his vision of an industrial and agricultural juggernaut. To oppose Stalin – indeed, to even think about opposing Stalin -- was cause enough for the dictator to employ his favorite tactic for compliance: cold blooded murder at the hands of the assassins who surrounded him.

On this evening, however, Stalin's dark side was well hidden. Surprisingly, he had elected to travel without personal bodyguards. "There are few men in the world that I trust, Mr. President. I sense from meeting you that you may be one of them," Stalin said. The dictator wore a business suit instead of his customary military garb. From appearance sake at least, the Russian dictator seemed ready to impress with his openness to whatever the President might propose.

Mussolini was an entirely unknown entity to the President except for what he had learned from the State Department and several meetings with the US Ambassador to Italy, John W. Garrett. The Secretary had lived in Rome for more than four years and had personally witnessed the rise of the Black Shirt Fascist government. While the others had boarded the *Titanic* without the pomp and circumstance they were accustomed to, "Il Duce" (the leader) made certain his arrival was noticed.

Preceding the dictator up the boarding stairs was a young dark skinned soldier, walking backwards, who fanned a plume of several gigantic ostrich feathers over the Italian's head. Wearing his full military dress, festooned with ribbons of medals and a brilliant red sash across his chest, Mussolini's arrival had a circus air to it, and the dictator proved particularly adept at playing the clown.

As he stepped aboard *Titanic*, the rotund, self proclaimed emperor of Italy threw open his arms and hugged the President like a long lost relative, then kissed him on both cheeks. Butt saw a mischievousness in Mussolini's eyes that was on the surface quite endearing. The warmth of the dictator's introduction suggested a kindness that the President knew was contradictory to his merciless rule of Italy. Thayer, observing the political charade, saw that Butt was not amused, perhaps because he had already endured Stalin's insincerity. The Chief of Staff moved quickly to escort "Il Duce" to his quarters, ducking slightly as the soldier with the feathers continued to fan the dictator.

Fittingly, the last to board was Hitler himself. Butt watched as the German dictator was helped out of the launch and made his way slowly up the boarding stairs, hesitating several times to look up at the *Titanic*'s grand superstructure.

"Herr Chancellor, finally the time has come for us to meet," Butt said in near perfect German, which he had been practicing for weeks. "It is destiny that has brought us here, and I look forward to forging new relations between our two countries."

Wearing his trademark light brown dress military uniform adorned with an Iron Cross and a black and red Nazi Party insignia armband, Hitler looked at his host sternly. Not the faintest glimmer of a smile had yet come to his lips.

"Yes, Mr. President," he replied in English, surprising Butt with his knowledge of the language, "it is good to finally meet you as well." He extended his hand in courtesy and Butt took it, shaking it vigorously. The handshake was surprisingly limp.

"As to destiny," Hitler continued, "I had hoped to have the opportunity one day - in private -- to discuss how we might go about preserving the peace between our countries on a more equitable basis. It seems we will not have that opportunity given the nature of these talks."

The President didn't flinch at the obvious upbraid.

"Herr Chancellor, the road to peace and the assumption of equality for the German nation - which I wholeheartedly, but conditionally support - may only come through the mutual agreement and dedication to honesty of the leaders of the nations represented aboard the *Titanic*," he said. "I assure you, our objectives are quite similar in that regard."

Hitler's eyes grew noticeably wide as the President stood his ground, refusing to be intimidated by the dictator who seemed already to be living up to his reputation. His face had turned red.

"We shall see, Mr. President," he said. "We shall see." He turned without another word and walked away followed by two uniformed military officers and a short, gaunt and physically frail appearing man who wore a long black leather trench coat despite the warmth of late summer. The President would learn that evening that the small man in the coat was Dr. Joseph Paul Goebbels, Reich Minister of Public Enlightenment and Propaganda.

Butt watched as Thayer led the Germans to their quarters. Slightly ashen, he turned to Millet who he thought was standing behind him.

"Well, that certainly lived up to its billing," the President said, but Millet had vanished.

Thirty-Nine

Aboard the *USS Augusta*, Admiral Nimitz fretted over the responsibility of protecting *Titanic* and was deeply troubled.

Under the rules set forth by the President, personal security aboard the *Titanic* was limited to no more than two men. Consequently, there were only two Secret Service Agents accompanying the American Commander in Chief. Jack Thayer and the members of Van Gogh were not allowed security details. The ships crew compliment had been slashed to forty, including Captain Murdoch and his officers, so most of the personnel working the voyage were stewards or wait staff. Deep in *Titanic's* bowels, another fifty firemen and engineers were working her furnaces and engines. Only a single communications officer was on board, a Navy man, but radio transmissions were to be kept to an absolute minimum. In fact, no radio transmissions – either in or out – were to be allowed once the meeting actually began, with one exception.

Titanic would radio *Augusta* every thirty minutes that all was well. In the event there was no transmission, the *Augusta* would immediately come to *Titanic's* assistance. The President was determined that this match would be played out by equally weighted teams, and no one man would have a decided advantage, save for his personal intellect and passion for peace.

But it wasn't the security on board the *Titanic* that had Nimitz worried. It was securing the area around the vessel that concerned him.

The President had decreed that Nimitz was to cordon off the waters in a twenty mile quadrangle around *Titanic*. No commercial or naval vessel were to be permitted inside the area no matter what flag they flew. Four US Navy destroyers were stationed at each corner of the quadrangle and would cruise the outside perimeter continuously. Nimitz, in his flagship would "freelance" the zone, moving quickly to intercept any indication of penetration by a vessel into the guarded area.

When Thayer outlined the President's wishes to the Admiral, he sat back in his chair proud of himself for having had a hand in the plan. Nimitz wasted no time in debunking it.

"Mr. Thayer," Nimitz said, barely containing himself, "what you have given me is the opportunity to protect the lives of the President of the god dammed United States and the heads of state of six of the world's largest military powers with four god dammed tin cans and a heavy cruiser in the middle of the frigging North Atlantic Ocean."

Thayer winced.

"Has it occurred to you or the President that a twenty mile 'no sail' zone amounts to four hundred square miles of ocean? I've got a better chance of finding a golf ball in a blizzard than I do in keeping that zone clear."

Thayer winced. No matter how hard he tried to explain the delicacy of the situation and the President's conviction that no further security was required, Nimitz refused to waver from his strenuous objection to the plan.

"I will follow the orders of my Commander in Chief," Mr. Thayer, and I will accept full responsibility for their execution. But between you and me son," the hard nosed sea veteran summarized, "you better god dammed well hope that he's right."

The plan went into effect two days before *Titanic* left Cherbourg. Nimitz's *Augusta* followed the great ocean liner from a distance of twenty miles, well out of view of any of its passengers. The Navy destroyers *USS Little*, *USS Sigourney*, *USS Gregory* and *USS Dyer* were waiting at their assigned coordinates, each at a spot twenty miles from *Titanic*'s intended arrival position: 41° 46' N, 50° 14' W, the exact location from which she sent out her first distress call at 11:40 p.m., April 14, 1912.

The precise location of their meeting had come at the suggestion of William Stead.

"That is where God intervened in our lives so that we might find real reason to be," he had written to the President. "If there is a spot on this earth from which to join our hands in the pursuit of peace, it is where *Titanic* brought us together."

Once at the desired location, Butt intended to entertain two days of discussions. Assuming that they had reached agreement by the end of the second day, the plan was for *Titanic* to make full steam for Cape Race, Newfoundland, escorted by the *USS Augusta*, where waiting naval ships from each of the countries represented would retrieve their leaders and head for home. At an agreed upon date within the following week, Butt and each of the heads of state would convene a press conference exposing the secret meeting and announcing the agreements they had reached.

As the sun finally set on the great liner, *Titanic* hoisted her anchors and steamed away from the French Coast towards the open ocean and New York City. Two decades before, her passenger manifest had included some of the world's most wealthy and influential people. As she left Cherbourg on this September evening, she carried the most important people in the world ever assembled in one place, let alone on an ocean going luxury steam liner.

The hyperactive Hitler, finding it impossible to remain in his cabin before dinner, took a stroll with his small entourage down the Promenade Deck to the bow. He turned and looked up at the main mast, squinting his eyes against the glare of the setting sun to see what flag *Titanic* was flying. He would be furious if it was the Stars and Stripes, after all the secrecy and boastful talk of equality.

Instead, he was quite surprised to see a large flag, flying from the very top of the main mast that seemed full of color but had no national markings that he could identify. He turned to Goebbels, always by his side like a small lap dog.

"Herr Goebbels, can you make out what flag that it is? I do not recognize it," Hitler said.

Goebbels pulled a monocle out of his jacket pocket and looked up. "It does not appear to be national flag, Herr Chancellor, it seems to be an inscription of some sort." He looked closer.

"I have it," he finally said, "but I do not understand the phrase. It reads:

'Come hell or high water'."

Forty

Thayer, Millet and the President met for a late brandy after dinner that evening to compare notes.

Miraculously, given the personalities involved, it seemed to have gone off without a hitch. Butt was somewhat disappointed by the obvious lack of interchange between his guests, who tended to converse with the members of Van Gogh. Indeed, John Jacob Astor, Benjamin Guggenheim and Margaret Brown held court with the heads of Great Britain, France and Spain. Mussolini, Hitler and Stalin had a brief informal conversation, or at least from appearances, as close to informal as possible. George Widener, of all people, seemed to attract the personal interest of "Il Duce", as did William Carter who pressed the dictator on the future of Fiat, the Italian national automotive manufacturer. But the President wrote off their animated conversations as the byproduct of the natural attraction between three such ebullient characters.

For his part, the President did his best to wander the room, making sure to spend time with each of the heads of state. Stalin was perhaps the hit of the party, regaling his audience time and again with bad Russian jokes, dutifully translated by his aid. "Uncle Joe" was certainly displaying none of the characteristics that had earned him the reputation as a butcher.

On the contrary, Hitler remained sullen, having little to say to anyone except Goebbels, with whom he spent most of the evening. He spoke cursorily to the President who was completely befuddled by the man, despite the repeated warnings of John Thayer, Secretary Simpson and other members of the State Department who had spent considerable time with the members of Hitler's hand-picked inner circle.

Following dinner, the President welcomed them again briefly and informed the group that their discussions would begin in earnest the following evening. *Titanic*, with three new huge Rolls Royce engines in her belly, was capable of making thirty knots now. With no concerns for ice being so late in the summer, Commander Murdoch steamed full speed ahead to her destination.

"I suspected the early going would be difficult," said the President in a strategy session with his closest advisors at the end of the evening. Unlike the group that joined the President – John Astor, Sir Cosmo Duff Gordon, John Thayer, Francis Millet and his Chief of Staff, there was little trust among the Europeans heads of state.

"These men are not comfortable together, and there are varying degrees of intimidation by our two friends from Germany and Russia," Duff Gordon observed. "'Il Duce' almost fawns over Hitler. I believe the Italian truly fears the man. It is almost embarrassing."

"It will be interesting to watch them tomorrow, Mr. President," Jack Thayer said. "We have intentionally not scheduled anything for the entire day, which should allow our guests to get their sea legs and perhaps loosen up a bit."

The President turned to Francis Millet, who had been strangely quiet all evening.

"Any observations, old friend?"

"No, nothing worth listening to," Millet responded, staring into his snifter, now nearly empty. "I am tired, gentlemen, I hope taking my leave will not disturb your conversation."

As Millet closed the door behind him, Thayer mentioned to the President that Millet had been acting strangely of late. "Nonsense, Jack, I'm sure it's the same problem most of us are having these days. We're running out of gas."

Thayer laughed. "You sound like my father, Mr. President. But by all means, whatever you do, keep your motor running.

"The finish line is within site."

Forty-One

On a parallel course fifteen nautical miles ahead of
Titanic, a killing machine drove steadily ahead at
seventeen knots, desperate to remain hidden in the black,
open ocean. Heavy cloud cover, obliterating any possible
reflection from the moon kept the six hundred forty ton
beast veiled from eyes that were just as desperately
looking for her. Even fully surfaced, she was virtually
impossible to detect from as close as a mile away.

The German U-47 Unterseeboot rode high on the
surface, completely blacked out, all running lights
extinguished. Only a dim red glow emanated from the
open hatch of the conning tower, nearly impossible to see
from any distance, but casting the two men training
binoculars over the horizon in a ghoulish blush. Only the
wash from her twin propellers gave her away, as the
calm seas allowed the submarine to knife ahead, nearly
invisible. This time was critical as they would need to
travel on the surface as long and as far as possible to
keep her batteries charged for when they would need to
submerge and become completely invisible.

Korvettenkapitän Günther Prien put the binoculars
to his eyes again and slowly turned a full 360 degrees,
searching for any telltale signs of another ship. Any ship.
To be discovered now would doom the U-47's mission.
What mission that might be was still a mystery to the
young Lieutenant Commander, whose instructions were
to proceed to a precise location in the middle of the
North Atlantic and only then to open his sealed orders

for further instructions. The only thing he knew was that he was to sail with the objective of remaining completely hidden and to remain submerged at his destination.

Günther Prien worried this. The location he was seeking was directly in the path of the large commercial ships sailing between Europe and the United States. Maintaining the U-47's invisibility could be a nightmare.

He could only guess at the true intention of his mission, and was eager to open his orders. Prien knew only that before he left the German Submarine Base in Bremen yesterday morning, he had been instructed to load his four forward torpedo tubes and a full compliment of eleven more torpedoes had been brought aboard the three hundred thirty foot long submarine. He had never sailed so fully armed and could not imagine why he would need to be. In the back of his mind was a constant nagging. We are not at war, he thought to himself. Are we to start one?

Finally satisfied that their invisibility had not been jeopardized, Prien instructed his accompanying First Officer to leave the conning tower and he quickly followed. The hatch was dogged tight and Prien felt relieved to be back on the Bridge where he was completely in charge. It was a small, lethal world where he was an absolute dictator. The twenty-four men aboard would respond to any order he gave without a second's hesitation. It was dark inside, at one moment brutally hot and humid, the next icily cold, and reeked of diesel oil, damp steel, perspiration and human body odor. It was Prien's favorite place in the world.

The Lieutenant Commander calmly gave the order to submerge and gave his helmsman instructions.

"Make her depth one fifty. Slow speed ahead, no more than five knots." he said. "We are well ahead of schedule. Let us reserve our batteries."

Turning to his First Officer, he suggested that the twenty-two year old junior grade lieutenant get some sleep. "I am assuming things may get exciting after we arrive at our destination. Have all hands that can be spared get some rack time as well." The junior officer turned and began to leave the Bridge without a word. Prein called to him.

"Heinrich, also make sure that the commando's get some rest. I have no idea why they are aboard my ship, but I am sure they will be needed eventually."

Why a team of highly trained special forces commando's had been brought aboard, without warning, just before they departed Bremen was still a mystery to the submarine commander nearly thirty-six hours later. The captain in charge of the commandos had entered his small cabin just before they left port, and had not emerged yet. Prien's curiosity was peaked, but his training restrained him from pursuing any answers – at least for the moment. Until then, his only job was to get his boat to the assigned position: "41° 46' N, 50° 14' W."

Forty-Two

The knock on the door came at three in the morning. Jack Thayer had turned in less than an hour before and was just settling into a deep sleep. It took him several minutes to understand the source of what had become a pounding irritation, actually a knock at his door. Several more minutes passed before he cleared his head enough to get out of bed and open the door. Ship's Communications Operator Raymond Flagler, a US Navy Ensign in street clothing was standing in the hallway, with a note in his hand.

"Awfully sorry to disturb you sir," Flagler said, "but I've just received an urgent message for you from Washington. A Mr. Maldonia is kicking up a hell of a fuss that he needs to speak with you immediately. Says it's a matter of national security."

Thayer yawned in the wireless operators face, rubbing his own to get the blood moving. "Doesn't anyone in that god dammed city ever sleep?" he said.

Flagler ignored the question. "I got a Morse message from the shore station in West Sayville, New York to call in by radio telephone. I did, and the shore station patched me through to a public switched telephone network and in a matter of minutes, Maldonia was on the line. I don't know who he is or what he's calling about but he insists on speaking to you or the President directly. Whoever he is, he certainly knows his way around radiotelephony."

"Yah, I know the guy," Thayer said. "And you don't want to know what he knows about telephones."

The President's Chief of Staff threw on a robe and followed Flagler to the radio room, just off the Bridge. The Ensign placed a set of earphones over his head and spoke into a large tabletop microphone. "Mr. Maldonia?" he asked and got a reply. "Just a moment sir, I have Mr. Thayer for you." Flagler placed the headset over Thayer's ears, adjusted the microphone and showed him how to use it. Then he left the room, closing the door behind him securely.

Thayer keyed the microphone. "This is Jack Thayer."

"Jack, it's good that I reached you," a voice crackled into his headphones. "I'm sorry about the hour, sir," Maldonia responded.

"Don't be. You've narrowed it down then?"

Thayer had actually been waiting for Maldonia to contact him. The MI-8 intelligence agent had been working non-stop for weeks trying to identify the leak within Van Gogh. It was clear that the President's top secret efforts had been compromised by one of the Apostles or a member of his own inner circle.

"No."

Thayer was silent in his frustration. The opening session of the European summit was just hours away and he still didn't know who the mole was.

"Actually, Jack, we've nailed him, we've got our man," Maldonia said. Thayer could hear the excitement in his voice. He was hesitant to ask the next question, but he didn't have to.

"Painter," was all he said.

Thayer winced. "Are you certain?" he asked with dread.

"Yes. I have intercepted transcripts, notes in his hand writing and we've already taken his contact into custody. A Bavarian art dealer in SoHo who also has a gallery in Berlin," he answered referring to the trendy art district in Manhattan. "He's singing like a bird. We noticed that Painter was calling him often. A radio message to his Berlin store usually followed within a few hours after their conversation."

"What was passed?"

"Just about everything, Jack, including the time and location. Berlin had that information within hours of the President making his decisions. They also know the full security plan. You should make Nimitz aware."

The news was catastrophic. "Any indication of Berlin's response?" Thayer probed.

"No. This was a one way street, Jack. Not even so much as an acknowledgement came back. A very well run operation. We believe the channel has been open for some time, probably preceding Van Gogh."

"The bugs?" Thayer asked, referring to the eavesdropping equipment found in the White House.

"Not there yet, Jack. We nailed a guy in a panel truck on Pennsylvania Avenue with a load of recording equipment within days after we found the devices. He's still being held, but as of yet, hasn't talked. Last night we were finally able to link him to the German Embassy, where he works under another name. We need a few more days to button up the case. Should be enough to close the Embassy if the President wishes."

One crisis at a time, Thayer thought.

"Good work, Robert, hell of a job. Just one last question. About 'Painter'. Do we know why?"

"Not a hundred percent certain, but it appears he was being blackmailed," Maldonia said. "He repeatedly refers to 'photographs' in his conversations with the guy in SoHo, demanding their return in threatening language. I'd say they got him by the balls, Jack. Don't know what photographs he's referring to, but in the after hours social scene our boy tends to enjoy, you can imagine."

"Shit..." was all Thayer could say.

"Yah. What do we do now?"

"Just keep doing what you're doing, Robert. If you've got any listening power in the Embassy, turn up the volume and let me know immediately. They might show their hand if 'Charlie Chaplin' has a trick up his sleeve," Thayer said, using the code name for Adolph Hitler.

Thayer ended the call and pondered his next move. The President would need to be informed that his best friend in the world had betrayed him.

Worse, Francis Millet was a traitor to his country.

Forty-Three

Thayer called the two Secret Service Agents detailed to the mission to his quarters. One had been keeping a close eye on the Presidential suite, the other had been sleeping. They were worried too. There wasn't a hell of a lot two men could do if the program went south.

Stan Harrington, lead man on the President's detail arrived rubbing sleep from his eyes. He was much too professional to complain about the hour, knowing without asking that the Chief of Staff wouldn't have dragged him out of bed unless there was a real concern. He'd been an agent assigned to three Presidents and knew when to just listen and when to open his mouth. This was a time to listen.

He sat with Thayer in his room in silence waiting for Roger Scovale, a five year veteran who had impressed Harrington with his cool demeanor, absolute attention to detail and various technical skills. He was one hundred percent confident Scovale was the right backup for this assignment – whatever the hell it was that they were supposed to be trying to prevent.

Between the two of them, they each had a military issue Smith & Wesson .38 caliber handgun and one sawed off shotgun. That's all they were allowed to bring on board, and that had been granted only after an argument with Thayer. Harrington didn't know what was up, but he was already feeling a bit bare ass naked in the weapons category. There was plenty of firepower just twenty miles away, but those were god dammed ship mounted cannons. Not of much use if they faced a fire fight on board. But he was getting ahead of himself, he thought, and hoped.

"Listen boys, we have an issue," Thayer began. "I can't give you all the details right now, because I don't have them all. But we're going to have to take one of the Van Gogh members into custody. Lock him in his room for the duration."

"Who?" Harrington asked, shocked and hoping Jack wasn't going to play games.

"Millet."

The Secret Service Agent winced, just as Jack had. "Shit, the President's buddy?"

"Yah. Life sucks and then you die."

"Can you tell me what we're going to hold him for?" Harrington probed, hoping that it might not have anything to do with the mission.

Thayer didn't dance. "Suspicion of treason. The FBI will take over once we get to dry land again. In the meantime, he is to be held in his cabin. I don't want him anywhere near the Europeans, their staff, ships staff or the Van Gogh members. No one gets near him and visa versa. Understood?"

Harrington thought for a moment. "Does the President know? He's not going to be happy about this."

"No. He needs his rest. I'll brief him at sunup," Thayer responded. "This thing needs to be handled delicately guys. I don't want anyone else on board to know that Millet's been pulled from the game. That's critical, understand? If anyone asks, he's taken ill."

Harrington studied the Chief of Staff. He was a straight shooter, the Agent knew from experience. Of all people. Millet. The boss would be shocked.

"Okay, Jack what's the rest of the story?"

"What do you mean? I told you I can't give you all the details," Thayer responded, slightly irritated.

"What I mean is what are you worrying about – or should I say what are you expecting."

Thayer swallowed hard. "Shit, I don't know. All I can tell you is that the god dammed location of the summit and our complete security plan was leaked to the Germans. How long ago, I don't know, but probably in plenty enough time for the bastards to develop some rough stuff if they're so inclined. And trust me. Adolph Hitler is not a guy you'd want you daughters to date."

Harrington turned to look at Scovale, who looked like he had just come down with stomach flu.

"Jesus Christ, Jack!" Harrington popped off. "There's only the fucking two of us. What the hell are we going to do if the Germans break out some hardware – or even worse, have a few friends waiting for us in the middle of the god dammed North Atlantic fucking ocean?"

Thayer was silent, his head down, deep in thought.

"Are you going to recommend to the President that we shut this caper down while we can?" Harrington asked more a demand than a question. "Our security has been completely compromised."

"No, I will not, Stan, because the President won't go along with it anyway," the Chief of Staff bellowed back. "You have no idea how important this is to him." He caught himself. "Christ, it's not about him, but it's his show and he's not going to back down. I know the man, Stan, forget it."

Harrington stared at him, not sure what to say next.

Thayer took charge. "We're not getting anywhere. The three of us are going to pay Mr. Millet a visit, see if we can get anything out of him. But I'm betting he won't have a lot to tell us. Tom, you keep a watch on the cabin. Make sure no one else tries to join us. Remember, this guy's a traitor and I'm thinking there's not much he and his friends aren't cable of."

They sat in silence for a moment. No one wanted to move first.

Harrington broke the calm. "You know I told my wife I was going to be with the President on the *Sequoia* for a few days, not to worry. You know what she said? 'Don't get wet'. Well let me tell you son, the safest place for the three of us right now is probably in the water in the middle of the god dammed ocean.

"And I don't even know how to swim."

Forty-Four

It was probably the hardest thing Jack Thayer had ever had to do.

Shortly after dawn, he found the President up as usual, already having his coffee. He was scanning some briefing notes for the meeting, set to begin that night, just after *Titanic* arrived at the designated position. He took one look at Thayer as he entered the room and knew immediately that his day was going to start out hard. His Chief of Staff's face never lied.

"Good morning, Mr. President. I hope you slept well last night," he greeted the President.

"Let's have it Jack," Butt replied, removing his reading glasses and putting his papers down. Thayer only knew one way to do it.

"It's Francis Millet, sir."

The President looked up at him for a moment, the message not registering.

"Is he ill… what is it…? he asked, and then stopped, realizing what Jack was telling him. "No," he said reflexively, "it can't be… His face turned ashen.

Thayer was silent.

"Are you sure? Because if there's any doubt let me talk to him…"

"He's admitted it, sir," Thayer said slowly, letting the President take it in. "I've talked with him at length. He is our spy, and has been for quite some time."

"Who…?"

"The Germans. They were blackmailing him."

Despite their mutual concerns about Millet's recent behavior, the President was still dumbfounded.

"What did he give them?" the President asked softly, struggling to mouth the words, frantic that there was some mistake.

"He gave them everything, sir," Thayer said. "A complete eyewitness account of the Chesapeake Bay meeting, our proposals and your intent to force Hitler to acquiesce, the time and location of the summit, and… the complete security plan."

Butt appeared stricken, unable to comprehend what he was hearing.

"He even informed them of your relationship with Mrs. Brown."

The President was staggered. Thayer felt like he had just punched the man in the solar plexus. Butt dropped his reading glasses to the carpet and leaned forward in his chair, shaking his head.

"God, no… not Francis. Anyone else, but not Francis." He was in agony.

Thayer stopped, allowing the man he respected most in the world a moment to reflect on the fact that he had been completely and inexplicably betrayed by his best friend. It took Butt several long moments to realize that Francis Millet, his inseparable companion since childhood, was also a traitor to his country. His most trusted friend… would be executed by the government of which he was responsible.

Butt finally stood up and walked out onto the balcony of his suite. It was a glorious day, with a full sun and not a cloud in the sky. The sea was calm, like plate glass. Like that night so long ago. Thayer followed him.

"Why, Jack… did he say why?"

"The details are quite horrendous, Mr. President." He hesitated.

"Tell me."

"It involved a fifteen year old German boy. Mr. Millet was somehow involved in his torture in some kind of sexual activity. It went too far. The boy died, mutilated. Hitler's agents photographed the entire thing."

Butt closed his eyes, grasping the railing with two hands. He felt sick to his stomach. Thayer continued.

"He was accosted by the Nazi's who showed him the photographs. They threatened to charge him with murder and release the details of the crime." He saw a tear role down Butt's face.

"They also threatened to link him to you. They would not only ruin him, they planned to create a scandal around your relationship. The Nazi's forced him to take advantage of his position with you, his access, and to spy for them. He has been in their employ for at least the last two years."

"Two years!" the President raged. "Why in God's name would that madman Hitler care about what I've been doing for the last two years? Our entire agenda was domestic, for Christ's sake. What could he have hoped to gain?"

"Apparently, the Chancellor fears you, Mr. President," Thayer responded. "Hitler knew it was only a matter of time before you expanded your agenda into the European situation. Millet's access to you was just too good an opportunity to pass up."

Butt slammed his right hand down on the railing, full of anger. "My God, does he realize what he's done?"

"Yes sir, and he is a pathetic sight. I fear that he may take his own life if given the opportunity."

The President turned to Jack with a look in his eyes the Chief of Staff had never seen before and hoped never to again. "Kill himself? Does he think that will satisfy me? That it will make up for the harm he's done? God help me I would strangle him myself before I would let him off that easy."

His rage spent, Butt returned to silence, working to calm himself. Finally he let go of the railing and walked back into the sitting room, sitting heavily back down in his chair. Thayer had never seen him look so tired, and suddenly, so old.

"And what of Molly?"

"He admitted to me that he was jealous of your relationship, sir. He included a report of Molly's visit to St. Simons Island in a fit of pique."

"How can one know a man his entire life, and yet not know him at all?" Butt asked sorrowfully. Thayer said nothing, leaving the President alone with his thoughts.

"Okay," he said, pulling himself back together. "At least we know what the bastards have." He stared ahead, unblinking, trying to think the situation through.

"What's your assessment?" he asked his Chief of Staff, willing himself back up on the saddle.

Thayer was prepared for the question. "Our position is completely compromised, Mr. President. I am certain Hitler has prepared himself with a response that will likely ruin any chance you have of success."

The President pondered the response. "You're right, of course. But let's look at this from another perspective." He always reminded Jack to come at a problem from every angle before settling on a course.

"Intellectually, we have scared the crap out of him, Jack," the President said. 'We can only imagine what went through his head when he learned the details of our plan. I will assume he was panicked, recognizing that if we were to succeed, the advantage of his emerging power in Europe – or should I say, intimidation – would be lost.

"So what response could he possibly have other than to somehow try to manipulate what he knows and use it to make a power grab?"

Thayer frowned. "I don't know if I follow you. You mean that somehow he will attempt to turn the tables on us - with a proposal of his own before we can back him into a corner?"

"Precisely. Remember what Sir Cosmo said about him being a caged animal? He will lash out Jack, I am certain of it. He will take the offensive, somehow. Hitler sees Europe as his personal chess board. Every move he makes is tied to an overall strategy of dominance - with the stakes being the solidification of his power over Europe."

"What might he propose?" Thayer asked, still unsure of the President's path.

"Frankly, I don't have a clue. And it would take a room full of experts and a week's worth of debate to even arrive at possibilities. We don't have the luxury of either."

Butt stopped and thought a minute longer, alarmed by another thought. "I cannot conceive that he would attempt to physically interrupt our meeting," he said, wondering even as he said it if he was underestimating the dictator.

"You mean with violence?"

"Yes. I know full well that the man is capable of murder, genocide, torture. My God, he is an animal. But even Hitler must know that if any harm were to befall the leaders of the six other most powerful nations on the earth that the entire world would want to hang him.

"He's not stupid, Jack, he's cunning. But he's stuck on *Titanic* just like we are, with no advantage other than knowing our game plan."

Thayer looked at him quizzically. "So what does that mean?"

"It means we stay the course. We offer our proposals as intended. We wait for him to move with the counter proposal we know he will try to bludgeon us with. He may succeed in wrecking the summit, but Hitler will not have the last laugh. As I have already indicated, I will speak before the League of Nations and lay the whole thing out for the world to see: the cruelty, treachery and deceit that are the hallmark of the Third Reich and the malfeasance of its Chancellor.

"Bottom line, Jack? We let the son of a bitch dig himself a hole so deep he'll never climb out of it. When the German people realize what he has done to them, when they come to understand the opportunities for them that he has squandered in pursuit of personal power, they will turn on him savagely. And our friend Hitler will end up as just another irritating footnote in the history books."

The two men sat in silence, gazing out at the empty, sunlit sea. "You are confident that he will not resort to violence?" Thayer finally asked.

"He cannot. He himself would be in the thick of it. He's just like you and me Jack. Passengers on a ship in the middle of the God dammed ocean. He can't possibly be contemplating any kind of physical action – he doesn't have an advantage."

Thayer clasped his hands together as if in prayer and brought them to his lips, reflecting on what Butt had just argued.

"Well Mr. President, I guess its back to Mrs. Brown's original plan," Thayer proposed.

"And that would be?" Butt asked.

"Come hell or high water."

Forty-Five

Commandant William Murdoch stood next to the young quartermaster who wielded the helm on the Bridge of *Titanic*. It felt good to be back at sea, he thought. The two years spent in retirement were filled with languor and a longing for the only world he truly knew. The *Titanic* had been a dream assignment for all the years he spent commanding the great ship between Southampton and Rio, every voyage an opportunity to make amends for the way he had failed her on the night of April 14, 1912.

Not a single day had passed since that he did not at least once see the gigantic white mass looming in front of his ship, and relived his actions. He had called it wrong, essentially steering the ocean liner into the iceberg, and if not for his bravery in the hours following, White Star would have buried him. His career would have been over.

Now at the helm again, he quietly celebrated every moment back aboard his ship, but each evening, before turning in, he strolled down to the Well Deck, climbed the ladder to the Forecastle Deck and slowly made his way to the forward capstan on the port side. Adorning the newly scraped and painted capstan was a large bronze plaque that had been cemented to the portside forward capstan a year after the *Titanic*'s accident. Freshly restored and polished, it was dedicated to the memory of Quartermaster Robert Hitchens who had given his life to save the passengers and crew of the

Titanic. This was where Hitchens had died coming to the assistance of then First Officer Murdoch. Every second of the events leading to Hitchens' death were etched into Murdoch's consciousness. Tonight, when *Titanic* arrived at the exact location where she struck the berg for the first time in twenty years, he would bring a gift to the grave of the young quartermaster.

Even as Murdoch was reminiscing on *Titanic's* Bridge, Admiral Chester Nimitz, aboard the *USS Augusta,* had just ordered his ship to a full stop, having arrived at the imposed twenty-mile perimeter location. *Titanic,* fifteen miles ahead of him, was closing in on the spot of her near fatal collision and the location of the European summit.

The seas were exceptionally calm and visibility was perfect. With lookouts posted at every corner of the heavy cruiser and quadrupled on the destroyers that were part of his small task force, they should have no problem spotting any vessel within several miles. But it was a big ocean Nimitz reminded himself. It would not be hard to sneak through their defense.

He called to the communications room. "This is the Commander," he spoke into the handheld microphone. "Are we receiving signals from *Titanic*?"

"Aye captain," a radioman responded. "Every thirty minutes, as arranged."

"Let me know immediately if that changes," Nimitz said in his most kick ass voice.

"Aye, Commander," the Ensign responded, thinking to himself what a great guy he was to have a beer with. Nimitz always had such great stories. Just don't mess with him when he's in charge.

One mile off to the north of *Titanic's* destination, the U-47 had also arrived on station. But she was invisible. The submarine lurked beneath the ocean, some one hundred fifty feet down. Below her was an abyss, stretching nearly two miles straight down to the sea floor.

Korvettenkapitän Günther Prien decided to take a look around.

"Bring the boat to periscope depth," he ordered, and waited as the U-47 blew ballast and slowly rose to a depth of fifteen feet. "Up periscope," he ordered again when the submarine had settled. He glued his eyes to the rubber cups of the periscope, and slowly rotated it three hundred sixty degrees around the horizon. It was late afternoon, and conditions were clear with a flat ocean.

He saw nothing on his first pass, but midway through his second look caught the slightest wisp of smoke from the southeast. He could not make out the vessel from this distance, but certainly it was a steamer of some sort. He watched her for several minutes more as the ship drew nearer. Finally, Prien he thought he could make out four funnels, probably a passenger liner which would not be surprising as the U-47 was submerged in the middle of the commercial North Atlantic shipping lanes. Is this what I'm looking for, he asked himself?

"Down scope, bring the boat to seventy-five feet," he ordered. The periscope was lowered quickly and he felt the vessel gradually sink to the level he had ordered. Despite their lack of combat experience, the crew of U-47 was well trained and Lieutenant Commander Günther Prien had complete confidence in them. He scanned the Bridge a last time before returning to his quarters to open the sealed orders. He was satisfied that no matter what the instructions required of the U-47, the crew was up to the task.

Arriving at his cabin, which was no more than a closet with a bunk, a small chair and a fold down desk, he locked the door behind him and retrieved the documents he had been given by the German Admiralty on leaving Bremen. The hot wax seal that kept the packet closed was embossed with the official German Naval insignia and the word "Spitzengeheimnis", classifying the contents as "Top Secret". He broke the seal with trepidation, the source of which he could not pinpoint, but nonetheless he was filled with unease. Collecting a pair of reading spectacles, he read the orders.

His eyes went wide as he quickly scanned the document, and he drew in his breath as he read them a second time, more slowly. Finally, fully satisfied that he had absorbed the contents completely, he refolded the document. His hands were trembling. Dazed, he left the cabin and made his way to the torpedo room where the only other private quarters on the boat was located. He knocked on the locked door and identified himself. It swung open a crack and he saw only a hand on the knob.

"Come in, please, Korvettenkapitän. I have been expecting you."

Forty-Six

Archie Butt sat alone on the balcony of the Presidential suite, a blanket over his legs. The late afternoon air had turned chilly. His briefing papers were open on his lap, but they did not have his attention. He listlessly stared out at the horizon. To the casual observer, the President of the United States appeared to be relaxing in the few hours left before a state appearance. He hadn't moved in several hours. In fact, he was dumbfounded by the betrayal of his friend.

Jack Thayer was urgently concerned over the mental state of the President. The news he had delivered to him in the early hours of the morning had devastated Butt, he knew. But now, with the most important diplomatic congress of his Presidency set to begin in little more than two hours, the Chief of Staff knew he had to awaken him from his deep funk.

Thayer had met with Molly Brown earlier in the afternoon, anticipating that the President's depression would worsen, and had informed her of Millet's betrayal. She was shocked beyond words. Not even the "unsinkable" Molly Brown could put her astonishment into words.

"It's incomprehensible, Jack." she said. "Francis was more than his friend, Archie thinks of him like a brother. He must be devastated… how could he…"

Thayer shook his head sadly, not knowing what else to do.

"After listening to Millet this morning, I can only tell you that the man was quite irrational in his fear of being exposed… for what he is, after all. I know he is Archie's friend. But there is a black creature that occupies his mind and body that the President is not aware of… even after all these years. He is a hideous man, Mrs. Brown, capable of nearly anything."

Molly's stomach was still churning from the description of the photographs Millet had summarized for Thayer. "Even in what should have been the darkest hour of his life, I would swear to you from the look in his eyes that he was enjoying some sort of sick sexual thrill as he described them to me. I was horror-struck as he talked. It was the most revolting experience of my life."

Thayer had asked Molly to visit with the President. "We must get his spirits up again, Mrs. Brown. He has worked tirelessly for this moment. It is the pinnacle of his life's work. He should not be deprived of it because of the betrayal of one man. Especially a man like Francis Millet."

A short time later, Thayer let her into the Presidential Suite. Archie was still on the balcony, where he'd been all afternoon. But his state of mind was even worse than Thayer had described.

"Archie," she said softly, approaching him on the balcony.

The President looked up, barely aware of her presence. "Hello, Molly," he said, his face emotionless. He looked pale and drawn, and his eyes were tired.

"Archie, Jack tells me we've had a fox in the god dammed hens house. Son of a bitch, who would have ever thought…" She stopped in mid sentence. He didn't respond.

Part of her wanted to reach out to him, take him in her arms and hold him. She thought for a moment that he was like that small child she had befriended so many years before on the stern of the sinking *Titanic*. The little girl had been completely lost, overwhelmed by her fear, not knowing which way to turn, what to do... She had just needed a hug, Molly remembered. But right now there wasn't time for hugs. She had already lost her patience with his lukewarm reception.

"Archie Butt, god dammit, are you just going to sit there like a lump or are you gonna get ready to kick some ass? Is this what you really are? A god dammed wimp?"

Butt turned back to her, and for a moment, she saw a spark of anger in his eyes. It passed just as quickly and he turned away.

"Now is hardly the time for one of your cowgirl tantrums, Margaret," he said, mumbling the words.

That did it. "You know what? You're god dammed right Mr. President. This ain't the time or place. Nor is it the time and place for the god dammed President of the United States to fold up his tent and paddle up creek!"

He stood up and looked down at her. "How dare you Mrs. Brown. I have never walked away from a fight in my whole life. But just in case you aren't aware, the battle plan has changed, and the odds are now very lopsided. One man has destroyed everything we've worked so hard to achieve – one fucking coward who betrayed his country."

Molly didn't wince. Cursing's good for the soul she thought.

"And the son of a bitch was my best friend! I would have done anything for him...anything," he continued, his voice dropping off as he sat back down.

Molly called out to Jack waiting in the sitting room. "Thayer, get off your lazy ass and bring us two tall brandies and a Cuban." They sat silently waiting for the Chief of Staff to return.

He was back with the drinks and the cigar in a few minutes. "Damn, I should have told you to pour one for yourself, Jack. You need to be a guest at this party too, seein's as how you're the best god dammed friend the President has now."

Butt looked up at her. "Yah, you candy ass, you're whining about that frigging sexual deviate asshole who stuck it to you good, and the real god dammed best friend you've ever had or will have is standing right next to you. And he, by the way, is counting on you, just like I am and another twelve god dammed Apostles who've risked everything to support you.

"So let's drink up, Mr. President, let's eulogize that sick sack of shit you thought was your friend."

Butt opened his mouth to say something, but Molly had the floor.

"Or, Mr. President, you can drink up with me and Jack here to celebrate the incredible loyalty you've found amongst a group of people that God himself couldn't have corralled before last April."

She was on a roll and Butt was speechless.

"And after you drink to that, take the last swallow in that glass and guzzle it in honor of the man with the biggest pair of balls I've ever known east of Kettle Creek: Archie god dammed Butt."

The President shook his head, then took in a deep breath and blew it out, like he was cleansing his palate of an unfriendly taste. He raised the brandy snifter in his hand, tipped it to Molly and Jack and then to his lips. He took a long drink. Then he laughed, and with a sparkle in his eyes, raised the glass to his lips and took a second drink.

"And now Mr. President, while we could sit here drinking and celebrating all kinds of good news, maybe we should wait until later tonight after the god dammed horse has been rode hard and put to bed wet."

The President stood again and took the two steps to reach Molly. He took her hands in his and raised her to her feet, wrapping his arms around her. "Oh, Mrs. Brown, what would I do without you."

Thayer cleared his throat. "Mr. President, we have a few things to discuss before we begin the meeting. If you'll excuse us Mrs. Brown."

"Why I'd be delighted, Mr. Thayer. A woman knows when her work is done." She winked at Butt and made her way to the door.

The President called to her. "Molly, just one thing. Where the hell is Kettle Creek?"

A wicked grin came to her face. "Why, it's where we're going to celebrate our honeymoon, Mr. President. Right after your re-election."

She slammed the door on her way out.

Forty-Seven

In his own cabin less than a hundred feet away, Francis Millet also sat alone in thought.

He had been locked in his quarters since early morning, and aside from his conversation with Thayer had not spoken to anyone. The hours of solitude had wreaked havoc on his mind. A fully stocked bar had only fueled the mayhem.

His twisted mind had vacillated between self-pity and remorse upon being discovered, then turned to rage over his persecution. In the hours of solitude, he had lost complete touch with the notion of right and wrong, and now, like the caged animal Sir Cosmo Duff Gordon had used in his description of Adolph Hitler, he was poised to lash out.

In his few moments of lucidity, he rationalized correctly that he had nothing to lose by continuing to contribute to Hitler's scheme. All that awaited him in America was a charge of treason and the media circus that would erupt. He was ruined. His life was over.

He contemplated suicide. Thayer and the Secret Service Agent had not been smart enough to search his belongings for a weapon, and the .38 caliber revolver he held in his hand made him feel powerful. He could use it on himself, or to help Hitler succeed. The life he had known was over. Was there a new life waiting in Berlin, he wondered? Wouldn't he receive a hero's welcome for supporting the Chancellor? Then the incriminating photographs would be destroyed. Wouldn't Hitler order it out of gratitude? Perhaps there was hope after all.

In the shadows of his mind lingered thoughts of his friend, Archie Butt. Each time they entered his consciousness, he pushed them back. Archie Butt was dead, or would soon be, he told himself.

Now, his plan set, he needed only to wait for the right moment.

Forty-Eight

At a quarter to eight that evening, President Archibald Butt, accompanied by his Chief of Staff and Secret Service Agent Stan Harrington, arrived in the purpose built conference room that had replaced *Titanic*'s First Class Lounge. He held his head high, there was energy in his step and a determined look was in his clear eyes. He looked every bit the part of the President of the most powerful nation on earth. While he didn't swagger, Butt walked with a confidence that set him apart from the average man. Thayer thought he hadn't seen the President this self assured and full of vigor since his first State of the Union address before both houses of Congress, when he had outlined his economic recovery plan for America.

Butt stopped at the entrance and took in the room where he would make his case for world peace. It was a masterful design by Thomas Andrews that brilliantly addressed the inherent protocol issues of the meeting the President was about to convene.

Taking full advantage of the historical significance of the summit, Andrews had let his creative energies run wild. What emerged from his vision was a sort of coliseum, albeit in a scale he could squeeze into a ship with a ninety-two foot beam. What the space lacked in dimension, Andrews ingeniously countered with the illusion of depth. By removing a number of suites below the First Class lounge, he was able to create an environment with two levels. On the floor level was the central meeting area. Surrounding it at the upper level where Butt had entered was a balcony with separate work stations. The room was sumptuously appointed with mahogany paneling and wainscoting. Three oversized crystal chandeliers hung from the ceiling, providing a balanced soft light.

Andrews had also been able to address Butt's concerns with the seating arrangement. To fulfill the requirement that each of the participants be granted a position at the table equal to all those present, Andrews had designed a heptagonal polished mahogany table. The resulting seven sided polygon allowed each participant an equal place from which to speak and be heard. Van Gogh participants sat above the meeting floor, on the balcony level overlooking the proceedings. Because of its amphitheater arrangement, the acoustics were superb, allowing discussions to occur with no more effort than casual conversation.

Each participant was also afforded an individual path to his section of the heptagon, down a flight of stairs off the balcony. Any man could come and go without disturbing the others.

Thomas Andrews was there to meet the President.

"Extraordinary, Thomas, absolutely extraordinary," Butt said to the designer.

"It's amazing what one can accomplish with a blank check, Mr. President," he smiled. "Let us hope Mr. Astor's investment pays for itself."

As Butt watched from the balcony, the European heads of state began to arrive with their aids and interpreters, and slowly took their assigned places around the table. The Van Gogh members began to fill seats on the upper level. All were present with the exception of Francis Millet. Hitler, as one would expect, was the last to arrive, and virtually every head in the room took him in as he walked dourly down the stairs to his seat. Goebbels accompanied him, stone faced.

Precisely at 8 p.m., the doors of the conference room were silently closed creating an almost vacuum like effect that made it nearly soundproof. The President of the United States, already at his seat, looked around the room. He could not help but be awestruck at the gathering. Around him sat the leaders of Great Britain, France, Spain, Italy, German and Russia, as well as the most powerful, influential and accomplished private citizens of the world. All, he hoped, shared his vision for the outcome of their meeting, but even as he stood ready to welcome his guests, he was not sure. The American President cleared his throat and began.

"Lady," he looked up and smiled at Molly who winked at him, "and gentlemen. Let me first begin by extending my humble, but eternal gratitude for agreeing to participate in this historical summit of the European leadership..."

Even as Butt spoke, his lifelong friend Francis Millet began to deliver his own well rehearsed lines in the solitude of his private cabin.

Knowing well Butt's propensity for timeliness, when the clock struck eight, he made his move. Clutching the cocked pistol in his right hand, Millet walked to the door of his suite and attempted to open it. As he had assumed, it was locked from the outside. He called to the Secret Service Agent he knew would be outside in the hall, standing guard by the door.

He jiggled the door knob violently hoping to attract the agent's attention.

"Help me, please, help me,' Millet hollered from behind the door. "I need help, please, someone."

In the hallway, Secret Service Agent Roger Scovale heard Millet's plea clearly, but took his time answering.

Good, I hope the bastard's cut his wrists, he thought. But remembering Thayer's insistence that Millet be guarded and protected, even from himself, he finally answered.

"What is it, Millet? You can't come out, you know that," Scovale said loudly, unconcerned at being overheard as the floor was now empty.

From behind the door, Millet smiled. "I need help," he feigned in a voice that would have done a dying man justice.

Scovale thought for a moment, unsure if he should open the door, then threw caution to the wind. What the fuck could a faggot like Millet pull? Nonetheless, he unholstered his weapon and had it at the ready as he turned the key in the door.

Millet was waiting for him. When Scovale opened the door and took a first step into the room, the traitor fired two shots from a distance of no more than three feet. Both shots hit the Agent in the chest. His eyes went wide with the shock of the assault and the excruciating pain, and Scovale fell to the floor, dying.

Millet studied his handiwork for a minute and actually felt a familiar stirring in his loins. Shaking off the bizarre pleasure, he grabbed Scovale's body by the belt around his waist and dragged him inside. He stepped into the doorway and looked down both ends of the hall. No one had seen the murder. Stepping carefully over the body and the pool of blood staining the pale blue carpet, he closed the door and reloaded the gun. He put on his suit jacket and left the room, walking down the First Class hallway towards the Bridge like he was taking a Sunday afternoon stroll. Escaping notice of the lookout posted at the bow of the *Titanic*, he ducked into the communications room of the great liner where Ensign Raymond Flagler had just finished his top of the hour coded message to the *USS Augusta*, on station, some twenty miles to the east.

Flagler, not aware of Millet's circumstances, looked up from his radio set as the artist entered the small communications room and smiled. "Good evening, Mr. Millet. How nice to see you. I'm afraid I can't help you with outgoing messages right now, President's orders you know."

"Ah, yes, I know all about the President's orders, Mr. Flagler," Millet responded. Pity I don't have much regard for them. I'll just have to send my own message." Without another word, he pulled the gun from his suit pocket, leveled it at the radioman's head and shot him in the center of the forehead. Flagler was dead before he fell forward off his chair, slumping to the floor with a sickening thud.

Closing the door and locking it, Millet pulled the body out of the way, and sat down at the radio set. He quickly pulled on a set of headphones and began tapping away at the Morse key with a seemingly innocuous message addressed to an art gallery in the SoHo area of Manhattan. He had been well trained on the device by the Germans and tapped out the message quickly. Finished, he glanced at his watch. 8:06 p.m. He would wait and send out the message to *Augusta* at 8:30, on schedule.

"Fuck you, Mr. President," he said aloud.

Eight hundred and fifty yards off the *Titanic*'s starboard side, a menacing pencil-like shape broke the surface. The submarine below it was at a standstill, so there was no wake from the periscope. On the Bridge of the German U-47 submarine, Korvettenkapitän Prien's eyes were glued to the eyepiece. He stared intently at the ocean liner a half mile away and marveled at the number of lights along her bow and superstructure. She's lit up like a Christmas tree, he thought, and wondered at her crews' obvious disregard for concealment. "She has been gift wrapped for me," he said aloud to no one in particular, noting as he did that there appeared to be only one lookout on the ship, on the bow. The submarine's lieutenant commander spent several more long minutes rotating the periscope in a 360 degree path, seeking any sign of a protecting warship. There was none.

"So odd," he said to his First Officer, as the periscope was retracted back into the sub. "The boat appears totally unprotected. Who in their right mind would leave such a precious cargo unguarded?"

"Remember, Captain," the First Officer responded, "she is surrounded by warships." Prien had informed only the second in command of the intent of their mission.

"Jah, but they are twenty miles away," Prein said. "With luck, we will be in and out before their fleet is even aware there is a problem."

They were interrupted by the sub's radioman, who informed the Captain that he had just picked up the message from *Titanic* that they had been awaiting. "The message is from a Francis Millet to an art gallery in New York City, Herr Captain. Is this what we have been waiting for?"

"Yes. Heinrich, signal the Commando's that the time has come."

He ordered the periscope up for one more look. Satisfied that their presence had not been discovered he gave the order to surface the boat.

"Heinrich, when she breaks the surface, open the forward hatches," he called to his First Officer, "and alert the gun crew to man their weapon. Are the forward torpedo's ready to be fired?"

"Jah, Herr Captain, we need only firing instructions," the First Officer responded.

"Set them for nine hundred yards and to run forty feet deep," Prien ordered, setting the torpedoes in the U-47's four forward tubes to strike well below *Titanic*'s waterline. "I do not intend to get any closer than this. Fire only on my command. Is that understood?"

"Fire only on your command, Yes, Herr Captain, it is understood," replied the First Officer.

"Come with me, Heinrich," Prien said as he climbed the ladder into the conning tower and opened the hatch to the night air. The hatch burst open with a strong push from below and he felt an immediate rush of fresh, salty air on his face. While the Lieutenant Commander was quite at home in the depths of the ocean, there was still nothing more he enjoyed than the first blast of fresh air after being submerged for long periods. He filled his lungs with the rejuvenating oxygen and climbed onto the conning tower, binoculars in hand.

As if on cue, the forward hatches sprung open. Men dressed from head to toe in black neoprene wet suits poured from the U-47's hull, pulling supplies and equipment from her hold. Two large, inflatable rafts were hurriedly pumped full of air and tossed over each side, clinging to the submarine by just a single line. Weapons, grappling hooks and other equipment were placed carefully in the boats, which were then boarded by ten commandos in each. In command was Kapitänleutnant Eric Straus, a veteran German Navy Special Forces officer.

"Hurry, quickly but silently," Straus ordered his men who settled into the boats in a matter of seconds. Then two men in each boat placed a four foot metal paddle in the water and awaited instructions. Straus turned and looked to the conning tower and gave Prien a thumbs up. A crewman handed him a note that the submarine commander had hastily scribbled. "There is only one lookout on the bow. God speed." Straus nodded in the direction of the conning tower to acknowledge the information, then gave each of the boats a silent command. He stepped into the port side inflatable as they simultaneously cast off their lines and made for *Titanic*. Stopped in the middle of the North Atlantic Ocean, she rocked gently on the calm sea, at rest in the serene quiet.

Onboard the *Titanic*, a lookout walked the Forecastle Deck, oblivious to what was transpiring just a half mile away. The night was calm, a bit brisk, but comfortable for the outdoor assignment. There was no moon, so visibility was limited. He had not seen the submarine surface in the blackness. He was on the lookout for ships lights on the horizon. It had not occurred to him to watch the surface of the ocean around the vessel. The U-47 blended perfectly into the dark waters, and even her conning tower light had been extinguished. It was if she was not even there.

Prien held his breath as the boats pulled closer to *Titanic*'s stern, which was their target. As he watched, they pulled into position below her stern rail, some sixty feet above, and one of the commandos threw a lightweight, rubber coated aluminum grappling hook over her side. It caught the railing on his first attempt, and Prien watched as the black figure pulled mightily on the rope, ensuring it was firmly set.

In *Titanic*'s small radio room, Francis Millet stared at the second hand on his wristwatch, ready to send the scheduled message to *Augusta*, still holding her twenty mile distance, at exactly 8:30 p.m. Precisely as the minute hand struck the numeral six on his watch, he keyed in the coded message to *Augusta*. Finished, he breathed a sigh of relief. In thirty minutes he would do the same thing again, fulfilling his role in the treachery that was taking shape. He expected to be handsomely rewarded.

Prien watched as the black clad commandos scurried sixty feet up the dangling rope to *Titanic*'s stern. He saw the first two men race up the Promenade Deck to the bow, hesitating for only a moment on the Well Deck below the Bridge before one of them came up behind the lookout. There was no scuffle. It was over in a second. Garroted, the seaman's body was unceremoniously dumped overboard. The ocean surface was so far below no one on the Bridge could have heard a splash.

The second man to die was Commandant William Murdoch, who had just begun his evening stroll to the forward capstan on the port side to pay his respects to the young quartermaster he had served with two decades earlier. Unaware of the danger, he had more spirit in his step this night, and he carried a brown leather case with him. In it were the binoculars that went missing on April 14, 1912 – the same binoculars that might have helped *Titanic*'s lookouts catch the outline of the iceberg a few moments earlier, possibly averting the accident entirely. Murdoch had retrieved the binoculars from the locked chest in the *Titanic*'s crows nest after the badly damaged ship had limped back to port in Liverpool, and had carried them with him on every voyage for the past two decades, waiting for the moment he might pass over this spot once more. He knelt quickly at the Capstan, said his usual prayer, then added a thought.

"See here, Mr. Hitchens, I've brought the bloody glasses that started this whole mess. You do have my apologies for bringing them so late, lad. You are the only man I know who deserves them." With that, he walked to the port side railing and tossed the case into the ocean. Just as he flung them over, a black-gloved hand clamped over his mouth and he felt a sudden rush of agony as a six-inch bayonet was plunged through his back and into his heart. He dropped to the deck without so much as a gasp and was dead before he hit the water. The lone commando assailant quickly crept back into the cover of the Well Deck shadows.

With astonishing speed and agility, the remaining German commandos made their way on board the *Titanic* and carefully converged on the Well deck. At a signal from Straus, four men, two on the port side, two on the starboard, silently climbed the three flights of stairs up to the Promenade Deck and waited outside the Bridge. Only the First Officer and helmsman were on duty. In place, Straus gave a hand signal to the commandos, who without hesitation, rushed onto the Bridge and silenced the two crewmen with almost no struggle. They were left for dead on the floor, the First Officer nearly decapitated from a slash across the throat, the helmsman draped over the wheel, stabbed in the heart.

The two commandos on the starboard side exited the Bridge and made their way to the Communications room, where Francis Millet sat silently behind it's locked door, waiting.

Millet abruptly heard two knocks on the door, then three more. It was the signal he had been waiting for. He jumped up from his chair and opened the door and was met by the masked face of a German commando holding a long bloody knife in one hand and cradling a submachine gun in the other. Millet had expected him, but still stepped back with fright at the visitors intimidating presence. "You have sent the signal, jah?" the assassin asked Millet. "Yes, all is in order," Millet stammered. "I must transmit again in 28 minutes."

"Stay at your post," the commando ordered Millet, who sat back down in his chair, nodding.

"We will come for you when it is done."

Back on the Bridge, the two remaining commandos quickly found and activated the ships electrical watertight doors. The alarm sounded in the bowels of the vessel when the switch was thrown, alerting the fifty or so men toiling in her bowels or sleeping in their confined quarters that the doors were going to be shut. With just thirty seconds to react, most never made it out. Every compartment below *Titanic*'s waterline was sealed off, leaving escape to her upper decks impossible.

About half of the crew compliment was working during the conference. Those not working were resting or passing the time in their small cabins. Doors at both ends of the crew compartment section were locked off with heavy chains by the commandos who had effectively taken control of the great ocean liner in minutes.

In the conference room, the talks continued as its participants were oblivious to the danger now gathering around it. At the exquisitely ornate grand staircase formerly used by First Class passengers, the handmade St. Alban's clock, flanked by two classical figures, "Honour and Glory crowning Time", struck 8:40 p.m.

Forty-Nine

With the *Titanic*'s decks now secure save for the few crewmembers who were on duty to support the meeting, Straus' men moved quickly to converge on the conference room. He could not hear what was happening inside but it didn't matter. There were entrances on both the port and starboard sides, and the Special Forces leader divided his men equally between them. With the blow of a whistle in his mouth, they exploded through the solid oak double doors with the help of small four-man battering rams, then streamed into the room and spread around the balcony level in seconds.

The sudden invasion caught John Jacob Astor in mid sentence as he was just concluding his analysis of the economic state of affairs on the European continent.

"What in the world..." Astor stammered, shocked by the presence of a small army, all brandishing menacing lightweight submachine guns. In their black uniforms and face masks, devoid of any military markings, there was no way to tell who they were, or why they had come. Straus remained silent, as he had been instructed, but took dead aim on Astor. Around the room, guns were leveled on every participant.

Before the President could say anything, Molly Brown stood up from her balcony seat, walked up to a commando and stuck her finger hard in his chest. "Who in the Sam Hill are..." Without hesitation, the commando smashed his gun down on the left side of her head. She fell to the floor instantly, not moving.

Archie Butt jumped up from his seat on the conference room floor and began to run up the stairs to reach her. A burst of fire at his feet from a commando at the top of the stairs stopped him dead in his tracks. Stan Harrington leapt in front of the President and shot the commando dead with a single shot. A hail of gunfire poured down on Harrington, who was killed instantly.

Butt was aghast. "Who are you? What do you want?" the President screamed, splattered with Harrington's blood, a sick feeling building in his gut. "How dare you," he said, moving up the stairs again. Another burst of gunfire answered his questions, this time catching him in his right knee. He fell heavily on the stairs, tumbling back to the floor, bleeding profusely.

Jack Thayer threw caution aside and rushed to the President. He was ashen. "Quickly," he hollered, "get me something for a tourniquet. He'll bleed to death!"

"Perhaps that will be the most merciful way for him to meet his end, Mr. Thayer," came a voice, heavy with German inflection, from the other side of the room.

"What...?" Thayer said, helpless to aid the President. All over the room, world leaders, diplomats and millionaires were all equals, searching desperately for somewhere to hide.

John Jacob Astor, in the center of the heptagon for his presentation, rushed to the voice. It was Hitler, and he was standing, holding a German military issue Lugar. He waved it at Astor, stopping his assault.

"Not even you, Mr. Astor, the wealthiest man in the world who can work miracles with his money, can overcome these odds." Hitler's eyes were huge and red rimmed. He was so enraged that spittle flew from his mouth as he spoke. Astor, a gentleman but no coward, took another step forward meaning to kill the dictator with his bare hands. Hitler shot him once, the bullet hitting him in the center of his forehead. Blood and brain matter spewed out of the back of his skull, spraying Prime Minister MacDonald with the ghastly mix. Astor fell backwards to the floor, dead.

There was a huge cry from the audience in the room, all shocked by the unimaginable terror that out of nowhere had interrupted their world. Some began to weep; others stood up and screamed at the madman to stop the insanity.

George Widener picked up his chair and turned on an attacker standing beside him. He only managed to get the chair up to shoulder level before he was gunned down in a burst of four shots that ripped up his chest. He too fell dead.

"Gentlemen, gentlemen. Please do not resist," Hitler said, his voice quivering with anger. "It is so unbecoming of people of your class and distinction. Better that you die as gentlemen, rather than cowering dogs, wouldn't you say?" Hitler was toying with them, exulting in the power at his fingertips.

He turned to Straus. "Bring me the traitor, now. But be sure he has sent the signal first," Hitler ordered him. With a simple nod, the Lieutenant dispatched two men to retrieve Francis Millet, still hiding in the communications room.

"My god, you are mad," Sir Cosmo Duff Gordon hollered from the balcony in utter disbelief of Hitler's actions. Straus turned his gun on the diplomat four seats away and blew his head off with a burst of fire from his submachine gun. Ironically, the weapon was one of tens of thousands that had been assembled in secret despite the restrictions of the *Treaty of Versailles*. The affable Scotsman's headless corpse rolled over the balcony railing and fell to the floor fifteen feet below.

Benjamin Guggenheim and William Stead made a run for the door and were about to be shot when Hitler ordered "Stop. Do not shoot them. Not yet. Soon I will have no one left to listen to the reason why this delightful party has been so rudely interrupted." Guggenheim and Stead were forced to the floor on their knees. Stead prayed while Guggenheim's eyes frantically looked around the room for a place to escape. He finally hung his head in silence, beaten for the first time in his life.

Archie Butt pulled himself to a sitting position, held up by his Chief of Staff. He was still bleeding heavily. He knew he would lapse into unconsciousness soon. Hitler wordlessly walked around the table and stood at his feet.

The President looked up. "Why?" he asked, the bitter taste of failure on his lips. "Why would you betray the German people?"

Hitler's head snapped back as if he had been hit with an uppercut. "Gottverdammt!" he screamed at the ceiling, his face hideously deformed in fury. "You idiot!" He lunged forward, bringing a heavy black leather boot crashing down on Butts wounded knee. A loud crack echoed across the room.

"Are all Americans so stupid? Did you believe for a minute that I would allow you to blackmail Germany and her allies? Did you not, in your astonishing arrogance, think for a moment that Germans and Russians would rather hold hands and march on you than allow you to ply us with your disgusting tricks?"

Hitler was out of control. He turned and randomly selected a target. Three shots sounded from his Luger, each hitting the Spanish President Niceto Alcalá-Zamora of Spain in the chest, knocking him backwards in his chair to the floor. The dictator calmly walked over to the Spaniard and shot him again, between the eyes. His body twitched as he died.

Stalin and Mussolini, visibly shaken by Hitler's insane ranting, sat silently. They had made their pacts with the devil. One false move or word could put them at the wrong end of Hitler's gun in an instant.

"Am I not correct, Joseph? Benito? Could we possibly have allowed this to happen?" The two dictators nodded. Mussolini was shaking in his shoes, a look of sheer terror in his eyes.

"But enough of this madness," Hitler laughed. Before you die, Mr. President, I want you to take a long, last look at the man who betrayed you and all in this room. Your best friend, Mr. President, the man whose loyalty you would not have questioned in a million years. Mr. Millet, please join us."

Millet had been dragged into the room by the two commandos sent to find him. They carried him screaming from the communications room just as he had finished sending the 9:00 p.m. message to *Augusta*. Hitler and his army had thirty minutes to finish their business. It wouldn't take that long.

"Mr. Millet, do you see how you have repaid the man who would have done anything for you?" Hitler reached into his breast pocket and retrieved a silk handkerchief, leaned down and doused it in the blood pooling beneath the stricken President. "Here, have a taste of your best friend," he said wiping the sodden handkerchief across the horrified artists face.

Archie Butt looked up at his friend, and locked on to his eyes. "Francis, how could you have forsaken me?" Pain stretched across Butts face as he waited for an answer. The pain in his wounded leg paled in comparison to his broken heart.

Millet was silent. Hitler ended the debate. "Friends should not have to debate such things," he said, and shot Millet point blank in the face. The artist fell heavily on the President. Butt reached up and grabbed Thayer by the collar, dragging him to his lips. "Survive, Jack. The world must know," he whispered into his grieving Chief of Staff's ear.

With the last two bullets in his gun, Adolph Hitler assassinated the President of the United States and shot Jack Thayer in the neck. His father, looking down on the mayhem beneath him, cried out in despair. The crazed dictator dropped his weapon and slowly walked up the stairs to exit the room. Goebbels, Stalin and Mussolini followed him, wordlessly.

As Hitler walked through the doorway to the fresh air on the Open Promenade deck he said to Straus, "Finish it." He turned and strolled down the deck, oblivious to the sudden explosive chatter of more than a dozen submachine guns being fired at once. The sound was deafening. He turned to Goebbels who was quiet. Even he was astonished at the dictator's cruelty. But as always, he was at his side, one step removed.

"It reminds me of a symphony," Hitler said, a sadistic grin coming to his thin, gray lips. "But they would not have enjoyed it."

Goebbels looked at him, puzzled.

"After all, Van Gogh had only one ear."

Fifty

A dense cloud of spent gunpowder hung over the conference room but did little to hide the carnage within it. Rivers of blood trickled down the staircases and pooled on the floor under the bodies of the Prime Minister of Great Britain and the Presidents of France, Spain, and the United States of America. Around the perimeter of the room, several bodies hung over the balcony railing. Molly Brown lay dead on the floor, having been machine gunned even after the brutal blow that had caved in her skull.

The interior of the magnificent conference room that just minutes before had held the hopes of world peace, now looked more like a Chicago slaughterhouse. It was eerily quiet. A spent cartridge shell fell from a step, breaking the cathedral like silence with a quick, but sharp, metal resound.

The body of Ernest Carter, which had been hanging precariously over the balcony rail, shifted from its own dead weight, and the automaker's body fell head first to the black marble floor some fifteen feet below. The crashing sound of his fall reverberated throughout the chamber, and he came to rest just inches from Jack Thayer whose body was draped over his friend, Archie Butt. The noise and jostle stirred him and he awoke with the acrid smell of gunpowder, blood and death in his nostrils. He was bleeding heavily from a single shot to the back of his neck. He reached up with his hand and felt the wetness, bringing it in front of his eyes. Only upon seeing his own blood did his consciousness kick in, reminding him of what had just happened.

Thayer quickly reached over and checked the President's pulse, but finding none, struggled to his feet. He recalled the President's last words to him. The Chief of Staff stood for a moment and took in the massacre around him. He gasped upon seeing his own father sitting dead in his chair, the remains of his skull flayed open to the brain. Resting against the edge of the table, Jack Thayer willed strength back into his body. It came to him that he had been spared, however accidentally, already taken for dead.

A rage began to bring his blood to a boil, and he exploded in grief, crying out in a guttural wail for the wasted lives all around him, for his dearly beloved father, and for his deeply admired President and friend.

"I will avenge you!" he screamed into the heavens, sobbing. He lowered his head, the pain from his neck wound almost unbearable. "You have not died in vain, I promise you. I will live to tell this story, I swear it."

He pushed himself off of the table and began the laborious climb up the steps to the balcony and escape from the slaughter. On reaching the deck, he steadied himself for a moment, clutching the ship's outer rail, and looked up and down each end of the ship for signs of life. Not a soul was visible. He wrongly assumed he was the only man left alive on *Titanic*.

Slowly making his way forward, he aimed for the Bridge and the Communications Room, hoping to send out a distress call. He found the two bodies on the Bridge and Ensign Flagler's lifeless corpse behind it. He could not find Commandant Murdoch and wondered if he had somehow escaped.

The radio set in the Communications Room had been destroyed by the fleeing commandos, machine gunned after having performed its part in the treachery. Thayer wondered if the last message to Nimitz on the *Augusta* had been sent. If not, help was already on the way.

As he stood in the doorway of the Communications Room wondering what to do next, he became aware of a banging sound coming from below him. It occurred to him that there might be survivors amongst the crew still below in their quarters. He climbed down the five flights of stairs to the entrance to the crew cabins and found the heavy, metal double doors chained and locked, but could hear yelling coming from the other side.

"Hold on, I'm here," he hollered back and began searching for something to break the chain. "Stay calm, I must find an axe," he yelled and climbed back up a flight of stairs searching for a fire cabinet. Blood continued to drip from his wound, but had seemed to slow.

The U-47, no longer concerned with surprise, had moved in closer to *Titanic* and picked up her boats. Korvettenkapitän Prien was shocked beyond words at the sight of the Chancellor of the Reich and the Russian Stalin stepping out of the inflatable boats onto the deck of his submarine. His orders had not indicated who he would be welcoming on board the U-47 from the *Titanic*. He did not recognize the Italian with the bright red silk sash across his chest, but assumed he was someone important.

With little time to waste as the next signal to *Augusta* was due in less than five minutes, Straus hurriedly ordered the boats unloaded and personally helped Hitler, Stalin and Mussolini through the forward hatches into the torpedo room. Bursts of gunfire rang out as two commandos riddled the canvas and rubber boats with bullets, instantly deflating them. Concrete blocks were retrieved from the hold and unceremoniously dumped on the floating remnants of the boats, sending them to the bottom. Straus took a quick look to ensure that no evidence of their presence was left on the surface and followed the remainder of his men through the hatches, dogging them as they closed.

Prien then shouted orders to his crew. "Full reverse, snap to it," he yelled down to the Bridge, backing up the submarine to a position about three hundred yards from the *Titanic*, lining his boat up for a clean shot at her starboard side. "Fire torpedoes one through four when ready," he commanded.

Almost instantly, a loud swoosh was heard from the submarine's bow and Prien felt the bow rise as first one, then the second, third and fourth torpedo's propelled themselves toward the great ocean liner, still sitting helplessly, riding high and unknowing on the mirror-like sea. The submarine rolled with the exit of the projectiles, her bow now lighter by several thousand pounds.

As the telltale track of bubbles followed the torpedoes racing toward *Titanic*, Prien sighed deeply. In the war, submarine captains had called this moment "die glückliche Zeit" or the "happy time." Strangely, Prien only felt sadness at the impending destruction of the world's most famous ocean liner. He did not find it a happy time at all, and tried not to think about what had happened aboard her in the last hour. Thankfully, he saw no one on her decks.

"Reload the forward tubes immediately," Prien called out even before the torpedoes already in the water had traveled half the distance to the steamer. Below decks, in the forward torpedo room, six men struggled to reload the tubes, using block and tackle to raise the monstrous projectiles into firing position. "Load the stern tube, as well," he called out, not sure of what to expect as they attempted to flee from the scene. He was aware only that the Americans had posted a small fleet in a twenty mile perimeter around *Titanic*, but did not at this time know if they were steaming towards him. If they were, the ships would be coming at the U-47 from every direction.

Wasting no time, he hurried down the conning tower ladder back onto the Bridge and gave the order to close the hatch. "Dive the boat," he ordered. "Bring her to a depth of one hundred twenty-five feet on a southern route. Navigator, fix our course for Bremen."

As the submarine dove for the safety of deep water, he ordered the periscope to be raised.

On *Augusta*, Admiral Nimitz faced an anxious radio man.

"The signal did not come, sir. It was due at 9:30 p.m. It is now three minutes after," the nervous Ensign reported.

"Was there any other traffic in the last hour?" Nimitz asked.

"Just one message sir, shortly after eight o'clock. Some silly thing about a meeting with an art gallery signed by a Mr. Francis Millet."

"You mean they broke radio silence?" Nimitz' ire was raised.

The Ensign squirmed. "Uh, yes, sir, but I hardly thought..."

"Right, Ensign, you hardly thought." He turned to his executive officer. "Sound battle stations and set a course for *Titanic*. Flank speed. And notify the *Little, Sigourney, Gregory* and *Dyer* to move in by ten miles and await instructions. Also tell them to double their lookouts." That was all he could do. It would take *Augusta* a little more than an hour to reach *Titanic*'s last known position.

Almost instantly, the crew of *Augusta* was summoned to their battle stations by giant klaxons that would wake the dead, and the heavy cruiser was steaming toward *Titanic* at twenty five knots.

On board *Titanic*, Jack Thayer had discovered an axe near the Second Class cabins and was hurrying back down to the trapped seaman when the first torpedo struck the second compartment. The massive explosion knocked him off his feet and he slid down the stairs. He felt the sickening crunch of his left shoulder as he landed hard on the deck in front of the still locked crew cabin doors. Struggling to his feet, he felt the ship lurch again with another enormous impact almost directly under his feet. He was propelled off the deck, hitting his head on the ceiling. Two more explosions came in rapid succession farther down *Titanic*'s hull, causing her to rise up out of the water, then slam back down to the ocean surface. Dazed, he lay on the carpet, trying to gather his senses.

From behind the locked doors, he heard screaming and panic, and a mass of humanity pushed forward seemingly at once trying to burst through them. The axe had been wrenched from his hands in the explosions and he was frantically searching for it on his hands and knees when the hallway went black. *Titanic*'s electrical system had failed, sending the eight hundred foot long vessel into total darkness.

He raised himself to his feet, still searching for the axe when he felt the deck beneath his feet lurch down at an extreme angle. The torpedoes that had struck the great liner amidships had ruptured her keel, effectively breaking the ship nearly in two. The bow, with two gaping holes beneath her waterline, hung precariously by the shattered remnants of the steel beams comprising her backbone. As the water rushed in, the weight of the salt water flowing into her exposed bowels began to pull the hull down deeply into the water, her bow rising higher and higher off the surface as it slid deeper into the water. In seconds, he was fighting to stand up against a violent torrent of icy cold water pouring up at him into the hull. It was if a giant had stepped on the massive boat from above, breaking her back.

As he tried to remain on his feet, the cries of anguish behind the closed doors quieted down dramatically then stopped altogether, the crewmen locked in their quarters having finally drowned. With the water now up to his neck, Thayer kicked off a bulkhead, and with his one good arm, struggled to swim to the staircase.

With all his might, he grabbed the stair railing and began pulling himself up toward the open air above. It was a race against the surging water that licked at the heels of his shoes as he climbed, the angle of pitch continuing to grow more severe.

With his last ounce of strength, he pulled himself onto the covered Promenade Deck, and at the junction of the Well Deck threw himself overboard as the bow section slid past him with speed and roar of a locomotive run wild. In the water, he swam for all he was worth trying to escape the vortex he knew would be created as the bow was sucked under the water. But with only one arm to propel him, he was trapped as the shipped finally slipped beneath the surface and dragged him with her.

Thayer felt himself being pulled down deeper and deeper in the water, perhaps twenty-five feet, until the vacuum suction on him was abruptly released. He kicked to the surface, nearly suffocating the last meter before his head broke into the night air. He gasped for breath, frantically looking for anything to hold onto to keep him afloat while he struggled to regain his strength. He could already feel the effects of the cold water on his body, numbing him to the bone.

With his lungs full of precious air again, he kicked off farther from the ship, the stern section of which was repeating the spiraling death dance. Finding a floating deck chair, he climbed on top of it, exhausted, and watched *Titanic* take her final plunge.

The stern section, where he and more than twenty-two hundred other passengers and crew had gathered to await their fate on that bitterly cold night two decades before, rose higher and higher into the night, her enormous propellers fully exposed. Framed against a brilliant, star-filled sky, the great ship hung for long moments in a perpendicular position, while the sounds of escaping air and the crash of fittings, china and furniture added to the calamity. He could make out the sound of her boilers exploding, one by one. It was a cacophony of terrifying sounds, a wave of noise that signaled the death throes of the greatest ocean liner ever built.

Thayer watched as the upright stern began picking up speed as it slid beneath the waves. As the water closed over the large, white letters displaying her name across the breadth of the stern, *Titanic* took her last gasp and knifed below the surface, beginning the long journey to her final resting place more than two and a half miles below. There she would finally find her own peace on a vast, sandy plain of the ocean bottom.

The exhausted Thayer was mesmerized as *Titanic* and the hopes she represented breathed their last. He prayed silently for his father, for his President and for all those who had perished in pursuit of their dream of peace. Then, mercifully, overwhelmed with emotion, he drifted off into unconsciousness with only a precarious grasp on the flotsam which kept him from following them to the bottom.

His final thought was that man had finally accomplished what God himself had not.

Fifty-One

As the U-47 escaped safely to the south on a track that would bring her directly away from the path of *Augusta*, Jack Thayer drifted in and out of consciousness while clinging to the deck chair that had become his raft. Even in late summer, the North Atlantic Ocean waters were bitterly cold and the effects of hypothermia were gradually numbing him to his situation. In a moment of lucidity, when the pain of his neck wound and broken shoulder jarred him into consciousness, he thought that there could be no lonelier place than the middle of the Atlantic. Unless *Augusta* found him, he would be dead within hours.

Afloat in a sea of wreckage, he knew he would be hard to pick out for a rescue ship, and willed himself to remain awake. It was his only hope. By 10:00 p.m., nearly frozen through, he felt himself drifting off to sleep again. To keep awake, he began to kick his legs behind the raft, swimming through the debris field to get to clearer water. Suddenly he saw the running lights of a large ship just over the horizon. It appeared to be steaming toward him.

He waved frantically in an attempt to attract the ships attention, but finally gave up. It was simply too dark and too far away. With all hope gone, he let himself go, barely clinging to the deck chair, but his brain continued to scream: "Jack... survive..."

Shortly, a lookout on *Augusta* waved his hands frantically from high above in the crows nest to seamen gathered below. "There, a man, eleven o'clock on the port side. I can just make him out." Floodlights hurriedly swung in the direction and Thayer was spotted. Under Nimitiz' watchful glare, a crew readied a launch to pick up the survivor. In less than fifteen minutes, they had him on board *Augusta*. He was unconscious and near death.

While ships doctors tended feverishly to him, the Admiral crisscrossed a tight path over what had been *Titanic*'s last position. He found nothing but wreckage and the body of Commandant William Murdoch, an old friend. "He was stabbed to death, sir, in the back," a seaman reported after *Augusta* had retrieved the body. It appeared that every other soul had been pulled down with the ship.

From the appearance of the wreckage, Nimitz hastily concluded that *Titanic* had suffered a violent end. But only Thayer held the key to what had happened. The Admiral held off on informing the Pentagon of his findings until he was able to speak to him.

Four hours later, having regained consciousness after undergoing surgery to close the jagged wound on his neck, Thayer received Admiral Nimitz from his hospital bed.

"Admiral," he greeted Nimitz.

"The President, Mr. Thayer...?" he asked, hoping not to hear the words he knew would come.

"Dead." He closed his eyes, trying not to remember the carnage. He winced at the extreme pain in his shoulder which was completely immobilized by a heavy upper torso cast. There was a rigid brace around his neck.

"All dead," he added with finality.

Nimitz' eyes widened in disbelief.

"Everyone?" he implored, recognizing the vast consequences of Thayer's answer.

"Everyone. They were all murdered."

The Admiral bowed his head, leaning over in his chair. It was incomprehensible to the naval officer. He sucked in his breath.

"Who?

"Hitler... the Germans, with a submarine."

Nimitz felt helpless. "I must inform Washington."

Thayer winced again, went to respond, but the words would not come to his lips. He was overwhelmed by the irrevocability of what he had to say. A minute went by while he fought for composure.

"Yes, inform Secretary of State Simpson that the President has been assassinated," Thayer said, his voice hoarse from the hours of immersion in the cold, salt water. "Vice President Moody should be sworn in immediately. The government must continue to function without waver."

The two men remained silent for long moments. Nimitz had to ask the question.

"Was it worth it, Jack?"

Thayer opened his eyes and stared the admiral in the face, his fists balling up in fury.

"Was it worth it?" he repeated the question, his voice rising. There was no hesitation in his response.

"Yes, the President would have had it no other way, even if he could have foreseen the ultimate consequences," Thayer responded. "He cherished the values for which he fought and he died defending them..." The last words caught in this throat. Thayer struggled again to control his emotions, knowing that only he was left to share Archie Butt's dream.

"I'm sorry, Jack, you should rest..." Nimitz too was on the verge of tears.

"No, Admiral," Thayer responded, "I need to answer your question. We owe him that much."

"Archie Butt believed in freedom, liberty and justice. He not only believed in the Constitution, he lived it. To answer your question, Admiral, if the President had known the outcome – if he knew it would cost him his life -- he still would have tried."

Nimitz hung his head, his eyes moist. "God bless his soul."

"Yes, God…" Thayer closed his eyes again. "Where are we headed?"

"Washington. *Sequoia* will meet us in Chesapeake Bay tomorrow night. There will be doctors on board to care for you."

"Good. Please notify President Moody that I intend to speak to the press upon arrival in the Capital."

Nimitz was surprised.

"To what end?" he asked.

Thayer paused before answering. His mind was turning back the hours to the final words of his beloved President. "Survive, Jack," he had said, gripping Thayer's collar with his bloodied hands. "The world must know."

"To what end, Admiral?" he finally replied.

"Hitler, Stalin, the clown Mussolini… they made one mistake. They depended on one thing to make their treachery an absolute success."

The Admiral's eyes narrowed as he listened.

"They counted on no one surviving, no witnesses to the murders," Thayer continued. "

"They almost succeeded, Admiral, save for your efforts to fish me out of the debris, and I am eternally grateful. Because, you see, I have one more mission to accomplish for Archie Butt.

"There is a story the world must hear, Admiral," Thayer continued. "It is a story about how good and brave men and a woman gave their lives in the hope of creating a lasting world peace. It is also a story about evil and treachery."

Nimitz was riveted by Thayer's explanation.

"Perhaps there is still hope of success, Admiral, if the story is told. Imagine the anger of people of free nations who have lost their leaders to the treachery of men who existed only to enslave their own countrymen. Imagine further the reaction of the German, Russian and Italian people when they realize what might have been, how there lives would have changed if but for the benevolent success of Van Gogh."

Thayer paused, the pain in his neck and shoulder almost unbearable despite morphine injections. He willed himself to go on.

"I believe these dictators, in their vile, duplicitous plot to murder Archie Butt, the leadership of free Europe and those who would have brought relief to so many, will be far too busy in the months ahead quelling revolution in their own countries to find the time or resources to prepare their war machines."

"At least for a time, Jack, at least for a while," Nimitz said, his head down, grieving for his lost President and his own failure – whatever the odds -- to protect him.

Thayer inhaled deeply and grimaced, then exhaled slowly.

"Perhaps you are right, Admiral, perhaps war is inevitable so long as men coexist in nations with borders. For now, however, perhaps Archie Butt did find a way to ensure that men will think about the consequences of war before waging it blindly."

Nimitz nodded. "I must leave you, Jack, I have much to do including getting you to Washington." With his good hand, Thayer reached up and shook the Admiral's. "Yes, we must get to Washington without delay."

The Chief of Staff closed his eyes, remembering his President's last request, which he knew was now the only way to stave off war. He allowed himself a last thought before exhaustion finally overwhelmed him. "I have a story to share with the world."

##

About The Author

 **F. Mark Granato's** thirty year career as a corporate executive in a Fortune 50 company brought with it extensive international experience in the aerospace and commercial engineering and building fields. Now that he has served his time, he is finally fulfilling a lifetime desire to write and especially to explore the "What if?" questions of history. In addition to "Titanic: The Final Voyage", he has published "Beneath His Wings: The Plot to Murder Lindbergh" and "Of Winds and Rage", an alternative history novel based on the devastating 1938 New England Hurricane. He writes from Wethersfield, Connecticut, with the help of a large German Shepard named "Groban", who occasionally asks probing questions.

Made in the USA
Middletown, DE
05 July 2020

11942860R00208